The authors are Jane Culley and Brian Taylor. After a career heading up the Marketing Departments of several major automotive businesses, Brian moved into market research and journalism speaking at automotive conferences throughout Europe and in the USA. He is also a published author and commentator on motor sport. Co-author Jane Culley provided much of the research for his special automotive industry reports. Before that she had a varied career path, including time spent as a private investigator, a sexual health worker, finding housing solutions for young people and working in a drop-in for young people with various problems. Their combined career paths enable them to draw on various aspects of life. This is their first novel.

Jane Culley and Brian Taylor

FOURTEEN DAYS IN AUGUST

AUSTIN MACAULEY PUBLISHERS™

LONDON * CAMBRIDGE * NEW YORK * SHARJAH

A CIP catalogue record for this title is available from the British Library.

ISBN 9781398473737 (Paperback)
ISBN 9781398473744 (ePub e-book)

www.austinmacauley.com

First Published 2023
Austin Macauley Publishers Ltd®
1 Canada Square
Canary Wharf
London
E14 5AA

Thankyou Mark Hope for your insight into the Gay World.
Thankyou Julie Knapman for your help with reading and feedback.
Thankyou Jericho Writers for your help in framing our submission and finding a publisher.

Fourteen Days in August is a fictional tale, but it is based on stories that have made the news over centuries. It is a frank and emotionally intense 14-day journey, covering a chain of events set in motion by pirate Robert Davies in the 1700s that smashes into the lives of several families in 2017. What follows promises them untold wealth. Some loves and friendships are cemented, and others tested when the quest to follow the road to their promised new futures threatens to spin out of control. They soon discover that the destiny they seek has many facets, including danger, love and sex. Desire is heightened in such a rarefied atmosphere and the threat of death is never far away.

The Players

Christina Kerensa Davies (Chrissie)

Writer/journalist; formerly from Falmouth but now living in Bristol. Married, with one son, Jonathan. Husband Cador presumed lost at sea in 1997. Long-term relationship with Barry. Loves horses and competes in local dressage events with her horse, Wiggy.

Cador Aled Davies/Edward Jons

Falmouth boat builder. Married to Christina and father of Jonny, but went missing while delivering one of his boats to USA. Presumed dead.

Barry Williams

Long-time lover of Christina. Professor of History at Bristol University. American classic car enthusiast. Lives in Bristol.

Isabella Sallis (Izzy)

Christina's best friend going back to their days in Falmouth. Now living in Padstow. Super-fit and a former International Marathon runner, she was in great global demand as a personal or team trainer. Single.

Jonathan Davies (Jonny)

Gorgeous, openly gay son of Christina and Cador. Studying art at Cardiff University.

Will Hurst (Will)

Jonny's on-off boyfriend. Will runs a bar called the Willcome Inn. Jonny's cocaine supplier.

Matthew Lloyd (Matt)

Matthew owns an art gallery in Cardiff. Jonny works there part-time, restoring and repairing paintings. Money earned helps pay his university fees and fund his drug habit.

Alexandra Dickens-Young (Sandy)

Like Jonny, studying art at Cardiff. Has a flat in Cardiff. Close friend of Jonny but not gay herself or a drug user. Loves horses. Her sister, Sue, is married to Lord Henry Mayhew.

Lady Susanna Mayhew (Sue)

Sister of Sandy and married to Lord Henry Mayhew. World renowned art expert. Lives in well-guarded manor house near Newport. Collects art.

Lord Henry Mayhew (Henry)

Husband of Sue. Successfully involved in financial dealings in the city and very wealthy. Has a stable of horses for the flat in the summer and for jumps in the winter. Holds grouse shooting in his Scottish estate. Has a hidden side.

Bryn and Margie

Married couple that has been with Lord and Lady Mayhew for many years. Margie is the housekeeper and Bryn the head gardener. Also serves as driver.

Anthony Brown

Head of the syndicate FIST—Foreign Intelligence Support Team.

Aled and Mary

Tenants of Lord Henry living in Home Farm on the Mayhew Estate and working the land.

Devlin

Stable lad at Mayhew and general helping hand.

Jacob

Very good-looking under-gardener at Mayhew.

Aiyana Jons

Daughter of Cador Aled Davies/Edward Jons and his partner, Sisika.

Arthur Robinson (Arty)

A friend of Jonny who is deep into the communications and tech world.

Holly

The manager at the stable where Christina's horse Wiggy is based.

Tony and Sully Cantana

The Cantana Brothers operate several criminal activities in the UK and report back to the crooked Religious Community Holding Company Accountants in Boston. They have a London base in Soho and a Bristol base at the Willcome Inn. Tony is a dangerous psychopath.

Sisika

The Native American partner of Cador Aled Davies/Edward Jons and the mother of Aiyana.

Charles Evans (Chuck)

Worked with Cador Aled Davies/Edward Jons at the Religious Community Holding Company Accountants.

DCI David Thomas and Inspector Ruth Davies

Senior members of the Cardiff Police Force; generally work as a team.

Superintendent Jack Clarkson

David and Ruth's line superior at Cardiff.

Captain Robert Davies

Pirate and direct descendent of Aiyana and Jonny.

Prologue

A phone rang in his office. The light was flashing on the red scrambled unit. He picked it up and an American voice said, "The messenger and the message have arrived in the UK. The bait is on the hook so we will see if it is taken."

He replied, "OK. We will take it from here. I will make contact when there is news."

"Good luck Sir. It could get messy."

Then the line went dead.

Chapter 1

The journey between who you once were and who you are now becoming is
where the dance of life really takes place.
(Native American Warrior proverb)

Day 1 Wednesday
16 August 2017

But the morning had started so well in Bristol. It was late summer and as Christina Davies looked out of the window of her flat just above Hotwells there was a slight mist shrouding the historic SS Great Britain in its dock on the Avon. The weather forecast was good and the mist was expected to lift soon; today was going to be a good day.

But then a glance at Sky News on the television spoiled the mood because it was all so depressing about the UK leaving the EU. Brexit was the word used for this process and she hated hearing it several times every day. She had always felt proud of being European—a continent with a wonderful history and culture. She loved to travel and she felt that being in the European Union created a wonderful bond with the other nationalities. But now, half the population in the UK seemed to want to remain European but the other half wanted to leave claiming loss of sovereignty, the need to take back control of our borders and so on. There was coarse ugliness in some of the debate taking place; particularly on social media.

It all left her confused and life was a constant conflict of trying to match her bond with Europe and the arguments put forward by those wanting to leave. Being a freelance writer didn't help much because experience had taught her never to take anything on face value so she was always searching for facts to get an understanding of the causes of this turmoil the country was in.

And she had personal ties to Europe too because her parents had decided to retire to a village near Benidorm in Spain. They were now very worried about their status in Spain after Brexit and whether they would still get their pensions paid out there. What a mess.

And Brexit stories on the news were followed by Donald Trump sagas. What should people think of this American President? Republican Bob Corker had evidently tweeted that the White House had become an adult day-care centre but the carers had gone missing. In truth, she was starting to have trouble making conversations with her American friends. Didn't they realise how he was making their country look so moronic? Mind you, on that front, we were doing a pretty good job with our own country.

So, although Christina was not a political activist, she did think about world affairs and cared deeply about her country's future. That was why she was in a constant state of stress. In fact, she had written a poem about her thoughts, called A Mist of Madness:

A mist of madness
has covered the world.
A fog so dense
that nothing makes sense.

Lies and hate
have replaced debate.
What was clear
is replaced with fear.

The desire to be led
rules our head.
The populists roar;
the crowd yells for more.

The loudest win;
truth drowned by the din.
Hope is the creed.
We wait for the deed.

You say déjà vu.
I say yes that's true.
And it did not end good.
It did not end good.

I feel sadness
in this mist of madness.

It was never published but it reflected her 2017 thoughts. And just writing it was very cathartic.

The news was beginning to make her feel angry so she soon turned off the television and had made her morning cup of Yorkshire tea—her preferred drink in the morning. That improved things. She had some more writing to do for a client and wanted to break the back of it that morning before going out for a training session on her horse Wiggy. She had entered a local dressage event and needed to focus on that.

She had a quick shower and caught sight of herself as she passed the hall mirror to do her hair and get dressed. She let her dressing gown fall apart so she could view her full body. Taking different poses, she thought, *Mmm. Not bad for a 45-year-old.*

Her boobs were not quite as perky as they once were and there were a few smile lines here and there—maybe a touch of cellulite on her thighs—but she looked pretty good. Anyway, her long-time lover Barry Williams seemed to like what she had. Barry had been her soulmate since her husband Cador mysteriously disappeared in 1997. In truth, he was on the scene before she was married.

The house phone started to ring while she was getting ready but she thought, *Let it ring. If it's important they will leave a message. Probably one of those nuisance calls trying to sell me something anyway. There seemed to be far too many these days.*

When she was ready, she checked for messages and dialled 1571 to see what it was. A voice said, *Hi. My name is Aiyana Jons. I am staying at the Premier Inn down by the harbour in Bristol. It is next to the Llandoger Trow pub. I am the representative of a Native American tribe from Massachusetts and I have some news for you about your husband Cador. I will send you an e-mail to confirm this message along with a photo so you can recognise me. I am in possession of some documents that Cador wanted you and Jonathan to see.*

The words were spoken with a strong American accent—probably East Coast. But she could also detect another dialect there as well. She quickly checked her e-mail box and Facebook messages and found the same words. The e-mail had a mobile phone number along with a jpg photo attachment showing a beautiful woman with long black hair.

As she tried to come to terms with the messages, Christina's mind seemed to shudder to a halt; as if she had driven a truck into a brick wall. Talking out loud to herself, a feeling of illogical anger welled up inside her. She tried to stop it but it kept coming like a boiling kettle.

"Oh my God! This can't be true. It has to be a hoax. Who the hell is this fucking Red Indian Squaw turning my life upside down? Cador is dead. I have the death certificate to prove it."

She regretted that racist description as soon as she said it, but she was very angry, confused and not a little bit scared. She didn't normally use the F word in general conversation either.

She was shaking in her state of blind panic and shock—pacing up and down as memories from her past were spinning around. Her thoughts raced back to her youth, her marriage and Cador's mysterious disappearance. She frantically searched for clues and as she tried to come to terms with the e-mail and the message; grasping at random thoughts that could help determine what it might mean and hoping to remember something that might help her make sense of it all.

She had to control her anger and get her thoughts into some kind of order so she shook herself and sat down to think. Cador was born in Falmouth, Cornwall and despite coming from Welsh stock his parents gave him a very Cornish first name Cador which means Cornish King. His middle name was the very Welsh Aled. They ran a cafe on Maenporth beach, just outside Falmouth on the way to Mawnan Smith and BudockVean. Christina used to work in the cafe part time and this is how she first met him. He went on to develop a very successful but small boat building business in Falmouth and had mysteriously disappeared whilst sailing one of his creations across the Atlantic to a customer based in Boston, Massachusetts.

At the time, he was busy tracking down the history of some pirate he was evidently related to—a man named Robert Davies. Christina had not thought much about the research at the time—putting it down to some 'Boys Own' adventure Cador was obsessed with. The research was leading him to a story about land given to the Davies family in USA so he thought delivering the boat in person could be combined with some Boston based research. Or that was what he had told Christina at the time.

Christina—Chrissie to her friends—was Cornish through and through. Her maiden name was Christina Kerensa Nancarrow. She and Cador both had an interest in horses and they were married in the Spring of 1992. They set up home just above the Helford Passage near BudockVean which was within easy commute distance of Falmouth. It looked out across the Helford River and you could see Helford village nestling in the hills on the other side. The beautiful Glendurgan and Trebah Gardens were close by and the 300-year-old Ferry Boat Inn was their local public house. You could get a passenger ferry from there across to Helford. Daphne Du Maurier had based one of her novels here— *Frenchman's Creek*. It was about pirates. Maybe this was where Cador got his interest in pirates?

They sometimes had a meal at the Budock Vean Hotel that was situated just behind their house. The hotel had a pretty 9-hole golf course and Cador was a member. Life was fairly good apart from the spark in her marriage fading faster than a shooting star trail. She enjoyed sex! She didn't think she was over-sexed but she was certainly highly sexed. Unfortunately, things in that department had become a bit spasmodic and unadventurous for her.

She thought back to the time of his traumatic disappearance in 1997. Following many attempts to find out what happened, life gradually regained some normality. Her son Jonathan, who was born a year after their marriage, was growing up and she had to earn money so had little time to mourn. She had to wait seven years before Cador could be officially certified dead and it was made more difficult because no boat or body was ever found.

And curiously, there was no paperwork concerning the planned voyage or the customer who had ordered the boat although a deposit had been paid. So fortunately there were plenty of funds and assets to cover monies due but a big void as to what had actually happened to him. After the death certificate had been released she settled the finances, sold the business and decided to move to Bristol where she continued a career as a freelance writer.

She now lived in an apartment just above Hotwell Road in Clifton. A large floor to ceiling window with French doors led to a balcony looking south towards the SS Great Britain, built by one of Britain's greatest engineers—Isambard Kingdom Brunel. He also designed and built the nearby Clifton Suspension Bridge. The outlook was certainly a view to cherish and visitors to her apartment loved it. And she was proud of her décor. The lounge had light oak flooring with beautiful Chinese rugs in hues of apricot and cream.

She had made a few close friends in Bristol—quite a few via her business contacts. Although it was a big city it retained a great community spirit with lots going on. She also retained relationships with some old friends in Falmouth and visited them when she could—especially her best and very close friend Isabella Sallis—or Izzy to those that knew her. Christina enjoyed the theatre—the Bristol Hippodrome was not far away, but there was also the Bristol Old Vic which was an original Georgian theatre, the Tobacco Factory and the Redgrave Theatre in Clifton. And she loved her horse Hartwig (Wiggy) who was stabled in Northwick overlooking both of the Severn Bridges and Wales. When time allowed she escaped to the countryside and competed in low level dressage events.

Her son Jonathan was now just turned 21 and studying Fine Art at Cardiff University. He was passionate about Renaissance Art and too much into sex, drugs and rock and roll for Christina's liking. Currently he was in a 'gay phase'. Well, at least she hoped it was a phase. She prayed that would change and couldn't say much about the sex, given her own love of sexual pleasure—must be in the genes—but he was a big worry and a constant drain on her finances.

As different aspects of her past bounced into her thoughts, her mind zoomed in on her best friend Izzy who was now a statuesque five-foot ten beautiful woman. Super-fit Izzy enjoyed cross-country cycling; usually up and down mountains; the rougher the better. She refused to let a silly thing like getting older slow her down. She was also a marathon runner and when she was younger she travelled around the world running in different locations. She was now in great demand globally as a personal trainer. She had never married although she has had many relationships with both male and female partners. She had usually been the instigator of these relationships but had always carried a torch for Christina. However, she knew in her heart that she belonged to Barry and always had done, despite her marriage to Cador.

Most girls or boys get their first taste of sexual pleasure by masturbating—not a word that Christina favoured at all. It was something out of a medical dictionary tainted by influences of old school religion, Victorian attitudes, guilt, self-abuse, sin and going blind. Self-pleasuring was much more apt in today's world. But it had been a girl who had taken Christina to her first proper orgasm—her dear friend Izzy.

She was nearly two years older than Christina and they had become friends working at weekends in the local stables. Her full orgasmic awakening happened when Isabella was 18 and Christina just turned 16. It was a day Christina would remember forever. Unlike Isabella, Christina had not had a proper boyfriend although there was one boy at school who she liked and who seemed to fancy her. They went to the cinema in Falmouth and held hands but he was too shy to go any further although Christina was keen to at least get to proper kissing and maybe a bit more.

With Isabella, it was really two young girls experimenting and learning about their bodies and started with Isabella taking the lead and demonstrating on Christina what a French kiss was. It developed into something very special with Isabella taking Christina to heights of pleasure she had never previously experienced.

Then her thoughts moved back to her soul mate Barry. They had met when Barry had a summer job on the tourist boats operating out of Falmouth when she was turned seventeen and had been sex partners before she got together with Cador—the latter a bit of an 'on the bounce' reaction to Barry moving away to Bristol to study history.

But the relationship with Barry continued when they occasionally got together on and off during her marriage and Barry's later marriage, particularly when Christina was away on writing assignments. But the bond between Christina and Barry was a true love affair rather than just a sexual affair. It was about pleasuring each other and sharing things rather than just seeking pleasure for themselves.

There was real affection as well as sexual attraction and it was Barry she would turn to in times of stress. He helped her after Cador's disappearance and was a very important part of her life. Indeed it was he who suggested she move to Bristol where he had become a Professor of History at Bristol University.

By this time, he was married to Trudi who had given birth to twins Thomas and Meghan a year after their rather large wedding in Trudi's hometown of Tewkesbury. They moved to Bristol for Barry's work and ease of commuting for Trudi who was a professional cellist. Her flaming long red hair made her very visible in the Soft Heart Orchestra under the great but difficult 60-year-old Maestro, Carl Rex.

She loved her twins, but due to touring obligations she left most of the daily chores of bringing them up to Barry, for whom it wasn't easy balancing these responsibilities with his career at the University. Her being away a lot also gave Barry ample time to continue his relationship with Christina. They were seen out and about and of course someone told Trudi who after several arguments about it decided enough was enough.

After seven years of marriage and a bitter divorce, they both realised that for the children's sake they should at least be civil to each other. Trudi moved back to Tewkesbury and Barry stayed in Bristol, keeping custody of the children which pleased them both.

Trudi became the 'other woman' in the life of Carl Rex. He was married to the author Genevieve Rex who was quite happy for Carl to carry on with Trudi, as long as he left her alone to write her slushy but successful romantic novels that appealed to older readers.

All in all Christina's life had been quite a melody of complex relationships. At 48, Barry was slightly older than Christina. Originally from Dinis Powys in Glamorgan, he went to school at the prestigious Public School Llanddan. He was very fit, passionate about Rugby and was a keen kick boxer. With dark hair and rugged good looks, at 6ft 3ins it meant that he was rarely without a girl although these days it was Christina who had first call.

He ran 5-10 miles most days with his dog Scrum, an 18-month-old liver and white German pointer that was very sweet-natured and devoted to Barry. He held a very special place in Barry's heart, being given to him as a puppy at six months old as a birthday present from his children.

He was a very much loved dog and when the twins were not at home Scrum was Barry's sole companion; you might say a canine soul mate. When Barry and the twins were all away for a day or more, Scrum was looked after by his neighbour Neil who had a young border terrier called Ted. During these away day periods, Scrum had his own special place in Barry's garage.

All these thoughts flashed through Christina's head as she gradually came to terms with this disturbing contact from someone called Aiyana. She knew where the Llandoger Trow was. It was a famous pub that was supposedly the inspiration for the Admiral Benbow in Robert Louis Stevenson's *Treasure Island*. It was in the old part of the city and she often went there because the pub opposite—The Old Duke—had great traditional jazz evenings.

At first she pondered about not meeting up but then her curiosity would not be able to maintain that line of thought. What was this documentation? The girl had obviously made a long trip to track her down so it must be important. And how did she know her telephone number and e-mail address?

19

Aiyana did look gorgeous anyway; quite fanciable really. And she said that she represented a Native American tribe. What was that all about? As her thoughts gradually settled into place she decided to contact Barry and try to persuade him to attend the meet with her. She trusted his judgement so she sent him a text:

Need to meet up and talk. Urgent. Please phone on mobile.

It didn't take long for the phone to ring. She briefly outlined the intriguing story and suggested they needed a quiet place to talk about it before arranging any meet up with Aiyana. Barry lived near Filton Golf Course, not far from the old Filton aerodrome where the first British Supersonic Concorde airliner was built and made its maiden flight in April 1969. The weather looked promising so they decided to drive out to the Ethicurean Restaurant in Wrington just south of Bristol Airport. Barry booked a quiet table on-line and arranged to pick her up from her home at 7.00pm.

The morning was slipping by to quickly so she finished getting dressed and rustled up a poached egg on toast and a Pink Lady apple. She then opened her laptop to complete her writing project. It was for a local monthly magazine and was about the history of the Bristol Hippodrome, a place she loved to visit so this contract was a dream. She had been able to interview some of those who worked at the theatre during the war years.

She completed the basic text but it took about three hours. She grabbed a quick bite to eat for lunch sitting on her terrace. The sun was now well out and it was a glorious day. Jumping into her riding clothes, at two o'clock Christina pointed her Land Rover Discovery towards the stables in Northwick where Wiggy was waiting for some schooling.

It wasn't a new vehicle but it was just what she needed for off-road work, towing and carrying all the horsey bits and pieces required. The schooling went well and she was full of confidence for the forthcoming event as she headed back home to get ready for an enjoyable evening with Barry.

Christina always wanted to look her best for Barry, as he did for her. Just in case there was time for a lover's cuddle or more in the car, she decided no tights, front loading low-cut bra and plenty of cleavage from a front-buttoned summer dress. All this excitement was making her very horny and she craved the closeness of a sexual encounter. In truth, she needed a good 'seeing to' because she hadn't seen Barry for a while.

She was an ex-Girl Guide so 'be prepared' was her motto, hence the box of man-sized tissues as well. Of course, they could have always spent time at one of their two homes to end off the evening but sometimes it was good to relive their youth and go for some in-car entertainment. The thought of maybe being discovered added to the excitement. When they were younger in Falmouth, it was often the only place to be together apart from the open air. It was then all very high on lust and passion whereas now it was more about pleasing each other and having some adult fun. Role-playing was all part of the action.

He arrived at 7 pm. As they hadn't seen each other for a few weeks a long kiss and cuddle in her hallway was in order before they left. She missed him terribly—even when they were only apart for a few weeks. She thought that if they lived together they would make love every day—several times probably— but they both liked their own space too much and decided to keep their own homes.

He had come in his '57 Chevy Saloon. He sometimes exhibited it at Classic Car Shows whilst Chrissie was competing in dressage at the same event. It was a left-hand drive with a column change and front bench seat. They had experienced lots of exciting fun on that bench seat over the years and the warm, cosy feeling of being together soon engulfed them. She started to review with him what had happened, phone call and e-mail wise, on the drive to Wrington as she snuggled across the bench seat to get close to him.

They drove over the Clifton Suspension Bridge and took the cross-country route passed a few of their secret lovers' park-up places, arriving at the restaurant around 7.30 pm. They were taken to their table overlooking the walled garden and the Mendip Hills and ordered a couple of drinks; she a large gin and tonic and Barry half of San Miguel lager as he was driving. The menus were on the table.

The food here was superb with local ingredients and all home-grown plants taken from their walled garden. When they were out together they usually ordered the same food. It started out by accident when they first met and they both seemed to like the same food. It was now more of a soul mate thing and this time they had the monk fish, chilli and chard followed by sticky toffee apple cake. They both had a small glass of the house Chardonnay (driving limits) followed by Americano coffees with cold skimmed milk and a couple of chocolate mints.

After they had finished and were sipping coffee, Christina said, "Well, what do you think I should do?"

They agreed that the meet should take place at the Llandoger Trow and while they waited for the bill Christina texted Aiyana for a suitable time and date the following day. She received an immediate positive reply:

7 pm. I'll be inside on the left.

Tomorrow they would learn more about this mystery. But right now she needed the comfort of some sexual activity. So as they got in the car she said, "Are we going to stop for some fun lover?"

He said with a knowing smile, "Is the Pope Catholic?"

Half way back out in the country he turned off the road down a lane she recognised and into a field so they were tucked behind a hedge. He turned the engine and lights off and they sat for a while with the moonlight shining through the windscreen. He moved along the bench seat to be close to her and whispered, "Well, sailor, what have you got to show me tonight?"

She said, "Mmm. Let's have a look shall we Captain?"

She then slowly unbuttoned the front of her dress, unhooked her bra, slid off her pants, slightly opened her legs and displayed her treasurers seductively saying, "How is this Sir? All ready for inspection."

He slowly moved over to caress what was on offer but Christina said, "Hold on. Haven't you forgotten something Sir? Lower half exposed please. It is the custom."

He unzipped his jeans and slid out of them and his shorts and murmured, "OK sailor. I'm ready for action; and you?"

Christina slowly moved her left hand to her mouth to wet her fingers and then opened the lips of her vagina to add to the moisture already there, "Ready and very willing Captain."

She put her arms around his neck and pulled his mouth to her right nipple that was very erect and very hard.

They were then swallowing each other's lust, kissing passionately, fondling with Barry's hand and fingers soon between her opening legs. Her nipples were tingling as she found his very erect cock. The word penis was not good enough to describe this totem pole of circumcised pleasure that she had loved for years. It was a super-cock and it was difficult to explain the excitement she felt by stretching her hand around its girth and length. It was big. Very big when judged with her other lovers and she adored it. Removed her lips from his mouth she gasped, "Permission to prepare it for entry Sir?"

"Permission granted sailor."

She bent over to gradually absorb its volume past her lips using her tongue to stimulate as she gradually took more of it into her mouth. Oral sex was something she really enjoyed. She didn't know why. It was something to do with the extreme closeness, trust and personal nature of the act and her ability to stimulate her lover this way. She was in control and she just loved it.

She could feel his excitement growing and her own juices were beginning to flow. She drew breath and said, "Permission to straddle the main mast Sir?"

"Oh Yes, Oh Yes. Please do. Permission bloody granted."

She got on her knees beside him and then holding on to the back of the bench seat she moved one knee across his thighs and straddled the mast. Looking into his eyes she slowly lowered herself onto his cock, feeling it fill her completely. When it was completely in her nipples were at his mouth level so she teased him by moving them across until he settled on one.

"Bite it hard, Sir. I want it to hurt."

She let out a gasp as she felt his teeth.

She put her mouth close to his right ear and murmured, "I'm now going to give you a good fucking."

His hands were now behind her thighs and he started to move her back and forth as she gradually settled on the rhythm she desired. It was glorious and she started to ride this joy stick with a climax in mind.

She could feel it coming but she didn't want it to end yet so she straightened up and rested her back on the dash board. This way she could caress one breast while her other hand went down to feel her hot spot and with his cock sliding in and out, she thought, *Oh God, I love this. Does it make me a sex maniac? If it does, I don't care. Sex is too good to be just about making babies.*

She could see Barry was really enjoying the show so she moved back towards him and thrust a nipple deep into his mouth again. His tongue got to work and she thought, *The next time they need to name a hurricane beginning with the letter B, it has to be Barry.*

She could also sense his cock growing and she felt a joint orgasm coming on. They were both uttering sounds of pleasure now. He was saying, "God I love you Chrissie."

"She was saying I love you too. Oh God, fuck me, fuck me."

They were then both overcome with animal sounds and the pleasures of two people who loved each other reaching the highest level of sexual pleasure—pumping juices that joined together in a cocktail of emotion as they totally melted into one body.

They rested in that position for a while before Christina grabbed for the tissues to tidy things up as she dismounted—*always an awkward performance*, she thought. After a while, she said, "God, that was bloody amazing. Nobody can make me cum like that. You certainly know which buttons to press and I don't know what I would do without you."

He smiled and said, "I will always be here for you babe; you know that. There may have been others but right from the time we first met it has been you that has owned my heart."

They stayed a bit longer using up all of the moment as the moonlight illuminated a couple of true lovers holding each other as if time had stood still. After a while he said with some sadness in his voice, "Much as I would love to stay longer we better get dressed and take this old Chevy home. We have a busy day tomorrow."

They got dressed and slowly drove back to Christina's with her snuggled as close to Barry on the bench seat as she could. Barry put on a Billie Jo Spears CD and they joined in the chorus of their favourite song:

They don't make cars like they used to.
I wish we still had it today.
The love we first tasted, the good love we're still living:
We owe it to that old '57 Chevrolet.

They kissed goodbye at her apartment and made their way to their own beds and their own homes. What a wonderful evening. Young love lived again—for a while.

Day 2 Thursday
17 August 2017

The next day went by slowly as she waited to meet up with Barry again for their meet in the evening with Aiyana, but after an omelette lunch she decided to write a lot more copy for her piece on the Bristol Hippodrome and edit her earlier work. Barry arrived in his day car this time—a Chrysler PT Cruiser. They had stopped making them but they both loved its 'sit-up-and-beg' retro style. They had decided to walk to the Llandoger Trow. It was warm and the weather was still holding fair. No high heels tonight though.

They went down Hotwell Road, Anchor Road, past the Bristol Marriott Royal Hotel and the Hippodrome Theatre before crossing to Baldwin Street and taking Welsh Back by the river side to the Llandoger Trow—or Admiral Benbow from Treasure Island if you prefer. They were both pretty excited at the prospect of meeting this attractive looking Native American girl.

They took time out for a quick minute steak and fries at the Aqua Italia and hung around by the river until the correct meet up time of 7 pm arrived and then entered the main door. They looked around but there was no sign of the beautiful girl in the photo sent to Christina so as it was a nice evening they decided to buy a couple of lagers and sit outside for a while. It wasn't long before a text from Aiyana came through:

Sorry; had to check out of hotel in a hurry. I have been followed by some bad people. Suggest you do not hang around at the Llandoger Trow in case they are there watching for people asking about me. It might be dangerous for you. Sorry. Will be back in contact ASAP.

Christina showed the text to Barry and checked her Facebook messages and the same message was there. They looked at each other and their unfinished lagers.

Barry said quietly, "I think it best if we leave."

As they left, a good-looking young man with very blond hair handed them a leaflet about the pub and hotel. They walked along Welsh Back and stopped by the bridge wondering what to do. Christina glanced at the leaflet and found a folded piece of note paper with a message. It said, *Don't meet up with the Indian.*

She showed it to Barry who said, "Bugger me! It reminds me of Blind Pew in Robert Louis Stevenson's book *Treasure Island*. The pirates had a method of issuing a death threat with small notes but theirs' had a black spot on one side. Sometimes they used the Ace of Spades playing card. In Treasure Island Blind Pew handed it to Billy Bones in the Admiral Benbow—The Llandoger Trow if you prefer. This is getting a bit heavy and very weird. Someone is playing a game with us or maybe it's a friendly warning."

They looked back towards the Llandoger Trow to check if anyone had followed them. It looked pretty clear but Barry thought it safer to take a taxi back home from the City Centre rank rather than walk. Again they checked for any suspicious characters before finding a taxi and even on the short journey back they kept looking out of the rear window.

They were pretty quiet on the way home; not wanting to share their thoughts with the taxi driver. But their minds were racing. What was going on? Was this for real or had they become embroiled in some new on-line Internet game? Maybe it was some kids playing silly buggers. Maybe it had a darker meaning. It was a frightening puzzle.

When they arrived back at Christina's apartment they talked a little and decided that even though they had Aiyana's e-mail and mobile number they decided that unless events dictated otherwise they would wait until she made contact again—if she ever did.

Barry decided to stay with Christina that evening as they were both a bit shocked. They made doubly sure that all the doors were securely locked. The place felt much colder than usual so they had a quick cream of asparagus cuppa-soup and snuggled up together for comfort. It wasn't an evening for sexual pleasure. It was one for thinking things through and seeking the protection and comfort that only love can bring.

The next morning, they decided to phone the Llandoger Trow to see if they could find out about those handing out the leaflets. The answer added to the puzzle:

"What leaflets? We had nobody handing out leaflets employed by us."

Chapter 2

A very great vision is needed and the man who has it must follow as the eagle
seeks the deepest blue of the sky.
(Crazy Horse, Native American Proverb)

Day 4 Saturday
19 August 2017

Jonny Davies just loved being at Cardiff School of Art and Design. He was in his second year of the Fine Arts course based at the Llandaff Campus in Cardiff Metropolitan University just north of the city. His accommodation was just south of the city in Tyndall Street, close to where Cardiff Docks once exported coal all over the world. It had become a thriving artistic community—quite Bohemian—although not too convenient for commuting to the University. Over time he had found a few short cuts to the Campus so he didn't have to drive through Cardiff City centre for the lectures and the practical courses he chose to attend.

This August morning after making himself a bacon and egg breakfast he was walking down Bute Street from his apartment, passing several familiar shops and galleries until he reached what had in truth become a second home in his summer break—the Matthew Lloyd Gallery where he earned some much-needed funds by renovating paintings. It was close to the Tiger Bay area of Cardiff and it helped with his tuition fees and his expensive coke habit. As he knew many of the shop keepers along the way, the walk usually took longer than expected due to stops for chats. Timing was not something he was good at anyway.

Jonny was gay. He had always fancied men although he had tried to conform for a few years. He even had a regular girlfriend or two but his sexual curiosity was still focussed on men. So he decided that he loved women but did not fancy them. He had several gay relationships in Bristol before he moved to Cardiff and life at the University. His first gay liaison was when he took some casual work in the stables at the home of Brigadier Dickens-Young near Newport. It was also when he met Sandy. He had helped his mother with horses so he was familiar with the work required.

One of the grooms was a New Zealander on a working holiday. His name was Colin and they had the use of the coach house. One night after a lot of alcohol and some weed the two ended up in bed. The affair lasted through the summer before Colin went home to New Zealand and Jonny started University in Cardiff.

As far as his personal image was concerned, something he was very conscious about, Jonny tended to favour the colour black. Black hair, black T-shirt, black jeans and black converse trainers. His looks were very striking and he knew it. Women would probably use words like gorgeous. Men might say that he was too pretty for his own good.

Arriving at the gallery and opening the door he was confronted by the eccentric blend of ancient and modern that was Matthew Lloyd. Dressed in a red velvet jacket, yellow corduroy trousers and about six silk scarves wrapped around his neck, he was every inch the archetype of what he felt an art gallery owner should look like. He played the part well. Jonny's nick-name for him was Matt the Twatt.

"Ah! Jonny boy; wonderful to see you. There is a piece of art awaiting you in the Studio darling. It would be super if you could start work immediately and there is a small bag of white magic for your nose."

Matt's feminine accent was deliberately accentuated as part of the act. Jonny replied, "Thanks Matt."

With an indignant huff Matthew replied, "Jonny, my name is Matthew!"

Jonny responded with a smile and a wink.

"OK Matt."

Jonny entered the studio and smelt the familiar aromas of paint and turpentine. It was almost as good as a line of coke he thought. On second thoughts, maybe not quite. There was the painting that Matt referred to. It was already on an easel under the skylight. It looked nothing special at first glance; or a second glance for that matter. Jonny shouted through to Matthew.

"What the fuck is this Matt? It's only good for a second-rate car boot sale. Looks like a bad copy of an old master."

Matthew replied with a sardonic tone to his voice and sounding more camp than usual.

"Darling boy, it is for an American client. They are paying good money so who am I to turn it away. Let's look at it together."

Jonny responded in a tone that inferred stay in your office and leave me alone.

"OK; No problem: leave me to get on with it."

Matt was a bit taken aback.

"Oh, but I thought we could chat a while."

This was Matthew's way of trying to pursue a more personal relationship with Jonny. Something Jonny definitely did not want; yet he needed to keep a good business relationship because the money was good and he loved the work. Jonny was in no mood for it and said abruptly, "No time Matt. Gotta get on with the painting."

Matthew flounced out clearly upset and closed the door to his office with a sulky glare back to Jonny. He couldn't resist blowing a kiss though.

Jonny turned his attention to the painting. Reversing it he realised that viewed from the back, the canvas, frame and mounting looked really very old. However, the painting on the front was definitely 20th century and not all that good. There was something odd about it. Viewed across the face of the painting it looked like someone had overlaid a second canvas over the original. He muttered to himself, "Curious and even curiouser."

Holding the painting up to the workshop skylight and viewing it from the back supported this although it was still unclear. But it looked like the painting on the back was different to the painting on the front. The canvass and mounting would have to be taken apart to be sure. His mind started to race and he thought, *Well, fuck a duck! What do I do now? I need to think about this.*

He picked up the little cellophane packet of white that powder Matthew had left for him. He didn't know whether Matt was a dealer but didn't really care anyway. Although he had done a bit of hash from time to time Jonny had his first coke line at a society party he had been invited to when he lived in Bristol. On entering the living room of the house, there was a glass table with lines of coke laid out on the top, Jonny was told to just help himself…so he did and liked it and it had since become a pretty expensive habit. He knew that it was damaging his health but he wasn't ready to quit yet.

Back to Matthew's gallery; he took out his pocket tool kit and measured out a small amount onto a square of glass. He then used two pieces of plastic to shape the powder into a neat white line. Taking a slim straw placed in his right nostril, he held the other nostril closed and snorted up the drug. He felt the familiar burn as it hit his membranes. He soon started to feel his mind and body light up and he murmured, "Oh that's good shit."

He knew the high would only last 15 to 30 minutes but in his mind it was time and money well spent.

He decided that he needed a second opinion on the painting and went through his iPhone until he found the number of his friend Sandy and made the call. After only a couple of rings he heard, "W'sup Jonny?"

Sandy saw it was Jonny on her phone screen and that always meant fun. Jonny replied, "Hi hun. I need your help with a painting I am cleaning down at Matts."

Acting a little surprised she responded, "Sooo spit on a cotton-bud and clean it. You don't need me for that babe."

Using a rather exasperated tone he answered, "No; it is much more than that! Can you get down to Matt the Twat's fairly quickly? I need your opinion."

"OK; see you in twenty babe."

With that she turned her phone off.

True to her word Sandy walked into the gallery about twenty minutes later. Although she didn't work there she was a regular visitor to the gallery because her sister Sue purchased paintings there from time to time, so passing by Matthew she gave him a wave and a smile and went straight to the studio.

She was 24 years old, about five feet, six inches tall with fluffy blue and pink hair and she wore a colourful mix of clothing that gave her a soft hippy look. Even her Doc Martins were hand painted with daisies. But she wore the jumbled ensemble with some aplomb and sexual allure. She was so gently pretty that she made people stop, stare and want to just be in her company. Her smile solved the problems of the world.

Her full name was Alexandra Dickens-Young, the youngest daughter of Patricia and Brigadier Hunter Dickens-Young. She was as beautiful inside as she was outside. She had one brother George who was at Sandhurst and her sister Lady Susanna Mayhew.

She was studying art at Cardiff University and had become best friends with Jonny when he worked for a summer at her parent's stable yard before getting a job at Matthew's. He was someone she found very interesting and although he was gay and they came from different backgrounds he was a kindred spirit in so many other ways. She felt very comfortable in his company and life was never boring when they were together. Their relationship was as friends although she had other boyfriends that she went out with and had experienced a sexual relationship that went wrong and broke her heart. Jonny helped her through the pain. She greeted her friend with, "Hi! What is so important Jonny?"

Jonny looked up and full of enthusiasm replied, "Take a look at this painting and tell me what you think babe."

After a quick glance she looked at Jonny with a questioning expression and said, "It's crap…Why would somebody pay good money for that?"

With some distain and impatience he frowned and said, "Hold it up to the light and take a detailed look at the canvas will you?"

This she did, feeling a bit embarrassed at being so glib at the first glance. After a while she gasped and slowly said, "Oh my God! It looks like there's another painting underneath."

Jonny quickly put his hand over her mouth saying, "Sandy. Shhh! Don't let Matt hear you. If you look at the back of the canvas, it is my guess that the original painting is about two or three hundred years old. I want to know what is underneath this more recent image."

Sandy gently removed Jonny's hand from her mouth and with a scornful look whispered, "So who owns it Jonny?"

Speaking in lowered tones now Jonny replied, "It's been sent over from the States. I'll ask Matt."

Jonny walked into Matthew's office and said in the most unassuming voice he could muster, "Matt; just out of interest who is the owner of the crappy painting from the States?"

Matthew looked under a pile of paperwork and withdrew a letter.

"Someone called Aiyana Jons."

Jonny looked back at Sandy in the studio with a questioning expression and thought to himself, *Huh. That's a bit of a strange first name. Sounds ethnic and I feel I need to know something about this lady and her fake painting.*

Responding to Matthew, he said, "Thanks Matt. Do you mind if I take the painting home to work on? I think I can finish it quicker that way. I'm sure it's not worth much."

Matthew nodded his OK and then as an afterthought said, "Oh and Sandy dear; can you take this Morley painting to your sister when you next see her. I know she collects them and I think she will like it."

While Matthew was getting the Morley painting for Sandy, Jonny slipped the letter from the American in his pocket and went back to the studio. He carefully put the painting being studied in a canvas carrying case and when Sandy came back with the Morley, in a loud voice that Matthew could hear he told her that they were going back to his flat.

Replying in hushed tones she said, "OK. But I guess we are going to my sister Sue's really?"

Jonny looked at Sandy and smiled. Sue was an art collector and there wasn't much she didn't know about paintings and their restoration.

"Well, she has all the toys for this kind of investigation. But first of all we are going back to my place and phoning the owner of this bloody painting for more info."

Jonny waved the letter retrieved from Matt at Sandy.

"The telephone number is in this letter. Now isn't that useful?"

With difficulty in stifling a giggle Sandy said, "Oh, well done you."

They walked back to Jonny's apartment that was above a row of shops in Tyndall Street. He unlocked the door and walked in. Looking at Sandy he asked, "Coffee Hun?"

Sandy nodded and threw herself down onto a chaise lounge Jonny had found in a barn and renovated.

As you would expect from an art student Jonny had decorated his apartment beautifully. The walls were stark white to show off some of the exquisite paintings he had produced during his studies. He had collected most of his furniture from second hand shops and car boot sales. Using his artistic talent's he had painted and modified these finds to give a unique but uncluttered look to the space. He had reupholstered the chaise lounge in royal blue crushed velvet and the effect with the white wall was stunning. This was the place where he could be himself and throw off the mantle of extravert that he had developed as a sort of armour against the world. Sandy felt very privileged that she was one of the very few he allowed into his home—or as he puts it his sanctuary.

Jonny put the correspondence from the American on a table. He fished his mobile out of the inside pocket of his Armani leather Biker Jacket (a present from an ex-boyfriend) and put in the number from the letter. He pressed the green phone icon and waited.

An American female voice answered but she didn't give her name.

"Ah! Jonny!"

Jonny was startled. How did she know it was him? He didn't have time to ask before she continued, "Wow! I wondered how long it would take you to call me. So have you figured out the painting puzzle?"

Jonny nearly dropped the phone in shock but managed to put it on loud speak so Sandy could hear.

"Whoa! What the hell. Yes I have seen the painting. Did Matt tell you I have brought it home to work on? How did you know it was me on the phone anyway?"

"I have my sources Jonny and no I haven't spoken to Matt. I was however confident that you would work on the painting and see that it was far from ordinary. I don't know whether you know but we are connected Jonny—through your father and your ancestor Robert Davies. I have been told that the painting is part of the key to a story that involves us all and could lead to a fortune."

Jonny was now confused and his head was spinning.

"I am sorry but my dad drowned at sea when I was a kid. What the fuck is this about? You have freaked me out. Who the hell are you anyway?"

In contrast to Jonny's rather hysterical conversation the reply was very calm.

"Jonny I don't have time to explain things at the moment. Just get the original painting revealed. Keep it a secret and don't spread it around that you have talked to me. I am sorry but there are some nasty people after the information that I have. Phone your mom and tell her you have spoken to me. She will give you more news. We'll meet up soon, I promise. But take care."

"But I need to know what's going on Aiyana."

His plea was not answered and he was left looking at the phone. Turning and gazing at Sandy he said, "She has hung up on me."

Sandy had heard all this on the phone loud speak and was by now just a little scared.

"Oh my God, how weird is that? Sooo what yagonna do about it Jonny?"

"Phone mum I guess hun. Shit my heart is pounding in my chest."

Sandy jumped up and went into the kitchen area that was separated from the main room by a breakfast bar. Jonny always kept his kitchen tidy and very clean and Sandy knew exactly where to find things.

"Before you call her I think you need that coffee babe. You have to get your shit together."

Jonny mused out loud, "What do you think she meant about nasty people and how does my dead dad fit into all this? This is like something out of a James Bond movie."

After taking time for a much-needed coffee Jonny called his mother.

"Hi mum. It's Jonny."

At the other end of the phone Christina could see that because his name came up on her phone screen. She briskly responded, "Jonny I am a little busy at the moment."

Jonny replied quickly, "Just one question mum please. It is important. Have you ever heard of someone called Aiyana"?

There was an audible gasp over the phone.

"Jonny! This is serious. How the hell do you know her?"

He recounted what had happened that day and then Christina explained her weird emails and the message from the previous day's trip to Bristol.

"Whoa mum this is scary. But what has this got to do with dad"?

Christina continued, "In truth I don't know. But from what your father told me all those years ago, it to do with his ancestor; a conscripted privateer ship's captain by all accounts who was pardoned for piracy by George II in the 1700's and given parts of Boston as a gift for protecting English ships from pirates and blocking Spanish gold from their South American conquests reaching Spain. Ironical really. That painting has something to do with it as well. It is a long story and I'm not convinced of it myself so we had better meet up."

They were interrupted by Jonny's doorbell.

"Hang on Mum. I'll just see who that is at my door."

He pressed the intercom and asked who it was. An American man with a heavy East Coast accent answered.

"A package for Mr J Davies."

A worried Sandy grabbed Jonny's arm shaking her head. Jonny's mind was also in overdrive now. *Take care*, Aiyana had said and his mum sounded concerned as well. Two and two were adding up to five so he said in the intercom, "I will be down in a mo. Just got to put some clothes on."

Jonny turned to Sandy and said, "Fire escape quick."

To his mum hanging on the phone, he said, "Call you later. I'll Facebook message or text you. Gotta hang up."

They grabbed the painting in its carrying case plus the correspondence from Aiyana and ran to a door in the kitchen that led to a pretty roof garden with a metal staircase at the end. They quickly descended to a lane at the back of the property where Jonny kept his immaculate five-year-old black Mini Cooper.

They got in and drove up the lane and onto the main road, joining the traffic and passing the door to the flat. Two men were outside the door still waiting for Jonny to let them in; but they had no package. Hoping that they hadn't been spotted, Jonny slowly drove by, keeping the deep throaty sound of the exhausts as low as possible.

They were quiet for a while. Jonny broke the silence.

"I am going to take this mystery painting to Sue right now and find out what is underneath. Then I am driving to Bristol to see mum. What do you want to do? This is getting to be a little mad and I don't want to be involving you in something dangerous."

Sandy responded sharply, "Fuck that. I want to have answers as well. I am with you on this trip hun."

They drove out of Cardiff and past the University heading East towards Newport for a few miles before turning off for Duffryn and eventually up to some imposing high metal gates with a security camera trained on them. Sandy got out and spoke into the intercom situated in the wall. The gates opened and they drove through parkland until they came to some more gates situated within a higher wall; more cameras and another entry system for Sandy to get through. After passing through these gates they drove up to a stunning mid-18th century property that had once been the home of one of the leading iron foundry owners in South Wales. They pulled up by the stone steps leading to the front door.

An attractive blond lady in her thirties was waiting for them. It was Sandy's sister Susanna who was married to the current owner; the fabulously wealthy Lord Henry Mayhew. In her own right she was highly respected and a renowned fine art collector/dealer with a laboratory that had X-ray, ultra-violet and infra-red facilities where she could check authenticity of her acquisitions.

She totally enjoyed her money and position in society and was a great party giver, mainly for charity and often procuring her private jet to host a party at one of their many homes abroad and in Great Britain.

Lord Henry was the eldest of two brothers, which meant that he was heir to the Mayhew title and Estate. Jonny had never officially been introduced although he had seen him around the place. The original estate in Berkshire had been handed over to the National Trust and they now lived in this 18th Century mansion. He was born with money but had an unerring capacity to make more.

He was generally known as the one to watch because he often made massive killings on the stock market where he had interests in several investment companies. He was also in a Lloyds Syndicate specialising in insuring fine art and certainly mixed in the right circles as an international player.

He kept a few horses in training at Lambourn and had a stable at his estate where he kept a few more quality horses for fun. He also liked to host pheasant shoots at his home in Wales and grouse at his estate in Scotland.

"Bore da, my dear little sister. What brings you and Jonny to see me? Let's have a hug then."

Sue liked to show off her command of the Welsh language even though it was quite limited.

They climbed out of the little Mini and gave Sue a hug and air kisses. Her smile was just like her sister Sandy's smile and she asked, "So what have I done to deserve a visit from you two?"

Jonny languidly stretched his arms. He thought he would play it cool at first and said, "Darling; I am in-love with your super sexy gardener. Does he still prune the roses in his shorts?"

"Oh get on Jonny. Behave will you? Come on in now and I will get some bubbles out of the fridge."

Jonny said in an apologetic voice, "I can't stay Sue. But I have a painting I would like you to look at. I think it's really interesting."

He picked up the painting case and followed Sandy and Sue into a beautiful hall and then through some high double doors into a drawing room decorated in soft blues and creams. He spied a small Turner on the wall; a new addition to the other old masters in the room. He opened the case and handed the painting to Sue.

Looking confused she said, "It's nothing! Just a pretty bad imitation. I am sorry but you should both know this."

Jonny thought, *Making decisions on first impressions must run in the genes.* Trying to hide the impatience in his voice, he replied, "Turn it over Sue."

After inspecting the back of the canvas, Sue sounded more interested.

"Oh! Now that is really something…old and another painting overlaid on top. I need to get this in the lab and take a deeper look."

That was just what Jonny wanted to hear.

"I hoped you'd say that Sue. I can't stop now so I'll leave it with you. I have to get over to Bristol to meet up with my mum but Sandy is staying to give you a hand."

Sounding very put out, Sandy said, "Hang on Jonny. I am going with you."

"No sweetheart. I am going to meet up with a couple of guys I know when I get there and if we go to see mum together she is sure to think you have turned me and will be arranging a wedding for us. I also think you need to be with Sue on this project and don't forget to give her the Morley that Matt gave you."

They followed him out to the car and waved him off. Sandy couldn't help being a bit worried about her friend and felt a lump in her throat.

It was now just after lunch time and before setting off he sent a Facebook message to his mum saying he was on his way. His main social media was Snapchat but his mum was only on Facebook and he liked it that way. Grabbing a takeaway Margareta pizza on the way he set off for the M4 motorway. Heading south he eventually joined the Portway heading towards Bristol. After cruising under the Suspension Bridge he arrived at Hotwells and took the turning towards Clifton. He was soon pulling up outside his mother's apartment and the whole trip took just under an hour.

He pressed the bell on his mother's entry system. There was a click and the door to the lobby unlocked so he walked in. He was excited to learn more about the amazing yet frightening story that was unfolding. But he also had other people to meet in Bristol.

Chapter 3

To remember who you are, you will need to forget what society has tried to teach you to be.

(Native American Saying)

19 August 2017

Saturday 1.30pm

Jonny took the lift up to the 3rd floor and walked along to his mother's beautiful apartment. She was waiting for him with the door open and greeted him with some excitement in her voice.

"Hello darling come on in. Barry is here as well."

Barry was seated on one of Christina's stylish cream sofas. He didn't get up to shake hands or punch fists but said, "Hello Jonny. Good to see you buddy."

Jonny responded with a

"You alright?"

Not waiting for an answer he walked over to the French windows. He took a quick look at the beautiful view; then turned around as Barry said, "We have arranged to meet Aiyana at 8.30 pm at Gordano Services just off the M5 across the river from Avonmouth. Hopefully she will let us know what all this is about."

Jonny had reservations about the venue being a bit public but decided to stay quiet and said, "OK Barry. I have to pop out to see a couple of mates first but I will be back at 7.30 pm. Must go."

As he headed for the door Christina pleaded, "Jonathan we hardly see you. Can you not spend some time with us? And what about something to eat before we go to see Aiyana?"

Like many mums she always used Jonny's full name when she wanted to show more authority. Using a quote from a Robert Frost poem Jonny replied with a wink to Barry, "Nah. Sorry mum; not right now. I have promises to keep and miles to go before I sleep. I'll grab something to eat before I get back."

Before Christina could say anything else Barry chipped in.

"Let him go Chrissie. We will talk later. But for God's sake be careful and watch out for any strange men Jonny."

"Oh Barry; you know I just looove strange men."

An exasperated and worried Christina gave in and said, "Please take care Jonny. I am not sure what we are dealing with here, or even if Aiyana is legit. And we can't call the police because I think they would not take this seriously."

"Yeah no worries mum. Love you guys; see you later."

Jonny then waved to Barry and hurried out the door after hugging his mum. As Jonny left the apartment Barry said with a rueful smile, "Don't worry love. My two are just the same. It's the way of young people."

"I know Barry, but I worry about him; he is so very self-sufficient. I suppose I feel sort of redundant as a mother. We never have proper heart to heart conversations like you do with the twins. I guess I am a little jealous."

Barry then rose to his feet and said, "On that note I am afraid I must get back and take Scrum for a run as well. He will be crossing his legs poor dog. I'll grab something from the Chinese takeaway on the way over tonight."

Barry enveloped Christina in a hug and gave her a kiss, telling her he would be back at 7pm. He looked back when he reached the door and for the first time thought that rather than the self-assured woman he had known for years she looked very vulnerable. He suddenly realised how much he loved her and felt a fierce need to protect her.

After Barry left, Christina looked at her watch. It was 4pm and she decided it was time for a glass of something. She wandered over to the cupboard and took out a glass and poured a lovely cold sparkly Prosecco from the fridge. She then walked out to the balcony and sat down on one of the lemon and white loungers to contemplate what had happened during the last few days.

She thought about Cador and their first years of marriage and suddenly felt quite guilty about how she had behaved. He had been second best to Barry but she had made her bed and maybe she should have kept faithful. But she was thinking only of her own pleasure back then. Cador was into his business and once he had made her pregnant he seemed to lose interest in sex. That side of her life was so important to her and she craved the closeness of the act as well as the eroticism. So it was his fault as well she thought.

She knew Cador had walked in on her when Isabella, Barry and herself had become wasted one afternoon and ended up in a threesome. She lifted a scarlet manicured finger and wiped away a tear that was slowly making its way down her cheek. Christina understood that her marriage had been in trouble at the time but sitting down with her thoughts she suddenly felt that it was selfish and a cruel way to treat him.

She had thought it was quite amusing to see the shock he displayed as he opened the door and was mildly surprised when he turned around and walked out without uttering a sound. Also it was most odd that he did not bring the subject up in the days following. She thought it best to stay silent as well; both hiding from the truth and delaying the inevitable perhaps.

At the time Christina remembered being happy and relieved when Cador said he was sailing solo to USA because she felt she could have some fun. When he went missing she had been shocked and upset, but on reflection, having a young son she was possibly more concerned with how she would cope being a single mum and in what manner things would pan-out financially.

Cador had not been a bad husband, but she now thought that maybe she had miss-behaved and she felt a sense of guilt for her actions that lead him to his untimely demise, even though, as she would find out, she was not personally responsible for that. She shook herself and said out loud.

"Oh for God's sake pull yourself together you silly cow. All this is history; it happened and cannot be undone."

The soft breeze of the Avon gently wafted up to Christina's balcony with the sounds of the people of Hotwell going about their daily business along with the bustle of the river traffic. Thoughts still drifted into her mind, *It's all still the same; so why do I feel so unsettled? If we don't go to meet this girl, will it all just go away?*

She reached over to a small glass-topped table and picked up her Samsung mobile, scrolled down until she got to her dearest friend Isabella's number. As Isabella had given Christina her first orgasm—an event that she thought of as her passport to womanhood—they had remained very close although Isabella had moved from Falmouth to Padstow. She touched the screen and waited a few beats until it was answered by Isabella's familiar voice.

"Hi Chrissie, my love. How are things?"

"A little bit weird I am afraid, Izzy. I really need to talk to you and just vent a little."

Isabella noticed the sigh in Christina's voice and replied, "Vent away, sweetie. I am all ears."

Christina then went through what had occurred over the last few days. Isabella listened in amazement.

"Oh my God Chrissie! Does that mean Cador is still alive? And if he is, could this girl be his daughter?"

Christina suddenly felt a bit stupid and slowly replied, "Do you know, with all this stuff going on I hadn't thought about that Izzy. Maybe he is still alive. I suppose it's possible that she is his daughter of course."

Isabella said, "Shit this is pretty scary. I don't like the sound of the criminal element either. I think maybe you should call the Police Chrissie."

Christina thought for a while and said, "And tell them what? Nothing has happened to us…yet Izzy. I wonder if it would be sensible to just not go to the meet up. This could just be a very elaborate scam, couldn't it?"

"Yes it could; and you could just put your head in the sand and hope it will all go away. But that's not the Chrissie I know. I think you need answers sweetheart. I also feel Jonny isn't going to let this go. There is that painting riddle that seems to have him captivated."

"You are probably right Izzy but I must go now, I need to shower and have a sandwich, before our meeting with Aiyana. I will let you know how it goes. How about lunch next week?"

"Yeah great. Can I stay over? We can drink too much and relive the old days."

"How about Wednesday 23rd Izzy?"

"That's good for me Chrissie. Bye, bye love. See you soon."

Christina hung up feeling a little better to have discussed things with her friend. She headed for the bathroom to have her shower. On the way she turned her iPad on and selected some music, a mix of Ed Sheeran, Limp Bizkit and Robby Williams—she turned it up loud so she could hear it easily over the sound of the water.

After about half an hour, she emerged naked rubbing her hair dry and noticed someone had called her mobile and left a message. On examination she decided she didn't know the number and would listen later.

Limp Bizkit was blasting out *Behind blue eyes* as Christina selected white linen trousers and a floaty apricot top. She looked at her bedroom clock. It was 6.30 pm; enough time to put on her makeup and be ready for Barry.

Task completed, she gazed in the full-length mirror and decided she looked OK, just as a 'ping' from the intercom let her know that someone was at the door.

She checked the CCTV to confirm it was Barry and pressed the unlock to let him in. Only dressed in her bath robe Christina looked up as Barry entered the room and smiled as he wandered over to her with his sexy loose walk. His hair was still wet form his recent shower and just looking at him gave her butterflies.

Behave nipples, she thought as she greeted him.

"Hi love; you're early. Did you have a good run?"

"Yeah. I quickly popped down to Eastville Park. It's a shame that they are thinking about building housing on that land. Scrum loves it down there. No Jonny yet?"

"No, there is still time though. I imagine he will leave it until the last second as usual. Oh, I've just remembered. I had a call from an unknown number. I must just see if there is a message."

Christina picked up her phone and looked at messages. Sure enough there was one. She pressed the button and put it on loud speak.

A familiar female American voice said, "Hya. When you get to Gordano Services, go to the Days Inn and I will be in room six."

Christina checked her Facebook messages but there was nothing there. Barry chipped in.

"OK. That is a bit less conspicuous than a service station. A lot more sensible I think."

"Yes I agree; much better. I cannot believe how nervous I feel. In fact I feel slightly queasy."

Sensing the concern in her answer Barry quietly said, "Come on love. Get dressed and we'll chill out for a while. I'll sort out the beef and ginger with rice that I brought over."

Barry raided the kitchen cupboard for plates and served up the meal. They sat on one of the sofas and tucked in to their meal. Barry put his arm around her shoulders. He gently kissed the top of her head, breathing in the scent of her recently washed hair. He murmured, "Don't worry, it will all be fine."

After he had left his mum's flat that afternoon Jonny went to a bar down by the river Avon called the Willcome Inn. He wanted to see an old friend for a catch up on the Bristol scene and to score some cocaine. The bar had its own mooring on the river and was decorated in blues and whites with a nautical theme. It was near the old slave trader area in Queens Square. His friend, Will Hurst, was sitting in the window checking up on Facebook. A gorgeous looking guy who did a lot of work in the gym and was as blond as Jonny was dark, he looked up as Jonny approached with a smile, then jumped up and hugged him.

Although there was some affection between them their relationship was very much based on lust and drugs rather than love. Jonny just thought Will was the sexiest man around and the feeling was mutual. Will was beaming.

"So good to see you my darling Jonny. Why didn't you say you were in town? I would have got the boys together for a party."

"Sweetheart, I would rather nobody knew I am in here at the mo."

With one eyebrow raised Will looked Jonny straight in the eye and said, "Oh dear. Got in a spot of bother have we Jonny? Do you want to spill the beans?"

"No and it's not what you are thinking. It's family business and it would be better if I was a little quiet for a bit. But I could do with a little charlie just to get me by."

"Yeah; sure Jonny; let's go up to the flat."

The two walked to the back of the bar. Will nodded to the bar staff and said, "I won't be long."

They went through a door marked private, then upstairs to Will's apartment.

Will put his arm around Jonny's waist and asked, "Coffee?"

"Yeah that would be great. But Will, I haven't seen you for a while. What about a real reunion."

Jonny placed his hand on Wills crutch; gently cupping him, then turning to meet his lips in an aggressive tongue tangling kiss. Will always aroused Jonny who immediately felt his own erection as he recalled their regular afternoon delight sessions before he left to go to Cardiff University.

They looked at each other and the coffee was forgotten. Will took Jonny by the hand and led him over to French doors overlooking the river. They sat down on a leather sofa and Jonny un-zipped Will's fly to release by now huge erection. Jonny murmured, "Hmm yummy; still going commando I see."

"Always like to be ready for some action Jonny."

Jonny then gathered Wills cock in his hand and lowered his head to slowly lick its rim, glancing up and enjoying the erotic thrill resulting from the satisfaction in Will's eyes as he tightened his grip around its base and slowly massaged it up and down. But Jonny needed more. He loved the feeling of a cock inside him and said,

"I need this baby inside me right now Will. It's been too long since the last time."

Will groaned in pleasure saying, "Oh God Jonny, pleeease. I'm ready."

Jonny stood up and with a cheeky grin said, "OK. Better get naked Will."

With a throaty voice a very aroused Will said, "Bedroom I think; and quick."

Will dropped his trousers and walked to a door to the left of the window and entered a Japanese inspired bedroom with genuine pieces of stunning black lacquer furniture and a huge platform bed in the centre of the room. Large French doors opened onto a sizable veranda over-looking the river.

He walked over to the bed, sat down and beckoned Jonny over saying, "OK. Let's have some fun sweetheart."

Jonny approached his eager partner, stood between his legs and thrust his bulge towards Will's face. Will stroked the eye level bulge—feeling the outline of a hard cock. He undid Jonny's trousers and pulled them down over his hips to land in a puddle on the floor. Jonny's shorts follow the same route. Will then slowly undid the buttons on Jonny's shirt from the bottom up until he was standing before him completely naked. Will then took his own shirt off and pulled Jonny onto the bed and onto his back. He started to kiss and lick Jonny's tummy—getting closer to his hard cock. He drew breath to whisper, "Jonny in the draw beside you; can you get the lube?"

Jonny reached over and took the lube from the draw as Will sat back watching—his eyes now only half open and the expectation bursting from his brain. He saw Jonny squeeze out some lube and felt him spread it liberally over his cock as well as his own arse.

Jonny then lay on his back and lifted his legs, allowing Will to slowly enter him with a groan as he watched Jonny's eyes close in pleasure.

"Oh my God, I am so turned on by you Jonny."

He started to pump in and out, slowly at first but then faster. All too soon he cried, "Oh fuck, I am going to cum, oh fuck, ahhh!"

He couldn't hold back and exploded into Jonny. After a short while a fairly disappointed Jonny opened his eyes and complained, "Well, that was a bit quick sweetheart. I think you now owe me a blowjob as well as some of your best grade 'charlie'."

Looking down at his now limp cock a slightly embarrassed Will said, "I'm really sorry about that hun. It's been too long since we have been together and I just couldn't help myself. Let's get showered and I'll sort out your coke stock and your cock."

Jonny followed Will into the large wet room shower and they are soon soaping each other down. Will knelt in front of Jonny and took his cock in his mouth. He expertly uses his tongue around the sensitive glands around the tip while moving his hand up and down the shaft. Jonny looked down at Will, water running down his well-muscled body. He put his hands on Wills head, gently caressing his hair and moving his hips in rhythm with Will's action, completely enjoying the moment until he felt his balls tighten.

"Will baby I'm cumming."

Will gamely took what Jonny had to offer, looking up at his lover's ecstatic expression as the erotic experience took hold and Jonny's gasps of pleasure filled the shower room. They both then sunk to the shower floor in each other's arms. After a while they kissed and finished their shower.

Will grabbed a couple of towels and passed one to Jonny saying with a sulk, "I suppose you are just going to leave me again aren't you? I wish we could meet more often."

"Sorry Will. Life is a bit complicated at the moment."

Jonny noticed that Will didn't look convinced about the sincerity of the remark and appeared worried as he replied, "Yeah! You know what? I just feel a tiny bit used. Just don't expect me to wait for you if you end up in real trouble. There are some nasty people out there. Come on; get dressed I will get you some Charlie."

Those remarks were to come back and haunt Jonny later.

"Thanks Will, you know how it is but I do think so much of you."

Will's reply was brief and sullen.

"Yeah; whatever."

They got dressed in silence and then Will walked over to a picture on the wall and lifted it off revealing an old school safe. He turned the dial backwards and forwards and the door clicked open. He reached in and brought out two plastic pouches and handed over to Jonny saying, "How much of this shit are you doing Hun?"

Jonny thought before answering.

"Between you and me probably too much. But it keeps me sharp."

Will looked deep Jonny in the eyes and said seriously with concern that sounded real, "Jonny; when the stash I have in there is gone I am stopping. My suppliers are getting heavy. Why don't you?"

Jonny replied without really thinking about stopping soon.

"Not yet love. But I will."

Anyway, Will had often said these words in the past so he thought his supply was pretty secure. Will grabbed Jonny and gave him a hug saying, "Please take care. It can be dangerous out there."

Jonny replied with a wink and a laugh but again was surprised at Will's obvious concern.

"I will."

They then wandered back down to the bar which was steadily filling up with people. Jonny looked at his watch and said, "Shit! I am late. See you later hun. I will pay you for the stuff before I go back to Cardiff."

Will watched Jonny exit his bar and muttered under his breath, "Bet you don't."

Jonny quickly walked to his Mini and got in. He took a look around the car park…just in-case he was followed. Heading for the Clifton McDonalds for a Big Mac and then to his mother's apartment he muttered, "Shit, I am getting paranoid."

Chapter 4

Certain things catch your eye, but pursue only those that capture your heart.
(Native American Proverb)

Saturday, 19 August

Jonny arrived back at his mum's flat just in time to depart for Gordano Services. It was getting quite humid and it felt like a storm was brewing.

He brought in his backpack and said, "Can I stay tonight, mum, in case our meet with Aiyana goes on late?"

"Of course you can. Dump your stuff here because we need to go now. Barry and I have already eaten so I hope you have."

As Barry had driven over in his PT Cruiser, they decided to go in that instead of Jonny's Mini. And rather than use the M5 Motorway they drove over the Clifton Suspension Bridge and then down to the Service area via Abbots Leigh. There wasn't much conversation as they were all thinking about what the meeting might reveal. And would she actually be there because last time she had to leave PDQ as did Barry and Christina? Barry was constantly looking in his mirror to see if anyone was following them. Jonny too was treating every car on the road as a possible threat. Christina was just numb with concern, yet excited to learn more.

They arrived at the service area and decided to park in the main car park and walk across to Days Inn. It was a pretty basic service area motel but the small reception desk was manned so they explained that they were there to meet a guest in Room 6.

The smart Eastern European receptionist/housekeeper rang the room and after a short conversation said, "OK. She is expecting you so go through. It's on the ground floor on the right."

With that she pressed a button for the entry system which buzzed as they went through. That buzz haunted Christina. It was like a Dentist's or Doctor's next patient call. After walking down a rather dark corridor, made gloomier by the décor that featured a dark magnolia paint scheme long overdue for a redec, they arrived at Room 6. Now for the moment of truth.

Barry knocked on the door and it was opened by the most beautiful amber skinned girl you could imagine; more gorgeous than the photo she sent before the aborted meeting at the Llandoger Trow. Her figure was classic—perhaps with larger breasts than usual—but the overall initial impact was Wow! She looked to be in her late teens or early 20s and she wore fashionable torn tight blue jeans with cream wedge sandals.

Her shirt appeared to have a traditional Native American pattern with the top buttons undone to show some cleavage. Around her neck she wore a multi coloured and stranded necklace of polished stones and a similar wrist band. Her face was very Native American with a long nose and dark eyes—a bit like the American singer Cher. Long black straight hair came down to her shoulders. Her perfume was very musky. Barry and Christina both immediately fell under her spell.

She spoke slowly but with an East Coast accent that was clearly bred in Boston.

"Hi; I'm Aiyana. I'm so pleased to see you."

Turning to Jonny she held out her hand and said, "I guess you must be Jonnie. So glad to meet you at last."

Jonnie shook her hand and said in the most casual and cool voice he could muster.

"Yep. Same here."

Then in turn she shook hands with Christina and Barry saying, "And you must be Christina and Barry. This is very exciting for me. I'm sorry it has been such a thrill ride to get to this stage but we made it."

Christina was still seduced by Aiyana's looks and said, "Please call me Chrissie. You're right about the thrill ride but I can't wait to hear your story. Is Cador still alive? What is your relationship to him? Who are the nasty heavies who seem to be following us around? There are so many questions Aiyana and it's very scary."

"Yes I know Chrissie. But pour yourself a coffee and I can tell you what I know. The room is a bit spartan but hopefully more private than the main service area. I have some very personal information to pass on and I thought privacy was best for that as well as our security. I've managed to get a couple of extra chairs and one of you can sit on the bed if you like. It's a long story so make yourselves comfortable."

They poured coffees and settled down to hear goodness knows what.

Aiyana started her story.

"First of all I'm sorry to tell you that Cador, my father, is no longer alive."

After leaving some time for that news to sink in she continued.

"As you have believed this to be the case for many years I guess this has not come as such a shock, but forgive me if I don't answer your questions now because the rest of my story will cover most of the answers. In fact I knew Cador as Edward because he had changed his name before he entered USA. But at first I knew him as a friend of my mother. I did not know he was my father for many years. However his money paid my way through Harvard where I achieved a first-class degree in Social Science and American history. This has led me to become an Honorary member of my native American Tribe Council of Elders who I am representing here today. You might recall that there were native American tribes that helped the Plymouth Brethren establish their colony in USA after they arrived on the Mayflower. . It is very unusual for one so young to be a member and the responsibility given to me is something I value highly. And I am bringing you gifts from my tribe."

She reached into a bag and brought out three wrist bands—just like the one she was wearing herself.

"These will bring you luck so I hope you will wear them."

"They are beautiful," said Christina, still reeling from the news that Aiyana was Cador's daughter.

"Thank you so much."

Still trying to remain cool, Jonny asked, "Are they ethnic tribal items?"

"Yes they are, Jonny. Made by tribe members in our community. The first part of my story is as told to me by my mother so nothing is written down in legal text. I only started to find out about Edward being my father five years ago. My mother died a year ago but left me some documents that she insisted should be kept private for twelve months after her death. Only then should I try to make sense of them.

"What I did find out before my mother died was that my father left the UK because his marriage was not really working. I hope you don't find that upsetting Chrissie but that is the story as relayed to me. He concluded that the marriage could not last and it would be best for everyone if he disappeared. He knew Jonny would be financially OK because the yacht building business was in a good state and could clear all its debts.

"His thinking was that his wife knew enough about the company to wind it up successfully, if that was what she wanted to do, or others were there to develop it further. A yacht requiring delivery to USA was a perfect vehicle for his disappearance. He took plenty of loose cash with him and after crossing the Atlantic he initially moored the boat that he was delivering in a quiet cove in Barbados in the Southern Caribbean Sea. The deposit was safe in the Falmouth business but there was a balance to pay on delivery so he sold it to the original customer at a knock down price on a 'cash and no questions asked' basis. With the money, and using devious means he was able to acquire an American passport under the name of Edward Jons."

Barry was dumbstruck and all he could think of to say was, "Wow! So he wasn't lost at sea. He was alive and well in USA."

"Absolutely correct, Barry, although not in USA at first. However, with this money and passport he travelled to Boston by sea and continued his quest for details about a Davies' fortune—the other reason for delivering the boat himself as you know.

"He did casual work in the city at first, gathering information where he could. Boston is a busy town, and like many big cities in the world, land ownership, big business and crime are often linked. It was during this time while working at a hotel that he met my mother Sisika whose tribal name is Singing Bird. These tribal names are very important to us as they represent our soul. When we die we cannot be buried without our tribal name being part of the ceremony."

"What is your tribal name, Aiyana?" asked Jonny, lightening the mood a little as he was coming to terms with the fact that he had a half-sister.

"Eternal Blossom. Do you like it?"

"It's beautiful, Aiyana; most suitable."

Jonny surprised himself making such a personal comment to someone he had just met.

She smiled and with a look that made Jonny feel an emotional tug deep in his soul said, "Why, thank you, my brother."

"My mother was working at the same building as Edward. The fact that she was a member of a native American tribe meant that they were kindred spirits relating to the Davies fortune and who gave the land to who, because the tribe had a claim on it as well—and still does. My mother and Edward soon started a relationship that resulted in my birth and I was brought up by my mother in in one of the two Native American communities of our tribe left—just outside Boston. Due to my father's illegal entry into USA on a forged passport, they did not marry for fear of his illegal entry being discovered, but the relationship was strong and it continued.

So there was my mother and Edward's life mainly in Boston and me and my mother's life in the Community. In many ways we were living parallel lives. In fact I was fourteen before I was told who my father was, along with the story of the Davies' fortune. However, by this time he had been killed in what the FBI called mysterious circumstances. I'll tell you more about that later because I'm getting ahead of myself.

As I have indicated, very early on in their relationship, and before I was born, Edward had told my mother the facts about the Davies' fortune and together they planned how best to assemble more information to substantiate things. My birth delayed this a bit but they used the time to create a strategy.

They found out that a Religious Community Holding Company building held the documents and those papers would hopefully prove or not whether the Davies family had any legal claim on land in Boston. This was where they decided to focus their quest.

That Religious Community Holding Company was—and still is—one of the largest land owners in Boston and the surrounding districts; the deeds of much of this land ownership went back to George II in the 1700s and other Monarchs before him. It made the Community one of the richest religious groups in the world. These deeds were held in the Holding Company Archives managed by a firm of accountants who in truth controlled things.

After my birth my father got a job at the Religious Community Holding Company. They thought it best not for both to work there in case events took a turn for the worse—a good move as it turned out. He did menial work at first but he managed to befriend and gain the confidence of an insider who had access to these archives; being responsible for filing the documents correctly and keeping them in good condition because some were very old and quite fragile.

That insider was Californian Charles (Chuck) Evans—someone else with Welsh roots. One alcohol fuelled evening Chuck revealed that there was one puzzling item in the archives—a fairly modern but pretty boring painting in an old frame. It was held in maximum security but seemed of little value. When he once asked about it he was told never to ask again and just file it as a maximum-security item."

Jonny was really hooked into the story and said excitedly, "I guess that must be our painting."

Aiyana replied with a smile that went straight to Jonny's heart.

"You're right; but you are getting ahead of me now Jonny. Let me continue the story. Chuck also revealed that he thought the Holding Company Board was being taken over by members of a splinter movement linked to the Mafia or at least some pretty heavy gangsters. Over a period of about ten years my dad had gained the trusted status of helping Chuck and he saw the painting himself. It was among several paintings and was of a woman handing a puppy to a child; a bit like a Gainsborough in style. On studying it closer it looked like another painting was hidden underneath the fairly ordinary looking displayed painting of the woman and the puppy. He couldn't be sure without taking out of the frame and didn't want to be caught doing that.

Going through some other documents relating to the painting he found a letter stating that the secret of the land offer to the pirate Robert Davies made by George II was revealed in the hidden painting. It stated that this should never be taken out of the archives. Dad took a photo of this letter and placed the original note back in its proper place.

He knew that if he ever was to solve the mystery of the land ownership he had to get that painting out of the archives; but how to do it without it being missed? He decided that the best way was to make a copy of the existing over-painted portrait and frame, then somehow replace the original and its overlay with this fake. The copy and replacement frame was to be created so that it could be assembled in the archive vaults after several visits to deliver the different parts. The fake would have to be good enough to fool the archive security team—at least for a while."

Barry chipped in.

"Now that was some plan Aiyana. And very risky as well."

Aiyana nodded and said, "Very true. Then they would have to get the original out of the vaults without being seen and without damaging the painting. This was the most dangerous bit.

"Dad came up with a plan to prepare another 'Old Master' style painting, but with a different image; one that could be temporarily laid over the original and its overlaid canvas. They would use a special water-based adhesive that would not damage the images beneath. This new false image could then be removed once the painting was outside the Community building and the original painting hidden away somewhere safe. If anyone stopped them as they were taking it out of the building they could say it had been damaged slightly and needed the attention of a professional restorer—the temporary fake overlay would show signs of damage. They could forge an official Religious Community 'take-out' pass to authenticate the procedure.

"Over a period of around four weeks the various elements of the fake picture and frame were brought together and smuggled into the vaults by hiding the pieces under clothing as he entered the building. It was highly dangerous but he could not think of another way. One evening he made the excuse to work late while Chuck was away on holiday. He assembled the fake and substituted it in the storage rack and, after carefully wrapping the original and frame with temporary overlay, walked it out of the building. There were few people about and fortunately nobody challenged him or asked for his fake pass."

Christina put her head in her hands and then looked up at Aiyana saying, "Oh my God. I can't believe what I'm hearing. It is like a film script. This is not the Cador I knew."

"Believe it Chrissie. Mum and dad decided to hide the original in a humidity-controlled container at a Native American Sacred Site near our home where few people would disturb it. They left it there while they decided what to do next; along with my dad's money left over from the boat sale plus some other relevant documents. So far they had only planned the painting's escape from custody. They now needed a plan to capitalise on their acquisition and this would take time and care.

It could prove that the Davies family were given the land although modern American law would make it difficult to make any claims such a long time after the grant was made by George II. But my tribe also had their claim on the land and refused to accept that George II had any right to give the land away as a reward for services to the Crown. At that time the tribe had nearly been wiped out by diseases brought over from Europe by the Settlers so it was important to their future. However, these tribal claims would be even more difficult to prove. But they thought there might be a way of rewarding both the Davies family and the Tribe by realising the value of the painting—if indeed it proved to be valuable.

Unfortunately Chuck discovered something was wrong a few weeks after he returned from holiday and reported it to the Managing Accountants. My dad found out via a friend giving him a warning with a phone call to his home and he knew he was in big trouble. He thought it best to disappear quickly. After a tearful goodbye to my mum, this he did. But, and this still upsets me when I talk about it so forgive me if my voice breaks, they found a body floating in Massachusetts Bay a few days later. There appeared to be no obvious injuries. But it took a long time before the body was identified as being my father."

Christina gasped out loud and Aiyana took a few breaths before completing this part of the story.

"The FBI never confirmed whether it was by accident or suspicious circumstances. I always felt they knew more than was being reported but nothing came to light. There was a rumour that the CIA got involved."

Christina said in a quiet voice, "How terribly sad. That must have been an awful time for you."

She knew the words were inadequate and did not convey the drama or the sadness that was being revealed, but it was all she could think of to say.

Jonny just stared at the floor and said nothing.

Aiyana replied to Christina, "It was Chrissie. As requested, twelve months after my mother's death I went through the documents and money and started to plan what to do next. Telephone numbers of family members in the UK were amongst the documents but some of these were out of date. However, he did keep up with what his British family was doing via social media, but just as a follower. I found this on his laptop that he left with my mum when he decided to disappear. That gave me some clues about how to make contact. One thing was clear in his Written Will and Testament that was amongst the documents. Whatever funds could be realised from the painting, then that money was to be split equally between the Tribe and his off spring. By the latter he meant me and Jonny."

With a touch of pent-up anger in his voice Jonny remarked, "That is one heck of a story Aiyana. But how did you find out about me working at the Matthew Lloyd Gallery in Cardiff?"

"Well, Jonny, you would be surprised what a trail we leave on Social Media and as I mentioned my dad left us his laptop."

Now coming to terms with his new status, Jonny leaned over and put his hand on Aiyana's arm saying, "Our dad."

Aiyana looked down at Jonny's hand and smiled.

"Sorry Jonny, yes, our dad. My feeling was that he wanted you to continue with the task of revealing the truth about the land ownership. He also left us his mobile and with the help a friend at Harvard I also tracked down other information. The Electoral Roll in the UK provides hard information about where people live. In today's world if you want to find out about people it is not too difficult as long as you are IT savvy. My Harvard friend is one of the best and does work for the White House."

Jonny then asked, "What about the painting? How did you get that out of USA and across to the gallery?"

"Yes; that was something of concern Jonny. Even though the main visible painting was clearly nothing to shout about, the frame was old. Once it was packed it wouldn't be visible of course but as an added disguise I had a sheet of modern ply fixed to the back. Fortunately I had a friend who was moving to the UK and she agreed to put the painting in the container with her other house items. If there was any Customs check I had my father's Will to prove my ownership. It was a risk but it came through unscathed.

I then came over to stay with her and help her move in and at the same time made some investigations about you Jonny and discovered that you worked at the gallery and were the only one working on the restorations and cleaning. Once I had this, and had removed the false painting my father had created, I sent the painting to the gallery. I had to get the painting to you so you could continue our father's quest. I have moved out of my friend's house and now have my own flat in Bath. My night at the Premier Inn in Bristol for our aborted meet was a one-off for the meeting."

Seeing the worried expression on Christina's face Barry immediately asked, "What about the nasty people that prompted you to cancel that meeting and was it the same two who tracked Jonny down to his flat? Who are they? Do you know?"

"In truth I'm not quite sure Barry. They could be FBI or even Mafia. But I think they might be something to do with the Religious Community Holding Company Accountants.

Although it is known as a religious community, as I have already indicated the accountants are said to have used heavy handed procedures since the gangster element took control and there is a lot at stake because this painting and the associated paperwork could cost them a lot of money. There could also be criminal charges because some think they were responsible for dad's death.

Somehow they must have tracked me and the painting to the UK. How they did this is a mystery to me. I don't think they have discovered how I got the painting into the country because there was no sign of them at my friend's house and I don't think they know about my flat in Bath. However I'm not sure about this. They clearly know something about you Chrissie because of the warning you received at the Llandoger Trow. Again, I'm at a loss as to how they knew. But someone has been tracking me."

Jonny added, "As Barry mentioned, they do know about me and where I live because they were at my door saying they had a package for me personally. I was with my friend Sandy and we scarpered pretty damn quick out the back with the painting because mum had warned me about things on the telephone. We could see them at the door when we left. They had no package that I could see and they didn't see us leave. They are getting information from someone; either in America or over here—maybe the gallery."

Christina looked forlorn and said, "I was scared enough before this meeting and I'm even more scared now."

Barry moved closer and gave her a squeeze and said to everyone, "So where do we go from here?"

Aiyana replied, "Well, I think we all have to take extra care and be aware of the people around us. But the next thing I think is to get the truth about that painting. Where is it now Jonny?"

"It's in a very secure place in South Wales Aiyana. My friend Sandy's sister Sue. is one of the world's most respected art collectors and dealers with a laboratory with X-ray and Infrared facilities. She is checking the painting for us as we speak and Sandy is helping her."

Aiyana came back with, "Great. Maybe you can check how she is doing on your way back to Cardiff?"

"Will do. But although I love your wrist bands Aiyana, like you I am concerned about our safety and I think we should be careful about using our mobile phones and social media.

The two heavies might be getting info from them. Use land lines where necessary. I have a friend in Bristol who might be able to help us on the security front. He is an IT genius and has friends at GCHQ in Cheltenham."

With a puzzled expression on her face Aiyana asked, "What's GCHQ Jonny?"

"It's the Government Communications Head Quarters that tracks info from across the globe. When hackers are at work they usually know about it. They might also have info on the two heavies."

Barry said, "Sounds like a plan Jonny. Are we all agreed?"

Everyone nodded in agreement. Jonny continued, surprised at his own confidence in taking control of the situation.

"As I have two important elements of the plan to complete—revealing the painting and getting advice on our security—I suggest I complete those tasks and then organise another meeting once I have some answers. In emergency any of us can contact each other on land lines but be aware of what is going on around you and keep off social media for now."

Christina smiled at her son and said, "It's getting late so I think we should get back to Clifton. You will probably want an early start tomorrow Jonny."

Barry agreed saying, "You're right Chrissie. Better get a move on. It's been quite an evening."

They all gave Aiyana a squeeze rather than shaking hands. A new bond had been formed. One based on intrigue, new family ties and fear. As they left the hotel they were super sensitive of everyone and everything around them. Similarly on the drive home—this time via the M5 Motorway before heading for Clifton after crossing the River Avon. Dark clouds were beginning to cover the moon and it looked like that storm was coming in.

Barry dropped Christina and Jonny off at Christina's flat and headed for his home. Once upstairs in the flat Christina and Jonny both had a stiff whisky to calm the nerves. Christina mused, "Well, my dear son, what has your father got us into here? I don't mind telling you that I am pretty spooked by it all and I doubt whether I will sleep much tonight. You take care tomorrow."

Jonny moved over and gave his mum a hug saying, "To be perfectly honest mum I am just getting my head around the fact that apparently my father was alive and cared not one jot about the fact he had a son apart from following him on social media. I'm going to crash out now. Try not to worry mum. It all looks a mess at the moment but I'm sure things will work out OK."

He knew he didn't sound very convincing about things working out because he was far from convinced himself. They both went to bed but the storm continued and Christina could not get to sleep. She got up and looked at the view from her window. The storm was right over head now and the lightning lit up the SS Great Britain and the riverside that had seen so much history; some to be proud of but others like the slave trade not. Her thoughts drifted across the last few days.

What on earth have we become involved with? A couple of nights ago I was reliving my teenage years on the front seat of a 1950s American saloon with Barry and now this.

A sudden large crash of thunder shook the flat accompanied by a huge flash of lightning that struck nearby. She suddenly felt very afraid for Barry as she wondered whether the two heavies knew where he lived. She returned to bed as the storm blew over but sleep did not come easy.

Saturday, 19 August

Christina's concerns about Barry turned out not to be misplaced. He had left her to drive home feeling quite bemused and thoughtful after the meeting with Aiyana.

Who would have thought it? Boring old Cador mixed up in stuff like this. I must do a bit of research on Boston and the Religious Community in the seventeen hundreds. Gotta find out more about this stuff.

He turned into his cul-de-sac and then left onto his drive with his mind on history. The twins were with their mother at this time so it was just him and Scrum at home. He opened the car door and turned for the house, pressing the button on his key fob to lock the car door while walking to the garage where Neil had left Scrum after walking him. The storm had just broken and crunching over the gravel in the heavy rain he looked up to realise the garage side door was open, which probably meant Scrum was out.

He was thinking it was odd because it was quite late. It was all quite worrying. He muttered to himself, "Must be next door with Neil."

He walked around to his own back door to open up before he collected his canine pal from Neil and saw Scrum asleep through the open door of the open porch. Relieved, but concerned in equal measures, he called as he opened the door.

"Hey mate; how is my best boy?"

Scrum lifted his head slightly and made a whimpering sound. Barry immediately realised something was seriously wrong. The dog had been sick and looked very poorly. Barry sat down on the door step, lifted Scrum's head onto his lap and reached into his pocket for his mobile. He then remembered Jonny's advice about using land lines so he placed Scrum's head back on his folded jacket for a pillow and headed for the phone in the hall. He needed to get hold of a vet.

He noticed a piece of paper attached to Scrum's collar but getting hold of a vet was his first priority. He took the number from his mobile phone log and dialled it on the land line but got an answer phone message telling him the surgery was closed and his call was being diverted to an emergency vet.

Barry was panicking by now knowing that his dog was very ill and all this was taking precious time. A lump began to grow in his throat and his heart was pounding as he feared the worst, but he had to remain focussed on getting help. Finally the call was answered. He quickly relayed the symptoms and the vet told him to take Scrum to the surgery immediately. The vet would meet him there. It was by now approaching midnight. Barry lifted Scrum into his arms and placed him gently on the back seat of his car. He took the note paper from under his collar and tucked in his pocket to check out later once Scrum was OK.

The drive to the surgery seemed to take ages. The storm was at its height and the windscreen wipers were having trouble clearing the rain from the screen. Torrents of water were rushing down each side of the road filling the gutters. The road was flooding in some places and the water grabbed on Barry's tyres making steering the car difficult. He kept talking to Scrum on the way, "Hang on my old friend. I'm here with you. We'll have you fixed up soon."

In truth he was really worried that he might lose him and the thunder and lightning added to his despair and growing gloom.

The vet was waiting when he arrived and Barry was soon rushing Scrum in through the main doors, past reception and into the examination theatre where the vet placed him carefully on an examination table. Barry watched with trepidation while the vet attached drips.

After a short while the vet asked, "What has the dog been eating because it looks like poisoning?"

"I don't know. I have been out and my neighbour was looking after him. I will call him. I hope he's still up."

Not wanting to use his mobile of course Barry continued, "Can I use your phone because mine is playing up."

"Sure. There's one in the waiting room."

Sitting down in the waiting room he grabbed the phone and dialled Neil's number. After a few rings it was answered by a voice that Barry recognised as belonging to Neil.

"Hello. Who's speaking please?"

"Neil, it's Barry and I'm at the vets with Scrum. The garage side door was open when I returned and Scrum was at the back porch. He is very poorly. Did he eat anything he shouldn't when you walked him?"

"No Mate. I put him back in the garage and shut the door as usual. Ted and Scrum didn't go off the lead tonight so I would have noticed. Sorry Barry. God I hope the lad is going to be OK."

"OK thanks Neil, see you later."

He put the phone down and looked up just as the vet walked out of the examination room and towards to him. He could see by the expression on his face and his sad demeanour that the news was bad. In his mind he tried to stop the words coming from the vet's mouth but of course failed.

"I am so sorry. I'm afraid he's gone."

Then it was if there was silence in the room—even though the storm was still raging outside. But in Barry's head that silence was soon replaced by a scream that got louder and louder along with a mind full of pain. He took a deep breath and tried to hold his composure.

A loud crack of thunder shook the glass entrance doors. Bending over he put his hands on his knees and screwed his eyes shut. But the tears he had been holding in while getting help for his canine pal now escaped. The vet handed him some tissues and after a while Barry walked over to the motionless Scrum, stroked his head slowly and bent down to kiss his forehead.

"Goodbye old pal. It was a fairly short life my boy but you were loved and you will be missed. Who's going to keep an eye on me now?"

He knew it wasn't much, but it was all he could think of to say in his grief absorbed state; and all he could get out of his mouth without choking.

After a while the vet said, "Call in on Wednesday and we'll sort out the paperwork Barry. I think you have enough to come to terms with at the moment. It is also important that we find out what poisoned him in case there is something nasty lying around out there so I will carry out an autopsy."

After thanking the vet he went out into the storm again with a huge lump in his throat and his tears mixing with the rain. He did not remember much about the drive home. He was now sitting on his sofa nursing a large single Malt and wishing he had some company to share his grief and the memories of his time with Scrum. He was heart-broken and in shock. The place felt very empty.

He then remembered the piece of paper in his pocket; the one that was attached to the dog's collar. He took it out and unfolded it.

Barry. The same fate will befall your kids if you go to the police.
Forget the Indian and they will be safe.

Barry felt his heart falter in his chest. In fact, he was sure that it stopped for quite a while as he realised that whoever the heavies worked for, they now knew where he lived and that Scrum had become a casualty of this saga. Where will it lead to? His first thought was his own children. He downed the whisky and using the land line called Thomas, his son.

Thomas was asleep and the ringing woke him up. He recognised the number on the phone screen through sleep filled eyes. Still in a doze he said, "Dad what the heck? Are you alright? It's gone midnight!"

Barry hadn't had time to think through what he wanted to say and he knew he sounded like a mad man and probably quite drunk.

"Tom. How do you and Meg fancy a holiday? My treat, how about Italy? Or Greece?"

Tom tried to wake himself up and understand what his father was on about.

"Dad you are babbling. Have you been on the vino? What's up?"

Barry swallowed hard to try and not let his emotions get the better of him and said, "Oh sorry Tom. There is no nice way to say this. I am afraid we lost Scrum tonight. The vet thinks he ate something he shouldn't."

"Ah no way Dad. So, so sorry. Is anyone with you?"

"No. I've just got in from the vet."

Barry continued trying hard to get some commitment about his holiday offer even though he knew he probably sounded like a lunatic.

"How about that holiday? I can book it for you tomorrow if you like. I can probably even get you a flight for tomorrow."

"Whoa slow down dad. You're not making sense. I know you are upset about Scrum but what has that got to do with a holiday. Anyway mum has got some things lined up for us."

Now using an almost pleading voice Barry said, "That's OK your mum can go as well."

Tom was by now sitting bolt upright in bed.

"Now I know something is up. Shall I come over?"

"No! no sorry Tom. I will call you first thing in the morning and explain things further."

He was now getting concerned about just how much he should tell Tom.

"Goodnight. I love you and Meg so much I just want you to have some fun."

"Love you too, Dad. Speak in the morning," replied Tom who was by now very confused and not a little bit worried. He knew how much his dad loved Scrum but something else was definitely afoot.

Barry thought about phoning Jonny and Christina, but then Jonny had said not to phone unless absolutely necessary until he had sorted out some additional security. Anyway it was now the early hours in the morning and he didn't want to disturb them. They couldn't do anything about it.

He didn't know that Christina was already awake due to the storm. He tried to get some sleep but his head wouldn't stop spinning; not from the large malt but from the terrible events that were now engulfing their lives. And how the hell did they know where he lived?

Chapter 5

Be strong when you are weak. Be brave when you are scared. Be humble when you are victorious.
(Native American saying)

Day 5 Sunday morning
20 August 2017

By the time that Jonny awoke at 5 o'clock the next morning the storm had abated. There were plenty of battered garden plants and debris about the place and some of the plants on Christina's balcony looked a bit sad. It had not been a great night's sleep for Jonny. As well as the storm, the events of the previous day kept going around and around in his head. Those events, coupled with the fact his father had been alive for a good part of his life and did not ever try and contact him, were bitter pills to swallow.

And it was Sunday. With all that had been going on he had lost track of the days. He got up, showered and dressed in a black tee-shirt and black jeans as per normal. The sun was just coming up as he wandered into the kitchen to find his mother already up and dressed in her riding clothes.

She turned around and said with a shrug, "I take it you didn't sleep too well last night either. I need to go for a ride to clear my head this morning. It's the only thing that helps when things are not so good. Better than seeing a psychiatrist I guess—and cheaper—but then again maybe not much cheaper when you think about it. How are you feeling this morning love? It was not a nice thing to hear about your father like that."

Jonny didn't look up.

"To be honest mum, I don't want to talk about it right now if it's OK."

Christina was a bit put out but understood.

"Oh! Fair enough. I just thought you would like to get it off your chest."

Shrugging his shoulders Jonny said, "Sorry mum. I will deal with it when I have time. Now how about a cup of tea and a bacon sandwich?"

He gave his mum a little smile and moved over to give her a peck on the cheek. She smiled back and said, "Kettle has just boiled and I'll put the frying pan on. There's some nice smoked streaky bacon in the fridge so I'll get it started. I am going to have my tea on the balcony if you want to join me. It needs a bit of a tidy up after the storm though."

Walking towards the hall phone he replied, "Yep. Sounds good to me. Be with you in a mo. I don't want to use my mobile; is it OK if I borrow your phone? I want to call Arthur Robinson. Can you keep an eye on the bacon for a while?"

By this time, it was just gone 6 am so Christina said, "OK; will do; though it's a bit early to phone love and it is Sunday."

"Don't worry he doesn't really sleep much mum."

Christina had spoken to Arthur on the phone a couple of times so she softly commented, "He is a little strange isn't he?"

Jonny smiled and nodded.

"Yeah; but geniuses normally are a little odd aren't they? And he is a mate so he is excused."

He picked up the land line phone and dialled a number that was quickly answered by Arthur's nervous habit and stammering voice.

"Um hhhello."

"Arty my friend, how goes life?"

Jonny spoke in his most enthusiastic voice. He liked to put Arthur at ease to calm his nerves and he had found from experience that being positive was a good policy.

"Um, JJJonny; um good to hear from you; um all OK with me. You OK?"

"Yeah I'm fine. Can I pop over to see you in a bit. I have a techy problem that I think you can help me with."

"Um, yes that will be fffine. Um when will you be over?"

"I shouldn't be long. I am in Bristol at Mum's. So as soon as I have had a cuppa and a bacon sarnie I will head down your way. Is that OK?"

"Um that's gggreat; see you soon."

The line then clicked and Arthur was gone.

After finishing frying the bacon and picking up his sandwich Jonny sat down with his mum on the balcony for a while and talked over the meeting with Aiyana the previous evening. As they spoke they watched Hotwell and the Bristol river side slowly awaken fresh from several hours of heavy rain. Although the sun was out there was still some mist over the water and it looked quite eerie. After a while he got up and tidied up the balcony storm rubbish before rinsing his cup out and wishing his mum a good ride on Wiggy. Christina said, "Hang on! I'll walk down with you love. I want to get a ride in before it gets too warm. My tummy feels like a washing machine every time I think about the situation we've found ourselves in."

Jonny opened the door for his mum to leave the flat and called the lift.

"Yeah it is pretty random all this stuff but dangerously interesting all the same."

He walked her to her car and gave her a quick hug and a kiss on the cheek. Christina responded and said, "See you soon. Keep in touch and take care darling. Phone Barry or myself daily on the landline to make sure we are all safe and keep us up to date about the painting and your ideas to improve our security."

Jonny waved goodbye with a quick

"Yep; will do."

Neither would know what news was about to break from across the Bristol Channel or what traumatic events Christina would experience that morning.

Sunday 20 August 2017
Cardiff Police Station

In Cardiff, Police Constable Hywel Jones was on the desk when the call came in regarding the body of a Matthew Lloyd being found. Two uniform police constables were sent down to secure the gallery and the serious crime squad was informed.

Detective Chief Inspector David Thomas had a difficult journey into his office dodging the debris of the big storm of the night before. He was just finishing his morning coffee and a cheese twist, while going through the many e-mails and administration documents that were now part of police work, when Inspector Ruth Chambers put her head around the door and exclaimed, "Bloody 'ell Dave. There is a right mess down in Bute Street! You had better put that paper work aside and come on down with me."

David Thomas jumped up, spilling crumbs all over his deck and papers.

"OK Ruth. Talk to me on the way. I hate admin so a bit of excitement is overdue. That was some storm last night though."

David Thomas had just recently been made a DCI; a position that has made his status conscious wife very happy, especially as he was still just 43 years old and had time to progress much further. However David was still coming to terms with the added responsibility that came with the rank. He was a quiet and unassuming man who followed the rules and generally came up with the goods. In truth, although he was handsome and fit, you would probably not look twice at him in the street. He sort of blended in, which was probably one of the reasons that he was good at his job.

Dave and Ruth had become close friends over the years and worked together well. They were often teamed up together. When they were off duty, or it was just the two of them, they were on first name terms. When on duty and others were involved then it was Ma'am and Sir.

Ruth explained the situation as they drove away from Cardiff Central Police Station.

"So evidently this Matthew Lloyd has been found dead in his gallery. Must be pretty bad 'cos PC Carl Jones had to go out and spew. He's only young, love his heart."

David wasn't sympathetic.

"Oh Jesus Ruth; I do hope he hasn't compromised the scene. Have the forensic people been informed?"

"Yes; they are at the gallery now Dave."

They turned into Bute Street to see that the protocol had been followed and the area had been cordoned off with police tape. On exiting the car David handed Ruth a plastic bag containing white disposable coveralls and plastic covers for shoes and then opened one for himself. They put them on, plus some latex gloves and entered the gallery. David asked the young constable he recognised, "Hello Carl. I hope you're feeling better now. Where is the body?"

Carl pointed to an open door at the back. Ruth and David could now smell something very unpleasant. As they entered the crime scene they were pretty shocked. The naked, flabby body of Matthew Lloyd was tied to a Louis Fourteenth style chair upholstered in pale green and cream stripes that was covered by a vile mixture of diarrhoea, blood and urine. The smell was vomit-inducing and flies had begun to gather. Someone had stapled Matt's penis to the wooden frame of the chair and also stapled his eyelids open, giving him a rather surprised look. In addition to this his throat had been slit right through to the spine. His head tipped backwards, lolling against the back of the chair. One of the forensic team turned and asked them to stay where they were for the moment.

David said quietly and slowly, "Oh, bloody ell Ma'am this is nasty... Ma'am?"

He turned around to see Ruth disappearing out the door to the other side of the street and throwing up her breakfast. He walked to the car and got out a box of man-sized tissues along with a bottle of water. Walking over to Ruth he wondered how she was going to cope with the autopsy. He thought how vulnerable she looked. Handing her a box of tissues and some water he said, "Here you go then, Ruth."

"So sorry, Dave. I'm not normally so squeamish and it will not happen again. It was just a shock, and that smell."

Thinking she would rather be in the open air, he said, "Would you mind getting one of your team to make some house calls to find out if anyone heard or saw anything? And check for CCTV. We also need to speak to who found him. I am going to talk to forensics. I think you need to get a clean overall on. You will find some in the boot of my car."

Glad to get her mind off the body and onto uniform police work, a relieved and grateful Ruth quickly replied, "OK. I will get someone on to it."

David nodded to Ruth before turning around to walk back to the gallery. He was thinking, *This is not an ordinary killing and not the sort of thing we are used to down here.*

Turning to one of the forensics team, he asked, "Do you have any idea as to when this might have happened yet Simon?"

"Bore da Sir. I would say about lunch time yesterday. But they sat him under the skylight and the heat from the sun has cooked him a little bit. It's a nasty piece of work this isn't it? If you give us half an hour we will have finished and you can come in to do your bit."

"OK Simon. Just let me know when you are ready."

His mind was ticking away as he thought, *Saturday lunch time; someone must have seen or heard something because people would have been about.*

Walking into the next room, he turned his attention to his surroundings. Everything looked as he suspected it should look. Paintings adorned the walls and appeared to be undisturbed; sculptures sat neatly on tables and the large antique desk looked neat and tidy and he thought, *OK, possibly not a robbery then.*

Calling forensics, he asked, "Can I open some drawers in here?"

It was Simon who answered.

"Yes Sir; all been dusted."

David wandered over to the desk. Opening the top draw he found a bunch of invoices and put them in a jiffy bag. The other drawers contained photographs of art work etc. Then he opened the last drawer *Eureka!* This one contained quite a few small cellophane packages of what David assumed was cocaine—plus a gay porn magazine. His thoughts were, *Could this be a drug or homophobic motivated killing? If so what had he done to deserve such a brutal demise? There was vengeance or a warning to others in this killing. It's almost like a ritual sacrifice. Someone with a much screwed up mind did this.*

He looked up to see Matthew's body had been bagged and placed on a trolley to be taken to the mortuary for the post-mortem. He asked, "Who is the pathologist for this case, Simon?"

"Leah Parton is on duty I believe, Sir."

"Ah that's OK; she is very good."

"And pretty damn gorgeous too, Sir. One wonders why she would want to be rummaging around in smelly dead bodies. But there you go."

David looked at him and winked.

"I can't say I had noticed Simon. I will stay here for a while to go over the scene and check in with your findings later."

The other thing he wanted to get in hand was a press statement. The media would soon be all over this and better to be ahead of the game with a plain holding statement. He dialled his office number and made sure things were in hand.

Sunday 20 August 2017

Christina, of course, was unaware of what had happened in Cardiff. After waving goodbye to Jonny early that morning, she got into her Discovery and drove to the stables in Northwick. When she arrived there were a few cars parked outside the stable as normal but she didn't take much notice because she was just enjoying the beautiful sunny morning after the terrible storm the night before.

There was still mist in the valleys and she guessed it must have been hanging around in the Bristol Channel because she could hear an occasional fog horn from ships leaving or entering Avonmouth. It was still very early but the yard staff members were already hard at work. Approaching one of the girls she checked if Wiggy had been fed yet and was pleased to hear that he had not. It meant that it was OK to ride him straight away. So feeling very content she walked over to the tack room to get ready.

In any stables the tack room is the hub of the enterprise and it was particularly true of Northwick Equestrian. It smelled of leather, horse sweat and coffee. Much discussion was carried out here about anything from the rights and wrongs of draw reins to who got off with who the previous night. A few naughty liaisons had taken place there when only the horses were witnesses. Christina loved it.

The place enabled her to have some quality time.

Breathing in the wonderful horsey smells she greeted Holly, the grossly overworked and underpaid head girl who was sharing an ancient brocade sofa with about four terriers and a scruffy brown and white lurcher called Mumbles. She was sorting out the horse out time rota for the day. Holly was in her early thirties and she spoke in wonderful soft tones with a slight Gloucestershire accent. She looked up and said, "You are an early bird this morning Chrissie. Wiggy was in last night but Jan lunged him for half an hour yesterday. He was a proper good boy. The school is free if you are schooling."

"It's fine Holly; I am going to hack him out today. I need to clear my mind. There is so much going on in my life at the moment that I just want to forget everything for an hour or so."

Holly looked straight into Christina's eyes and said, "I am here mind if you need a friendly ear Chrissie. You know that."

"Thank you Holly. You are a dear friend. See you in a while."

Christina lifted down Wiggy's saddle and bridle from the rack while Holly got back to her rota, but a little worried about Christina's mood. Christina then walked over to Wiggy's stable and as she walked in she saw that Joe, one of the lads, had just finished grooming him. Admiring her superb horse Christina remarked, "Thank you Joe. He looks very smart. What stars you and Wiggy both are."

She started to tack up her horse, avoiding his teeth as she did up the girth and telling him to pack it in. This was the regular banter between her and Wiggy as they prepared to ride. She then led him over to a concrete mounting block, got on and was soon hacking up the lane. She hadn't taken too much notice of the red Range Rover Evoque with blacked out windows quietly start-up further up the lane and passing her slowly further down, although she thanked them for passing wide and slow.

She continued on her leisurely ride out into the countryside letting the stress of the previous few days drift away. The fields were still wet but the water was slowly draining into the ditches and gullies by the side of the lane and into the streams that were getting flooded.

The lane surface was already dry in patches. However, she did notice the Evoque parked a few miles on and thought it was a bit odd and too early for courting couples even if it had blacked out windows. Suddenly someone opened the car door just as she was passing making Wiggy shy violently to the right. This possibly saved her life because the sunlight glinted on polished steel and the man who opened the door was brandishing something that looked like a bloody great Samurai sword. He was trying to take a swipe at Wiggy. Fortunately he missed.

But the horse took great exception to it, along with the flash of reflected sunlight, and shot off very fast down the road with Christina hanging on for dear life. Although she was scared the shock kicked in the adrenalin and she went into a sort of automatic survival mode. Her initial thoughts to herself were to get away and keep Wiggy from slipping on the tarmac.

Where can I go? Where can I go?

The lane had high hedges and she was hemmed in. She had just managed to regain some sort of control of her beloved horse when she heard the slamming of a car door and an angry revving V8 engine. Taking a quick look back, she saw the Evoque speeding towards her and she screamed out loud, "No!"

This only upset Wiggy again who put on a spurt of speed galloping further up the lane. Christina then spotted an open gateway to a field about twenty-five yards ahead. Taking control of her horse to get him balanced enough to make the turn without slipping, she pushed him forward until they reached the gateway. She then pulled him up and executed a perfect turn on the quarters shooting into a still wet stubble field, just as the Evoque raced straight past, slamming on the brakes making the tyres screech as the rubber burned on the tarmac.

Christina didn't stop. Putting her horse into an extended canter she rode to the other side of the field looking for a different way out. Even though she tried to steer her horse towards the drier patches, the muddy soil slowed her down and took much of the strength from Wiggy She spied another open gate in the left-hand corner. Looking over her shoulder she saw the Evoque was now making the turn into the field but its four-wheel drive was struggling to cope because the tyre treads were not really a match for the mud. They were more for cruising in Chelsea than going off road. She looked to her front and murmured to herself, "I can make that gate."

Pushing Wiggy into a gallop towards the opening they went flying through. She pulled up sharp and turned on the quarters, grabbed the gate and pulled it towards her until it clicked into place and she thought, *That will slow them down a bit.*

Then, turning Wiggy, she cantered the bewildered horse through a second field praying for another gate.

She pressed on through this field, starting to take stock of her surroundings. This second field was larger—about ten acres and laid to grass, making it a bit easier on Wiggy. She was on top of a ridge which was drier and the field sloped sharply down to her right ending in a partly mist shrouded flooded stream at the bottom. Through her panic she saw the stream as an escape route for a horse but perhaps not an Evoque. She only hoped Wiggy was up to the challenge as he was more used to trotting around doing pretty circles in a ménage than running in a cross-country event or hunting.

Taking a quick look around she could see those chasing her with the Evoque had opened the gate and were again driving or sliding towards her. She turned Wiggy down the steep slope and into the mist without a problem. The Evoque drove to the top of the ridge and also turned down following slowly on the slippery grass. Wiggy was practically sitting down on his haunches as they neared the bottom of the hill but the Evoque kept coming.

Suddenly her horse shot forward, nearly losing his balance and coming close to unseating Christina. She heard a dull thud and something whistling by her head. In horror she realised they were now shooting at her with a silenced gun.

She did the only thing she could and pushed Wiggy faster; knowing it could possibly end in disaster. Luckily he kept his balance until they got close to the stream. She found a pretty hard bit of ground and hoped the other side of the stream was also sound. She backed up enough for Wiggy to get his stride and then pointed his head towards the flooded stream and pleaded aloud, "Don't fail me now Wiggy. JUMP!"

Just as another bullet whistled past and embedded itself in a tree at the other side of the stream, the horse launched himself up and over the wide ditch landing safely on the other side. The ground stood firm and Christina put her legs to Wiggy's side and shouted, "*GO, GO.*" Glancing over her shoulder, through the mist she was relieved to see the Evoque now nose down stuck in the swollen stream with the water above bonnet level at the front.

Three men got out—two middle aged and one younger with blond hair. For a moment Christina thought she had seen him before, but now out of breath she didn't have time to think about it as she leaned forward urging Wiggy to go faster up the hill in front of her and away from the stream and her pursuers. He was soon out of the mist and into the sunlight again—goodness knows where he found the strength.

After a few minutes she had slowed down to a canter and was patting and thanking her dear now profusely sweating horse for trusting her and doing things totally outside of his dressage training.

Christina regained some composure and started to think quickly. She was pretty sure the Evoque would be stuck for some time, but they could still follow on foot and they had guns that they were prepared to use for God's sake. Talking calmly to the horse she said, "We need to find a way out of here and go back to the stables a different way Wiggy."

As she got to the top of the hill to look around she could see both bridges across the Avon and so got her bearings. She spied a gate onto a road she recognised. Cantering over she breathed a sigh of relief when she saw that there was no padlock on it. Opening the gate was easy because of Wiggy's beautiful schooling. Even though he was still puffing he stood perfectly still for her to lean down and unlatch the bolt, and then the same for her to close it again. She turned his head towards home and trotted down the country lane, using breathing exercises to calm her nerves.

Her head was still spinning when about half an hour later Christina and Wiggy were turning into the yard. She jumped down off her very hot and sweaty horse and led him over to his stable. Looking around she spotted Joe.

"Please Joe can you wash Wiggy down for me? I have an emergency."

Joe said, "Yeah no worries."

Then looking at the horse he gasped, "What have you been doing for goodness' sake? He looks like you've been out for a day's hunting rather than a quiet hack."

Christina looked at him and surprising herself with her composure said, "Hunted more like I'm afraid Joe. Do you know where Holly is?"

Joe replied, "In the school."

Christina rushed around to the all-weather arena at the back of the stable yard without a glance, leaving Joe wondering what the hell was going on. Holly was schooling a lovely big grey over some fences but Christina didn't wait for her to finish before calling her name.

"Holly! This is an emergency! Please can I borrow the yard phone."

"Yes of course you can. Whatever is the matter Chrissie? You alright? Is Wiggy OK?"

"Yes fine. Please Holly; I really need the keys to the office. I must make a call."

Holly looked at the normally cool Christina and could see she was in a very stressed state. Jumping off the horse she passed the reins to one of the working pupils before hurrying over to a red brick single story building that was part office and part Holly's living accommodation. With a curious expression on her face she asked, "Have you lost your mobile then?"

"No. But it is important that I use a land line. The reason I'll explain later."

Holly unlocked the door and Christina rushed in to a small kitchen area and over to a scrubbed pine table littered with 'Horse and Hound' magazines, bills and unwashed breakfast dishes. She picked up the handset that was sitting amongst the clutter.

"Press nine for an outside line. I will leave you to it. Shout if you need me mind."

Holly then left the room and closed the door behind her. Christina took a deep breath and dialled Barry's land line number. It rang twice and Barry answered with a quick, "Hello."

Now sobbing Christina cried, "Barry! It's Chrissie. I've been chased and shot at."

She then let it all get to her as she crumpled down onto a chair, fighting the tears and lump in her throat as she tried to get the words out to tell him the story. It took some time. The previous hour's drama hit her like a brick as she relived the real danger she had survived and the realisation that she was still in a lot of trouble.

Barry gently got her to calm down enough to tell him the complete chain of events before she added, "We have to call the police Barry."

"OK love. I'm afraid I also have some bad news as well. Scrum was poisoned last night. He died at the vets. The bastards left a note saying it will be my kids next."

This sent Christina spinning out of control.

"Oh God Barry! Why didn't you let me know?"

73

"I have been trying to Chrissie. I've called you all morning on your land line! But we need to get hold of Jonny before we do anything else. Get in your car and come straight to me. Don't use your usual route though. I suggest you go north and come in via Patchway. It will take a bit of time to get their Evoque out of the ditch but we have to stay several steps ahead so keep your eyes peeled. I will have to call Jonny on his mobile. I know we shouldn't but we have no choice at the moment. In the meantime I'll also rustle up something to eat."

"I'm not really hungry Barry. I can't stop shaking. I've just been shot at for God's sake. How the hell am I going to drive let alone eat?"

With a serious note in his voice Barry said, "Because you are a much stronger woman than you give yourself credit for. I think if they had wanted to kill you then you would now be dead. I think they wanted to kill Wiggy and frighten you silly. Now move Chrissie. Go to your car and get to me ASAP."

Christina felt a bit chastised and was not really convinced with Barry's explanation about the shooting. But she recognised that he was right about getting to his place.

"OK. See you in fifteen minutes or so but I'm really scared. And how the hell did they know about Wiggy and the stables?"

Sunday 20 August 2017

After waving goodbye to his mother that morning Jonny walked to his Mini and slung his rucksack in the boot. Like Christina he was not aware of the dramatic events across the Bristol Channel. It was only a short drive to Arthur's house—particularly this early in on a Sunday morning before the Bristol traffic built up. Arthur lived with his mother in Montpelier—a suburb just north of the centre of Bristol. It had been named the 'hippest' district in the UK by one travel index and had been a bustling hub since the late 18th century when baths for inner city dwellers were established there.

A bohemian hotspot, it still maintained its unique and artistic vibe with its quirky street art much-beloved by residents. He was soon pulling up outside a Victorian villa, the name plate reading 'Sapere Aude' that translated into 'Dare to be Wise'.

To enter the grounds there were large wrought iron gates operated by two intercom buttons on the brick gate posts with cameras mounted on top. Jonny knew what to do as he had visited his friend here many times so he pressed the button on the right and after a few seconds the gates slowly opened. He drove in and parked his car on the neatly brick paved drive and walked around to the back. As he looked up to the top of the building Arthur opened a door in the roof and stepped onto a fire escape waving to Jonny. He then let down a metal ladder for Jonny to climb up.

Once in the room Jonny looked at the little guy before him. Arthur was no more than five feet tall with lots of blond curls. He was also of slight build. Jonny put his hand on his pal's shoulder and said with a smile, "Hey buddy, how are you?"

"Um yyes, ggood. Um lots to kkeep me occupied."

Arthur's large attic space was furnished wall to wall with computer screens all with a different view. There were loads of electrical parts on shelves and a small bed in one corner with a large curled up ginger cat called Icon who was staring balefully at him. There were two doors in the room—both metal clad with multiple locks.

Arthur had an acute personality problem. He could only really relate to a computer, although he could talk to Jonny. This problem meant that he rarely ever left the house because the outside world terrified him. He had many on-line friends around the world that he played competition computer games with and he also talked daily through his computer to many like-minded nerds. In many ways he was a bit like an old-fashioned radio ham.

He had been friends with Jonny from the first day at junior school. Jonny would often stand up for Arthur as he always seemed to attract the bullies. So to Arthur Jonny was a hero and they communicated with each other on a regular basis.

Arthur was a mega genius with computers and the associated technology. He was able to work from this fully equipped converted attic base and earn a sizable amount working for several industry giants checking the cyber security of their systems. But he also had many contacts within GCHQ in Cheltenham for whom he worked on an advisory basis.

With a more serious tone to his voice, Jonny said, "I need your help Arty. We have a problem and I think you can help."

Recognising the change in Jonny's demeanour Arthur replied, "Of ccourse. If I ccan."

Jonny then went through the events of the last few days. It took some time and Arthur was totally absorbed in the story making some notes on his iPad along the way.

When he had finished the saga Jonny asked, "So I just wondered if there was a way to improve our security like masking our mobiles so we can't be tracked for example?"

Arthur thought about it and looked up saying, "Um so um, I think I ccan help you. Ffirst of all we need to mmake ssure that your phone has not been hacked. I want you to change your ppassword to artymax1. This wwill um ccancel any existing hhacking and enable me to be alerted if anyone ttries to hack you again. If they do, I can clear it immediately. Nnot only that, I wwill um be able to llocate where any hhacking is coming ffrom. Over ttime we should bbe able to llocate where they are living or bbased. I have a ccontact that operates a ssquadron of drones and these can be um useful along with CCTV. You ccan do the ssame to seven other um mmobiles in yyourtteam and issue ppasswords up to artymax7.

"Ddo the same to any other um ddevice that you use for e-mail or social mmedia. When all this is over you can go back to your own um personal ppasswords again. I have also been developing this little chip to um stop um anyone tracking mmobile phones. It wwill be available on the open market soon. This ccan pprovide extra ssecurity."

He was getting quite animated now that he was into the subject he lived for.

"Oh and um if you want I have this little gizmo."

He shot over to a filing cabinet and rummaged around before producing a zip lock bag with what looks like small red and blue buttons.

"With this, I can ttrack you through CCTV almost anywhere in the wworld. Um, so I can um check you are ssafe. But one of these um babies can also be used to ttrack the unpleasant people if you get um, close enough to stick one on them or their um, ccar for example.

"The um ddrones can again help where there is nno CCTV cover. I'll pprogramme the red buttons for your team members and the bblue ones for the enemy. Make sure you ddon't mix them up when applying them. How mmany of each do you need?"

Jonny looked at him and shook his head in amazement.

"About seven red and maybe five blue I guess. Arty my buddy; you are a genius."

Arthur smiled and said, "Um yyes. I suppose I am. Each bbutton has a piece of peel off um plastic and underneath is an extremely sticky bbase. Um don't allow the sticky part to touch anything other than um, what you need it to sstick to, bbecause you will be unable to get it off in a hurry."

Arthur chuckled and continued, "Um, now pass me your phone and I will show you how to place the um, anti-tracking chip."

"Have you anything that we can use to check if we have already been bugged by a similar button placed on our vehicles by those chasing us Arty?"

"Yyyes. I um ccould um loan you a couple of special wands but I have developed an app that you can download to your phone and use the ccamera function to identify any um enemy bbugs by pointing it at any ssuspected carrier. I'll tell you what let's um do bboth and you can wwand your car before you leave today."

Now on a roll, Arthur continued, "Oh and um I've jjust remembered. I will also ddownload a program that will scramble your wwords to um anyone except the person you are calling from your phone. That ccould be very useful."

All Jonny could think of saying was, "Wow. Can I do that for the other phones?"

"Um yeah. I'll sshow you how."

He took Jonny's phone and started a download. In five minutes the download was completed.

"Ah! Something else Arty. Hopefully you can help but if not I will understand. I wonder whether you could see if your friends at GCHQ know anything about the Religious Community Holding Company Accountants in Boston and whether the two heavies that appear to be following us are connected to them in any way?

We have information that the Board operating the company is dominated by a splinter Mafia or other gangster mob and that they might have been responsible for my father's death. I wouldn't be surprised if they are involved in other criminal stuff in the UK. It would be useful to know who or what we are dealing with."

Arthur looked very concerned but after some thought he replied, '

"Um I'll ssee what I can do. I have some other ccontacts that um mmight be able to hhelp as well. Bbut it is important that my involvement is er kkept secret."

"Fantastic Arty. I'm going to go back to Wales now to see what Sandy and Sue have discovered about the painting. Is there anything I can get you before I leave? Also what do I owe you?"

"Um I hhave all I need and you um owe me nothing. This is rresearch."

Jonny looks at his friend with compassion.

"Ah Arty you worry me. You need to get out and see some life. Get a girl friend or something."

Arthur wrinkled his brow.

"I ssee all the life I um nneed through my ttechnology. I don't like the wworld out there. Um it is nnot for me."

"OK my friend; I will go now. But take care."

Jonny hugged Arthur before collecting all his new security aids. Arthur then pressed a button and the locks on the fire escape all clicked to unlock. Jonny waved as he stepped out onto the fire escape landing.

"See you soon Arty."

"Um I will be wwatching you. Don't forget to apply the bbuttons I gave you ccorrectly. Um I want to see you on ttelly. And I'll wait on the fire escape so you ccan ggive me the thumbs up after you have used the um wand on your ccar. If you um ffind one, disarm it by ppointing the end of the um wwand in the centre of the bbutton and pressing the red um trigger. When the ggreen light comes on it has bbeen disarmed.

"Once disarmed, um try and gget one off and over to mme. It will be very difficult bbut it ccould also be um useful in tracking the bbad guys ddown."

Jonny trotted down the steps and used the wand on his Mini; going over it very carefully and paying special attention to underneath the vehicle. There was no bleep from the wand so he gave the thumbs up to Arthur. He decided to apply a button to an inside pocket in his wallet rather than on the car. That way he could be tracked when not in the Mini.

As he turned his car towards the gates they slowly opened and he headed for Wales, but not before stopping for a take-away cheese sandwich at a local cafe. He was soon on the M4 Motorway listening to the car radio and keen to get back to Sandy and Sue.

It was now mid-morning but the roads were still pretty clear of holiday traffic as Jonny pulled up at the toll booths to cross the Avon and paid the fee. Once across, it didn't seem long before he arrived at the turning towards Duffryn and Jonny was looking forward to receiving the latest news about the painting and getting his new security kits in place. In fact he was feeling pretty pleased with the progress he had made.

The car radio was giving out the news and weather. A recent terrorist attack in Barcelona was the lead story and of course there was a lot about Brexit and how good or bad it would be for the country. The romance between Prince Harry and his American actress girlfriend Meghan Markle was receiving more attention from the gossip columnists. Then something that shook Jonny rigid.

The body of a gallery owner has been found in his shop in Bute Street Cardiff. He has been identified as Matthew Lloyd and it is being treated as murder. Police are on the scene and an area has been cordoned off. A further statement will be given later today.

Jonny swerved to the side of the road in shock. Hooting motorists made him realise that it was not a good place to pull over, so he drove until he could park up and get out of the car. His heart was hammering in his chest and he felt very queasy. After giving himself a few minutes to think things through he reached for his now secure phone and dialled Sandy on her sister's land line.

Fortunately it was Sandy who picked up the phone.

"Hello. Who's speaking please."

By her demeanour it sounded as if she had not heard the news about Matt yet, but not thinking about breaking the news gently in his highly stressed state Jonny yelled down the phone.

"It's Jonny! Matt's dead! It's just been on the fucking radio! Shit Matt's dead, they say murder. Fuck Sandy; fuck!"

There was a short silence before Sandy said slowly, "Oh my God! Sooo do you think it is connected with the painting hun?"

Surprised and a bit annoyed at Sandy's calmness Jonny replied, "A bit of a bloody coincidence if not Huh. I am on my way to you now. I'm off the motorway and have just pulled over near Newport. I won't be long. Don't use your mobile phone until I get there."

He then hung up and got back on the road; his mind reeling all over the place. He just wanted to get to the safety of Sue's high security home to think things through. It wasn't long before he was rolling up alongside the stone steps. Sandy was waiting by the door and hustled him into the drawing room.

Making the understatement of the day, an upset Sandy said, "This is sooo not good, Jonny, is it? Matt was a Twat but …dead…This is pretty heavy news, mate. Wow! I can't quite get my head around it."

Jonny put his head in his hands and then ran his fingers through his hair, before looking up at Sandy and saying, "Thinking further about things, the painting may not be connected to Matt's death of course. Right now we don't have proof of this. But I need to tell you the story Aiyana gave us yesterday. It's strange as shit. I am so sorry to get you involved in all this Sandy. I think Sue needs to hear this as well."

"Okey dokey. I'll go and grab her. Lord Henry is here as well. I'll bring him through. He'll want to know what is going on and I hope he might be able to give us some advice hun."

Jonny put his arm around her shoulders and looked at her pretty little worried face. He really cared about Sandy and she cared about him.

"Sounds like a good idea. I think I need to go to the police in Cardiff. This is beyond us now. I also need to call mum and Barry and then Aiyana."

Just at that time there was a call coming through on his mobile and he could see on the screen that it was Barry. He swiped the green button on the screen and said, "Hi Barry wassup…?"

"Hi Jonny. I know we agreed not use mobiles and I'm sorry to call on this number but we have some serious problems and I had no choice."

Jonny could tell he was really worried and explained that the mobile was cool because Arthur had given him some electronic kit that has made things more secure on this number now. He would be able to secure all their phones when they next met up. Now more relieved Barry quickly explained the harrowing chase that Christina had just experienced and the death of Scrum and the attached note threatening his children.

"Jonny this is bloody scary. How do they know so much about us? Are you safe?"

Feeling a bit numb Jonny waited before he spoke, gathering his thoughts about how to tell Barry about Matthew Lloyd. He said, "I'm safe for the moment Barry. But have you seen or heard the news this morning?"

"No. I've been sorting out things with the vet. I'm going to have Scrum cremated. They are sending samples off to toxicology in the morning and I should get the results back in a day or so. We need to know what killed him. I've also been trying to contact Christina on her land line but of course she was out riding so it took ages. I didn't want to use her mobile. I have also spoken to my ex-wife because I wanted to get my children to safety. I gave her very little details but my insistence made her as mad as hell! However I managed to get her and the twins to take the next train to London and stay with some friends; just for a day or two until I can sort out something else. I told her about Scrum but not the note. Anyway what is the news Jonny? What have I missed?"

"Sounds like a good plan about the twins Barry but you had better sit down while I tell you the latest news here."

Jonny then told a shocked Barry about Matthew Lloyd's murder. All Barry could say was, "Ooooh shit!"

"I'm sorry to cut you off now Barry but I can't say any more at the moment. I have to go. Lord Henry has just arrived. Don't go to the police just yet. I will let Lord Henry know what is going on. He has contacts and will be able to give us good advice. I will call you as soon as I have spoken to him. Bye for now."

As Jonny ended the call Barry walked to the window and looked out on his calm suburban garden thinking about his dog, Christina's close call and the events that were escalating at a furious pace. There were lots of berries already forming on his holly tree and he thought that it might be a sign of a hard winter to come. He then slowly moved his head so that he was looking up at the sky and cried, "Oh God! What have I done to deserve all this."

He then curled up on his sofa and burst into tears.

Chapter 6

Be strong enough to stand alone, be yourself enough to stand apart, but be wise enough to stand together when the time comes.
(Native American saying)

Sunday Lunch Time
20 August 2017

Back at the Mayhew Estate Jonny put his mobile back in his pocket and turned to face the room. Lord Henry and Sue had just walked in through the French doors. He had just flown in from his estate in Scotland after organising a grouse shoot. The 16-seat Eurocopter was still on the front lawn.

Jonny observed Lord Henry's cool nonchalant entrance that was preceded by a black Labrador and a Springer spaniel who both insisted that Jonny said hello with a stroke and a pat. Lord Henry was dressed in a beautifully cut country tweed jacket and moleskin trousers. Jonny thought, *He is bloody gorgeous. Shame he's straight.*

Sandy was also thinking, *Shame, he is my sister's husband.*

In a deep, wonderfully enunciated voice, Lord Henry said, "Sandy; good to see you. And Jonny; good to meet you at last. I understand you have found yourselves in a spot of bother?"

A shaken Jonny replied, "I am afraid it's just got a whole lot worse Sir! I really could do with your advice."

Lord Henry sat down saying, "OK let's hear it then? And please call me Henry. Take your time because detail can be very important."

Jonny then related to him the ever-increasing catalogue of events including details about Arthur's security gizmos and the necessary secrecy about his involvement. It took some time.

After some silence Lord Henry drew a long breath and said slowly, "OK. Let's think this through. The first thing we need to do is to get your mother and Barry up here, and possibly the horse. These people sound pretty nasty so your family's safety is paramount. If they had wanted to harm Aiyana they could have

82

done that some time ago so hopefully she should be safe for now but we will have to think about her situation as well.

You and Sandy will also need to stay at Mayhew. Sandy has her own room here anyway and plenty of clothes to change into. We will prepare a room for you Jonny. It is not safe to return to your flat until this business has been sorted. But you will need to get hold of some extra clothes. We have an excellent level of security in place here so once inside I'm confident we can keep everybody safe. Then I believe you should talk to the police with regards to Matthew Lloyd's murder because you and Sandy were probably one of the last to see him alive and obviously the police will have looked at CCTV and seen you both in the area. As somebody who worked regularly at the gallery that is reason enough for them to want to interview you anyway.

However, at the moment I'm not sure whether you need to tell them about the other events because as of right now we cannot be sure that the murder is to do with the painting, although it is highly likely of course. It might be to do with something else altogether. And we can't talk about Arthur's involvement either. So before you meet the police I will need to talk to some pals in security and law to confirm the best way forward. They could advise something different and you might need a legal representative in with you."

Jonny heaved a sigh and said, "I'm really sorry to get you all mixed up in this. It started out with a contact from a stranger that intrigued me and my mother but has since exploded into something that is getting out of control. None of us ever expected to arrive at this crazy situation—particularly so quickly."

Lord Henry placed a friendly arm around Jonny's shoulder saying, "Don't worry about it Jonny. From what you have told me, curiosity would have led me to follow the same clues. Someone tells you that the father you thought died around twenty years ago was in fact alive and living in USA until just a few years ago—you had to follow it up. I will organise a horsebox to go down and pick up your mother's horse, and I think you should go and pick up her and Barry. I will lend you one of our cars because your Mini might have been spotted on CCTV by the police and it could be on a stop list. It will not take them long to track down where you live so time is short."

A much-relieved Jonny replied, "Thank you so much. I was beginning to panic."

He took his phone out of his pocket and called Barry's number. It was answered very quickly.

Jonny asked, "Hi Barry. Has mum arrived at your place yet?"

Walking over to the window to look up the road Barry replied, "Nope, not yet. I'm feeling sick with worry."

"OK. I'm sure she will be there soon Barry. Here's the plan. Lord Henry is going to send a horse box to pick up Wiggy and a car for you and mum. I'll be driving the car. It will be a whole lot safer with you guys up here. You will need to pop back to mum's place to pack some clothes for her and can you ask her to pack some for me. I have some in my old wardrobe at her flat and she knows my size and what I like if she needs to buy extra.

Then take yourselves somewhere to have something to eat and let us know where you are so we can pick you up. So bring with you essentials and changes of clothes for you as well; you might be here for some time. And don't leave behind passports just in-case. The enemy is probably still trying to sort out the Evoque so you shouldn't be followed, but be alert anyway."

"OK Jonny. But I think I will park my car at the university campus after picking the gear up from Christina's and then take a taxi into Bristol. That way I'll not have to worry about parking. We can leave Christina's car in my garage. There's room for my Chevy and her Discovery."

Barry breathed a sigh of relief when he looked outside again and saw Christina turning into the drive.

"OK Jonny. Your mum has just arrived. I'll get moving."

"Phew! Great news. Keep in touch. Let us know where you are when you get to your café or bar."

Jonny switched off his phone and looked at Lord Henry.

"I think I should get going straight away. Barry sounds pretty spooked."

Lord Henry, leant down and stroking the head of his spaniel said, "Right then let's get this organised."

He got up and wandered over to the French doors saying, "I will chivvy up someone from my stables to pick up the horse. Can you find a post code for Wiggy's stables?"

Jonny replied quickly as it sounded like an order, "Can do. I just need to look it up on my phone. I'll also ensure Sandy's phone is secure with Arthur's chip and make sure she has a CCTV locator button on her person."

Sue got up and as she walked out to the kitchen she told them she was going to get some sandwiches for everyone.

"I've already made some and you can take them with you if you don't have time to eat them now."

Lord Henry was also walking out and looked back over his shoulder saying, "Oh, and Jonny! After I have taken advice and when Christina and Barry arrive, I will try and arrange for the police to come here to interview you and Sandy. I think I can pull a few strings. Of course we will need to meet up first and discuss the advice I receive."

He didn't expect a reply. Again it was more of an instruction as he was now taking control. By the time he had finished he was outside followed briskly by his dogs.

As Lord Henry and his dogs quickly disappeared towards the stables Jonny raised an eyebrow and looked at Sandy saying, "Do you think I should follow him?"

"Yep. I would get after him if I was you hun. He's now on a mission."

Jonny put on his best pleading look and voice and said, "But I'm hungry again! I don't function when I am fucking hungry. Can you bring me out some sarnies Sweetheart? Pretty please."

Sandy laughed and said, "OK. I guess you will be in the stable yard, as Henry will be organising a box for your mum's horse. So you had better get out there PDQ and have that post code ready for him hun."

Jonny blew Sandy a kiss and took out his mobile to Google post codes. At the same time he quickly walked through the French doors, across the lawn towards a beech hedge and an ornate metal gate. In truth he was almost running. He passed through the gate to the beautiful old red brick stable yard that included about 30 loose boxes and an archway with a clock tower at one end. It was very impressive.

When he eventually caught up with Lord Henry he found him talking to an attractive, tall dark-haired man of about thirty years old, dressed in a check shirt tucked into brown well-fitting jodhpurs and long tan riding boots.

The word that came into Jonny's mind as he walked over to the two men was, *Yummy.*

Lord Henry did the introductions.

"Ah Jonny, this is Devlin. He will be picking up the horse and he will be using a box that is not sign written in case those villains are still about. Do you have the post code?"

"Yep here it is. The stable block is just before you enter Northwick."

Jonny showed his mobile screen to Lord Henry who immediately wrote down the details and handed them to Devlin.

Jonny then walked over and shook Devlin's hand saying, "Hi Devlin. Nice jodhpurs."

Devlin looked slightly amused as he responded with a quizzical expression, "They are Cavallo; a present from my ex—girlfriend. I must say they are very comfortable."

Jonny recognised the strongly coded answer and thought, *Hmm. Possibly not gay but a nice one for Sandy perhaps.*

He turned around to see Sue and Sandy walking through the gate with trays of sandwiches in their hands. They walked over to a stone bench and table and placed the trays on it.

Sue called out, "Lunch is ready. Devlin there is plenty here for you. Do help yourself. Oh, and Devlin, have you met my sister Sandy?"

Addressing Sandy with a smile in her voice she said, "Henry poached him from the Cuthbert-Clawley's in Cambridgeshire. What a bloody mouthful that is."

Devlin looked on the prettiest vision of cuteness he had ever seen and said, "No I er, don't think we have met. Hi Sandy."

"Hi there Devlin good to meet you."

Sandy smiled prettily from under her long eyelashes while thinking, *Oh, sexy man alert and God, doesn't he look amazing in those Jodhpurs.*

Then she realised she was staring directly at his crotch. She quickly looked up but knew she was blushing as she stared at kind brown eyes that were smiling knowingly back.

Jonny walked over to the table to grab something to eat, smiling to himself as he saw a new relationship on the horizon for Sandy. Sue had put smoked salmon and baby spinach in brown bread and roast beef and horse radish in white. He grabbed one of each and said, "I think I had better call mum, so she can contact Holly the head girl at the yard to let her know that Devlin will be picking up Wiggy. Sandy should possibly go as well. Holly knows her and Sandy also knows the way."

Lord Henry looked at Devlin.

"Is that OK? Probably a good idea. Always sensible to have an extra pair of hands when travelling horses; especially a horse you are not familiar with. Sandy is very competent around horses so she would be an asset."

Devlin couldn't believe his luck but answered nonchalantly, "Yeah; sure. As you say an extra pair of hands is always welcome."

As he bit into a delicious roast beef sandwich, Jonny thought, *Ha-ha; just call me cupid.*

He then said, "They'll have to make sure they stay close to the horse box when they arrive at the stable because the bad guys might still be around the area sorting out their Evoque. Leaving it un-manned could be asking for trouble."

Lord Henry agreed.

"Good point Jonny. After you've phoned your mother take the black Freelander to pick up her and Barry. Here are the keys. It has tinted windows."

Jonny thanked Sue for the sandwiches and Henry for the car and took out his phone to speak to his mum.

"Hya mum! Where are you now?"

"We're just starting out for my place to pick up some things love; and then we will take Barry's car to the University and make our way to a café somewhere easy for you to find. How have things progressed at your end?"

"All OK here mum. I guess Barry has told you that Lord Henry thinks it would be a good idea if Wiggy came up here as well-until this is all over. It's best for his safety. Can you call Holly and let her know? Tell her it is only temporary but don't let her know all the details. It will be Sandy and a guy called Devlin. The box will not be sign written. I will be with you and Barry soon driving a black Freelander with tinted windows. Let me know when you get to your café and try to get something to eat."

"Will do. I'll make the call to Holly now using Barry's land line. Barry has made some sandwiches that we are going to eat as we drive to my place but I'm not really hungry. My stomach is still doing summersaults. You drive safely. I'll be glad when we are all safe."

"See you soon Mum. Must go now."

Jonny ended the call and turned to the others and said, "OK. I will see you all in a bit. Mum is calling the stables now to let them know Devlin and Sandy are coming. Let me have your mobile Sandy so I can secure it with this special chip from Arty. You can then use your mobile without fear of someone tuning in to your conversations or texts.

And fix this button on something you carry with you all the time—maybe your wallet or purse rather than the phone. See you all soon. He suddenly felt that he sounded like Lord Henry giving out orders."

As Jonny walked to the front of the house, he saw Sandy and Devlin getting ready to pick up Wiggy. He opened the door of the freshly valeted black Freelander and was soon some way ahead of them heading for the main gate and onwards to Bristol. He thought how nice freshly valeted leather smelled and promised to tidy up and refresh his Mini as soon as possible.

The road was pretty quiet and it took him under an hour to get down by the river under the suspension bridge. The tide was in and there was the wonderful sight of the Matthew sailing boat bringing trippers back to the city. The Matthew was a replica of vessel used by John Cabot when he discovered Newfoundland in 1497. He thought, *How lucky I am to have grown up in a city with such history; even if some of it associated with slavery is unsavoury. It certainly makes you think about our past.*

Barry had called him to let him know they were at the Grain Barge which was a pub overlooking the river on the Hotwell Road. He phoned back saying he was just a minute away and continued heading down Portway and on to the Hotwell Road where he soon spotted them standing outside waving. He did a U-turn, pulled over, got out, gave his mum a peck on the cheek, and as he opened the rear door he said, "Hi! Your carriage awaits you."

He placed their belongings in the back as they settled themselves in. Christina seemed to have packed for a month away and she sat in the front with Barry in the back. Jonny checked his text messages before driving off and there was one from Arthur saying, *I can see you on TV on Hotwell Road so all working OK.*

At least that was another level of security up and running. As soon as they were buckled up in the Freelander, they headed back down the Portway and on towards Wales and safety.

Apart from a few words of greeting and admiration for the Freelander, Barry and Christina were pretty much silent and Jonny felt very concerned. Understandably they seemed to be in a complete state of shock. He decided to try and get a conversation going to lift the mood so using a quiet voice he said, "Sorry to hear about Scrum Barry. He was a dear sweet dog."

Barry muttered something Jonny didn't quite hear apart from the word.

"Bastards!"

He continued his task.

"Mum; are you OK"? "By what Barry told me it must have been terrifying. Thank God you and Wiggy are alright. We will be safe once we get to Sandy's sister's place. Because of Sue's artwork collection and some top-class stallions, it is like Fort Knox."

Because there was no reply he decided to continue the conversation that was beginning to sound a bit like a monologue.

"The place is an art appreciators' heaven; like a mini National Gallery. You will love the stables. Oh, and Barry, you must get Lord Henry to show you his classic car collection."

Jonny knew he was gabbling but the silence from Barry and his mum was deafening. Christina had been staring out the side window and suddenly said, "For Christ sake Jonathan we are not going on bloody holiday! There has just been an attempt on my life. Why the hell did that stupid American kid have to get us involved?"

Christina's voice was now high pitched and panicky as she continued, "How do we know they are not following us right at this moment, Huh? We have no idea what we are up against but we do know they are capable of murder."

Jonny sheepishly responded, "Sorry. I just wanted to take your mind off things. You will be safe once we get there."

Barry chipped in using a nearly whispering tone while at the same time giving Christina a sharp stare.

"We know Jonny. Bear with us because we are pretty shaken up at the moment and we have been trying to come to terms with what has happened in our own way. I'm sure you are right. We will feel a lot better when we get there."

Jonny took the hint and they continued the drive in comparative silence; until they got to the first gates of the Mayhew estate that is when Barry commented on the stunning wrought iron gates with the entwined Mayhew family crest.

Christina however remained silent; sitting rigidly in her seat; that is until they passed through the second gate when Jonny noticed his mother visibly relax by taking a deep breath and letting it out slowly. Jonny thought he would venture conversation again and commented, "There are CCTV cameras everywhere and the whole place has a state-of-the-art alarm system. So just relax. It shouldn't be too long before we have Wiggy back here as well.

Once I have you settled in and secured both of your mobile phones with Arthur's chip I am going to call Aiyana to update her and make sure she is OK.

She has probably heard the news about Matthew's murder and will be wondering what to do."

Christina put her hand out and touched Jonny's face and said, "Sorry for earlier. I can't believe what a sensible and caring person you have grown up to be."

Jonny was slightly embarrassed and he knew he was going red.

"Yeah, yeah, whatever. Let's get inside now. Look; Sue and Lord Henry are coming down the steps to greet us."

After Jonny had introduced everyone, Sue invited them in while Jonny retrieved the extensive luggage from the Freelander with the help of Barry.

Barry noticed Christina looking up at the impressive building and there were tears of relief in her eyes. He took her hand, raised it to his lips and said quietly, "Everything will be fine now luv."

He too then gazed at the beautiful building they were about to enter.

"You have a stunning home Lord and Lady Mayhew. Thank you for your help."

Lord Henry boomed back, "Absolutely; no problem Barry. We have plenty of room. And please it is Henry and Sue. The house was originally built for one of the Iron Barons in the early 1800s. But Jonny tells me you are a bit of an American classic car fanatic. I will show you around the garages later. Classic cars are one of my indulgences."

Sunday Mid-Afternoon
20 August 2017

As Jonny was heading for the Freelander to pick up Barry and his Mum, Sandy followed Devlin to the lorry parking area which was situated around the back of the stable yard. She had to admit that his back view was as good as his front; nice broad shoulders tapering down to a seriously nice arse.

They stopped in-front of a silver, three-and-a-half-ton horse box. Devlin whistled and shouted, "Jimmy!"

A small tan and white Jack Russell came shooting across the yard and launched himself into the open door. Devlin then set the Sat Nav and turned to Sandy saying, "His Lordship thinks this van is a little less conspicuous than one of the larger boxes and it is brand new."

"Mmm. Sounds like a good idea Devlin. So I think the route should be over the old bridge, down the M5 to Junction 17 and back towards the Bristol Channel. You can see both bridges from the stable."

Once they were moving off and little Jimmy was happily curled up on Sandy's lap, she asked, "So have you always worked with horses, Devlin?"

"Nope. I went to Uni and got a degree in economics. My father got me a job in the city with a bank. I hated it so much—every day was torture. Everywhere I looked there were cars spewing fumes, and in all directions all I could see were buildings. I missed my horse and my dog because I wouldn't expose Jimmy to those fumes so I left him at home with mum. I was desperately lonely without him so I jacked in my job and went to work for the Cuthbert-Clawley's; riding their show hunters. My father was furious and complained that he hadn't spent a fortune on my education for me to be a shit shoveler. He hasn't spoken to me since."

They were heading for the main gate and they could see Jonny just disappearing up the road. Sandy looked at Devlin's sad eyes and said, "Yeah. I feel your pain Devlin. I just couldn't imagine working for a bank if my heart was with animals and the countryside. But were you happy with your last place?"

Devlin looked at Sandy and grinned.

"Well now; there is a bit of a story to that as well Sandy."

"Ooh! I am all ears Devlin. And we have plenty of time to kill."

Devlin looked at Sandy and said, "I am not sure that I should tell you about it really. I have only just met you and well, it's a bit um naughty; well very naughty really."

Sandy laughed nervously and said, "Oh my God. Soo now I absolutely have to hear about it. And please spare me no details. I have to know it all."

She was a bit shocked at herself being so forward with someone she had only just met but somehow felt very at ease in his company. Like good mates. It was if they had known each other for years.

"OK then. You asked for it. Let me know if I go too far with the detail though. Have you met Jolyon Cuthbert-Clawley's wife Monica?"

Sandy thought about it and was very intrigued by the question.

"I might have at a function I suppose. But I don't recall ever talking to her."

"Well, Sandy, although she is closer to forty than thirty she is pretty hot and she knows it; keeping very fit by riding and going to the gym three times a week.

At work and in company she was very straight and a bit of a disciplinarian but I hadn't been working for them very long, when she started to get me on my own and come on to me! You know; a bit of cheeky talk, lots of cleavage and when she passed me would make sure she accidently on purpose touched me. Being only human, I was really turned on. She knew that she was getting my attention.

At first I resisted because I wanted to keep my job but she could be very persuasive. Anyway they both invited me over for dinner one night—well probably Monica I expect. The wine was flowing and inhibitions gradually faded away. She manoeuvred me into the kitchen while Jolyon was dosing off the wine. She was wearing one of those dresses with the top cut right down to her waist with no bra and revealing far too much, I really did not know where to look. She was actually enjoying my discomfort.

I made it back to my flat over the stables and thought I had escaped but I had just got undressed when in waltzed Monica wearing a buttoned-up coat and high heels."

She slowly unbuttoned the coat and let it slip to the floor Oh my God she was completely naked apart from the shoes! I thought I was having an erotic dream. She walked over to me and pushed me back down on the bed, and well I am only human I am sure you can guess the rest concluded Devlin.

Jolyon, was twenty years older than her. I assumed he had not been paying enough attention in that area. That and the fact that Monica was really horny and just loved sex."

By this time Sandy's imagination was doing summersaults.

"Oh my God! Did Jolyon catch you at it?"

"I haven't finished yet Sandy."

He glanced at Sandy in the rear-view mirror and said, "Are you OK?"

"Oh yes. Dooo carry on. It's a bit x certificate but I'm enjoying the story."

As soon as she had said the words she knew it sounded far too enthusiastic. In truth it wasn't just the story she was enjoying. There was another very pleasurable feeling building up.

"So er what happened next?"

With a wicked and knowing smile Devlin continued, "Well, after that we started to get together regularly and the sex was pretty good. There was no love; just hard-core sex; toys as well. Sometimes it was in my flat and other times in her bedroom when Jolyon was away. They had separate bedrooms and hers had mirrors all over the place because she loved to watch herself. There was a big screen TV as well and she sometimes had porn films showing while we were at it.

One night in her room she appeared dressed in leather. You know—the works, boots up to her thighs, thong, bra and a whip. Now I don't mind a bit of roll-play but I was not happy about the whip and told her so.

Anyway we were doing what you do with me on top and Monica more horny than usual when I felt hands on my bum. I knew that they weren't Monica's because she had her hands either side of my face. I turned to look and there, standing at the bottom of the bed, was a naked Jolyon; wearing a Gimp mask and sporting a massive erection and I was pretty certain I knew where he wanted to put it. I have never moved so fast in my life. The next day I phoned Lord Henry because he had offered me a job when he saw me working in a horse at the Royal Welsh show. The rest is history."

Then, as if he had just told Sandy about a rugby match he had played in he said, "What about you Sandy? What have you been up to?"

By this time Sandy was still imagining the scene described by Devlin and it took her some time before she could gather herself together. She had trouble getting a picture of Monica and Devlin having sex out of her mind so there were a few moments of silence before she could answer.

Eventually she managed, "Phew! Well, compared to your life hun I am pretty boring really. I went to Cheltenham Ladies College and then on to Cardiff University where I study Art. I have to admit it doesn't sound terribly exciting after your story."

"I'm sure it's fantastic. What about Jonny? You seem close."

Sandy was beginning to feel calmer and replied, "Sooo I met Jonny when he worked at my parent's stable yard one summer. We hit it off immediately. He is studying art at Cardiff as well and is so much fun. But also he has been there for me when I needed a friend."

"He is gay isn't he?"

Sandy immediately turned on Devlin being very conscious of homophobia saying,

"And you have a problem with that?"

Devlin came back quickly with a smile.

"Good grief no! I just wanted to make sure there was no competition."

A blushing but relieved Sandy who was very protective of her friend replied, "Oh! Now I don't quite know what to say to that."

"How about saying yes to a drink with me later Sandy? We could go to the pub, or I could buy you dinner."

Sandy's first thought was, *OH YES!*

Then she remembered that there was a lot going on and Jonny's mum and Barry were staying over and her mind was racing.

Oh God; he is so yummy; what to do?

Before she could say anything, Devlin's disappointed voice said, "Ah. I guess as it's taking so long to answer, it is a no then."

"Oh no! It's not that, Devlin. I would really love to go out with you. But there is so much going on at the moment. And don't you think it would be a bit rude of me to go out tonight with Jonny and his folks staying?"

Devlin turned and smiled at her.

"I totally understand. Another time then? But I am not going to just fade into the background. We will go out; I feel it in my bones."

In truth he was feeling it elsewhere.

The Sat Nav disturbed their private world with a metallic female voice squawking, *In three hundred yards, you have reached your destination.*

Sandy thought to herself, *Where has that time gone?*

Now more composed and thinking about the current task, she looked up the road through the horsebox windows as they arrived at the yard gate and said, "Jonny said to take extra care and to look out for any suspicious looking vehicles hanging around."

Devlin drove into the stable yard and parked up and asked, "Do you want me to go and check the road? I am not really sure what is going on, but hopefully you will enlighten me on the way home."

"Ooh yes please Devlin. But please be careful because something happened to Chrissie out here this morning and it was pretty nasty. I will go and find Holly and get Wiggy sorted. And don't let the horse box out of your sight."

With that they both got out of the horse box and walked in different directions, leaving Jimmy in the passenger seat.

Holly had heard the horse box doors close and was walking across the yard when she saw Sandy. She gave her a big hug saying, "Hey! Where you been keeping yourself girl? It's been ages. Do you still have Damit? I used to love watching you jump that horse at shows."

Sandy returned the hug. It felt good to see Holly again. Until Sandy went to Cardiff University they both did the show jumping circuit and there was always a party in someone's horsebox.

"Yes, Damit is at home with my parents now Holly. Mummy did try drag hunting him but he got over enthusiastic and poor mum got carted over some big hedges and a few gates. She said never again. At the moment he is playing at being an uncle to some foals. They follow him about like the Messiah."

Looking at Holly Sandy realised that she had lost her attention and she was looking over her shoulder towards the entrance to the yard. There was desire in her voice when she gasped, "Oh my Gawd Sandy. Who is that by the front gate? Is he a present for me? Blimmin love it! Very sexy."

Sandy turned around and seeing Devlin looking up and down the road she laughed.

"Oi! Hands off Holly 'cause that one's mine; or at least he will be soon."

"Get on. He is probably gay anyway. He is far too good looking to be straight."

Mimicking Holly's Gloucestershire accent Sandy said, "Nope. In fact mind he asked me out on the way here. So stick that up your blimmin' jumper."

"Fair play Sandy."

They were still laughing when Devlin strolled over. Sandy did the introductions and while they were walking over to the stable block she explained about their shared show jumping days.

They soon saw Wiggy looking absolutely gorgeous after his adventures earlier. He was tied up and a stable lad was fitting travelling boots on his legs. Holly put her hand on the horse and speaking softly in his ear she told him that he was going for a little holiday and that she would miss him. The relationship between those who love horses and their four-legged friends is very special and is really only understood by other horse lovers. Wiggy was calm and seemed to understand so she then untied him and handed the lead rope over to Devlin who walked the horse to the horse box without any problems.

Holly said, "While you are loading him Sandy and I will pick up Chrissie's tack and bring it over."

They walked to the tack room and Holly said quietly but with a frown, "Sandy; I am worried about Chrissie. She was in a proper state when she came back from her ride this morning and Wiggy had obviously been ridden blimmin' hard. I wondered whether everything was alright between her and Barry. There have been some proper goings on around here today mind and I wondered whether they were related.

A Range Rover Evoque got stuck in a flooded stream on Charles Younger's land. One of his lads, Sam Ablett, had to pull them out with a tractor and the vehicle was in a right manger state with the engine bay completely flooded. They gave some cock and bull story about getting lost and looking for a short cut. But Sam didn't believe a word of it because they were well away from a road.

He said there were three of them and they sounded as if they came from America. One of their names was Sully; a right nobber. The third one was younger. Really blonde hair and Sam thought he might be local because he looked a bit familiar. They called the Bristol Land Rover dealer who sent a truck that took the Evoque and its passengers away. All very jubby."

Not wishing to give anything away or risk getting Holly involved Sandy replied, "No worries hun. Barry and Chrissie are fine. Like an old married couple sometimes. Yes there is stuff going on but the least you know about it at the moment the better. I'm sure they will tell you about it when it's all over."

Holly didn't seem assured so Sandy gave her a big hug. They both agreed not to leave it so long and would definitely organise a girly night.

Devlin completed loading Wiggy into the box and they were soon on their way back to Wales. Sandy took out her phone and called Sue's mobile to let her know they were on their way back. It took some time for it to be answered. When it was Sue sounded out of breath and there was the sound of Katherine Jenkins singing Pia Jesu somewhere in the background.

Sue, immediately recognised the caller from her phone screen and said, "Hi Sandy. Sorry I took so long to answer but I had miss laid my phone again.

Found it hidden behind some cushions. Doh."

Sandy laughed and replied, "It's OK Sue. No problem. Just to let you know that the horse is loaded up and we are on our way back. So let Chrissie know Wiggy has been a good boy and Holly sends her love."

"Good news Sandy. See you soon and I'll let Chrissie know all is well."

The trip back was pretty straight forward. They had a CTV camera to keep an eye on Wiggy who seemed to be very content. Sandy told Devlin more about her show jumping with Holly. He did probe for more information about what was going on with Christina but she said to bear with her because it was probably best at the moment if he remained in the dark. But she did promise to ask the others if it was alright that he should know more as he was getting involved on the fringes anyway.

There were no more stories about Devlin's sexual adventures with Monica, which was just as well because Sandy thought she couldn't take more of that sort of excitement at the moment although the prospect of a future relationship with Devlin had an extra glow. She concentrated on making friends with Jimmy who was curled up on her lap again. They arrived at the Severn Crossing toll booths and sailed through because Lord Henry had season tickets for all of his horse transporters. It was not long before they were turning into the stable yard at the Mayhew Estate.

Devlin unloaded Wiggy who stood proudly in the yard; taking in his new surroundings with his head up and his black coat glistening in the late afternoon sun. Christina walked across the yard to take the lead rope from Devlin, relieved that her darling boy had arrived safely without incident. She asked, "Thank you Devlin. Was he a good boy?"

"Yes he was a super star. He really is an absolutely stunning horse isn't he?"

She couldn't help feeling a bit proud that someone else thought the same as her about her horse.

"I think so Devlin. But I am biased of course. Lord Henry said to let you know there will be a barbeque in the walled garden at around seven if you would like to come."

Devlin smiled and said, "That would be great so I had better get on with the evening stables. Are you OK with Wiggy? He is in stable fourteen—right by the tack room where you will find the tack that we picked up from Holly."

"Thank you and I'll be fine Devlin."

Christina led Wiggy over to his stable and removed his travelling boots. She was happy that he seemed to be taking everything in his stride. But she made a thorough check over to make sure there were no lumps or bumps from their morning escapade. She shivered as she thought back but thankfully he appeared fine so she closed the stable door and left him tucking into very large hay net.

She was gently humming 'Fly Me to the Moon' as she walked back to the main house, thinking how wonderful to live in a beautiful home like this. She spotted a young man talking to Jonny. He was working in the rose beds and was wearing just a pair of cut off denim shorts. She thought, *Hmm. That could be painful with all those thorns.*

Then she laughed to herself as she realised she was more concerned with him getting hurt than appreciating his good looks. She muttered to herself, "I must be getting old."

She went straight to the kitchen where Sandy and Sue were getting things ready for the barbeque and discussing the merits of Devlin over a glass of Bollinger champagne. Sue called, "Chrissie. Would you like some bubbles darling? Henry and Barry are over in the garages looking at the car collection."

"Oh yes please. I am rather partial to bubbles. Oh and Devlin said he would like to come to the barbeque."

Then, chinking her glass against Sandy's who responded with a slightly embarrassed smile she said, "Excellent. That will make you my little sis' very happy."

Just then Jonny wandered in clutching a red rose saying theatrically, "A rose by any other name would smell as sweet."

He then made a beeline for the Bollinger and Sue poured a glass.

"I take it you have been talking to my gardener?"

Jonny strutted around the kitchen with his rose and champagne and said, "Oh yes. But I had to be careful not to get pricked."

A joint groan of derision came from all three girls as they mocked his very corny joke.

Chapter 7

After dark, all cats are leopards.
(Native American Proverb)

Sunday Evening
20 August 2017

By 7.30 pm the barbeque was well and truly on the go. Lord Henry had assumed responsibility for grilling the steaks and there was a fabulous aroma in the air. Plenty of salad, relish and buns were available and of course Bollinger. Everyone was tucking in. Jonny wandered over to the barbeque and Lord Henry served him his third beautifully cooked medium rare steak. Jonny searched out some cheese and relish and then heaped it all into a bun. Sue looked on with envy and said, "Why the hell don't you get fat Jonny? Every time I turn around you are eating."

"Fast metabolism darling. This is only my third."

Then he looked over to one of the elegant patio tables and noticed Sandy and Devlin looking very cosy chatting to each other. He decided he would join them.

"Hello! You two look cosy—if you know what I mean? I thought I would disrupt the conversation and get to know Devlin just to make sure he is not going to take advantage of my bestie…or to make sure he will."

He then added with a dirty laugh, "I just hope someone will be getting sausage surprise later."

A blushing and embarrassed Sandy replied with a nervous giggle, "Oh for God's sake Jonny. Sometimes you can be sooo inappropriate."

Unperturbed Jonny sprawled himself nonchalantly on a chair and poured himself some rather nice champagne from the bottle on the table.

"Chin, chin darlings. I have a feeling I am going to get a little pissed tonight and maybe I could get lucky with rose boy."

Sandy reminded him, "Er not too pissed please because you have an appointment with the law tomorrow morning hun—remember."

They were laughing and chatting away when Jonny's mobile started to play Madonna's like a virgin (his call tone). He spoke so everyone could hear.

"I must take this call. It's my genius friend Arty. I'll just find a quiet place because he might have some crucial news for me."

He moved further into the garden and answered the call with, "Hi buddy! How ya doing? Do you have any news for us."

Arthur's familiar stuttering voice replied, "Hi JJonny. Er hope you are all ssafe and wwell. Yes I do have some nnews and it needs to be taken very seriously. I don't want to um pput it in text or pprint so you will need to remember the details as I relay them to you. And apart ffrom those directly involved, er you must never reveal where this news came from. I kknow I've said this before but I mmust stress the importance of this."

"Sounds serious Arty. Of course all this will remain secret within our group. Fire away."

"Um well, ffirst of all I think I know who the ttwo heavies are. They are the Cantana Brothers—a ddangerous American duo with a UK operation in South London and er links across the UK and a West Country bbase in Bristol. They are into pprostitution using Eastern European illegals and have several mmassage pparlours. They are also into drugs with the er Bristol drugs hub bbased in a bar by the river supplying distribution partners in Falmouth, Newquay, Pplymouth, Exeter, Weymouth, Bbournemouth, Yeovil, Taunton, Cardiff and Ttorquay. They target ttowns with ttourism and er universities. They are also into mmoney laundering and probably much else besides."

The mention of a bar by the river made Jonny's hair stand on end.

"Do you know what bar it is Arty? It could be very important."

"Ern not yet but I'm trying to find out and will let you er know when I do. According to the Drug Squad information ffile Tony Cantana is a psychotic, mmasochistic and a nasty ppiece of work. He is just about controlled by his half-brother Sully. They have the same father but um ddifferent mothers. They were bborn into a Mafia family but are now ffreelance. Sully is tall, ddark haired and extremely charming if needed. His mother was the ddaughter of a Mafia Don. Tony is shorter with ffairish hair and ppiercing blue eyes. His mother was a show ggirl from Las Vegas."

There was a pause before he continued.

"They appear to be ppart of a Global crime syndicate and are UK agents for BBoston gangsters who are linked to the er Religious Community Holding

Company accountants that you told me about. A Boston gangster came over at about the same time as Aiyana and they have made er regular visits during the past um few years.

There was another short silence. Then Jonny said, "Bloody hell! This sounds big; much bigger than I thought Arty."

"It is bbig Jonny, and very er ddangerous. I am quite wworried about you all. The digital chchatter during the past couple of days confirms that they er really want that ppainting back. Once they found out that Aiyana had got it into the country and they tracked it to the Matthew Lloyd Gallery they were um content to let things take their ccourse and ppick it up again when they thought it would be ffound to be of no value; er not thinking that someone would discover the hidden ppainting. I ththink they must have bbeen er watching the gallery when you and um Sandy left with the ppaintings. They then ffollowed you to your flat.

"The kkilling of Barry's dog and the chasing of your mother on her horse were like the original bblack spot warning. Just that; er warnings to kkeep out of their wway I think. Bbut they are ggetting information from er ssomewhere. They do not appear to know about the bbackground story with Aiyana and yourself being related or anything about the written letter Aiyana has in her ppossession stating what should become of the ppainting in inheritance terms. They er just think that you are ffriends of Aiyana. They are nnot even sure how she er ggot hold of the ppainting or where it has been hhidden all these years.

"The Religious Community Holding Company has no written ddeed of ownership of the ppainting because it is likely that many years ago they er stole it from the pirate Robert Davies who originally commissioned and owned the um ppainting. They might have stolen it from his relatives in later years.

"Bbut they have now lost ttrack as to where the painting is. That is probably why Matt was er mmurdered. After losing track of you and Sandy they returned to the gallery and under torture he probably told them that you had the painting along with the fact that Sandy had an art expert sister. They still do not know where Aiyana lives but they are now after her, bbelieving that she knows the whereabouts of the um painting. They will find out that she is in Bath and my advice is that she should gget out of the UK pretty ddamn quick—within hours if er ppossible. They have pproven to be capable of murder and the feeling is that she is in immediate ddanger.

"Um maybe she should return to her Native American ccommunity in North America for a while? There are two Native American ccommunities of her tribe left in USA and her status as an Honorary Tribe Elder should result in her being absorbed un-noticed if she returned by a non-direct route, so llimiting the chchance of being er ttraced. She hasn't been out of USA many days so locally, apart from the Religious Community and the Tribal Elders, most might not even know that she has been in the UK. Maybe flying out via Madrid or another European city rrather than use a UK airport; or ppossibly Eurostar and then a flight. She could um return once things have quietened down, bbut right now they appear to be closing in on her and she should er disappear."

A now very concerned Jonny said, "I agree. Having only just discovered that I have a half-sister I don't want to risk losing her. But she might take some persuading because she is a strong woman on a tribal mission with a mind of her own. I'll discuss things with Lord Henry first because he might be able to help getting her out of the country un-noticed.

Sandy and I are due to be interviewed by the police tomorrow so we haven't much time. Should I still meet up with her to secure her mobile phone? Do you have international coverage on the scrambling and tracking?"

"Um yes. Still secure her phphone if you can and we do have ffull global tracking. I'll leave it to you to ddecide what to do but er do it quick and llet me know the outcome. You had bbetter get on with things as time is crucial. Involving um Lord Henry ssounds like a ggood idea. Ggood luck."

"Oh and I have just received an e-mail about that bar. It is the Willcome Inn down by the river."

Jonny drew breath.

"Oh shit!. That is a mate's bar. I know him quite well. Thanks buddy. Is there any way the bar can be watched?"

"Oh yes I umm have hacked into their umm CCTV and a friend has a ddrone popping over the umm bar, every nnow and then."

"I owe you one Arty, catch you later."

He thought for a second that he should speak to Lord Henry immediately but decided to try and get hold of Aiyana first to see that she was safe and whether she had any plans. The phone was soon answered with Aiyana saying, "Hi Jonny. I was waiting for you to ring. I hope you are all safe. I'm staying in a hotel."

"Yep; all safe here. Sorry I have not been back to you sooner. Before we speak I want you to phone me back using the hotel land line."

"OK. Will do."

Aiyana recognised the urgency in Jonny's voice and switched off her mobile phone. It wasn't long before she phoned back. Jonny logged the phone number she was on for future use saying, "Sorry about the subterfuge but I will secure your mobile when I see you. How are you anyway and what's this about you staying in a hotel again?"

"All OK but I decided to make some moves when I heard about Matthew Lloyd. One thing about being brought up as a Native American is that you learn to use your intuition or sixth sense. The Great Spirit moved me and I felt the need to disappear or melt away in case the heavies started to track me down. I packed my bags ready for an escape route and took the bus. I'm now ensconced in the Snooty Fox in Tetbury. I think I am safe here for a while anyway."

"Good. When you hear my latest news you will see what a good move that was Aiyana. Things have taken a few dangerous turns and it will take a few minutes to update you."

"That's fine Jonny. I'm all ears. The main thing is that we are all safe at the moment anyway. I feel so guilty about getting you all involved in this."

Jonny then went through all the events regarding Christina, Barry and Matthew and how Lord Henry had provided a safe haven for them. He also relayed the latest news from Arthur and confirmed that he and Sandy were to be interviewed by the police the following morning. He went on, "I know that you would like to stay here and be part of all this but we are afraid for your safety now. Also if you remain the police may want to interview you. You have completed the first part of your tribal mission by making contact and getting the painting to us. We are now on the way to releasing its secrets. Having only just discovered that I have a half-sister I don't want to lose you Aiyana. It would be best if we got you out of here very quickly.

There are several options but I think the best plan would be for you to return to your tribe until we sort out the heavies and the police investigations about Matt have been finalised. You can then come back to the UK and we can complete the mission in hand. In the meantime we can continue to unravel the mystery of the painting over here and keep you up to speed via e-mail, Skype and phone calls. What do you say? Lord Henry will be able to help with travel plans to keep you under the radar."

After some moments of silence she said thoughtfully, "I know that is the sensible thing to do Jonny but as I got you all into this mess I really feel I should stick it out with you."

Jonny replied with some impatience, "We all joined in willingly Aiyana and we will get through it. But right now your safety is paramount. The Elders of your tribe will not thank us for leaving you in such danger. For the moment Lord Henry has provided good protection for me, Sandy, Barry, my mum and the painting. Let me talk to him and come back with a plan later tonight. I'm sure we can find a way of getting you back to your community without being seen by the bad guys."

"OK; I know you are making sense Jonny. I have all my travel documents with me and please pass on the thanks of myself and my tribe to Lord Henry for his help in this. He must be putting himself and his reputation at some risk. I'll sit tight here and wait for your call later."

With some relief Jonny said, "Thank goodness. Lord Henry may need to phone you direct for travel document details and he will use the landline number you are on now. I assume it is your room number?"

"Yes. It is the room phone Jonny and I'll wait here until I get a call from him or you."

"Good. Stay put Aiyana. It will not be long before you will be able to return to the UK and we can really see what this painting has to offer us all. I'll talk to Lord Henry right away. Speak to you later; stay safe; bye."

He turned off his phone and went to find Lord Henry and pulled him aside to relay details of his conversations with Arthur and Aiyana before asking, "Do you think we should involve the others in this—particularly Sue, Sandy, Barry and my mum? And what about Devlin? He knows little about what has been going on although his trip to pick up my mum's horse would have given him a few clues. What he doesn't know would give him some protection from the villains but not a lot."

Lord Henry looked concerned and he thought deeply for a while before saying, "I think we should involve them all. I believe I have a contact who can help get Aiyana away safely provided you can take her from Tetbury to Gloucestershire Airport straight after your interview with the police tomorrow. I'll gather everyone in a huddle now before I make some calls."

His strong tones bellowed out as if he was the Speaker in the House of Commons.

"Gather around everyone. We have some news. Jonny will update you."

Jonny relayed his conversation with Arthur and Aiyana—adding a bit to keep Devlin up to speed—and then handed back the proceedings to Lord Henry who continued, "Aiyana's presence in the country at this time makes a complicated and dangerous situation even more complex. If she agrees to my plan I think I can help her quietly get back to Boston for a while. I have a friend who owns an Executive Business Jet airline operating out of Gloucestershire Airport. With GCHQ being close by he has regular flights and one leaves late afternoon every day for Adolfo Suarez Airport, Madrid. There are always spare seats so I'm pretty sure I can get Aiyana on the flight tomorrow, although I will need to check things out. She will then need to stay one night at a Madrid airport hotel and catch a flight the next morning to Bangor Maine. She can take a train from there to Boston and so slip back home in a fairly inconspicuous manner.

I can arrange all the flight tickets and hotel bookings this end but will leave Aiyana to buy her train ticket to Boston in Bangor Maine. So all we need to do is make sure she is at Gloucestershire Airport on time. It takes about one hour to get from here to Tetbury and another 40 minutes to get to the airport where a Bombardier Challenger 850 will be waiting. Jonny's interview with the police should be over around lunch time so he can take the Freelander and take Aiyana to Gloucester Airport. I will need to phone Aiyana for the details required to book the tickets and when everything is confirmed Jonny can phone her back with the transfer details. What do we think?"

Sue suggested that it would be prudent to have copies of the documentation proving Aiyana's ownership of the painting but everyone agreed that getting Aiyana to safety seemed the best idea. So taking a note of Aiyana's room telephone number Lord Henry retired to his office to make the arrangements.

After an hour Lord Henry returned and said, "Right! Everything is arranged and paid for apart from the train journey from Bangor Maine to Boston. Her airline tickets and hotel booking details can be picked up from the Executive Business Terminal desk at Gloucestershire Airport tomorrow afternoon. I have spoken to her and she knows the routine. It just needs Jonny to phone her back with the pick-up details. The flight to Madrid leaves at 5 pm so you need to be at the airport by 4 pm Jonny."

Jonny said, "Thank you so much Henry. It is most generous of you. I'll phone her now to confirm things."

Jonny phoned a by now much relieved Aiyana who was waiting for his call and confirmed that he would be at Tetbury at around 3 pm. She confirmed back that she had the hotel photocopy key ownership documents regarding the painting and he could pick them up tomorrow.

When he had finished Barry took him aside. He had a bit of perturbing news after a conversation with Sandy.

"Jonny! I think we might have a bit of a clue about those on our case. Chrissie and me were talking with Sandy and she told us about a conversation with Holly when she and Devlin picked up Wiggy this afternoon. Evidently there was a lot of action after Christina left because the Evoque had to be towed out of the flooded stream. In the end it was taken to the Bristol Land Rover dealership.

Holly said that two of the men who chased Christina had American accidents and the third one was younger with blond hair. The American accents line up with what we already know but the man who pulled their Evoque out said he thought he recognised the blond boy as a local Bristolian. Christina reminded me that the guy who gave us the leaflet outside the Llandoger Trow on Thursday night was also blond. Might be a coincidence but then again maybe not. What do you think?"

Barry saw a worried expression on Jonny's face as he replied, "No. Unfortunately I think there might be something in it because added to information Arty gave me earlier it looks like I might know the blond guy. It could be that we have a fifth columnist in the mix; one that I thought of as a friend. Don't worry I'll sort it."

On the positive side Sue indicated that she was making progress in discovering the secret of that painting—the cause of the predicament in which they found themselves.

Chapter 8

Sometimes it takes a little kindness from one hurting soul to another to change us forever.
(Native American saying)

Day 6 Monday Morning
21 August 2017

DCI David Thomas was back sitting at his desk in Cardiff Central Police Station, looking at the various reports from uniform regarding the murder of Matthew Lloyd, when an email came through from the superintendent requesting his and Ruth's presence. He muttered to himself, "Well; better not keep the boss waiting."

He wandered off to collect Ruth from the office next door. Putting his head around the door he said, "Hey Ruth; the boss needs to see us. Better trot upstairs quickly."

Ruth looked up from her PC.

"Yep just logging out."

She then got up and followed David out and up the stairs to the Superintendent's office. David knocked once and they entered.

Superintendent Jack Clarkson was a big man; not fat, but around six foot three he was fit from regular visits to the gym. Fifty years old he got to his rank through hard work pounding beats and study so he knew how most things worked in the service. However he did not suffer fools gladly and he wasn't happy when he received a call from his top brass that morning requesting two of his senior staff do a home visit to interview a couple of students who believe they were two of the last people to see Matthew Lloyd alive.

David and Ruth entered and said, "Morning Guv."

Jack looked at his two best detectives and spoke in a sarcastic tone, "OK. It appears that you guys are off on a jolly. You need to pop down to the Mayhew estate that is owned by someone called Lord Henry Mayhew, down near Duffryn. There you are to interview Alexandra Dickens-Young and Jonathan Davies who saw the deceased the morning of August 19th before he was murdered. It's all on the CCTV coverage. In fact it looks like they were the second to last to see him alive."

David asked, "Is there a reason they can't come into the station Guv? I am up to my ears with follow-ups on this case."

"Sorry but no."

Pointing to the ceiling the Superintendent continued, "I had a call today that said it's a home visit and that is that."

As he was talking he handed David a piece of paper with the address and names on it.

Ruth asked, "Could just one of us go down Sir?"

"Nope. I think it would be better with you both. Whoever Lord Henry is he obviously has contacts in high places so we will be watched. Anyway sometimes one of you can pick up what the other doesn't. See you both later."

The Superintendent then looked at his computer screen indicating the meeting was over. Ruth and David both turned around and said in unison, "Thanks Guv."

They then left the office—closing the door behind them.

David looked at Ruth and said, "We'd better get going then. I'll drive so I'll see you in the car park."

"It's a bit strange isn't it Dave? I don't think the boss was too happy about the situation. He hates being told what to do. On the way down I'll pop into my office to pick up a laptop and see what we have on these people."

"Good idea Ruth. See you in a mo."

David called into his office to pick up his car keys and walked outside to wait for Ruth in his car. As he got in his phone began to ring. He noticed it was his wife and answered with a frown.

"Hello love. Can't talk now; just about to head off to do an interview. Yes I'll call into the supermarket on the way back. Yes I will get washing up liquid and cat food. No I will not forget. Got to go now… bye."

He hung up just as Ruth opened the passenger door.

"Remind me I have to pop into the shop for the wife. I'm bound to forget."

Ruth nodded knowingly and plugged in the charger for the laptop.

"Yeah no worries."

David set up the GPS and off they went heading out towards Newport.

Ruth started to search the internet but found little of substance. By the time they reached the outskirts of Newport and were heading for Duffryn she said, "There doesn't seem to be any significant info about out two witnesses online David, although Alexandra's family looks like an excerpt from Debrett's Peerage. There is a reference to Jonathan being caught with a small amount of Marijuana in his possession when he was sixteen but he wasn't charged; just warned. Both are currently studying Art at Cardiff University. I'm guessing they are probably girlfriend and boyfriend."

It didn't seem long before the Sat Nav was telling them that they had reached their destination and they found themselves outside some very imposing gates. Ruth gazed at them in some awe and said, "Well, this looks very nice, I must say. I think I need to go and talk to that box in the wall."

She got out of the car and wandered over to the gates. Speaking into the intercom she held up her badge to the camera. The gates slowly opened, so she walked back to the car and they drove through and up to the second set of gates which opened on their own accord.

"Bloody hell Ruth! It's a bit posh isn't it?"

They drove slowly until they came to a halt beside the steps leading up to the house main entrance. Standing at the top was a tall man dressed in country clothing and an attractive blond woman. David and Ruth got out of the car and ascended the steps to the attractive couple. The man greeted them with an outstretched hand.

"Good morning DCI Thomas and DCI Chambers I presume. I am Lord Henry Mayhew and this is my wife Lady Susan. Thank you for agreeing to carry out the interviews here and do come in."

They shook hands and David wondered what the protocol was. Should he refer to his host as Lord Henry or My Lord? With not much time to decide he just replied, "Good morning Sir."

Ruth followed his lead.

Lord Henry ushered them into a side room that looked like a well-appointed office and asked, "Would you like to interview them together or separately?"

Ruth replied, "Separately please Sir."

"Fine. I'll send the first one along. There is a coffee machine set up on the side for you. Help yourselves to biscuits."

Lord Henry and his wife then left the room, shutting the door behind them. David and Ruth drew breath and took a look around them. There were a couple of wooden desks with computers; a wall with a full bookcase; a filing cabinet with a coffee machine, cups and a plate of assorted biscuits on the top. Against one wall was a red settee with a coffee table and two red easy chairs in front of it.

"Shall I be mother and pour the coffee."

said Ruth gravitating towards the filing cabinet.

"Thank you Ruth; and a biscuit would be nice."

Ruth poured the coffee and sat down on one of the red chairs next to David. She took a sip and in an exaggerated upper class voice Ruth said, "Don't forget to hold your little finger out while taking little sips. And no dunking your biscuit. We're with posh people now."

Just then there was a knock on the door and David answered.

"Come in please."

It was Jonny; he stood by the opened door looking very smart and dressed in black of course.

"Good morning. I'm Jonny Davies."

He strode purposely into the room. Lord Henry had briefed both he and Sandy about the best way to handle the interviews. Clearly it was vital to truthfully answer the questions asked, but at this stage not to offer extra information. The threats that had been made so far were only personal to Christina and Barry. Matt's murder may or may not be related to the painting. With Aiyana soon to be out of the country, for now her involvement should not be introduced into the investigation unless asked. Likewise Arthur's involvement must remain a secret.

If asked later why these facts were not declared earlier, the fear of further personal injury is a reasonable answer. We wanted to be certain everyone was safe before introducing them into the investigation. The fact that the Morley painting and the American painting had been taken from the gallery could be discussed—if asked.

"You want to talk to me about Matt Lloyd?"

"Ah yes. Good morning. I am DCI David Thomas and this is DCI Ruth Chambers. Would you like to sit down?"

They waited a moment for Jonny to get comfortable on the settee.

"Now then, we will be recording this interview."

David said the date, time, place of the interview and asked, "First of all can you just give us your date of birth, full name and your address please?"

Jonny gave them the information. Ruth then came in with, "As you have heard, Matthew Lloyd was found dead at his gallery. Now please can you tell us your relationship with the deceased?"

Jonny told them that he supplemented his university grant by helping Matthew in the gallery by restoring some of the artwork. He finished with how shocked he was at the news.

David asked when he last saw Matthew. Jonny answered truthfully, even though he knew they would have the information. Ruth then asked what the purpose of his visit was. Jonny knew he had to be careful but Lord Henry had briefed him on this question and they had decided that as Lady Mayhew purchased paintings from the gallery that would be the best route for now, along with mentioning another painting from an American client that needed to be cleaned.

"I was cleaning a painting for an American client and Matthew had a Morley painting that Lady Mayhew might like as she collected them. So he asked Sandy to take that to her sister."

Ruth asked, "Are the paintings here?"

"Yes. The one from the American client is in the lab being worked on."

David turned to Ruth.

"I think we should see the paintings before we leave Ma'am.

He then turned back to Jonny and abruptly asked, "Do you use cocaine?"

Jonny was a bit taken back as he was not expecting that question. He defensively asked, "What has that got to do with things?"

The reply from David was immediate and brusque.

"Please just answer the question Mr Davies."

Jonny thought quickly that he had to be semi honest.

"Yes, I have had a line or two in the past."

David looked at Jonny as he answered thinking, *Hmmm. That shook him a bit.*

So he continued with the topic.

"Did you take cocaine in the gallery on the morning of Saturday the 19th of August?"

Jonny thought, *Shit, they have probably found traces of Charlie.*

So, still feeling a bit rattled, he answered, "Matt asked me if I wanted a snort, so yes I did."

David piled on the pressure.

"Were you having a relationship with Matthew Lloyd?"

Jonny was even more shaken and replied in a rather insulted tone, "Christ no! I am not into middle aged queens. Yes, I am gay but please give me some credit."

Trying to keep a smile off her face Ruth then asked, "When you left the gallery did you come straight here to the Mayhew Estate?"

Jonny told them truthfully that he went to his flat, then to the Estate to drop off both Sandy and the paintings before heading down to Bristol to see his mum and a friend.

David took his time writing down some notes before saying, "Thank you Mr Davies. That will be all for now but we will probably need to speak to you again. Would you mind asking Miss Dickens-Young to come in please?"

Jonny got up and walked towards the door. Just before he got there he turned and asked where they found Matt. Ruth answered, "In the gallery, but we can't say any more I am afraid."

Jonny nodded and opened the door. Ruth went with him and watched as he walked across the spacious hallway to a door opposite and she heard him say to someone inside, "Your turn sweetheart."

Ruth heard a muffled reply and Jonny saying, "It was OK."

Jonny disappeared inside and was replaced by Sandy with her multi-coloured hair and dressed in jeans, floaty white top and Doc-Martins with primroses painted on them. Ruth accompanied her back into the office and the same introductions were made and information given. Ruth then asked, "Miss Dickens-Young, can you please tell us about why you were at the Matthew Lloyd Gallery?"

Sandy explained that her sister Lady Mayhew occasionally purchased paintings from Matt Lloyd and sometimes used the gallery for cleaning works of art she had purchased elsewhere. Her friend Jonny did some part time work there and he had phoned her to check it was OK to bring a couple of paintings back to her sisters. So she went to the gallery to pick up the paintings and go with Jonny to visit her sister. Ruth continued, "What is your relationship with Mr Davies?"

"We are friends. Jonny worked at my parent's stables for a summer before he went to university. We love art and are both studying at the same university in Cardiff."

"Did you also work for Matthew Lloyd?"

"No. I know him because of Jonny, and Sue—I mean Lady Mayhew—occasionally sourced paintings through the gallery."

Sandy was asked about her movements after she left the gallery. She told them everything but left out the two men at the door to Jonny's flat.

Ruth looked at Sandy and asks bluntly, "Do you take cocaine?"

Sandy looked Ruth straight in the eye and answered with a bit of anger in her voice, "Nooo."

Ruth then asked, "May we see the paintings that were at the gallery please?"

Sandy got up and walked to the door saying, "The Morley has been hung in the dining room but the other one is being worked on in the lab. If you bear with me a mo, I will get them."

When Sandy had left the room Ruth said, "They seem genuine David. But we can get more info off the CCTV cameras in the area?"

"I agree in principle Ruth. But I can't help feeling there is an involvement somewhere. I'm not completely convinced and something tells me something is not quite right."

He looked at Ruth, spread his hands and said, "But it's up to us to find out I suppose. That's what we are paid for."

After a while Sandy walked back in carrying the paintings which she held up for them to see. The Morley was framed for hanging but the other one was just on its stretch frame.

She said, "So this one is by the Devon Artist Sheila Morley; painted in the mid 1960's. Lady Mayhew collects her work. The one from the American client is more of an amateur project we think."

They both looked at the paintings. The Morley was of a woman dressed in a long blue skirt and white blouse standing by an open window with white muslin curtains blowing inwards. It was a very gentle piece of art. The other was of a woman handing a puppy to a child. David explained for the recording device that Miss Dickens-Young had brought in the paintings and also said to Sandy, "Thank you for your time. We will probably need to speak to you again soon and we'll need to measure and photograph the paintings for the record before we leave so we can do that now."

After the painting details had been logged and photographed Sandy escorted David and Ruth to the front door. David asked for contact telephone numbers for her and Jonny and Ruth took down the details. As they got back into the car David took a last look at the beautiful property.

"My wife would love this house you know Ruth. I think she feels I have failed her somehow. Oh well; I wouldn't want the upkeep or their heating bills that must be enormous."

Ruth laughed and agreed with him saying, "You're right on both counts. But my flat is fine."

But she suddenly felt a warm glow of affection for David as she thought that his wife would still be discontent if she was the Queen of England. When they got back to Cardiff they both went into the operations room and looked at the timeline they had started. Ruth chipped in first.

"OK. According to what Jonny Davies says he arrived at the Gallery at about 9 am. Sandy Dickens-Young says she arrived at about 9.45 am. They left the Gallery at approximately 10 am; CCTV will back this up."

David stood with one hand under his chin studying the timeline wall then he turned away adding, "I am going to check if Uniform has got all the CCTV coverage in yet and then I will call the mortuary to see if we can pop down and observe."

Ruth felt sick and went pale at the thought.

"Oh er Dave; maybe I can stay here?"

"I think you should come down Ruth. It's no good putting it off. You will just build up a fear and it will get bigger and bigger each time you need to absorb that level of information. Come on now; let's do this. Besides, they will give you a bowl to be sick in."

The last sentence came with a chuckle in his voice as he looked her in the eye and winked. One phone call later and they were both on their way. On arrival as they entered the pathology room Ruth commented to David, "These places are always so cold."

An attractive redhead who was holding an electric saw and leaning over a mortuary slab with the body of Matthew Lloyd laid out on it looked up and said, "No choice I am afraid. It would get a bit smelly if we allowed it to be warm in here."

David greeted the pathology team that consisted of the woman and a small pale balding man of about fifty who was standing beside her, holding a large stainless-steel bowl with what looked like a liver in it.

"Good afternoon Leah. Hi Alan. Do you have one of those cardboard sick bowls for my esteemed colleague? She gets a bit queasy in these situations."

Leah answered as she smiled at Ruth and handed her a bowl.

"Aw, don't be insensitive Sir. Lots of people are sick just at the thought of an autopsy. Try standing back a little Ma'am, just in-case. We don't want you to be poorly over our Mr Lloyd. You can go to the viewing gallery if you like."

Leah turned back to the body. It had been cut through the abdominal cavity with a Y shape at the chest. The proceedings were being recorded as she said, "I have inspected the body and it would appear Mr Lloyd was killed by a single cut to the throat by a very sharp knife—possibly slightly curved like a samurai sword. However, he had endured various injuries to the body before the killing blow. This was not a good death. He would have suffered for some time while he was tortured. Alan would you weigh the liver please?"

She then showed them what looked like a metal butt-plug with a loop attached saying, "Oh, and forensics also found this on the floor. It had been inserted into his rectum that has some burn marks. This would indicate he would have had an electrical current put through it. Very nice."

A by now slightly grey looking Ruth said in a quiet tone, "Oh dear God! Whoever did this is a sick bastard."

Nodding his head David commented, "They knew exactly what they were doing to give maximum pain before they killed him. It looks like we are dealing with a gangland type killing. They were after information I think. Or maybe just to scare off others. I'm not sure. What do you recon' Ma'am?"

"Well, it isn't something we deal with every day Sir—thank God. And it sure wasn't an accident."

Ruth then turned to Leah and asked if she had found any trace of Narcotics?

Leah replied, "Not so far but I will run some more tests and let you know in a few days."

David and Ruth thanked Leah and Alan for their time and as they walked away they heard the electric saw start up. David turned around to see Leah begin to cut through the top of Matthew Lloyd's head. He ushered Ruth through the swing door saying, "It's not a good idea to turn around Ruth."

When they arrived back at the station they sat in the Operations Room discussing what they knew. Looking at CCTV they saw the two men that entered the gallery half an hour after Jonny and Sandy left; one tall and slim the other short and stocky.

They were both wearing hoodies so their faces were obscured but the shorter one appeared to have something strapped to his back under his jacket. The other one carried a large briefcase. Ruth and David looked at each other and said in unison, "Matthew's killers."

It was gone 9 pm before David got home and just as he put the key in the door of his home he suddenly remembered the cat food and washing up liquid. He muttered to himself as he saw his wife waiting the other side of the door.

"Oh shit! Now I am in trouble."

"Where the hell have you been? Dinner was ready two hours ago. It's ruined. You could at least have called me. Where is the cat food and washing up liquid? For God's sake David can't you do anything right?"

David said nothing. He knew from experience it would just get him into more hot water. Being in the Police Force didn't always sit well with being a husband and at this moment he wished he was back in the incident room with Ruth.

Monday 21 August 2017

Back at the Mayhew Estate, as soon Ruth and David had left Jonny prepared for his trip to pick up Aiyana and take her to Gloucestershire Airport to catch her business jet flight to Madrid. Sue made a few sandwiches and he left in the Freelander just after noon taking the M4 west and then the A46 heading for Tetbury. He stopped at Doughton to phone Aiyana so she could be ready outside the Snooty Fox with her luggage.

She was there when he drew up to the main entrance. Jonny placed her luggage in the back of the Freelander and they drove off. Heading for Stroud he then followed the signs to the M5 and Gloucester Airport. On the way he updated Aiyana with more details about what had happened and when the drew up in the airport business lounge car park he made her mobile phone safe using the down loads and button provided by Arthur.

Aiyana looked at him and said with a very serious expression on her face, "Thank you for all this Jonny. But please keep wearing the wrist band I gave you. I will send strong thoughts from our Guardian Sprits to it every night to keep you safe."

Aiyana handed over the copies of the painting ownership documents and Jonny placed them safely in a locked compartment on the Freelander. They then went to the Business Centre Departure lounge where Aiyana's flight tickets and hotel booking documents were ready for collection. Lord Henry's arrangements had all worked out as planned; but then again why wouldn't they?

They had time for a quick coffee and a hug before it was time for her to board. She turned and waved as she said, "I will let you know when I arrive in Boston and please thank Lord Henry for everything he has done and keep me up to date with developments. Wow; a real English Lord. They will not believe me when I tell the Tribe. Speak soon. Hopefully it will not be too long before I return."

And with that Aiyana—his newly found exotic half-sister—was gone. As he watched the jet take off, although he had only known her for a few days he felt a strange emptiness as the plane disappeared into the clouds. He made his way back to the Freelander and headed back to Wales with some sadness in his heart although he knew it was the best for Aiyana's safety. It had been quite a day so far.

Chapter 9

Everything comes to you in the right moment; be patient.
(Native American Saying)

Monday Late Afternoon
21 August 2017

Jonny arrived back at the Mayhew Estate still thinking about Aiyana. Sue was waiting to greet him and asked, "You look thoughtful Jonny. All went well didn't it? Aiyana on her way home and to safety?"

"Yep; she is flying home. But it's a strange feeling ; I have only known her a few days but I miss her already."

He then noticed that Sue was beaming and was very excited. He looked her in the eye and said, "You look happy though. What's up?"

"I have been working on the painting and it is beginning to throw up some rather exciting surprises. I'll tell you about them later."

Now Jonny was interested and wanted to know more, so in his best pleading voice he asked, "Awe; come on. Can't you just give me a clue darling?"

The secretive smiling Sue became the stern and serious Sue.

"No I will tell you when we are all together. Sandy, Chrissie and Devlin have gone for a ride around the estate and Barry and Henry are playing with the cars down in the garages. I have told them dinner is at 7 pm on the terrace, so you will just have to be patient."

"OK I will go for a walk around the rose gardens and enjoy the view."

Sue looked at his grin and with a knowing smile said with an edge in her voice, "That's nice Jonny. Jacob, the gardener is just about to finish his shift so you will probably find him getting ready to go home. You might catch him if you are quick. He keeps his motorbike behind the stables."

"Right then I had better be going. See you in a while crocodile."

With that Jonny shot out of the door and disappeared in the direction of the stables.

Sue watched him go. She smiled and thought to herself, *He has no idea just how exciting this painting really is. None of them have apart from Henry. At the moment, it is our secret.*

She then turned and walked back into the kitchen where her housekeeper Margie was just putting the finishing touches to a beautiful dressed salmon that had been brought down from their Scottish estate. Margie and her husband Bryn had a cottage on the estate. Bryn was the head gardener and also doubled as a driver when Sue and Henry were at home. Bryn's Father had worked for the Mayhew's until he had a fatal heart attack fifteen years previously. Bryn had been in the Army at the time but left to take over his father's roll. Margie and Bryn had become more like family friends than staff members.

The salmon had been gutted, boned and scaled before being wrapped in foil and cooked in the large oven. It was then placed on a plate and let to cool before applying mayonnaise and thinly sliced cucumber to represent the scales.

"That looks amazing Margie. Shall I put it in the fridge for you? Then you can get yourself home."

"Thank you Lady Mayhew, I have a houseful at the moment with the two boys down from university, and guaranteed they will have some friends back at the cottage who will also want feeding."

"Yes; but it must be fun having them home Margie."

"It is but it makes for a very busy life. But you have a houseful yourself at the moment so I'll get out of your way."

Margie washed her hands and dried them before saying goodbye, leaving by the kitchen door.

Sue liked to do some of the cooking when she had the time but Margie was the mainstay because as well as being a housekeeper she was in charge of the kitchen and prepared delicious fare. This Monday evening Margie had prepared several different salads to go with the salmon along with a soured cream sauce. She had also made her famous and very delicious raspberry pavlova for dessert.

As everything was more or less ready Sue decided to just spend a little time in her laboratory looking again at the painting that could change the lives of those around her. Intriguingly, she had also discovered an additional little surprise tucked away inside the canvas and the wooden stretch frame. At first glance it looked like parchment or very old paper. She thought to herself, *That needs extra care. I'll try and get that out tomorrow.*

Her studio was a hexagonal room that went up into a beautiful domed opaque glass ceiling, shedding light in every part of the space. There were no side windows for security reasons but a sophisticated lighting system had been installed for when she was working in the evening.

She had put the painting on an easel getting the maximum light from above. She grabbed a chair and placed it in-front of the painting and sat down marvelling at her discovery. She had confirmed that a second canvas had been applied over the original. A water-based glue had been used to hold it in place and it would take time to reveal it all.

However, taking a guess that any signature would be in the bottom right corner, using some water on a pad she had slowly separated the two paintings in that area. And Bingo! There was no mistaking the signature and the style of a truly great master.

She was very excited and in a celebration mood. This looked like being her life's big discovery. She heard a sound and turned around to see Henry smiling at her from the open doorway. He half turned and shut the door, locking it at the same time. He walked over to Sue who knew exactly what that wicked smile and the locked door meant. Rising from her chair, she turned to face him with her longing quickly taking hold. It had been some weeks since they last made love and the excitement of the painting discoveries meant that she was now really in the mood; some might say gagging for it.

Henry took her by the hand and led her over to an authentic Chinese rug. He moved up close and placed his hand beneath her chin—just raising it a little before he pressed his lips gently on hers. Kissing her with tenderness, he then, without a word being spoken, reached down and slowly lifted her tee-shirt up and over her head dropping it to the floor. Her bra followed suit revealing breasts that any man or woman just wanted to caress. Reacting to the moment she placed her hands on either side of his head and pulled it to one of her by now very hard nipples.

She had always loved her lovers paying attention to her breasts. They were one of her most erogenous zones and she could reach orgasm by caressing them. She gasped when his tongue started to massage and encircle her nipple and had to use her thumb and finger on the other one as she became engrossed in her own sexuality. After a few arousing seconds Henry raised his head and lowered his hands to undo her jeans—gliding them down over her slim hips and revealing long shapely legs. He then hooked his fingers onto each side of her panties and slid them down.

He lowered himself down onto his knees in-front of her, kissing her body as he moved down. Sue leant back on a table and opened her legs. Henry moved his hands onto her bottom, gently drawing her closer to his face until she was close enough for his tongue to find her clitoris, slowly encircling it until she felt she would collapse as she held his head close to feel it moving in time with her hips. She knew her sounds of pleasure were getting very loud and hoped nobody was outside to hear.

Sensing and hearing her arousal and his own, Henry stood up and unzipped his trousers to release a now very large and hard cock leaving Sue to self-pleasure herself while he did it. When he was naked she lowered herself onto the rug and lying down with knees apart she urgently pulled him down on top guiding his cock with her hand.

She needed him inside her now and he slid inside without resistance because she was now so wet. He started to move in and out—very slowly at first, letting her feel the whole length of him—before gradually getting faster and faster. He looked at her and without a word he knew when she was ready as her eyes partly closed and her short sighs reached a crescendo. They both reached their climax together with a chorus of sighs and groans. After the noise—a short silence. Then some quietly spoken words that meant everything.

"I love you Sue."

"I love you too darling."

They lay entwined on the rug for a short while enjoying the intimacy of the moment. After a while Henry raised himself up on one elbow and looked at Sue, breaking the moment by saying, "I take it you have not told them about your intriguing discovery yet?"

"Nope. I will tell them at dinner. I am so excited. They won't believe it."

"Yes; they have all been through a rough time so some good news will be welcome. In truth I think it is Jonny who is holding them together at the moment. He has got more backbone than I first gave him credit for."

Sue replied thoughtfully, "Hmm; don't ever underestimate that young man Henry. There is so much more to him that he keeps hidden under that perceived persona."

She reached over to his face and kissed him passionately with tongues entwining and said with a cheeky smile, "That was wonderful darling. Thank you. We must do it again sometime; soon."

Sitting up, and reaching for her clothes she then said, "But sadly we had better get moving now. Let's freshen up and I will take the food out. Would you mind laying the table on the terrace darling? It would be a great help."

Then with a second thought and a giggle she said, "Oh. We'd better get dressed before we leave in case anyone is about."

Henry smiled and said, "Ah; good point. I will see you in the kitchen in about twenty minutes sexy."

Meanwhile, elsewhere on the estate, Chrissie had just got back from her ride with Sandy and Devlin. Although she had totally enjoyed her ride she had felt a bit like a gooseberry because it was obvious that the two young people were infatuated with each other. There was definitely some electricity in the air.

She lifted her leg over the back of the saddle and lightly dismounted Wiggy. Devlin's little terrier came out of the tack room at a run eager to see his beloved master. He was bouncing up and down on his short little back legs as if he was on springs but all he got was a pat on the head. Undeterred, he shot back into the tack room and picked up his latest great achievement; a half-eaten rat that he dropped on Sandy's foot. It was as if he was saying, "Bet you couldn't do that."

Devlin came to the rescue. He picked him up and looked him in the eye shouting, "Jimmy you little shit."

The dog just belched and gave him a lick on the nose.

Sandy, who was well used to terrier personalities, just laughed and told Jimmy that he was a very clever boy. Christina on the other hand felt a little queasy as Sandy wiped rat entrails off her boot, so she started to lead Wiggy over to his stable to get his tack off. She looked up to see Jonny going through the Archway to the staff parking area behind the stables. It might have been a mother's intuition but he seemed to be in deep thought and very angry about something. He looked up, smiled meekly and waved at her, but there was something about his demeanour that worried Christina.

In fact, although Sue's positive indications about the painting had cheered him up a bit after waving goodbye to Aiyana had made him gloomy, he was now thinking about the information that Arthur had given him the night before regarding Will. He had put this to the back of his mind while whisking Aiyana to safety and now wasn't sure how he was going to deal with it. With the stress of everything that was going on around him at the moment, his mood was jumping between highs and lows. But to be honest, deep down he was incredibly angry about Will and it was this news that dominated his thoughts at that moment. Will had been his friend and lover for a couple of years and at one time he thought they would end up together once he had finished Uni. He was also his supplier. He murmured under his breath, "Fucking little bastard."

He looked up as he reached the other side of the archway and painted a smile on his face as he saw the good-looking gardener just pulling on his motorbike leathers beside a matt-black Moto Guzzi Audace motorbike. It's V-twin engine and big fat tyres really looked the dog's bollocks. It was time for another high.

Admiring the machine Jonny slowly said, "Oh very nice bike Jacob. I will expect a ride up behind you on that piece of kit."

Jacob flashed a big smile and unhitched a spare helmet from the side of the bike which he handed to him.

"No time like the present Jonny. Hop on."

"Wow! OK; just a quickie then. I can't be very long I am expected at dinner at 7 pm."

Jacob put his leg over the bike and kicked up the side stand and turned around patting the seat behind him saying, "Have you been on the back of a bike before Jonny?"

As he took his seat behind Jacob Jonny's quick reply was, "Oh yes; plenty of times. I just love the feel of a big V-twin between my thighs."

Jacob started the bike and the V-twin burst into life. Proceeding down the drive at a leisurely cruising pace they pass through the security gates and then Jacob opened the throttle, quickly accelerating down the road at speed as the torque kicked in.

Jonny held on tight to Jacob, enjoying the thrill of the powerful bike and the closeness to Jacob. All this meant that he had no control over the major boner straining against his jeans. He thought to himself, *I need some good hard sex.*

He called out to Jacob, "Where are you taking me?"

"Just up the road for a short ride. We can't be long because it's already a quarter to seven so we had better turn back now or I'll be in trouble with his Lordship. But if you like we could meet up tomorrow. It's my day off."

Jacob turned the bike around and headed back. Right at this moment Jonny and his boner would have rather spent more time with Jacob and then have dinner at the estate, so feeling horny and disappointed he replied in a sulky voice, "Yeah. Whatever."

They arrived at the estate gates and Jonny asked Jacob to drop him there and he would walk back. They exchanged mobile phone numbers and looking straight at Jonny's groin Jacob laughed and said, "That's a nice bulge you've got there."

He gave Jonny a wink and a wave and then roared off down the road.

Feeling a bit cheered by that thought Jonny pressed the security button in the wall and the gates slowly opened. His mind switched back to Will as he stomped up the beautifully landscaped drive, devising plans regarding what he will do to him when he caught up with him—none of it is very nice.

As he got to the steps to the house he put his head up and shoulders back and put a false smile on his face. He needed to rid himself of his anger. As he went upstairs to his room, he thought, *What I need is a snort of Charlie.*

Humming happily on the back terrace, having quickly composed herself after her enjoyable session with Henry, Sue had put the food on the table. Chrissie was admiring the beautifully prepared salmon and telling Sue it was almost too lovely to disturb while Henry and Devlin were discussing the financial market. Barry had just walked through the French doors and made straight for Chrissie. He put his arm around her and told her that he has just seen Jonny walking up the drive looking like thunder.

Chrissie replied in a flippant almost dismissive tone, "Yes; I saw him earlier and he looked peeved. Probably fell out with his new found friend the rose boy."

Barry remained worried.

"Hmm; he didn't look happy to me at all. It looked a bit more serious than that."

Sandy was next to arrive wearing cream shorts topped with a pretty shoulder exposing floaty top and cream Doc Martins—painted with sunflowers this time.

Devlin looked up and watched her arrival, thinking, *Dear God, but she is stunning.*

Last to arrive was Jonny—all smiles now and looking as if he had just walked into a party. Everyone turned to look at him and smiled. He just had that effect on people—or maybe it was something else this time. He checked his fly but that was complete so he said, "Hi folks. For those who don't know, Aiyana is on her way back to a safer—I hope—Boston, and... Oh my God! Look at that food. I am starving."

Sandy quickly moved over to Jonny and whispered, "Wipe your nose. It is ringed with white powder. Not a good look at all."

With a slightly embarrassed laugh he wiped it off with a napkin and quietly replied, "Oh shit! Thanks darling."

In truth he didn't really care much that it had been observed. But it mattered that Sandy cared because they were in her sister's home and if she thought it important then it was.

When they had all assembled Sue clapped her hands together to get the attention of everyone.

"Sorry to interrupt the conversations but before we eat I have a little news with regards to the mysterious painting."

She waited until everyone was silent before delivering the news in her most dramatic style.

"As you know, I have only had the painting since Saturday but by using x-ray, ultra violet and infra-red lights I can confirm that it is in fact two paintings on two separate canvases; one laid over the other. It will take a long time to fully reveal what we have but I have managed to carefully lift a corner of the top canvas which revealed a signature. It looks like it is by no other than..."She paused for effect..."Thomas Gainsborough."

Everyone gasped. Chrissie put her hand up to her face.

"It is dated 1753. He was not so well known outside Suffolk at that time and was living in Ipswich painting landscapes and some local portraits. I have checked the type of paint used and it is the sort of paint that Gainsborough was using at that time. His famous painting of Mr and Mrs Andrews was done at that time and there are many similarities in the materials used as well. There is still a whole lot of work to be done before I can prove that to the artistic community but this painting could be worth a small fortune. It is an incredible find. The discovery of a painting of this magnitude is certainly not something that happens every day. It is a shame that we have no sale's history at the moment. This will make it more difficult to prove its authenticity."

Sue looked at the faces of her guests and felt a happy glow at being able to impart good news to her new found friends.

"I have checked the current auction prices and it would seem that your painting could be worth in excess of £6.5 million"—more gasps. "But it does depend on the subject and that still has to be revealed by further work in my laboratory. It is very important that this remains our secret until the work is completed and the authenticity and ownership has been ratified so please do not tell anyone else about this yet."

The party became very excited and they all started to talk at once about what an incredible discovery it was and its unbelievable value. All except Jonny who just looked thoughtful and nibbled on a piece of cucumber that had been on the dressed salmon. He had absorbed the news of course and was excited; but his thoughts were still on Will's betrayal and what to do.

Sue smiled at their almost childlike excitement and said, "I have opened a few bottles of bubbles to celebrate darlings so let's eat and enjoy the moment."

They all took a plate while Sue cut into the fish, serving them all a slice. They helped themselves to the various salads before taking a seat around the table.

Jonny managed to place himself next to Barry who, after some conversation about the painting, asked quietly, "What's up Jonny? Something is bothering you. I've known you all your life and I know when you are putting on a show."

"Yeah Baz. Got a lot on my plate at the mo. Perhaps we could meet up in the gym early tomorrow and do a bit of the old kick boxing?"

Not wanting to take their host's hospitality for granted Barry turned to Henry and asked, "Would it be OK to use your gym in the morning Henry?"

Henry smiled and replied, "Yes of course. It's there to be used."

"Thank you Henry. I could do with a workout."

Turning to Jonny he said, "Is 7am OK? We could go for a run afterwards if you like."

Jonny replied with a grimace, "Yep. The gym sounds good to me; but I will skip the run if you don't mind."

Barry smiled but thought, *I must ask Jonny to stop calling me Baz. I hate it.*

The evening was very pleasant with everyone chatting happily. The news about the painting was to say the least, very encouraging and it helped release some of the stress of the previous few days. Chrissie was describing the beauty that she observed while riding around the estate between the inner and outer security walls.

They had passed a lake with willow trees hanging their branches, as if they were combing the water in the gentle August breeze with moorhens and ducks making their way blithely in and out of the rushes. It was like a deep cleanse treatment—washing out all the nastiness of recent events.

Sue agreed.

"I have sat on that bank and painted that very scene. It is absolutely blissful isn't it? There is a lot of history associated with that part of the lake. In fact the lake was created from an underground stream and inlet that links to the River Ebbw at the Southern end of our land. The Ebbw flows into the River Usk close to where the Newport Docks used to be—most of which have now been closed or filled in. Before the docks were built there used to be some wharfs that smugglers used and then ferried their ill-gotten gains up the Ebbw for disposal. Boats can't get past some of the silt banks these days but our inlet is said to be one of their storage areas. You might have noticed a big boulder in a wood on a small hill. That is said to be the point where the goods were off-loaded. You can see the ruins of some small buildings when you get close up."

Henry joined in while filling his brandy glass and offering the same to his guests.

"I'm glad you like the place and feel at ease. I always consider this estate as home, although we acquired each of our properties for their individual interest or beauty; and of course investment. But I feel that I can relax here. It would be the one place I would endeavour to keep if things went tits up at any time. I do have the family pile in Berkshire that has been in our family for a few hundred years, but my younger brother is living in it with his wife and ever-increasing brood—six at the last count."

He laughed as he said, "I think they want to fill all of the fourteen bedrooms."

The evening progressed in the same convivial manner, and as night started to envelope them the wonderful aromas from the night scented flowers filled the air. Moths begin to flutter around the lights on the table. Christina thought, *Could this be an omen about people gathering around the painting's ownership once its authenticity had been clarified?*

Sandy and Devlin excused themselves saying they were going for a walk around the gardens. Devlin whistled for Jimmy who got up from under the table where he had been competing successfully with Henry's dogs for scraps. As they walked away, the knowing looks from the others seemed to reflect a mixture of nostalgia and jealousy—young love blossoming in a world full of danger and unknowns.

Jonny smiled but his mind was still on other things. He got up to lean against the balustrade and looked out at the gathering dusk. Still trying to get his head around Will's betrayal, the situation was now gnawing away at his heart and stomach.

Christina and Barry got up and helped Henry and Sue carry the dishes back to the kitchen. Barry looked over his shoulder at Jonny and felt really unsettled at the downhearted set of Jonny's head and shoulders as he looked out at the estate. He thought to himself, *Oh well, maybe we will have a talk tomorrow.*

Jonny straightened up and walked to the table to help with the clearing away. He painted on his best smile, thanked them for a lovely evening and went to bed. But sleep didn't come easy.

Day 7 Tuesday
22 August 2017 6.30 am

Jonny woke up from a restless night. He put on a tracksuit and wandered down to the gym in the basement. Barry was already there and was doing some stretching exercises. They acknowledge each other with a "Hi" and a smile. Jonny started to loosen up before putting on boxing gloves and kick-boxing foot guards. They started to warm up, taking it in turns throwing punches and kicks at hook and jab pads; increasing the speed and power as time went by.

With the warm-up over they faced each other with their gloves up and they started to spar. Barry was quickly taken back a little with Jonny's over-reaction to a punch but found it easy to defend because Jonny was not focussing on placing his punches and kicks; although his speed and power was impressive.

Barry shouted, "Stop right now!"

After Jonny drew back Barry continued, "OK; let's talk about your aggression shall we tiger?"

Jonny was puffing hard and was bent over with his gloved hands on his knees so didn't say anything.

Barry went on, "Look; all you achieved there was to tire yourself out. You have to control your anger Jonny and focus on your actions. Now do you want to talk about what has got you so worked up?"

"I don't really want to go into details just yet Barry but you are right; I have a problem with a person I trusted and I have found out he is mixed up with all this shit. I will sort it and get my anger under control. Let's do some more boxing."

"Don't do anything rash Jonny and keep us in the loop—OK?"

Jonny nodded his ascent and they tapped gloves to continue. Thinking about Barry's words Jonny managed to land a few well aimed kicks on Barry and vice versa. The session became much more positive.

Barry changed into running gear while Jonny went into the shower before going back to his room to get changed. Just before Barry was leaving for his run Jonny called out, "Catch you later and thanks."

Back up in his room, Jonny sat and looked at his phone and a plan started to form as he thought things through.

Barry is right. I must control my anger and focus or I will be putting us all in more danger. First of all I must not let Will know that I have found out about his involvement in this. Right—let's get started.

Jonny pressed in Will's number and it was answered pretty quickly.

"Hi Jonny, how are things?"

"Yeah good thanks hun. I have a couple of days free, do you fancy a meet up tomorrow?"

"Er yeah. But I am in London for a meeting at the moment. How do you fancy a night out up here?"

"Sounds good. I would love that. We could go clubbing or something. I will call when I am on my way—probably tomorrow."

"Excellent. I look forward to your call. Gotta go now. See you tomorrow."

With that the line went dead.

Jonny sat back and drew breath. Right; we are on our way. But I'd better check out things with Arty just in case he is telling more lies.

Jonny rang Arthur who told him that Will left the bar last night and had not yet returned. They had a brief conversation to confirm that everyone was safe including the flight details for Aiyana who was on her way back to Boston, and to check everything else was in order as far as Arthur could see. He confirmed all looked good so Jonny said, "Thanks Arty. I have to go now but we'll catch up more later."

Time for some R&R before that trip to London so Jonny phoned his new rose gardener friend Jacob. The phone rang for a while before being answered by Jacob. Jonny said, "Hello Sweetheart. Fancy that day out with me today? You can show me the local beauty spots."

"Great. I will pick you up on the bike in an hour by the main gate. See you there."

Meanwhile Sandy and Devlin had just brought the horses from the paddocks into the stables to protect them from the heat and flies because another sunny day was forecast. Devlin asked, "Would you like a spot of breakfast Sandy?"

"That would be nice but I have to get back to the house. Sue wants a hand with the painting. I will be out later to ride though."

She gave him a peck on the lips before turning to go.

As she disappeared through the gate in the hedge she heard Devlin call, "I am missing you already."

She smiled to herself and thought, *I like him; I like him a lot. He makes me feel warm and safe. Please let him like me the same way.*

She wandered around the back of the house and entered through the kitchen door, saying good morning to Margie before taking an apple from the fruit bowl and proceeding on to the laboratory. Sue was already there. She had the painting face down on some padded velvet.

She greeted Sandy and asked, "Sweetie, can you give me a hand with this?"

Sandy took a closer look and said, "Hmm; intriguing. So is that a piece of parchment or vellum under the stretch frame?"

"Yep. I think it is vellum. It may be nothing but it has been carefully placed in here and I need to be very careful not to damage it. I've removed the tacks from one edge of the canvas, so if you can pop some cotton gloves on I would like you to hold the canvas strait. You will find some gloves in the top drawer on your left."

After putting on the gloves, under Sue's instructions Sandy held the canvas so it didn't bend and damage the painting.

"OK, now lift it slightly Sandy."

Being very careful Sandy slowly lifted the canvass and Sue carefully removed the piece of vellum from between the canvas and the frame before placing it on the work bench.

"Right now place the canvas back on the frame and hold it while I tack it back in place."

After that process was carefully completed Sandy said with not a little excitement in her voice, "So; shall we have a look then?"

Sue nodded with a smile and Sandy watched as she unfolded the document and placed paperweights on each corner. The vellum hadn't aged too well and was quite brown in colour. The writing had also faded. But they could see that there was quite a bit of writing at the top and what looked to be a crude map underneath.

Sandy gasped in astonishment and said, "Oh my God. Wow! Is this a pirate's treasure map then?"

"How very amusing dear sister. I think you may be right. And there appears to be a lot of text to go with it; maybe instructions about what it all means."

At about the same time Jonny had walked around to the back of the stables to meet Jacob for their day out. He was early so he took a seat on a low stone wall and sent a text to his mother saying he would be out with Jacob all day. He then received a call from Arthur.

"Umm hi JJJonny. I fforgot to tell you earlier. Umm I have a ggadget for you."

"Cool Buddy. What's this then?"

"Umm I hhhave an um earpiece so I can talk tto umm you wwwithout anyone hearing and um a bbutton mic so you can ttalk um back."

"Awesome! I am off to London tomorrow so I will drop into see you on the way and pick it up."

"Ccool. Um see you tomorrow."

Jonny heard Jacob's motorbike coming down the drive so he said, "Gotta go now Arty."

He jumped off the wall to greet Jacob who handed him a helmet and they were soon travelling through the sunny Welsh countryside before turning onto the M4 heading West to one of Jacob's favourite places near Carmarthen.

After about an hour and a half they pulled into a car park by the Taf estuary and Jacob said, "This is where Dylan Thomas spent the last four years of his life Jonny. They say he wrote Under Milkwood in the boathouse. I thought we could go for a walk along the estuary before we have a spot of lunch in the Boathouse Tearooms."

Jonny looked at Jacob and smiled.

"Nobody has ever taken me out on a proper date before. This is lovely."

Jacob continued, "I used to come down here a lot; I did my dissertation on Dylan Thomas. I would stand and look at the view and imagine the great man standing in the same place. I felt inspired."

Jonny looked at him and said, "I didn't know you were at Uni!"

"You didn't ask. You just assumed I was a gardener. I love gardening and have worked for Lord and Lady Mayhew every school and uni hols since I was a kid. But I also went to Cardiff and took my degree in English lit."

Jonny laughed, "Well, it just goes to show you should never judge a book by its cover."

"Damn right Jonny my dear. Damn right."

Jonny looked at Jacob and smiled to himself thinking, *Yep, I like him.*

The two wandered back to the boathouse after their walk. Both were happy and comfortable in each other's company. They found it easy to talk to each other without the usual first date embarrassing pauses and talked about anything and everything, discovering they had much in common but enough differences to be interesting.

Jonny glanced at his watch and exclaimed, "Good grief, it's nearly four o'clock, Jacob! I can't believe the time has gone so quickly. We had better get back or it will appear very rude to Lord and Lady Mayhew. I feel a bit guilty that I have just pissed off for the day and left them with my mum and Barry. Mind you, they all seem to get on really well."

Jacob stood up saying, "OK let's get moving then. But I'm sure it will be alright."

It was five forty-five when Jacob Dropped Jonny off behind the stables. They both removed their helmets and Jonny pulled Jacob towards him. They looked at each other and kissed. Jacob placed his hand on Jonny's crotch and playfully traced the outline of his erection with his finger.

Jonny murmured, "Fucking hell Jacob I really need to have you right now."

"Not yet Jonny, but soon, maybe."

With that he straddled his bike. But before he put on his helmet he turned to Jonny and said, "Look Jonny. I really do like you and I want to keep seeing you. But I won't be used. I am not into casual sex so let's just enjoy each other's company for a while."

"Awe come on Jacob! I know you are gagging for it. Or are you just a cock tease?"

"Think what you like mate. But if you want me in your life you will wait."

And on those words he placed his helmet on his head, started the bike and rode away—leaving Jonny standing with his mouth open. He was feeling pretty confused and a bit stupid during his walk up to the house.

Sandy saw him walk through the stable-yard and ran over to greet him full of sunshine and smiles; stopping when she saw his scowling face.

"Sooo things didn't go well then? Do you want to talk about it hun?"

"Yeah Babe. There is a lot I need to get off my chest. Let's grab a coffee and sit in the garden."

A worried Sandy said, "But everyone has gone out to the pub for dinner. We are supposed to meet up with them."

"Nah. I am not in the mood but you guys go."

She saw he wanted to talk so replied, "Well, actually I would like to spend some time with you my friend. Come on hun; let's get coffee and I will ring them to make our excuses. Are you hungry?"

Jonny smiled and said, "Don't ask silly questions. You know I am always hungry."

Sandy rang Sue and offered their excuses and they were soon sitting down on the terrace with coffee and cream cheese filled bagels. After a few mouthfuls Jonny started to tell Sandy about Will's betrayal.

"So you are just going to go up to London and meet with Will without a plan in place. Do you think that is wise hun?"

"Probably not to be honest but I can't just let it go. It's driving me crazy. And what if I can get some information about everything that is going on?"

"Huh; And what if you get killed? How do you know that the two thugs won't be with him? They have guns and big pointy knives. For God's sake my friend, you could very much end up dead!"

"OK then, lets come up with a plan because I am going to London tomorrow whatever happens."

They then spent some time talking over different scenarios and Sandy persuaded Jonny that she should go up with him. They were pretty sure she would not be recognised and that could be useful in some of the scenarios discussed. She also thought at least she could act as some sort of restraint on Jonny's more extreme tendencies. Mind you, she had to blackmail him with the threat of telling the others if he went without her.

Once they had an outline plan Sandy said, "So we'll keep this to ourselves hun. We can let everyone know that we will be in London by sending texts once we are well on the way. By then they will have no chance to try and stop us; which they will if we tell them early. Anyway, we can make up our minds about that later. But what about your day with Jacob?"

Jonny replied with a perplexed look on his face, "I just can't understand it. We had a great day today. We really got on well and it's obvious we fancy each other. So why won't he…you know…"

"Have sex with you?"

"Yeah."

"Oh for heaven's sake hun. You have only had one date. Jacob's a nice regular guy and not into casual sex."

Jonny responded with a knowing smile, "Oh sweetheart there is nothing casual about sex with me—but you are probably right. I'll just have to wait. But as you know, patience is not my best quality."

"What about you and Devlin? Everything is looking pretty cosy."

"Ah I really like him but it is too soon to tell really. He is a lovely guy and I would like to continue seeing him and God he is hot. But we have not made love yet. He says I am worth waiting for. Bless him."

They were interrupted by the sound of the two families and Devlin returning from their meal at the pub, so they got up and went into the kitchen to have a coffee with them before going to bed. However, as agreed they did not mention their plans for the next day. They knew that would just cause problems.

Chapter 10

A man must make his own arrows.
(Native American Saying)

Day 8 Wednesday 7 am
23 August 2017
Padstow, Cornwall

Down in Cornwall, Christina's friend Isabella Sallis was an early riser, and at 7 am had already finished her run to St George's Cove and back. It was a particularly beautiful morning. As the sun came up it turned the sea a light blue colour; almost white in places, while out on the horizon the sky was a hazy orange. Having had a shower, she was now on her sunny beach-facing decking marvelling at the view across the Camel estuary to Rock Sands while enjoying her first black coffee of the day.

Sometimes she took the ferry across to Rock where she could run for miles, but today time was of the essence. She was looking forward to her trip to Bristol where she would be staying with her friend Christina and she had decided that she would come off her strict training diet and have a few drinks during her stay.

As she thought about how their special friendship started, the stirrings in her body were interrupted by her Bengal cat Paula—named after marathon runner Paula Radcliff. She was winding herself fluidly around her legs, meowing loudly demanding to be fed. Isabella picked up Paula and laid her cheek against her own saying, "Come on then little one. Let's get you some breakfast. Uncle Pete from next door will be popping in to feed you but I will be back here on Friday."

After feeding Paula she walked into her very minimalist white bedroom and took off her bathrobe, admiring her fit body as she passed by the full-length mirror. She had tummy muscles most men would be proud of so she gave herself a wolf whistle. Picking out some Bo Ho yellow cotton hareem pants and a fitted navy T-shirt she got dressed before wandering into the living room to phone Christina and let her know she was starting out.

Using the landline she dialled Christina's house phone number. After a few rings the answer phone kicked in so she left a message giving an estimated arrival time of around noon or just before—thinking it a little odd that Christina did not answer. As it was still early she concluded that she had probably stayed at Barry's that night.

She had decided to drive to Bristol. The air fare from Newquay was not cheap and there was all the bother of parking at Newquay Airport and getting from Bristol Airport to Christina's flat. There were a few trains from Padstow to Bristol but there were changes to be made along the way and it was just as quick to drive and more convenient. So she grabbed her luggage and called goodbye to the cat before loading the gear into the back of her metallic silver Land Rover Defender. And after popping the key next door to Pete she got in her car and headed off to Bristol

She loved her Landy. It had been on many an excursion both abroad and in Great Britain. She even had a name for her...Dirty Gertie. She was no speed machine, but she could take her half way up a mountainside and then back down again. With big knobbly off-road tyres and a snorkel exhaust, Isabella and Gertie were ready for anything.

As well as convenient, the road trip was interesting and took in some wonderful scenery during the first part of the drive. She drove via Wadebridge and then down to Bodmin to join the A30. This route took her right across Bodmin Moor and then past Dartmoor. The forest scenery around Oakhampton was still at its summer best—all reminding her about how lucky she was to live in such a beautiful part of the country. Once on the M5 at Exeter it was inside lane only. The knobbly tyres on Gertie were not the best boots for motorway driving.

She stopped at the Sedgemoor Service area that was overlooked by Brent Knoll. Starbucks provided a much-needed Granola Bar and black coffee plus a glass of water as she sat outside and watched the well-tanned holiday makers returning from their two weeks in the South West. Then it was on towards Bristol, over the River Avon and along Portway towards Bristol. The trip with a stop had taken just under four hours and full of excited anticipation she was at last pulling into the parking area at Christina's apartment, looking forward to a long welcoming hug and kiss. It had been a long time and she felt like a teenager on her first date.

She noticed Christina's car was not there—which was odd. Still, she got out of the Landy, leaving her back-pack until later in case she had to drive home again. She also left her keys in the ignition. She then walked over to the intercom. Pressing the button to talk the door clicked open before she could say anything. She thought, *Hmm, that's weird.*

She always like to use the stairs as part of keeping fit and when she arrived on Christina's floor, she found the door to the apartment was closed. Christina would normally be there with the door open to greet her. So she knocked on the door but there was no answer.

Trying the door handle, it opened so she stepped gingerly into the flat and called out, "Chrissie. Are you there?"

All of a sudden, she was grabbed around the neck from behind. She quickly brought her elbow back and connected with someone's solar plexus with a satisfying grunt but whoever was holding her did not release his hold. The smell of aftershave indicated it was a man.

Another man walked towards her with a devious smile and said slowly in a strong American accent, "Hello Izzy. Don't bother to struggle. You will only make things a whole lot worse for yourself. In fact you could end up dead. So be a honey and just cooperate with us."

Isabella tried to take a breath but couldn't. She felt that she was about to pass out.

"My brother Tony here likes to see people in pain. He likes to hurt people a lot, so I am going to ask him to just loosen his hold a little. But if you cause any trouble for us I won't be able to stop him. Now be nice Tony; let the lady breath. We need to ask her some questions and she won't be able to talk if you destroy her throat."

Tony released his grip and Isabella took in a ragged breath. She turned to see a sneering Tony who said in what she thought was a strong New York accent, "Just give me an excuse baby and you and I will have a little fun."

She was then manhandled into the living room and shoved onto one of Christina's settees. Her mobile phone slipped out of her pocket as she sunk sideways into the cushions. She was now looking at both of them. One was tall and dark the other one who had grabbed her was short and blond. She managed to croak, "Where is Chrissie? What have you done with her?"

The tall man replied with a laugh, "We've done nothing with her yet. And we are wondering where she is as well. But she has something that is ours. So it looks like we need to take you on an adventure. We'll let her know where you are and she might come and find you."

Wednesday 23August 2017
The Mayhew Estate

In the same morning back at the Mayhew Estate, Jonny had been in the gym for about forty-five minutes. He was giving the punch bag some real grief. Every punch was to Will's face. Every kick was Will's crutch. He felt fit and ready to meet the lying bastard. He knew what he was going to do and it felt good to be actually doing something. He returned to his room and showered. Checked his phone he noticed a message that brought a big smile to his face. It was from Aiyana:

Back home with my tribe in Boston safe and sound. Take care and keep me in the loop. We are all willing the good spirits to protect you.

He then sat on the bed and called Arty. He passed on the good news about Aiyana but of course, Arty already knew this because of his tracking. He also outlined his plans and they arranged that Jonny would be with him before noon. He then got dressed and went down to the kitchen.

Christina and Barry were sitting at the breakfast bar having a cup of tea. Barry explained he was just waiting five minutes until 9 am to call the vets as they should have the Toxicology Report on what had killed Scrum. Jonny nodded his head and poured himself some tea and made some toast, putting butter on so thick that it was soaking through to the plate. Christina looked on with a grimace and said, "Sue has asked us to meet us in the lab at 9.30 am. She says it is very exciting and she wants to show us personally what she has found out about the painting so far."

"Ah OK! I can't stay long. I have to go to see Arthur at lunch time. Sandy's giving me a lift as she has some stuff she needs to do."

"Fine! You do that; but for God's sake take care."

Barry picked up his phone.

"Right then; let's do this."

He speed dialled his vet and explained the reason for calling. The receptionist told him the report had been completed but that Vet would like to talk to him personally; so she transferred the call.

"Good morning Mr Williams. I am afraid the autopsy has shown that Scrum had been given an overdose of an opiate. It looks like heroin. I am so sorry; he probably picked up a piece of steak that had been injected with the drug while out on his walk. You may want to contact the police to let them know and warn local dog walkers."

Barry thanked the vet, paid the fee by card and organised for Scrum to be cremated. He ran his hands through his hair and with eyes glistening he said with contained emotion, "Dear God! What absolute bastards. They gave my poor boy heroin."

Christina puts her arms tightly around him and said, "I am so sorry love."

Jonny clenched his fists, stared at the wall and with a curl of the lip, muttered, "Another nail."

He had to wonder what the next few hours would bring.

Barry glanced in his direction and hoped he was not about to do anything stupid. He didn't want to say anything in front of Christina because he knew she would go off her head at Jonny if she even had a suspicion that he was planning something.

Jonny made himself relax and said he was going to have his breakfast out on the terrace. He picked up his cup and plate and walked out of the kitchen door into another beautiful day. He heard the sound of an acoustic guitar. He looked around the corner and there sitting at the table was Sandy. With a guitar in her arms she was accompanying herself while singing Rag and Bone man's 'Human'.

He sat himself down with a gentle smile and listened to his friend. He knew she was putting herself into a calm space that only music can achieve. The words seemed to talk to his soul. When the song finished Sandy turned to him and said, "Sooo are you sure you want to go through with this hun? You could get into big trouble."

"It's all I can think about at the moment babe. I need answers. I know it might be a bit irresponsible but I can't think of any other way to sort it; can you? You don't have to join me you know."

"Hmmn! You don't think I'm going to let you loose on this one on your own do you? I'm coming with you and if you try and stop me I will let Lord Henry know what you plan. I will bring my car around to the front at about 10.15 am. Best to use my car as it is not known to those chasing us."

"Right then. But now I guess we had better go to see your sister. She says she has something to show us."

He picked up his cup and plate and wandered back into the kitchen. Putting on a fake smile for his mum and Barry he said, "Come on then guys let's go see Sue."

The four of them followed him down to the studio. Sue and Henry were both there waiting for them. Sue said, "Good morning all. Come over here. Sandy and Henry already know this but I have something interesting to show you."

They all gather around a table on which the old piece of vellum was placed.

"OK. This was placed under the wooden frame of the original painting. Now I am sure you will all agree that it looks suspiciously like a treasure map with some additional instructions that I've yet to decipher. However, the strangest part is that it appears to be a map of our land here at Mayhew. Not as it is now; but as it was back in the 18th Century."

She paused and looked at their surprised faces.

"Actually, it's not as strange as it sounds. We know that your ancestor was from around these parts. We also know that we have that ancient mooring on our tributary off the Ebbw that feeds the lake; moorings that were used by smugglers. I have painted in the area often and you will recall I pointed it out to you Chrissie. Look! They have even indicated that rock.

It is not beyond the realms of possibility to imagine pirates rowing up to here to stash their ill-gotten gains. We might learn more when I completely reveal the original painting."

Looking hard at the map, Jonny mused, "Oh…My…God! Eat your heart out, Captain Jack Sparrow. But please, please can you wait before you all go treasure-seeking? I don't want to miss it but must pop over to Bristol today."

Christina scowled and said pointedly, "Can you not postpone your trip, Jonathan? I think this is quite important, don't you?"

"Yep I do think it's important but nope I can't change my plans. Sandy and I have stuff that we must do and we can't put it off. I am only asking you guys to wait one day."

With some impatience Christina said, "So what is so important that it can't be put off? And we can't impose on Sue and Henry's wonderful hospitality for much longer."

Lord Henry thought he had better calm things down and said, "Whoa! We absolutely love having you here. It's not as if we don't have the space and it is rather exciting. We can check out the site today and possibly do some excavating tomorrow. Now I think that should keep us all happy. But what is so important that cannot be put off Sandy?"

Sandy didn't like telling lies but needs must. Thinking on her feet she thought her investment flat in Bristol offered a good excuse. Her father had purchased it for her as a present on her 18th birthday and it was now a student let. Crossing her fingers behind her back she replied, "I have to sort out my flat in Bristol. I have a student coming to view for a house share and it is the only time she can make it. Sooo housework is a priority and Jonny said he would help me. Jonny also needs to see Arthur. He has info and some more security gadgets for us."

Adding some support to his friend who he knew would be hating this subterfuge Jonny chipped in, "Yeah Arty wants to go over CCTV coverage with me."

Not completely convinced Lord Henry replied, "OK. But keep in contact."

Wanting a quick exit Jonny said, "Right need to get going. Love you all. See you later."

With some tension in her voice Christina asked, "Just hold on one moment. What time will you be back?"

"We are not sure but may stay over at Sandy's place in Bristol if there is a lot to sort out. Don't worry; we will keep you in the loop. Just got to pop upstairs to get some gear. I will see you around the back Sandy."

He planted a kiss on his mum's cheek, waved to the others and strode quickly out of the studio in-case anyone asked more awkward questions.

Within ten minutes, he was around the back of the stables waiting for Sandy to pick him up and to have a quick word with Jacob.

Jacob wandered over; he was shirtless, and the sun was glinting off his beautifully tanned and toned chest. Jonny thought, *God, he is sexy.*

Jacob knew something was up. Looking straight into Jonny's eyes, he said, "You off somewhere then?"

That look made lying very difficult so Jonny looked down at the floor before answering.

"Yeah; got a lot to sort out in Bristol. But should be back in the morning. I will text later, OK?"

Jacob could tell there was more to it and said, "Yeah, but if you need me, or if things get difficult, call! I will be there."

141

To stress the point Jacob put his hand under Jonny's chin and lovingly raised his face so he could look into his eyes.

"Whatever it is you need to do, for my sake and your own take care."

He didn't wait for a response but putting his shirt back on he turned away and walked back to his work in the garden leaving Jonny looking after him. At the same time Sandy drove into the yard in her relatively new white Beetle. She kept it at the Mayhew estate as she didn't need it in Cardiff. She stopped to let Jonny get in and said, "All OK?"

"Not really. Too much left unsaid babe. Let's get this over with."

Their Journey into Bristol was mainly spent in silence; each lost in their own private thoughts. They took the M4 and then dropped down towards Bristol via the M32. Within an hour they were pulling up outside Arthur's house.

Sandy looked at Jonny and said, "OK then; I will go into the city and do a spot of shopping. I'll be back to pick you up at around 12.30 pm and then drop you at Temple Meads station."

Jonny leant over and gave Sandy a peck on the cheek saying, "That's fine babe. I really do appreciate this. See you in a bit."

As Sandy drove off, the gates to Arthur's house started to open and he walked around the back. Looking up he saw Arthur with his cat on top of the fire escape platform just starting to let down the ladder. The cat came down with it and wound itself around Jonny's legs.

He leant down to give the cat a stroke and said, "See you later Icon."

The cat just looked up scornfully and wandered off for his afternoon constitutional.

Smiling at how cats can make you feel insulted Jonny climbed the ladder rungs to Arthurs' room and was welcomed by his friend.

"Hhhi JJJonny, Umm so much tto um show you. Ccome in."

As Jonny went in, he could see dozens of monitors now all turned on with each displaying something different. Some were showing street level scenes; some were from the air and many other things that were quite beyond him. Arthur spent some time explaining the basics to him.

"Rrright then umm er let's just get yyou um up to speed with wwwhat's going on."

"Fuck me, little buddy! It looks like you have been really busy."

Arthur blushed but agreed with him.

"Yyup; you ccould ssay that."

Then recognising the Mayhew estate and grounds in real time on one monitor Jonny said, "Oh my God! That's Mayhew. You've hacked their CCTV."

"Umm Yes; ssort of. I nneed to know where everyone is and um if any tthreat is um imminent."

Arthur sat down in his red and black custom leather gaming chair in the middle of the monitor city and motioned Jonny to sit next to him. He then looked at Jonny and said, "Are you um ssure you wwant to ddo this? I'm nnot comfortable with helping you bbecause of the ddanger."

Jonny replied, "I have to do this—with or without your help Arty. Sorry."

"Um right then. I am watching a club in Soho that I um have ttraced actual ownership to our American chums. The um gguy from um The Willcome Inn is there. Um not sure where the others are nnow, um sort of lost ttrack, but um I have ppeople looking."

Arthur pointed to the screen.

"This is the outside of the cclub. Um it is in Dean Street and goes under the nname of Slap."

He touched the screen and it changed to a semi-dark interior. He went into the touch screen menu and made some adjustments so the room quickly lightened.

"This is the inside. You um will nnotice there are several ddoors, but the one in the left hand ccorner leads to offices and a small lliving area. It has um a ddial lock thing. The nnumber to open is 1954. The same code is used for the back door."

They spent some time enabling Jonny to memorise the scene before he changed the screen again and they were looking at a corridor with more doors. Arthur said, "Unfortunately there is nnot CCTV in all of the rrooms."

The view changed and they were looking at a small living room with Will sitting on a couch. It looked like he had a games console in his hands. Jonny muttered some expletives and told Arthur in a sarcastic tone that he was really looking forward to his meeting with him.

"Can you check up on Sandy? I just want to see she is OK."

Arthur spun around and touched another screen.

"Um here she is; um arriving at St Nicholas Mmarket."

Jonny watched Sandy wandering around the historical glass arcade. She seemed happy chatting to several stall holders. She was that kind of person. He also saw that she had several carrier bags.

"OK; she is fine. Let's have another peek at Mayhew?"

Arthur spun around until he was facing the Mayhew screen and switched through different views. Jonny could see the stable yard and his mum grooming Wiggy. He could also see Jacob in the gardens working on some of the raised flower beds. He felt his heart miss a beat and butterflies in his stomach and thought, *Jesus! I have got this bad. I just want to be with him.*

As if Jacob could sense him, he stood up and looked directly at the camera. He took his tee-shirt in his hands and pulled it up over his head exposing his amazing body. Jonny groaned and tried to rearrange himself discreetly saying quietly, "Oh my God!"

"Umm, I will gget your earpiece and mic sorted—one for you and one for Ssandy I think you said. They um bbasically work on the cell-phone nnetwork but our channel is for our exclusive use and it has hi-sensitivity to ppull in signals where they are weak. I um will be able to hhear you and um ttalk to you and visa-versa. We can have three-way cconversations and the um mic vvolume is set to enable you to sspeak in hushed ttones."

Arthur picked up one of two small blue boxes and opened it to reveal a very small clear plastic ear piece and a shirt button size mic.

"Umm pput this snuggly inside your ear; ppush it right in so um it is unlikely to come loose. I expect you will change cclothes later so the mic just ssticks to your clothes."

He then assembled two more boxes and opened one.

"This um bbattery pack and cell-phone unit just clips to your cclothing. It is operated by a ssimple on/off switch that can access our ddedicated channel. Um the link bbetween the mic/headphones and the cell-phone pack is wi-fi but I ssuggest you use the um separate wwire to plug the headset/mic into the bbattery/cell-phone pack in case you are in an area without ggood wi-fi. The um additional lleads enable you to charge the bbatteries just like a cell-phone. Although it is an extra-long life bbattery—um 24 hours continuous use—I um suggest you pput it on charge when the um opportunity arises. There is a separate um lead for charging in a car.

"Don't forget to test it with um Ssandy when you hand over her equipment. I'll bbe here all afternoon so um we can check the three way llinks are working OK. You can um do it ssitting in the car."

"Thanks Arty, I owe you big time my friend."

"Ummm…It is what friends are fffor. Bbut please ttake care."

They stayed chatting for a while before Sandy phoned to say she was outside to take Jonny to the station. Arthur had spotted her on camera anyway. It was just turning 12.30 pm and Jonny was getting quite hungry so once in the car he suggested that he and Sandy should grab something to eat at the station.

Bristol Temple Meads is the oldest and largest railway station in Bristol. It was opened in 1840 and like the Clifton Suspension Bridge and the SS Great Britain was designed by Brunel. It is an important hub with trains from the South West right through to the Midlands, North West, North East, Wales and Scotland as well as to London.

They found a space in the car park outside the main entrance and Jonny went over the communication technology with Sandy, checking the three-way link between the two of them and Arthur was working OK. He then handed an ear piece, mic and charger to Sandy before they walked across to the station. Jonny purchased his single to Paddington and they sat in Bonaparte's for a coffee and snack. Jonny's train was due to leave at 2.30 pm so at 2.15 he and Sandy moved towards the platforms. Jonny stopped and said, "No need to come to the platform babe. You'll need to be on your way anyway because you've got some driving to do."

He gave her a hug and then looked straight into her eyes and whispered, "Is everything in place?"

She winked and said, "Oooh yes. Good luck hun and have a good trip."

With that Jonny walked to his platform. Waving to Sandy, he thought, *My God! I'm lucky to have found a friend like that.*

At the same time, he tried to forget about the danger he was about to put her in.

Wednesday 2.30pm
At Mayhew Estate

Meanwhile, back at the Mayhew Estate, Christina's memory was about to kick in with a vengeance. Barry was giving her a hand mucking out the stable while Wiggy was having a bit of time in the paddock. In the summer he was usually in the stable during the day to keep him away from the flies and sun. But because of all the things going on his routine was a little messed up and he seemed more content in the paddock. Barry was on wheelbarrow duty, emptying the barrows when they were full after each stable was finished. He laughed and said, "Who needs a gym if you have horses? I'm knackered."

Christina smiled and replied, "We will have to get you a horse darling. It will probably be cheaper than your gym membership."

He turned to Christina and took a good look at her in grubby jodhpurs. With no make-up and her hair pulled back in a crocodile clip, he thought, *God, she has never looked more beautiful.*

He returned to his wheelbarrow duty saying, "Well, this is certainly a different way to spend a Wednesday, isn't it? Who would have thought that we would be caught up in all this and staying here in this beautiful place."

There was no reply so he looked up and saw that she had dropped her pitch fork and grabbed her mobile phone with panic written all over her face. He asked, "Chrissie what's up? Are you OK?"

Christina was clearly in panic mode and not OK.

"Oh my God! I've just remembered that Izzy was coming to stay at my place today. With all this stuff going on it went completely out of my mind. I must get hold of her—but why hasn't she phoned me?"

She punched in Isabella's mobile number and waited. But there is no answer. She then tried her landline number in Cornwall but no reply again. So she decided to try her own landline in Bristol and there was no reply there as well. She then thought to herself, *Jonny is in Bristol; I will get him to call around to the apartment to see if there is any sign of her.*

She dialled his mobile. The phone rang but then it went to answer phone. She called again with the same result. She started to panic.

"Barry, we have to go back to Bristol—right NOW. There is something wrong; I just feel it."

She started to run towards the house before he could empty the contents of the barrow or try and calm her down. When he eventually caught up with her she was already in the house talking to Sue and Lord Henry who was also trying to calm her fears saying, "Chrissie take it easy. You might be getting stressed about nothing. But if you are sure you want to go down to Bristol in person I will ask Bryn my driver to take you. He can stay with the car and act as a sort of lookout. You can rely on his discretion as well."

Christina smiled weakly and replied, "Oh thank you both so much. I don't know how to repay for you kindness. I must get changed."

With that she gave them both a hug and turned to run up the stairs to her room; with Barry following trying to catch up with her recent phone contacts— or lack of them—and what she wanted to do. He managed to de-stress the situation, talk things through and agreed that they needed to get to her flat and suss things out.

They were soon on the road with the amicable Bryn driving the Freelander. He told them his family had lived and worked on the estate for generations and laughingly said the grave yard was full of his relatives. He talked a lot, but didn't really expect an answer as long as Barry and Christina made the right noises at the right points during the conversation. This they did in between trying to come to terms with the situation in which they had found themselves.

Before long they had crossed the Severn bridge and half an hour later they had pulled up outside Christina's apartment. She immediately noticed Isabella's Land Rover and said, "Look; there's Izzy's car so she must be around somewhere."

On Bryn's advice they sat in the Freelander for a while in case anyone up to no good was around. There were no other strange cars that they could see, so with Bryn keeping watch, they cautiously ventured out.

Checking Isabella's Land Rover first, they noticed she had left her back-pack in the vehicle with the driver's door unlocked. With some trepidation and continued awareness of their surroundings they entered the building—not knowing what to expect. Once upstairs the first thing they noticed was that the door to her flat was unlocked. But there was no sign of a forced entry or of her friend. And otherwise it was pretty much the same as she left it, with no obvious or visible signs of a struggle of any kind. Barry suggested, "Try calling her again Chrissie. Perhaps she has popped down to the shops or something."

Christina took out her phone and called Isabella. This time they could hear the ring tone coming from the settee and they saw a part hidden mobile flashing. It was Isabella's phone.

"Well, that settles it. Something has happened to her; I just know something is wrong."

Christina's voice had gone up at least two octaves in her panic. Barry said in a calming voice, "Chrissie you are still jumping to conclusions. Just calm down a bit. Let's think things through."

But Christina was having none of it.

"Don't bloody patronise me Barry."

She immediately regretted her tone and said, "I'm sorry love but I just know she is in trouble. If she was OK she would have called me to let me know she was here. I will try Jonny again just in case she is with him although I don't know why she would be."

She got the not available message from Jonny again. She walked over to check her land line for any messages and saw that Isabella had tried to phone her earlier in the morning. She showed it to Barry.

She looked out of the French windows and gazed wistfully down on the river saying, "Well, she definitely has been here. What do we do now Barry? Do we call the Police?"

Barry took his phone out of his pocket saying, "I am going to call Henry; in case he has heard from Sandy or Jonny. Let's see what he thinks we should do next."

The phone rang a few times and eventually Henry's dark chocolate voice answered. Barry put the phone on loud speak so Christina could hear.

"Hello Barry. How's it going"?

Barry quickly explained what they had found. After a short silence Lord Henry said, "Right; she's obviously been there. I think I am going to give Jonny's friend Arthur a quick call. Sue has spoken to Sandy but felt there was something not quite right. And before he left I asked Jonny to contact me regularly but I have heard nothing at all. Get yourselves back into the car; but drive around a little in case the property is being watched. I will call back soon."

Before Barry had time to say thank you and goodbye Christina was on her way out of the front door. He followed close behind, just getting out before she shut and locked it—double checking that it was secure. They then took the stairs and made their way quickly down to the car and Bryn. Before driving off they took Isabella's backpack out of her car.

As suggested by Lord Henry they drove around a bit before heading back to Wales, deciding to drive south before joining the M5 at the Gordano Services junction. They were crossing the Clifton Suspension Bridge when Lord Henry called back with information from Arthur who had said that Jonny and Sandy were safe. Arthur had put a device on them both so he could monitor and be in-touch with them at all times. However they were not in Bristol but in London.

Barry's mobile was on loud speak and Christina looked incredulously at the small screen with her mouth open. Barry had a clue what Jonny was up to after their kick-boxing conversation the previous morning but he didn't want to let Christina know about this or she would have gone ballistic so he replied, "What the hell are they doing in London, for God's sake?"

Lord Henry revealed, "Well, evidently they want to get answers from someone called Will who they are meeting in the American hood's bloody club in Soho. Arthur has promised to keep me updated, but I can assure you I am not happy because my reputation is on the line here as well. Worse than that; Jonny has put my sister in law's life in danger. Arthur says they are both safe at the moment and will let us know immediately if something happens. He's a strange guy but he knows his stuff.

And this bit will be of interest to Christina because he also said a female was recently taken into the club under duress. I could be adding two and two together and making six, but this could be her friend Izzy. We'll talk when you get back when hopefully we might get some news from someone. See you soon. And you might as well bring Christina's friend's bloody Land Rover back with you."

With that he put the phone down and was clearly very angry. They looked at each other and said in unison.

"Oh shit."

Bryn just said knowingly, "Oops! Better turn around and pick it up then."

Chapter 11

Fly like an eagle; soar above the storms of life.
(Native American saying)

Wednesday 4.15pm
23 August 2017

Jonny was, of course, unaware of the latest developments in Bristol. His train arrived at Paddington around 4.15 pm. He had received a couple of calls from his mum that he decided not to take until he was on his way back to Wales. He changed clothes in the toilets as planned, posting his dirty clothes back to the Mayhew Estate at a nearby post office. And having time to spare he decided to visit the National Gallery that he knew remained open until 6 pm. Taking the Bakerloo line to Piccadilly Circus and walking the rest of the way he was there by 5 pm and spent a rewarding hour looking at paintings from the Great Masters. He checked out those by Thomas Gainsborough of course and hit the jackpot because Gainsborough's Blue Boy was on loan from the Huntington Gallery, California. What a special treat!

It was still a nice late afternoon so he decided to go through Admiralty Arch and enjoy the evening sun in St James's Park before heading back towards Soho to get some food. He picked up a couple of hoi sin duck wraps and was able to sit in Leicester Square as there was a music evening taking place so it was open late.

He phoned Will as arranged. Arthur's work had discovered he was at the Slap club and had further identified where it was in Soho. Will didn't know that and it was important to keep up the act. So he feigned ignorance and pretended to note down the details.

The Slap was at the Oxford Street end of Dean Street so he dropped in to the French House at the southern end so as not to bump in to anyone he wanted to avoid—like the American hoods. By this time it was around 8 pm and after doing a line in the toilets he settled down to a sparkling water.

The buzz and speed of London was enhanced with that snort of Charlie which left him feeling totally hyper while it went through his system. He was trying very hard to sit still but had to wait until 9 pm before he could get into the Slap club. As usual he was dressed in black, but he was wearing a fitted shirt with crystal buttons and skinny fitted trousers. He was aware he was looking really hot and had been getting admiring glances and several offers of drinks from both males and females. But for once he could not care less. Right now all he wanted to do was to get this over with and head back to Wales.

At 8.45 pm he got up from his seat and went to the toilets to put on his communication equipment. He was by then more in control so he quietly told Arthur and Sandy that he was going to make his way slowly to the club. They responded so he knew it was all working OK and they could both hear every word he said. Arthur told him that the two thugs had arrived at the club and appeared to have brought an unwilling woman with them and put her in one of the back rooms without a camera. He didn't recognise her.

Soho is a strange cosmopolitan cocktail of tourism, crime and entertainment mixing music, food, theatre, dance and sex. And sex wasn't just an evening activity with some lap dancing clubs operating from lunch time. Street girls had long ago moved indoors and on-line although most public telephone boxes in the area still had an interesting display of business cards offering very personal services. You could almost smell the electricity in the air and at this time of the evening it was beginning to come alive with people and sharp lights.

Serious looking door men and women stood at their post ready to welcome or repel customers from the different Dean Street clubs they were guarding. He walked past the modern looking Soho Theatre that was opened in the year 2000. Tonight was Stand-Up Comedy Night. He wondered whether that was an omen. Before long he was standing outside Slap and took his place in the queue. He used this time to check out the punters in front of him and there were some weird set ups.

There were a couple dressed in strips of leather—the male wearing a dog collar with a lead attached that was held by a skinny woman with a shaved head. In front of them was a young woman with a scarlet short bob. She was wearing very tiny red shorts, thigh length red boots and a black corset tied with red ribbons. Over her shoulder she had draped a plaited leather hunting whip. He thought to himself that if he wasn't gay he would really fancy that. She turned around and he briefly caught a look at her face. Her eyes had been outlined

151

sharply in black and she was also wearing black lipstick. The whole look was an incredibly beautiful dominatrix. She raised her eyebrows and he smiled as somewhat surprised, and hardly believing the transformation before him, he recognised who it was.

The queue moved slowly until there was only the black and red vamp and the couple with the dog lead in-front; then it was just Jonny to pay and he was soon in the club. The synthesiser dance music was very loud and there was a huge mass of moving bodies whose owners had drug induced zombie eyes. There were several raised platforms lit by flashing lights. Some had acrobatically moving poll dancers dressed in small bits of ripped leather that did little to cover their athletic bodies. On other platforms were cages where people were performing various S&M acts that left nothing to the imagination. Directly in front of him was the bar.

"OK Arty I am in. Can you see Will?"

"Um yes, hhe is um with the Americans at the bar."

Jonny walked to within a couple of feet of the bar.

"Ah yes I see them on the right-hand corner."

Arty said, "It is obviously very um nnoisy in the cclub so I will have to um keep the headset volume pretty um high. You will hhear each other's conversation and it might be a bit um distracting bbut there is nothing we can do about it. Kkeep messages brief and um loud if you can. If you can't answer bbecause others around you will hear then just um lower your head near the mic and ssneeze. This will be the ssignal that you have um heard the message."

Sandy chipped in, "OK. Got it. I'm going in for operation distract chaps. Gotta get these hips going. Here we go. Sooo wish me luck."

Sully Cantana and his brother Tony were sitting at the bar discussing Izzy who they had kidnapped earlier and explaining to Will that it would be in his best interests to contact Jonny who they had been unable to meet up until now. Will had indicated to Tony that Jonny might be at the club that evening. Then this vision in black and red sashayed over and laid a whip thing across the brothers' laps. Tony the psychopath was immediately interested.

"Oh baby; we could do something interesting with that."

He grabbed her around the waist and pulled her close. Sandy stroked her finger down his nose and whispered, "Oh yes; but some bubbles first please."

"Sully! This little huni wants some Champagne."

Sully turned around and ordered her a drink. He looked her up and down and thought, *She is hot.*

Sandy drew a breath and remembered that this was for a good cause. She then got down to some serious flirting.

Breathing a sigh of relief as the brothers were distracted, Will was now looking around and spotted Jonny. He made his way over to him. Chatting was impossible in the club. The music was loud resulting in the general level conversation being even louder. Jonny shouted in Will's ear.

"Can we go somewhere quieter?"

Will nodded and took Jonny by the hand to the door to the left of the bar. He punched in the code and led him into a corridor. The first door on the right led to the living area and they entered. The main door to the bar automatically closed behind them and they were in an environment that shut out most of the club sounds.

Will turned around to face Jonny with a smile but before he could offer his lips he met Jonny's fist smashing into the side of his face. The force twisted Will around so fast that he fell backwards over the arm of the sofa. Jonny looked down at him and snarled, "That is for my mum you evil cunt."

Will got up slowly rubbing his face where Jonny's punch had landed. He didn't think anything was broken but by Christ it hurt.

"I didn't know it was your mum."

He saw Jonny coming for him again so he made a wild punch that Jonny easily ducked, spinning on one leg and flooring Will again with a kick in the chest.

"You were fucking shooting at her you lying bastard. You tried to attack her horse with a bloody sword."

Will was now having a little trouble breathing and wisely stayed where he was.

"I didn't; it was Tony! You have to believe me."

Jonny put out his hand to help him up but when he was standing Will pulled Jonny forward and brought his knee up and connected briefly with Jonny's testicles. Not a sensible thing to do because Jonny was alive to the move and very quickly jumped back.

"Oh, want some more do you sweetheart?"

Still holding Will's hand, he pulled him back and head butted him on the nose hearing a satisfying crack as it broke. Blood gushed from his nostrils, soaking his shirt front.

"Oh fuck! Oh fucking hell. You broke my fucking nose."

"Oh dear. Does it hurt? Now sit down and stay down or so help me God I will kill you. I just need to check in with my friends, then I am going to ask some questions and you will give me some answers, OK?"

"Yeah OK."

"Sandy are you OK?"

Sandy was still busy keeping pawing hands off her body, wishing her shorts weren't so short, and she replied with a coded sneeze.

Jonny got the message and replied, "I hear you. Arty, is the coast still clear?"

"Um yyes; all ffine. Sandy is kkeeping them occupied."

He then turned back to Will and gave him a tea towel to handle the flow of blood from his nose.

"Right then Will. How and why did you get involved with these evil arseholes?"

Will put the towel over his nose and tilted his head back.

"They use my mooring at the Willcome to bring in drugs. Where do you think your Charlie came from? They paid well, and anyway if I didn't cooperate I would probably be dead. They are into all sorts of other evil stuff. It wasn't just drugs being brought in. They have high level contacts in USA—criminal and political."

"Why are they chasing my mum and what the fuck was killing Barry's dog all about?"

"I don't know the details but it is something to do with a Native American girl. They think she brought something into the UK that is their property and they believe you have it—a painting I think. They somehow tracked her to the Premier Inn in Bristol. I was told to keep an eye on her and report back if she met anyone. I tried to warn your mum and Barry when I spotted them both at the Llandoger Trow. These guys are frantic to get whatever you have back. They are under big pressure from their bosses in Boston but they are not sure where you have it stashed."

"Yeah; that more or less confirms what we know. But who is the woman brought in earlier?"

"Not sure but they called her Izzy. She is tied up in the office next door. How do you know about her?"

Jonny glared at Will in shock and thought surely there can't be more than one Izzy linked to this mess? That would be too much of a coincidence. He had to find out.

"Jesus! Is that my mum's friend Izzy? What has she got to do with this mess? Is the office door locked?"

"Yeah door locked."

"Where is the key?"

"For fuck's sake Jonny! They will kill me—no joke. Tony Cantana is a sadistic psychopath. He will enjoy it."

Jonny moved in close and put his hand around Will's throat, applying pressure on his windpipe and releasing just before he was losing conscious. At the same time he whispered, "Ah Will my sweetheart. Believe me, if you don't give me the key I will kill you anyway."

By now Will was seeing stars and he could tell that his ex-friend and lover was very serious.

"OK but you will have to make it look good by knocking me out so that when they find me they will think I was overpowered. The key is on the wall by the door. It's on the hook marked Room 4."

Jonny looked behind him and saw a row of keys on hooks with coloured tabs.

"Right. Before that, you owe me loads, so where is the Charlie?"

"There is some in that drawer. It's not much but you can have what's there."

Jonny gathered up the stock and put it in a hidden shirt pocket.

"Now stand up buddy. I'm going to enjoy this."

Will stood up and pleaded, "Jonny I am sorry."

"Yeah; you will be now."

Jonny brought his fist back and hit Will a beauty on the chin, dropping him like a stone.

"Sandy, I will need your help back here in a mo. Be ready to move. Arty is the back door clear?"

Arty replied yes while Sandy just sneezed again. So Jonny walked quickly to the kitchen area and took a sharp knife from a drawer. Grabbing the right key he left the room and headed for Room 4.

Meanwhile Sandy was getting quite nervous. Her flirting skills were working at their limit but she needed self-defence skills to keep Tony's wandering hands in check. Taking the tassel end of the whip he put it suggestively in his mouth and before Sandy could resist he grabbed her hand and put it on his crutch. She felt his hard cock pressing against his trousers and started to feel sick.

"Hope you've got a deep throat cos you're going down on this very soon."

Trying to stop herself vomiting Sandy slowly removed her hand and said in the most sexy voice she could muster under the circumstances, "Maybe sweety. But don't be so impatient. Remember, everything comes to he who waits."

Somewhat destroying the mood Sully turned around and said, "I've looked around the club. Where has Will fucked off to?"

Disappointed at the interruption Tony turned away from Sandy and asked sarcastically, "What's wrong? Lost your little fuck buddy. He's probably gone for a cocaine break."

"Yeah but he sort of mentioned that the little scrote from the art gallery may be popping in and we need answers. The Family is getting edgy and they want a result little bro. I don't know about you but we got it good here and we don't need family sticking their nose in."

"Yep. But in the meantime me and this hot little bitch are going to have a play with the whip. What do you say darlin?"

Tony put his tongue on Sandy's face and licked it from chin to cheek.

She felt her stomach turning again but just in time Jonny's message came through, "Sandy we need to go! Get here NOW!"

Sneezing and trying not to show her relief Sandy smiled and while licking her lips said to Tony, "Hold on big boy. So I just have to visit the ladies first to stop this sneezing and then you will have my full attention—I promise."

Tony patted her bottom as she wandered off in the general direction of the loo. It was getting busy in the club and it was difficult for him to follow her progress, but anyway his mind was full-on looking forward to a session of rough sex.

As he waited he thought how strange it was that he had never seen her in the club before and he could not recall her around the district. She also appeared to be alone which was quite unusual. If she was a working girl then she would be in trouble if she was trying to trade in their club without their authority. However all that could wait until after he had sampled what was on offer.

As she disappeared Sully was having similar thoughts and was beginning to think that something was not quite right. He said, "She is really hot but who is she? Why haven't we seen her before? I would have recognised her. She kinda stands out and she ain't one of our ho's. She walked in and came right over to us, Something ain't right here Tony."

Not wanting to spoil his opportunity for some great sex Tony said, "Relax. I will find out where she is from. You go find your little Willy."

Sully slid off his bar stool and headed for the back rooms grunting, "Yeah. I will do just that. Something definitely ain't right."

Meantime, while Sandy had been fighting off Tony's advances, Jonny had been busy in the back rooms. Making a silent prayer he put the key in the lock of room 4 and opened the door. He breathed a sigh of relief as he viewed Izzy, apparently unharmed, but with cable ties around each ankle attached to another that was attached to the legs of a chair. With her hands behind her he assumed she had also been tied to the back of the chair. Duct tape was stretched across her mouth.

This was when Jonny called Sandy with, "Sandy we need to go! Get here NOW!"

As he spoke he was across the room and cutting through the ties. As soon as her hands were free Isabella gently took off the duct tape.

"Jonny. What are you doing here? What's going on?"

"Talk later Izzy. We need to get out of here quick."

He grabbed Isabella's arm and pulled her to the door, entering the corridor just as Sandy rushed in from the club door.

Jonny shouted, "Let's go babe. Out the back."

With Jonny still holding Isabella's arm they all headed for the back door. In the stress he fumbled with the code and got it wrong first time. They heard someone starting to unlock the door from the club so he got his act together and punched the right number, pushed opened the door and they all ran out slamming the door closed. There was an angry shout behind them. They didn't turn around but sprinted down the back ally and onto Dean Street just south of the club entrance.

The unknown voice was from Sully coming through the club door just as they had reached the exit door. Seeing the woman hostage being pulled out of the back door by the redhead and some young dude he shouted, "What the fuck!"

He ran down the corridor towards the back door but it was slammed in his face. By the time he put in the code and was out into the night they were gone.

He quickly spun around and ran back to the club. He grabbed a confused Tony who was waiting for his red-head to return, pulling him off the chair and shouting, "They've got the woman."

They both ran out to the front of the club and looked up and down the street. Sully spotted Sandy's bright redhead and then the others.He yelled at the doormen pointing at the red head, "Get after the red head and the other two with her. Bring them back here."

He then rounded on Tony angrily and yelled in a sarcastic voice, "What the fuck is goin' on Tony? Who do you think has stolen our guest? I'll tell you who! Your fucking red head bitch has got her. Now stop thinking about your cock and get running. Bring them all back here or don't come back at all. I'm going to find Will."

Sully stormed back into the club, pushing people out of the way as he got through to the back room living area where he found a very bloody and dazed Will sitting on the floor. Sully grabbed him by the shoulders and threw him on the sofa.

"Right then, how about you tell me what just happened? Coz those fuckers didn't find her by accident. Apart from me and Tony you are the only other person with unaccompanied access to this area."

Gathering his senses as best he could and shielding himself from any more punches that might come from Sully he stammered out the first excuse he could think of.

"It was Jonny. He knew you were holding someone here. I have no idea how he found out but he knew."

Sully snarled, "And I suppose you very conveniently gave him the fucking key to Room 4. You were supposed to tell me when he arrived, you little cunt."

"You were busy, so I thought……"

"You are not supposed to think you little pervert! Have you any idea what this means? We are in a whole pile of shit. If we don't get that fucking painting back in the time frame given by Boston we are so fucking dead."

While Sully was organising the chase with the doormen, Jonny was working out an escape route. He had looked wildly up and down Dean Street. There appeared to be no taxis on ranks or passing by, so rather than go north past the club entrance they start walking briskly south, dodging in and out of people on the street. He knew it was urgent to get off this street fast.

Isabella was by his side and looking over his shoulder to check Sandy was with them he shouted, "Take your wig off Sandy. You stand out like a beacon."

Sandy ripped off the red hair and dropped it into a convenient bin along with the grips holding her hair in place. She closed the lid as she said, "The wig is the least of my worries hun. You try walking quickly in these thigh length boots with heels. Wait up a mo."

She stopped to unzip her boots to below the knee and roll down the tops. As she did this she looked behind her and shouted, "Shit they are outside the club, with four doormen. We are going to have a few heavies after us very soon. So we need to move fast. Can you run Izzy?"

Isabella answered over her shoulder, "It's what I do sweetie; but I'm glad I don't have those boots. I think we need an escape plan; I don't know Soho well at all."

Jonny said to Sandy, "The plan was for your car to be at Canary Wharf Sandy; right?"

"It's there hun."

Jonny called in Arthur.

"Arty where should we go buddy? Gotta make Canary Wharf fast."

"OK, Umm Keep um going the way you umm aare going. On your left you'll ccome to a Ppizza Express on a ccorner. The um street on your lleft is Ccarlisle Street. Tturn left there and head um to Soho Ssquare. There is a ddance festival on there and if you are quick you should be able to um lose yourselves in the ccrowd. You nneed to make for the road on the um opposite side of the Square. It is ccalled Sutton Row."

"OK Arty. Hold on to my hand Izzy so we don't get lost in the crowd. Sandy is wwired so if she does get lost we can easily make contact again. Now all of us run like hell."

Jonny, Sandy and Isabella make the dance festival crowd before Tony and the doormen make the corner of Carlisle Street. This meant the heavies were unable to see the threesome weaving their way through to Sutton Row. After a while Jonny was back onto Arthur.

"OK Arty we are at the Sutton Row junction. Where to now?"

"I'm ggetting you to Charring Cross Road. You um mmight find a ttaxi there. If not you will be cclose to Ttottenham Court Road Underground Station so there will be um ttransport options. Mmove up Sutton Row until you see a left turn into Falconberg Mews and ttake that left turn."

"Got it. We are running up the Mews now but it looks like a dead end."

"Nno it's not. There is an alley at the end to the um right that will ttake you to Charring Cross Road. With a bit of luck you sshould lose the um heavies. I have a CCTV shot sshowing them ccaught up in the er ddance crowd."

"I see it. We are at the alley now. I can see the main road at the end. I'll get back to you when we all get there."

It didn't take long. By this time they were walking briskly rather than running.

"No sign of a taxi being available Arty. I think we need to take the underground option. Did you get the Oyster Cards Sandy? We don't want to be messing around buying tickets."

"Yes hun. Luckily I bought three day cards in case we were taking Will back with us. So Izzy can use that one."

"Great. Which way to the station Arty? Oh I can see the sign up on the left. We are heading that way."

"Um good. Keep up some sspeed. You sshould be clear of the heavies because they are um still in Soho Square working out where you went. Jjust in case they get llucky make sure you each have an Oyster Ccard ready and head for the main um tticket hall. You'll need to ttake an escalator ddown to the um Central line and you are ggoing East. If you are qquick, according to one of my sscreens there is an Epping ttrain um coming in within the next ttwo minutes. Gget on that and you will be um out of ddanger. The fourth sstop East will see you at Bank and that is where you nneed to get off. It should ttake you about fifteen um minutes."

The station was quite busy so they ran to the main ticket hall, Oyster Cards in hand and double stepped down the escalator; Sandy with some difficulty in those boots. The Epping train was just pulling in to the station. It seemed to take ages before the door opened. They couldn't see three seats together so they decided to stand at the front of the carriage. Sandy received some admiring remarks about her outfit from a bunch of well fuelled 'jack the lads' out on the binge. Right now she could have done without the banter. They breathed a collective sigh of relief as the doors closed and the hum of the electric motor pulled them away from the platform and into the tunnel. There was no sign of the enemy and the comforting dusty, metallic smell of the electricity arcing from the power rails was very welcome.

It must have been around fifteen minutes earlier that the four doormen—Carl, Tyson, Jack and Scott—had joined Tony and rushed down Dean Street after Jonny, Isabella and Sandy. They caught sight of them heading for Soho Square but Tony stopped running before they got close to the dance festival thinking that with so many witnesses in a crowded Soho it was not a great idea. There were plenty of police about and they didn't really want to involve them. He called the heavies on the walkie-talkies they all carried and said, "I think we are too fucking obvious. Carl and Tyson follow discreetly and see where they go. Jack and Scott get back to Slap if you can't find them here."

Tony stalked back to Slap. Not bothering to walk around people he just ploughed on and people got out of his way. A couple of men protested and almost had a go, but one look at his face was enough to dissuade them.

He stomped through the club without stopping and went through to the back. He took a thump at the wall and put his fist through the plaster board. But it didn't make him feel any better.

He shoved open the door to the office and threw himself into the revolving chair. Sully was by a desk with Will, who was feeling pretty sorry for himself with one eye swollen shut and turning a vivid shade of purple and red. He also had a horribly swollen jaw, that he was quite sure was broken. Tony snarled at him, "We were set up! That bitch was a fucking diversion so your mate could get into the back! She is mine I will show her what I am capable of. She'll look like you when I'm finished."

The walkie-talkie crackled into life. It was Scott letting them know that he and Jack were back in the club. Tony told them to come to the office.

Before the two heavies joined them they started to go back over the club's CCTV coverage that showed what and who entered. Sully froze the screen showing the outside of the club and pointed to someone in the queue. He turned to Will and shouted, "Is that your fucking cock-sucking mate Jonny?"

It was pretty painful for Will to speak so he just grunted and nodded his head. They let the CCTV play on and the cameras in the interior of the club clearly showed Jonny entering the club. They also saw the red head walk up to them at exactly the same time as Will got off his stool to go to meet Jonny.

There was a knock at the door and a mumbled, "OK to come in boss?"

Tony got off his chair to let the two heavies into the office. They were sweating profusely; the guys were built for physical strength not running. The fact that they were dressed in black suites didn't help on the warm summer evening. Sully motioned for them to gather around the screen. Pointing out Sandy and Jonny he said, "I want these two scrotes and you are going to find them for me. Drive to Bristol tonight. Carl and Tyson will join you. Tony will give you two addresses that I want you to watch. And report back to us any people you see entering either property. Take photos of them if you can. Take it in turns to sleep in the car. One address is in Filton and the other in Clifton.

When Carl and Tyson get back they might have some news—or even have caught up with the bastards. If so we don't have to rush down there but I will still want the premises watched because other people are involved. If they come back empty handed don't let me get near them because I might kill them. Let Carl and Tyson know what is happening, and before you go take screen shots of the two targets so you each have a copy on your phones. Then close the club and get everyone out. The punters are not gonna like it but tough shit.

We can pull some bouncers from one of our South London clubs for tomorrow or get the manager to go to our usual rent a doorman agency. Oh and get changed before you go so you can blend in because it will be early morning by the time you get there.

Take the BMW. The keys are in the room next door. When you get to Bristol hire another car as soon as you can. Keep in pairs so you can cover both addresses. Tony, me and this damaged ass hole here will follow in the Evoque and get back to the Willcome and then to Cardiff to watch the little bum boy's flat."

They nod and say yes boss and Sully wrote down the addresses of the premises they were to watch. As they left the office and closed the door they heard the theme tune to 'The Godfather'. It was Tony's mobile. He answered with an abrupt, "What!"

It was Carl to say they lost the targets. They looked around Charring Cross Road and Oxford Street and guessed they must have bolted down the underground at Tottenham Court Road. Tony threw his phone across the room. It hit the wall and smashed. He shouted, "Shit! The stupid bastards have lost them. They could be fucking anywhere by now."

A worried and exasperated Sully tried to calm his brother down a bit.

"For fuck sake Tony; get a grip. You are not helping by throwing a tantrum."

Tony's replied with a sort of roar and turning around he picked up the swivel chair and threw it at the door. There was a loud crash and the wheels on the chair made holes in the panelling where it made contact, the chair sticking in the door for a few seconds before its weight dragged it to the floor.

Sully was now worried. His brother's eyes were wide open and nearly bursting out of their sockets. He had seen him in this kind of rage before and he knew it would be hard to bring him down to a manageable level again. Will on the other hand was absolutely terrified and was crouched down behind the desk with his hands over his head.

Sully said, "Come on; let's get our stuff together and head for Bristol. Looks like we've got a lot more work to do before that fucking painting is back in our hands."

Back on the Epping train Jonny and Isabella gave Sandy some protection from the leering looks from the alcohol fuelled lads and Isabella said, "How did you survive the trip to the club on your own dressed like that Sandy?"

"Simple hun. I took a taxi."

They remained silent for the rest of the short journey and wary of those around them until they were just about to approach Bank. Jonny said, "We are at Bank Arty. Where to now?"

"You will nneed to make your way to the er Docklands Light Railway pplatforms. They jjust use the initials DLR. At Bbank it is underground and um you will have to ttake the escalator down to Pplatform 9. Nno need to rrush now. The heavies lost you at Ttottenham Court Road Station. You will need a ttrain going to Lewisham. The next one is not due just yyet so you will have ttime for a sit down."

They followed Arthur's instructions and arrived at a fairly empty Platform 9. Finding a seat with some privacy they started to plan their next moves. Sandy had booked a three-bed room at the Britannia International Hotel on Canary Wharf so they could either stay the night there or make the long drive to Wales overnight sharing the driving. After some discussion they decided that after freshening up in the room they would get as far away from the heavies as soon as possible.

Sandy had her suitcase in the room so it would give her a chance to change out of the 'show stopping' gear she was wearing and into something more suitable for a long drive. The Lewisham train pulled in and it was fairly empty. It felt weird being in a train without a driver. Within twelve minutes and four stops later they were above ground and approaching Canary Wharf DLR Station near Canada Square. It was now about 11 pm.

They walked to the hotel with Jonny updating Isabella with more details about what had happened over the last few days. Once inside they went up to the room, showered and got ready for a four-hour car ride back to Wales. Sandy lent Isabella a change of clothes as her travel bag had been left in her car outside Christina's apartment. Jonny contacted Arthur to let him know they were safe and about to head back home so they would be going off line. Arthur said, "OK. Ttake care. Bbut keep your mmobile phone open. Oh and um Lord Henry has bbeen on asking where you are. Evidently you were ssupposed to stay in ccontact. He also seemed to er know that Izzy was mmissing. Something about her ttravel bag and Land Rover being ffound at Christina's place in Bbristol. What should I ttell him?"

"Oh shit! With everything going on I forgot. I don't really want to get into a long conversation with him now. It's only 11.30 pm so text him saying we are safe and to tell Christina that Izzy is with us. Say I will explain everything tomorrow. I think I might be in for a bollocking but hopefully rescuing Izzy might save the day. Thanks for all your help today my friend."

"Nno problem. I enjoyed the er ride. Vvery exciting. But I think I'm in trouble too. Have a ggood trip."

Sandy settled her hotel bill but not knowing when they would next eat they decided to get something in the Hotel's Pizzeria that remained open late. Isabella and Sandy both had a lighter Cannelloni Verdi vegetarian dish from the pasta menu. Jonny went for a pizza; choosing the After Work pizza that had a mixture of everything on it. Being Jonny he had an extra cheese topping of course. They took some bottled water with them and headed to the underground car park to find Sandy's white Volkswagen Beetle.

They agreed to share the driving and with Sandy taking the first stint they headed East past the Excel Centre and London City Airport until they reached the roundabout adjoining the old North Circular Road. Heading North they followed the signs to the M11 and then headed West on the M25. It was just around Midnight.

Isabella and Jonny caught up with some sleep as Sandy headed for London Heathrow where she turned on to the M4 heading West. They planned to change drivers at the Reading Service area and then later at Leigh Delamere. After just under an hour on the M4 she pulled into Reading Services. Feeling physically and mentally exhausted Jonny and Isabella had been snoozing in the back seat and had to shake some sleep out of their bodies, so a quick walk around the car park was in order before they all wandered into Costa to get some strong coffee and some pastries. As it was 1.30 am it was pretty quiet and Jonny called Arthur on the mobile to check all was well.

"Hi Arty; any news about the enemy?"

"Um yyes. Um, they have left London. And it looks like four um of the um doormen are also in convoy with them—in a, um silver BMW. I'm not uup on makes but um sporty looking. The bbad guys aand Will are in a bblack um Range Rover Evoque. The rred one must still be in for repairs. They are about um thirty mminutes behind you."

Jonny thought about it and said, "They won't know the car we are driving so that's a comfort if they do catch up with us. I suppose it's possible that they might split up; one car going to Bristol and the other to Cardiff. My thoughts are that we should drive straight to Mayhew. At least we should be relatively safe there."

He turned to Isabella, "Are you OK with that?"

She replied, "Sounds good. I just want to feel safe at the moment. But I think we should hit the road straight away to keep ahead of them?"

Jonny got back to his conversation with Arthur who said he would keep them updated so keep the phone on hands free. But he agreed they should either get back on the road pretty damn quick or take a trip towards Basingstoke and wait up in a lay-by for a while in case they too decided to take a break at Reading Services.

Just as Jonny ended the call his phone rang again; this time with an unknown number. He answered it with a cautious Hello and then registers shock as the caller said in an American accent, "Hello you little mother fucker! We want that painting. We know you have it and if we don't get it, I personally will take a great pleasure in cutting you into pieces…or maybe someone close to you. Yeah that would be good wouldn't it? That painting does not belong to you OK? Just return it, back off and leave us alone."

Jonny heard a hard-unpleasant laugh in the background and then, "Sad sack that you are, you have no idea who you are dealing with. And you can forget the cops 'cause they are in our pocket. See you soon sweet-cheeks."

Jonny was about to answer but the caller hung up. Just as well because he had no idea about what to say anyway and the background noise might have given a clue as to where they were.

Feeling pretty shook up and slightly queasy he looked at the others and said, "Shit! That was one of them. They must have got my number from Will's phone."

He relayed the bones of the conversation to them and Isabella was first to speak.

"Right then. No more messing about. We go straight to the police. This has gone far enough now. I was kidnapped. I feared for my life and God knows what else has happened."

Sandy put up her hand and reasoned, "Hang on just a mo. There is a lot you still don't know Izzy. Let's get back to the car. We need to get to Mayhew and the sooner the better. In particular we need to speak to Lord Henry. I fear it will not be a comfortable conversation."

Jonny checked back with Arthur who confirmed that they were still twenty minutes or so ahead of the heavies who appeared to be sticking to speed limits. He agreed it was safe to get back on the M4 and continue to head for Wales as long as they did it now. They walked quickly back to the car feeling pretty freaked and looking all around just in-case. Bundling into the VW they all of the same mind…getting some miles between them and the thugs and back to the safety of Mayhew.

Jonny took over the driving and looked at the car clock. It was now 2.30 am Thursday the 24th of August. As he drove out he found it difficult to believe just how much their world had changed in six short and terrifying days. He kept the speed at around 70 mph. They had enough to worry about without attracting the attention of the motorway police.

He thought over what had happened and realised that now back on the road he was actually not feeling too scared; just a feeling of adrenalin coursing through his body and a desire to find out all there was to the mystery of his ancestor, the painting and the possible treasure.

He was soon driving past the Chieveley Services and just as he could see the mast next to the Membury Services. Arthur came through and confirmed that the two cars following had stopped at Chieveley for a break. Jonny gave a sigh of relief so he decided to stop at Leigh Delamere for petrol but not bother with a driver swap. He was feeling OK so he would just complete the trip.

The black motorway road lined with the different coloured cat's eye road studs seeming to be never ending. There was very little traffic on the road; just the occasional articulated lorry. Sandy and Isabella were not much company as they had fallen asleep so Jonny just had his jumbled thoughts to keep him company.

As they crossed the River Avon the mist started to drift across the motorway in waves and it was a relief to get past the Bath junction and the lights of Bristol to the south and see the Severn Crossing just up ahead. He was by now feeling pretty knackered and just wanted to get some sleep. At approaching 5 am on Thursday morning he was rolling up to the gates of Mayhew. Sandy roused herself to get out and open them, and before long they were pulling up outside the front door. They were safe. But they were really hoping that they could get some sleep before facing Lord Henry.

Chapter 12

Seek wisdom, not knowledge. Knowledge is the past. Wisdom is the future.
(Native American saying)

Day9 Thursday 5 am
24 August 2017

Sandy had her own key to Mayhew. She opened the front door and quickly disarmed the alarm as it started to bleep. Unfortunately the noise was enough to disturb Lord Henry. The worry about their activities in London had resulted in him being unable to sleep and he had been cat-napping in his study.

Stepping out of into the hall and wiping the sleep from his eyes, he was greeted with the sight of Jonny, Sandy and Isabella creeping towards the stairs. He fixed Jonny with a look as black as thunder. Still half asleep himself after that long driving spell, it made Jonny shiver. But almost as if he was a different person Lord Henry then turned to Isabella and said with a smile, "Welcome to Mayhew Isabella. I understand that you have had quite an adventure. Christina has been worried sick. Sandy will show you to a spare room because I am sure you are exhausted after your ordeal. Try and get some sleep and we will talk later."

Then turning to Sandy he said more sternly, "Sandy! As soon as you have shown Isabella what's what, come straight down to my study. Jonny! Study; now."

Lord Henry turned on his heels and marched to the study door, holding it open for Jonny to enter. Feeling as if he was entering a Head Master's study for six of the best, Jonny held his head up as he walked past him. He felt his actions were justified and was ready to put forward his side of the story. But before he could open his mouth Lord Henry spun him around to face him and roared, "You stupid, selfish little fool! Have you no respect for your mother and Barry, not to mention Sue and me? Whatever possessed you to run off and put yourself and Sandy in danger like this? You have no idea about the people you are dealing with and you could have both been killed. This is very serious and it's time for you to grow up. Now I suggest you try and explain your actions before I decide what to do next."

With that he stalked over to his desk and sat down before slowly looking straight into Jonny's eyes and saying with a glare like a laser beam, "I don't want excuses. I want facts and they had better be damn good ones."

Jonny shrugged his shoulders and lowered his eyes to the floor. Regaining some composure he looked up again and said slowly, "Before all this mess, I had been seeing Will on and off for some time. He was my friend, my lover and he supplied me with cocaine."

Jonny stopped to see if his words were having a shock effect. But Lord Henry's expression was as stony as before so he continued, "I had seen Will the day before those bastards made an attempt on my mother's life and I found out after that he had been in the car with them. So in my mind he was just as guilty as they were. Arthur's surveillance confirmed his involvement and I wanted answers. I was angry, but because of our relationship I wanted to give him a chance. I confided in Sandy and we came up with a plan. I tried to talk her out of going to London, but she said that if I planned to leave her behind she would tell you I was going, which meant you would stop me. Arthur also tried to persuade me not to go but agreed to help when I said I would go anyway."

Jonny glanced up at the clock on the wall behind Lord Henry just as the door behind him opened. He turned around to see Sandy walk into the room.

She saw that Jonny was under pressure and wandered over to touch his hand reassuringly before saying in as confident manner as she could muster in her tired state, "Izzy has gone to bed. She is exhausted and much shaken of course. I was going to wake Christina to tell her that her friend was here, but then I thought sleep would do Izzy good. So; how far have you got into our little adventure hun?"

Jonny spoke quietly but without any real resolve. He was really looking for some support from his friend in the light of Lord Henry's anger.

"I have explained the reason why we went up to London."

Looking towards Henry with a defiant smile Sandy said, "Did you tell him you tried to stop me from going but I insisted with the help of a little blackmail?"

Henry turned towards Sandy and with a raised eyebrow said, "He did, but I still can't believe that you put yourself in that kind of danger and the fact that you lied to your sister and me is something else I didn't expect. I have learned more about our American friends and they are Villains with a capital V. Now both of you tell me the full story."

Jonny and Sandy related the happenings of the previous evening and early morning hours, only interrupted by the odd grunt or tutting from Lord Henry. He asked to see Jonny's knuckles when they got to the part where Will got beaten up and was satisfied that they were not broken although very bruised. When they had finished their story Henry stood up and shaking his head said, "I am not sure if you have been bloody brave or very stupid. Maybe your ignorance about the true nature of the situation led you to some unwise conclusions. But whatever it was you have been incredibly lucky and I want you to promise that you will not attempt any further privateer activities to do with these people.

Just focus on the map discovered on the mysterious painting for a while. It is not just your own safety I am concerned with but my own credibility because remember I have made certain promises to the police. Now go and get some rest; you both look done in. I will see you both at mid-day and we will have a chat with Arthur with regards to what the yanks and Will are up to now. Isabella can also fill us in with additional details in case they said anything useful to our understanding about their activities."

Jonny and Sandy mutter OK, but Lord Henry insisted, "I said make a promise. This time without crossing your fingers Sandy."

This they did and then turned to leave the room. Once they had shut the door.

Jonny turned to Sandy and said, "Well, it could have been worse I suppose."

Sandy nodded and said, "Yep; but we made a promise that must be kept hun. I think Lord Henry knows more about these people than he is letting on. So let's go and try and get some sleep."

Before he crashed out Jonny sent a quick message to Jacob; just to let him know he was home. He received a 'thank you for letting me know' message. And it came with an X which he thought was encouraging. He lay down on top of the bed and before he knew it fell into a deep but troubled and weird sleep dreaming of being chased by giant caterpillars.

Thursday 24August 2017
Cardiff Police Station

Back at Cardiff Police Station DCI, David Thomas was going over the crime scene CCTV coverage of the Matthew Lloyd murder. The techies had managed to sharpen up some of the images and also get some stills of the two suspected murderers which he had already circulated throughout the British constabularies. He was pretty sure they would get a result quite soon.

Ruth had just returned from the staff kitchen and moved the photo prints and a neat pile of papers out of the way so she could place a coffee and a packet chocolate Hobnobs for herself and David on the table. She then took a seat and started to put the photos in order of sequence. Looking closely at images of two hooded men entering the gallery she remarked, "I would say that the smaller suspect had definitely got a concealed weapon strapped to his back. If you zoom in on the screen version you can see part of the hilt. I don't think it will be long before someone recognises them and we will have this case in the bag. What do you think Dave?"

David peered at the photo and mused.

"Hmm; yes Ruth it certainly looks like a weapon. And we also have these images of two similar sized men without hoods at the front door of Jonny Davies's flat. I think we need another chat with the two youngsters at the big house. We will take along the photos. I have a hunch those two students are somehow caught up with all this. I will clear it with the Super. Maybe we can get them to come to us this time?"

Ruth chipped in with a disappointed look, "Oh; I rather enjoyed our little trip to the big house in the country. And that lord Henry is pretty gorgeous!"

David laughed and nearly choked on his coffee.

"Calm yourself Ruth. I will give the boss a call and arrange a meeting to update him on what we have and to fix another interview with the students."

He picked up the phone and pressed Superintendent Jack Clarkson's extension. He answered with a gruff no nonsense, "Superintendent Clarkson."

David said, "Ahh good morning Gov. DCI Thomas here. Can we have a quick meeting to go over our findings on the Lloyd murder?"

The abrupt but polite reply was, "Yes David. Pop up now. I have about half an hour free. See you both in a moment."

David put the phone down.

"Bloody hell Ruth he wants us now. Let's gather up our papers and get upstairs because he will be a grumpy sod if we are more than five minutes."

Ruth gathered up the papers and photos as she replied with a laugh, "It's just as well that I have put them all in order then, isn't it Dave? You can thank me later."

David grabbed a Hobnob and looked sadly at his partly drunk coffee before dunking his biscuit and eating it quickly before following Ruth out of the door.

They were soon outside the main man's door. They stop; look at each other, knock and entered when summoned. As they walked towards his desk Superintendent Clarkson said without looking up, "Right then. Let's see what you've got?"

Ruth placed the photos on the desk and both she and David explained the time frame of each photo and who had received a copy within the constabulary. David also shows a blurred CCTV image of two men outside Jonny's flat and the gallery—one tall and one short. He explained, "So you see Gov, just as I thought in the beginning. I believe the owner of this flat, Jonny Davies—is somehow involved; maybe innocently, maybe not. He worked at the gallery and these two nasty looking reprobates are suspects in the murder and visited Mr Davies's flat. I certainly think he knows more than he is telling us at the moment. Uniform also did house-to-house and several owners stated that they thought they saw two men matching the description getting into a red Range Rover Evoque. We are going to widen the CCTV search in the area to try and trace number plates on red Evoques in the area. There can't be many in that colour. We also need to interview those two students again."

The Superintendent studied the photos closely. He then took a deep breath and sat up and said, "OK. Good work. As it seems we have to go through certain channels to get to them—God knows why—I will sort out another meeting with the students for you."

David and Ruth both said thank you Gov and left the office, closing the door behind them, confident that progress had been made.

Thursday Lunchtime
24 August 2017

Jonny awoke with a start with Sandy standing over him and shaking his shoulder.

"It's gone twelve noon, hun. We need to go down to Henry's study. He wants us to be there when he calls Arthur. Apparently, he's already spoken to Izzy."

Jonny sat up feeling very disorientated; the strange dream still in his mind.

"Just give me five mins babe. I need to have a quick wash and a pee. You go on down; I won't be long—honest."

Sandy left saying, "You'd better not be or you will be in even more trouble—with me as well as Lord Henry."

Jonny got the message and threw his legs over the side of the bed. He wandered over to his bathroom to get ready. He was very conscious of the fact his hand was now very swollen and pretty painful. He thought, *Bloody hell; I hit that bastard hard. I wonder if his jaw hurts like my hand?*

Barry was on his way out to give Christina a hand in the stables when Jonny passed by in a rush towards Lord Henry's study. Barry had heard that Isabella was now safe but not much more so he gave Jonny half smile and said, "I hear your trip was quite successful. That hand looks bad so please omit any gory details when you talk to your mother. No need to send her into orbit. OK?"

Jonny smiled as he walked by and said,

"Yeah no worries Baz. Tell you more later."

Barry frowned at the use of 'Baz' as Jonny continued down the hall and walked into the study. Sandy was sitting on a Chesterfield leather sofa, but there was no sign of Lord Henry.

"He had a phone call on his mobile and shot out like a scolded cat. Sooo my lunatic friend, something's up. Sit next to me. He shouldn't be long."

After a few minutes Lord Henry strode in, shutting the door purposely behind him before taking a seat behind his desk. He switched on his PC and while waiting for all the programmes to open he looked up and said, "I think we will talk via the computer. I like to see who I am chatting to."

He logged on and after a few moments he beckoned them to move around to his side of the desk so they could all see the screen that featured a very anxious looking Arthur in his attic room. Jonny knew that Arthur always found interaction with people he didn't know well very difficult.

Henry said, "Good afternoon Arthur. Thank you so much for talking to us. I'm a huge fan of your work. You are an extremely talented young man. At first I was angry that you helped Jonny in his Soho jaunt but I understand that you were given little choice. I wonder if you could let us know what our American friends and associates are up to at this particular time?"

Jonny thought, *Hmm; that's strange. He's talking to Arthur as if he had known about him and his activities for some time—unless he was just trying to be friendly of course.*

Arthur replied, "Umm wwell um, Ssully and Ttony are in um Cardiff wwatching Jonny's fflat. They lleft Will at the Willcome Inn. Bbut hhis um mmen are um in Bristol; ttwo of um them are at Jonny's mmum's flat and two at um Bbarry's house."

Arthur turned his chair around and pointed to a screen that showed a black Range Rover Evoque parked outside Jonny's flat.

Jonny chipped in with, "Well, they obviously don't know where we are, thank goodness."

Lord Henry was deep in thought and after a while said very slowly and purposely, "No they don't at the moment. But Jonny—does Will know who Sandy is?"

A startled Jonny suddenly realised that Will knew a lot about him and his friends.

"Yeah; we talked because I thought we were close. He knows Sandy is my BFF.He also probably knows about Sue and her art collection and restoration business."

By now Jonny was feeling pretty sick at the thought that his friends and family could all be in danger.

"Oh shit! That could be where they are getting their information from. That and from Matt before they murdered him. It won't take much for them to figure out that I have brought the painting here. And I used Sandy's name in Soho when we were escaping from the club. What have I done? Henry I am so sorry. We have dropped a whole lot of mess in your lap. I just thought it was about a cool painting and it has sort of snowballed."

He put his head in his hands and groaned. Sandy touched his arm and unconvincingly told him everything would be OK. At the same time she gave Lord Henry a worried look.

Lord Henry looked back at the computer screen and said, "Arthur can you keep an eye on these chaps and let me know if they show any signs of coming to Mayhew? If there seems to be unusual activity around the perimeter let me know straight away. I have CCTV that I can train on them. I am sure they will have other resources at their disposal. Use a drone if you have to."

Arthur replied, "Yyes Ssir. I will ddo that."

Lord Henry ended the conversation with, "Thank you Arthur. I will let you get on with your work."

He then shut down his screen and looked at a very dejected Jonny and Sandy. Breaking into a smile and with a completely different and confident tone he said, "Right then; it's now one o'clock. Who's up for a spot of treasure hunting?"

Jonny looked up and shook his head in amazement, wondering how Lord Henry could change from concerned to jovial in a blink of an eye.

Sandy was more used to it and quickly replied, "Ooh yes! We are well up for it. I will get some sandwiches and fill some thermos flasks with coffee."

Jonny perked up at the mention of food and said, "Hey wait up hun. I will help. God I am starving!"

Lord Henry continued in his positive vein, "OK. I will see you in the stable yard in fifteen minutes and I'll get the long wheelbase Land Rover started up. It will seat everyone and could be useful for the terrain on the other side of the lake. Can you shut the study door as you leave."

As soon as they had left he locked the door and opened up a draw with a key. This revealed another draw with a fingerprint scanner. He put his finger on the scanner which slid the draw open. Inside was a red phone.

Thursday 24August 2017
Cardiff Police Station

David and Ruth were happily back in the incident room thinking about lunch when David got an email from the Metropolitan Police to say that they had recognised the two people from the crime-scene. David punched the air shouting, "Look Ruth, we've got them."

Ruth read the email and danced around the incident room crying, "Bloody marvellous."

Picking up the phone and dialling the direct number to his contact at the Met David said, "I'll give the Met a call to confirm the details"

It was answered pretty quickly although it seemed ages to David who said, "Hello, its Chief Inspector David Thomas speaking from Cardiff Police Station. Do you have names and any background on the two people you have just identified for me?"

He wrote down the information given and said, "Thank you. That is most helpful."

He put the phone down and looking at what he had written he gave a grim sort of smile. An impatient Ruth said, "Well, come on then Dave. Don't keep a lady waiting. What have we got?"

David answered slowly and dramatically, "Well, it would appear that the two fellows are definitely yanks; brothers going by the names of Antonio and Sully Cantana. They own a night-club in Soho plus a few other pleasure centres. But

MI5, MI6 and the Met are on to them and they are pretty sure that they are mixed up in drugs, vice, money laundering and possibly people trafficking and fostering subversive activities."

Getting very excited Ruth chipped in, "They sound delightful people. We need to get them in for questioning ASAP, don't you think? This could be the collar of our careers; we will be bloody famous my dear friend; the new dynamic duo of policing."

Just then the internal phone from the Superintendent rang. David picked it up and still buzzing with excitement said, "Sir we have done it."

But then there was a short but deathly silence and Ruth could see the rage in David's face as he went red and said, "What! You have to be bloody joking! No way is this going to be dropped. It's our case. Sir, please."

David slammed down the phone and looked at Ruth, who was shaking her head saying, "No, no, bloody no. Why?"

David grunted, "Bloody MI6 and MI5. They want all the information we have gathered sent to them today. We are off the case Ruth; with immediate effect. I am going to the pub to get pissed. You coming?"

Still shocked, Ruth looked around at all their hard work and asked, "What about the information they want?"

David just replied, "The overpaid posers can fucking wait."

Ruth tried to calm David a bit although she felt the same.

"Your wife will bloody brain you if you go home in a state Dave."

He replied, "I don't give a stuff. She can leave me if she wants."

On those last words he strode out of the room with a worried Ruth trailing behind to keep him out of trouble.

As she ran past the desk she said to the Desk Sergeant, "Cover for me. We have an emergency. You have my mobile as well as my police emergency call number."

The Sergeant had seen David storm by and knew what that mood meant. He said, "So I see. Good luck Ma'am. I've got your back."

Once outside she quickly caught up with him as he was going for his car. She said, "Stop right there and calm down. If you are going to get pissed you do not need your car. And if you want me with you we can't go to a pub because I'm in uniform and it would not look good. I've got a special bottle of Malt back at my flat so let me drive you there and we can sample the best that Scotland can offer. I can get some lunch for us if you like."

David stopped and turned to Ruth saying, "Are you sure? I know you are making sense but fuck it Ruth; I'm not in a great mood. And you'll need to drive me home afterwards."

Ruth could see that she had cut through some of the anger and gently said, "Yes I'm sure. What are friends for? Anyway I'm as pissed off about this as you so I could do with a drink or two. Come on; my car is parked over here."

They got into her unmarked Seat Cupra and headed towards her flat in South Penarth. It was just off Lavernock Road overlooking the Glamorganshire Golf Club. He had been there before because the gym they both used was not far away. The journey took about 20 minutes or so which left David time to let off more steam. By the time they had arrived he was much calmer due mainly to Ruth's patience. Before they got out he turned to Ruth and said, "Thank you for being such a good mate Ruth. You know you have been very special to me although I know the job and other stuff means I can't always show it. I find it difficult even in private."

David rarely ever spoke about his feelings and Ruth was a little surprised, but also pleased that he should confide in her.

"I know. And you are special to me as well David. That is probably why we work so well together. Fuck the job; let's get that drink."

She then smiled before they both got out and approached her flat. She put the key in the front door lock and said, "Let's have a stiff Malt first and then you can help me make some lunch. Ham salad OK?"

David replied, "Yes that sounds fine. Where's the Malt? I'll pour the drinks and bring them into the kitchen."

Before replying she thought carefully about continuing the new closer level of friendship and using the Welsh for darling she said, "It's in the cabinet cariad. I have ice in the fridge."

As soon as she said the words she knew that this could lead somewhere they had not been to before and was scared that it might be at the expense of their friendship and working relationship. And he was married for God's sake—albeit not vey happily.

Her head was spinning. It was if a switch had been thrown and the whole dynamics of their relationship had changed and she felt nervous about the consequences. If their relationship became even deeper then who knows where things could end. It was all too much to contemplate while her heart felt a drum beating in her chest. It was if she was on a runaway train that she couldn't get off so she settled into thinking, *Fuck it. Let things take their course. If it happens, we will face the new future.*

She started to prepare the lunch and David came in. He took ice out of the fridge and handed a glass to Ruth; he said, "Here you are luv. Thanks again for being there when I needed you."

Although still nervous and now very conscious of him being in the room with her, she felt relief and a warm glow engulfed her body at him returning the familiarity.

"I'll always be here for you my friend. On that you can rely. And I know you will always be there for me. Can you butter some French bread? We can then drink down our remaining anger and eat."

She turned around and looked into his eyes that were now full of affection and something else—desire maybe. Holding up her glass she said, "Cheers. Here's to us. Sod the rest."

David responded with a smile and touched glasses saying, "I'll drink to that."

They carried their lunch into the dining area and sat down at the table to eat with small talk between mouthfuls. She could feel the nervous electricity between them and knew that something important was happening.

When they had finished David poured two more large Malts and they sat down on the sofa. Ruth opened up the conversation with, "Why did you not have children David? You would make a lovely dad."

He smiled and said, "Well, thank you my friend. We did try for some time when we first got married but nothing happened. Then the job got in the way; you know long hours and awkward shifts. Somehow we just drifted apart. To be honest we haven't made love in four years. Maybe that's why she is always so bitchy but I just don't fancy her any more. I think she has someone at her tennis club and I suppose we stay together for convenience as much as anything."

Ruth looked at him and said, "Oh I am sorry sweetheart. I didn't know things were so bad. It must be awful for you."

David put his drink down, turned towards her.

"It's OK. You get used to it. But it's good to talk to you about it though. And what about you? Why is such a wonderful woman like you on your own?"

Ruth thought she would continue with exchanging confidences and looking him in the eyes and said,

"Oh you know; like you the job just gets in the way. And maybe the right man has not come along or been available."

She winked at him when she said that and continued, "When I was a Sergeant I was in a relationship with an Officer based at another station. His name is Oliver and we still meet up occasionally but there is no spark there anymore. We just tend to have dinner and talk. There is no sexual side of things at all. We don't even revisit the memories.

And something happened a couple of years, back, just after my mother died. I was very low after nursing her for many years and I had a fling with the most attractive young girl that I met during a training week. She was only 23 and beautiful inside and out. She helped me over my grief. One night she came to my room for drinks and we watched a girl-on-girl adult movie on the hotel TV channel. Somehow we ended up naked and well, you know, things sort of happened. There is something a bit forbidden feeling another woman's naked body against your own that makes it exciting.

She is based at a Bristol station and we kept up the relationship for a while staying at each other's flats when the shift pattern allowed. It gradually fizzled out though and I am really a man's girl anyway—when the right one is around that is.

But while it lasted it was very exciting and I'm feeling aroused just thinking about it. I'm quite physical and I love sex with the right person. Maybe I just wear partners out. But like you I have not made love with someone of the opposite sex for years. Oh my God look you David. Whatever are you doing to me? I am normally a very private person."

David put his arm around her and with the other hand moved her chin to face his saying, "Good grief Ruth. That's a lot of information. What a strange couple we are my friend and what a bundle of surprises you are."

Then fidgeting a little and smiling he said, "I must say that thinking about you and another woman has made me a little, er uncomfortable somewhere; but in a very pleasant way."

Then with some seriousness in his voice and taking a deep breath, he said, "I don't know about you, but right now I want to live for the moment. Do you feel the same?"

Knowing where this was going but unable to get her words out Ruth just nodded her head thinking, *Oh God yes. Let it happen.*

Then he said, "Can I kiss you?"

Ruth nodded again and feeling as nervous as a kitten she moved her lips close to his and softy replied, "Oh yes. I would like that very much. I think it's time, don't you?"

David kissed her lips gently at first and felt Ruth's tongue searching for his. The kiss soon absorbed both of them and the years of affection and abstinence burst through into a celebration of love and a mutual desire to satisfy each other's sexual needs. Ruth moved one of David's hands to her breasts and he was soon undoing the buttons of her uniform shirt to caress what he could feel were her now erect nipples. Her hand had moved to the top of his thighs where his cock was now growing as she felt and caressed it through his trousers. She moved her mouth from his and whispered, "God David we are behaving like a couple of teenagers. Are you sure you want to go down this route? I do, but then I'm not married. We have worked together for years and I consider you my closest friend but it could change everything."

His reply was, "Oh yes. I want it too. I feel like a teenager about to have sex for the first time. It is as if it is meant to be. I'm with the most amazing woman in the world; a friend who I adore but have been unable to show it. We both need this and I know this moment will be very special."

Without moving his hand from her body, or hers from his, Ruth sat back a little and said, "You are right cariad. After four years without a man inside me this will be like the first time for me. In case it turns out to be just a one-off bad idea or memorable bit of afternoon delight I want it to be the best ever. I'm going to get out of this uniform, shower and glam myself up for you. There is another shower room through there and you'll find a robe on the door. When you've finished put it on and wait for me on the sofa. I'll let you know when I'm ready."

David groaned, "Oh; and I was so looking forward to making love to someone in uniform."

Ruth giggled, got up and walked towards her bedroom smiling as with a chuckled she said, "Don't worry sexy. All might not be lost in that department. Do you want the handcuffs as well? And no more Malt. We don't want a loss of performance on our first date."

Then, with a wink and a blown kiss she was gone. David thought, "Wow! I'd better do what I'm told then."

With that he made his way to the shower room and had a good wash down and soaking. There was some cologne on a shelf. He didn't know what type it was but figured that if it was there Ruth must like it so a bit of 'splash it all over' was in order. He took his time and heard Ruth humming while she showered in the en-suite that adjoined her bedroom. He put on the bath robe and returned to the lounge.

Looking at her bookcase, as well as the usual books on law and order he noticed some very raunchy titles; including '50 Shades of Gray' of course, but there was Lady C, the Perfumed Garden, the Kama Sutra and even the Virgin Soldiers. Her selection of videos was just as hot and if the images on the outside were anything to go by Ruth loved adult reading and viewing. He had just sat back down on the sofa when he heard, "What do you think then lover?"

He turned around and there was Ruth with her back leaning on the doorframe of her bedroom. She had done something to her hair that made her look quite different. It was tumbling over one shoulder when usually it was tied back severely because of the job. Some of her hair had fallen down to her eyes like a windswept fringe.

She was also wearing some small gold earrings and a matching necklace. Her smoky eye make-up gave her a sultry look and her carefully applied makeup made her appear even more beautiful.

She had on a crisp new uniform shirt with epilates and her best uniform jacket slung over her shoulder. Her shirt was completely undone, the two sides hanging over her breasts just revealing her nipples. Her chequered uniform cravat was just loosely hanging around her neck. Other than that she was completely naked apart from a pair of black high heel shoes that showed she had fabulous legs. Sexily rubbing one leg against the other she said with a very cheeky grin on her face, "I bet you haven't seen a Woman Police Inspector dressed like this before sweetheart."

David just looked and gulped. The description sex bomb came to mind. His normally fairly ordinary looking friend had turned herself into a vision of glamour and raw sexuality mixed with affection and a nervousness that was almost virgin like. She was every man's ultimate fantasy and she wanted him. His cock was standing to attention by now as he said, "Wow! Only you in my fantasies Ruth. You are the most sexy looking woman I have ever seen. Where have you been hiding this person? You are drop dead gorgeous sweetheart."

She replied, "She has been beside you for years, but our relationship didn't seem to develop in that direction. But draw the curtains before I come over. We don't want the neighbours to get too excited do we?"

David drew the curtains closed and once he was back on the sofa Ruth slowly walked towards him, the heels giving her a sway to die for and a walk that a police officer should not be capable of at all. She stood in front of him for a while swinging her hips from side to side and thrusting her pelvis forward so he could see everything. She parted her uniform shirt to show off her breasts and looking at David she grinned and said, "Do you like what you see? I hope you like big boobs darling because they are an important part of what's on offer."

David replied, "God. They and everything else about you are beautiful. I must be in a dream."

Still standing in front of him and looking straight into his eyes she cupped one breast and moved her mouth on to the nipple using her tongue to massage the large areola. This movement immediately sent her pleasure points into overdrive and her nipples and areola grew. She couldn't help herself moan as the feeling reached her clitoris.

With his hand on his cock David moaned, "What are you doing to me sweetheart? This is driving me crazy. I must have you."

She held out her hand and said, "You will soon. Come on; Let's go into my bedroom and have some fun."

Using her most flirtatious voice and looking down at the tent pole that was holding out David's robe she continued, "And you can introduce me to that friend of yours who seems so eager to meet me. I think he and I are going to get on really well."

He took her hand, got up and pulling her close he gently kissed her on the forehead. With arms around each other they slowly walked into Ruth's bedroom. Ruth said, "Are you nervous? I am because it has been so long."

He replied, "God yes. But I want you so much. I know this is right."

The curtains in the bedroom had been drawn and the only light was from a small table lamp on a bedside table. They kissed with an extra urgency and Ruth said, "Lay down on the bed David but leave room for me. I want to properly welcome your friend. He is standing so nicely to attention."

David lay down on the bed as Ruth kicked off her shoes and slung her jacket over a chair. She left on her shirt and cravat to keep the uniform theme going as she was as excited about that as David.

Kneeling down beside him, she slowly undid the belt on his robe while David watched. As all was revealed she gasped, "Well, who's a big boy then? He's gorgeous. She circled her hand around it and slowly massaged it up and down.

With David making erotic sounds and her gazing at his cock she said, "Welcome to my bed my new friend. I hope you enjoy your visit. I think you will do very nicely."

With that she bent down and after kissing the top and encircling it with her tongue she took as much as she could into her mouth in a tongue massaging kiss that lasted for ages. She then moved her lips slowly up and down its length. What she couldn't attend to with her mouth was receiving the willing attention of one of David's hand moving up and down the shaft. With the other hand he stroked her hair and applied pressure with the motion of her head as she worked her magic. He groaned, "Oh God! That's amazing Ruth, but you'll need to stop or it will all be over too soon."

Ruth came up for air grinning at his enjoyment and said, "Now wasn't that worth waiting for?"

Watching him still caressing his cock she murmured, "God! Watching you do that turns me on. Make more room for me beside you because I want to feel your lips on mine again. And as you can see from my nipples my boobs need some urgent attention."

David murmured, "Come here darling. I'm learning about your needs fast."

They embraced again with lust engulfing any inhibitions they might have had earlier. Their hands were now all over each other's bodies—Ruth's on David's cock and David's between Ruth's legs massaging her clitoris as he used his fingers inside her. Moving his hands to her breasts he used his tongue on her nipples and around her fascinating large areolas. Ruth found this wildly exciting and held his head tightly saying, "Ah; be harder with your tongue darling. I really love this feeling."

As he pressed harder with his tongue he felt her nipples harden and grow further and she cried, "Oh yes. That's it darling. God I love this. You have the tongue touch. Just feel what it's done down below as well."

He slowly moved his attention lower, kissing her body with his tongue as he went down. Sliding his fingers between her thighs he found her juices were in full flow and her clitoris was protruding like a small stiff cock. He ran his tongue over it and found that he could hold it between his lips moving it in and out. Ruth started to move her hips and he heard, "Yes; yes. Oooh! Oh yes. I love that. Do it more."

Looking up at her as he continued, he saw she had both breasts in her hands with her teeth about to surround one nipple. Her eyes were looking down at him.

183

As her hips moved faster she said, "Oh stop before I cum darling. Taste my juices and then come up and kiss me again."

As she groaned in pleasure he moved his tongue inside her vagina as deeply as he could. Then moving his body so his head was close to hers she put her fingers in his mouth; withdrawing them slowly and running her tongue over them tasting her own juices as she looked into his eyes.

She sat up and said, "Jesus I have to cum now. Lie down on your back. I want to fuck you my friend."

He rolled over with his cock still in full working order. Ruth straddled his body and looking down on him with her cheeky smile, she used her hand to slowly guide him inside saying, "For both of us it has been a long wait so let's savour every moment."

David was in heaven and said, "Oh that feels good Ruth. I never thought having sex with anyone could fill me with so much love as well as desire. I just want to make you happy."

As she absorbed all of David's cock inside her she bent down and kissed him and said, "You don't know how happy that makes me darling. With you now inside me I am a new woman. Let's do it."

With that she straightened her back and started to move her hips and use her fingers on her clitoris. Slow at first but then faster as the feelings inside her increased until she felt that she was going to explode. Her tits were bouncing, a feeling she loved, and she could see how excited it made David. But she couldn't stop herself from reaching a climax even though she knew her lover was not ready. She cried, "Sorry darling. I have to cum now. I can't wait, Ooh! Ooh! Fuck…"

With that she increased her hip movement and arched her back as she shuddered to the most wonderful and long-lasting climax she had ever experienced.

She remained on his stiff cock for a short while, eventually bending down to kiss him. Then letting her breasts sway over his mouth, teasing him with her nipples she said, "Sorry I couldn't wait but it's your turn now. I think I can cum again I feel so sexy."

They rolled over with David still inside her but now on top. He started to move in and out saying, "I'm going to give you the best fuck you have had darling."

She smiled and said, "You already have lover. But let's complete the job because my clitoris is on fire again."

With that she put her legs behind his and started to move in tandem with his ever-faster thrusts inside her. They were both moaning in pleasure and could feel the ultimate joint climax approaching. David said, "I'm going to cum soon. I have never felt like this before."

In between gasps, she replied, "I'm cumming again ooh, ooh …"

Then, both crying out together, their pumping climaxes came in unison and they were joined together in a new beautiful union of desire and the ultimate pleasure of satisfying each other's basic needs.

They stayed locked together in each other's arms for several glorious minutes, holding each other tightly while kissing. Eventually he rolled over and Ruth handed him some tissues. It had happened at last. An afternoon that started out in anger about the job had ended in the most emotion engulfing sex either of them had ever experienced.

David was the first to speak.

"That was the best sexual experience of my life. You have made sex so much fun as well as erotic and the most and wonderful act of personal commitment between us. I had no idea what a little sex pot has been hidden inside you."

Ruth leant over and gently kissed him on the lips and said, "It was wonderful wasn't it? The best for me as well. I have never been so uninhibited with anyone. You have released the new Ruth. But what have we done?"

David looked at her and said, "One thing is for sure my friend. This is not just a one-off. It was not just a good fuck. It was an act of real affection between us. This afternoon has changed our lives and we both know it. We will have to come to terms with any consequences."

Just then his mobile phone rang. It was in the pocket of his robe that was on the floor beside the bed. He reached down and saw that it was his wife and immediately turned it off not wanting anything to destroy the moment. Ruth said, "Was it work darling?"

A sad looking face replied, "No it was my wife."

Ruth said, "You had better phone her back or go home. I'll drop you off at the end of your road if you like."

David said, "I would rather make this moment last longer Ruth. I don't really want to go anywhere just yet."

Ruth snuggled up to him again saying, "I know. I feel the same. But we now have to work out how we are going to handle our new relationship—with your wife and at work. And we will have to decide where it is going to go as well. It will take time and we will need to keep it a secret until you have sorted out what you want to do with your marriage. Now you've rediscovered your libido you might want to improve things in that area with your wife."

David quickly replied, "No. That's not going to happen Ruth. What happened today was because it was you and me consummating a relationship in a way we should have done years ago. My libido is directly linked with my feelings for you. Life plays some inconvenient tricks. I agree we need to keep things secret while we sort things out, but one way or another I would like for us to be together. I don't know how but if that is what you want too then that is what I will work towards."

Ruth smiled and kissed him before saying, "You can move in here with me if you like but not before you sort things out at home. You know that is right and there are financial implications as well."

David said, "I know darling. You are right and I will need to get my head around things. This afternoon has put many things into context and I know what is important to me. It is making you happy. You are the woman in my life now."

Ruth replied, "And you are the man in mine. You have made me very happy. I knew I had a good friend. I now have someone who satisfies me in every way and whatever happens I feel blessed."

Then, looking at her watch and getting up she said, "But I need to take the glam off and get back to the station. What are you going to do?"

He replied, "I think I need some time to process my thoughts. Just drop me off by the local bus stop and I'll make my way into Cardiff and then home. You can tell them that I had a meeting with an informant. I'll be in tomorrow and we must remember to behave in a professional manner ma'am. No touching now."

She laughed and said, "Certainly not Sir."

She went back into her bedroom, changed her hair and make-up and put on a new uniform. David got dressed and they were soon ready to go back to their normal world.

Before they opened the front door they held each other and kissed passionately.

Ruth said, "OK. Let's get back to our normal life. Mind you, I will have trouble keeping a smile off my face now."

David squeezed her bum and they left. There was much to fix outside this bubble of contentment they had created and that would not be easy.

Chapter 13

Give me the eyes to see and the strength to understand.
(Native American saying)

24 August 2017 Thursday 1.05pm
Mayhew Estate

Sandy was in the kitchen making the sandwiches ready for the treasure hunt and Jonny was hindering; eating the cheese and ham before Sandy could put it on the bread. Through a mouthful of nicely matured cheddar cheese he said, "Have you seen the sexy Devlin yet?"

Sandy replied while using the butter knife to smack his hand that was making another attempt on the cheese, "No; not yet. Have you spoken to Jacob?"

Jonny answered with a cheeky smile, "I got a text with a kiss, which I think is good. But we've not spoken, which is not so good. Can I have a piece of bread and butter please?"

Sandy sighed, buttered him some bread and handed it to him. He asked, "Do you have any peanut butter?"

Sandy pointed to the cupboard behind him.

"Should be in there hun."

Jonny grabbed the spread and dolloped it on his bread so thickly he could only just take a mouthful without dropping it all down himself. Sandy looked on with an expression that was a mixture of amazement, scorn and dismay.

Turning around she picked up the kettle and filled two flasks with hot water, instant coffee and milk, before firmly twisting down the tops. She then popped the sandwiches in plastic containers and packed the whole lot in a rucksack that she handed to Jonny saying in a very upbeat tone, "Right then; let's go my friend. Henry says for us to gather in the car park behind the stables."

It was a beautiful sunny afternoon with a light breeze that was just enough to stop it feeling too warm. They walked through the gate in the hedge and into the stable yard. Jimmy, Devlin's little Jack Russell terrier flew across the yard as soon as he saw Sandy—jumping up excitingly at her legs as she bent down to greet him. She said, "Sooo where is your dad then Jimmy?"

She looked around until she spotted Devlin putting a saddle and bridle away in the tack room. He turned around and flashed a blinding smile at her. After he completed putting the tack away he strode out and placed a kiss on Sandy's forehead. Looking her in the eyes he said, "Hello beautiful; how did your trip go?"

Sandy nodded and told him it went OK. Devlin continued, "That's good. How about dinner tonight? I'm cooking."

Sandy felt all a-glow at the thought of being alone will him thinking, *I think this could be the night. I had better find time to freshen up my Brazilian.*

She replied, "Mmm, lovely. I will look forward to it."

Jonny raised his eyebrows and then mimed being sick. In a sarcastic voice, he said, "Oh dear God; give me a sick bucket. You two are just too cutesy to be real. Come on babe; let's go find the others before they leave without us."

Sandy narrowed her eyes and kicked the back of Jonny's leg so he nearly fell over and said in the most sarcastic voice she could muster, "OK sweetie. Oh dear, did you nearly fall? Sooo sorry. Let me help you."

As she offered her arm, Devlin laughed saying, "See you later. Have a good time."

With a wave a limping Jonny assisted by Sandy walked through the archway and into the stable car park. Christina and Barry were in the back of a cream-coloured long wheelbase Land Rover and Sue and Henry were in the front. Jonny and Sandy climbed into the rear and sat on the flip down seats in the back.

Lord Henry started the engine and said that he was going to keep to the estate tracks across country, so they needed to buckle up because it was going to be a bit bumpy.

Jonny leant over the back seat to talk to his mum. It was the first time he had spoken to her since his return from London. He asked, "No Izzy?"

Christina replied, "No. She is staying back at Mayhew to get herself together. Rather than use her own Land Rover that could be recognised by our villainous friends, Bryn is going to drive her into Bristol to get the train back to Cornwall this afternoon. She is still pretty shaken and wants to be at home with her cat. We can get her Land Rover down to her later when we have more of an idea of how things are panning out. She told me all about what happened."

She then gave Jonny a weak smile and a nod. He knew there was a lot more to be said when they were not in the company of others.

They were soon driving along the fields and tracks of the estate with the windows open; the fields have had their second cut of hay and the smell of the grass being turned by the tractors was intoxicating. If you didn't know better you would think it was Lord Henry taking some guests around to view his empire; not a group of people caught up in a mystery and murder plot on their way to hopefully find buried treasure.

The Land Rover bumped up a muddy track making Jonny and Sandy hang on to their seats for grim death because there were no safety belts on the rear flip down seats. They were screaming with laughter. One huge bump resulted in Jonny landing on the floor Sandy tried to give him a hand up but they both remained in a heap on the floor because every time they nearly found their feet there was another bump and they fell over again. There was much laughter from the front and they realised Lord Henry was looking at them in his rear-view mirror. He was doing it on purpose. Jonny cried, "Oi! Pack it in. We are going to be all black and blue."

Sue also joined in although she had trouble keeping a straight face.

"Yes Henry. Behave. Stop and let them get back into their seats."

Lord Henry stopped laughing and brought the Land Rover to a halt. Sandy and Jonny got back into their seats and they found they were on top of a small ridge, looking down on a river running into the Mayhew Estate lake, with the estate buildings behind and the inner security walls on the other side. It was fringed with weeping willows that threw their reflection onto the gently rippling water. There was an old arched, stone bridge over the narrowest part of the river that looked as if it had been there for hundreds of years. The whole vista was of calm serenity and everybody was silent as they took in its beauty.

It was now just gone 2 pm. Lord Henry's booming voice broke that silence.

"OK then people. Let's find some treasure."

He put the Land Rover into a low gear and drove down the slope (possibly a little too fast for comfort) heading towards the lake before stopping beside the bridge with a jerk.

He said, "We had to take the long way round because I am not sure the bridge would take the weight of the Landy. The ruins of what we have always assumed to be a smuggler's cottage are just in that small copse to the right."

They all clamber out and Lord Henry handed out shovels, a couple of petrol bush cutters already fuelled up, a mattock, some pruning shears, gloves and a metal detector that he had in a large container on the roof of the Land Rover. In truth there was not much left of the cottage. With no roof and a few half walls it was very overgrown with trees growing inside and brambles covering almost everything. It was quite clear that accessing it was going to take some time.

Donning a pair of gloves and starting up a bush cutter Barry said, "Right then let's get started. And we must take photos before we leave. Aiyana will be interested in our progress."

After about a noisy hour of cutting, digging and picking they stop for a well-earned rest and some sandwiches. They were hot and sweaty but Sue produced some hand wipes so they could freshen up a bit. They were also being plagued by midges and they hadn't thought to bring fly spray. Jonny mentioned they should have brought swimming gear when his phone rang. It was Arthur so Jonny answered, "Hey buddy what's up?"

"Umm the four heavies are driving over the Prince of Wales bbridge in another um bblack Evoque. I think they um have Will wwith them. Um I think tthey will be on ththeir wway tto join the Cantana Brothers who are no longer outside Jonny's flat but are heading East. Mmaybe Will has ggiven them more er information about Ssandy and Mayhew."

Jonny replied, "Oh shit! We are out on the estate at the moment. Keep us posted Arty. I'll inform Lord Henry."

"OK. Speak ssoon."

Lord Henry heard Jonny's half of the conversation and saw his worried expression. Finishing a sandwich and giving Jonny his full attention he said, "What's the problem Jonny?"

Jonny exclaimed, "The bouncers with Will are on their way in another black Evoque. Arty says they are on the bridge and could be joining the Cantana Brothers who have left outside my flat in Cardiff and are heading East."

For a moment, with a mixture of expressions showing amazement and concern, all five of them stopped eating and stared at him. After a few moments silence Christina looked at Lord Henry and asked in a slightly panicked voice, "But we are safe here aren't we?"

Barry put his arm around Christina's shoulders as Sue also glanced at Lord Henry and anxiously said, "Don't worry Chrissie. Mayhew is like Fort Knox and the hoods have no idea we are here at the moment."

Lord Henry looked thoughtful before saying, "That might not be true Sue. Putting information from Jonny and Will together plus what they might have gathered from Matt, they could have concluded that we are all here; particularly if they have not seen any sign of you at your homes.

I think I will call the staff at the house and tell them not to go outside the inner boundary walls, just in-case."

With that Lord Henry reached for his phone. Sue then jumped to her feet and picked up some equipment saying, "OK then while Henry is on the phone, I think we should pack up and get ready to move."

Before long they had all the picnic and work gear back in the Land Rover. Lord Henry finished giving his house staff instructions over the phone and climbed in the driver's seat saying, "I think we should go back via the main road using the rear entrance access gate by Home Farm; it will be quicker."

They were soon driving at speed and this time there was no laughter with less bumping around just some serious thinking. They gritted their teeth and hung on tight until they passed through the Home Farm outer wall security gate and on to a tarmac road. Before they knew it they were soon driving through the main gates of Mayhew; everyone glancing for any signs of the hoods. Continuing past the inner wall security they drove around to the parking area at the rear of the stables. Noticing the Freelander parked up Lord Henry said, "Ah! I see Bryn is back so he must have got Isabella away. I will get him to locate Jacob and Devlin. Can the rest of you go inside? We need to get the staff together to brief them but I will need to make some phone calls first so let's gather in the kitchen in about 20 minutes. In the meantime can you get some coffee on the go Sue?"

With Lord Henry in his 'I'm in charge' mode they all quickly walked off in the direction of the house. As a result of his earlier phone call made when they were out on the estate, most of the staff had already assembled in the kitchen so as she put the kettle on Sue said, "In a few minutes Lord Henry will be in to let you know why you have been called in this morning. Who wants tea and who wants coffee?"

She looked up to see a forest of worried faces so she said in a calm voice, "Don't worry; your jobs are all safe and we are not about to sell Mayhew."

There was a collective sigh of relief as the tension went out of them.

Devlin walked around to stand by Sandy. He took her hand and kissed her fingers quietly asking, "Are you OK?"

She just nodded her head saying with a smile, "I am fine hun."

Jacob was the last to enter with Bryn and searched the room until he caught Jonny's eye and smiled as he mouthed, "Hi."

Margie, Sue and Christina handed out the drinks to the staff. There was a soft buzz of conversation in the room but when Lord Henry entered, they all stopped and turned towards his commanding presence. It was now 3.30 pm. When there was complete silence he said, "Good afternoon everyone. I have gathered you all here because we have a situation outside of Mayhew that could be dangerous. I am afraid that you will have to stay here for the time being until we know it is safe. I would like to ask you to keep within the inner walls and also let your family know that you possibly won't be home tonight. Don't alarm them and please bear with us and I am sorry for any inconvenience."

The Staff all started to ask questions at once but Lord Henry just put his hands up to stop them saying, "We will answer your questions as soon as we know more. Bryn, can I borrow you for a moment?"

He then turned and left the room closely followed by Bryn, leaving Margie and Sue to dodge questions and sort out sleeping arrangements. Jonny got out his mobile and texted Arthur, *Where are they, buddy?*

The answer text came back quickly, *They are already outside the outer wall near the main entrance. You just got through the gate in time. There are the four bouncers and the Cantana Brothers. A couple of them are walking around to see if there is a way in. Tony Cantana is getting something out the back of one of the Evoques. Oh, that's not good. They have a drone and it looks like there is more than just a camera fitted to the undercarriage.*

Jonny left the kitchen and went down the hall to Lord Henry's study. The door was shut so he knocked and the door was opened by Bryn. Lord Henry boomed, "Come in, Jonny. We are watching our friends on the CCTV."

Jonny relayed Arthur's test message about the drone and Lord Henry said, "Yes. We have spotted that. It looks interesting and I'm not sure what they are up to. Bryn can you bring me a gun? Twelve gauge under and over should do it."

He handed some keys to Bryn who walked over to a door to the right of Jonny. He opened the door using the key and behind it was a metal door with a combination lock that Bryn obviously knew. Once open Jonny was surprised to notice there was a walk-in room lined with stainless steel and it had metal cupboards of various sizes attached to the sides. Bryn walked into the room and selected a cupboard. Opening it revealed a shotgun. He opened another cupboard below it and took out a box of cartridges. He then walked out of the room closing the cupboards and both the metal door and the outer door making sure both were locked. He then handed the gun and the box of cartridges to Lord Henry.

With a wink and a smile Lord Henry said, "Right then; let's go do some drone shooting shall we?"

Breaking the gun and placing two cartridges in the barrel, he then nonchalantly walked out of the study to the front door with the gun over his left arm. Just as they got to the door there was an explosion as one of Lord Henry's cars went up in flames. It was a 1961 E Type Jaguar convertible; one of the first vehicles off the production line. The hood was down ready for Bryn to carry out an internal valet but fortunately there was no petrol in the tank and it was parked away from buildings or more damage would have been done. The vibration had set off alarms in the house that created a din and anxiety amongst those inside and unsettled the horses.

Through gritted teeth Lord Henry said, "Bastards. That car was special."

He opened the door, snapped the gun shut, pointed it skywards, aimed and pressed the trigger. The drone and whatever incendiary devices were attached exploded harmlessly in the air like a clay pigeon shoot. A few remaining pieces fell into the yard.

Henry then broke the gun again and walked back into the house with a serious expression on his face saying, "Shut the door Jonny. And Bryn; get the fire extinguisher and save what you can of the car. Come into the study when you've done what you can. And get Devlin or the others to check the horses. I'll turn those bloody alarms off."

Jonny shut the door and ran to catch up with Henry who was just disappearing into the study. As he ran, he thought, *Oh my God! That man is so fucking cool. I want to be him when I grow up.*

Lord Henry turned off the alarms and then positioned himself in front of his computer screen saying, "Right then Jonny; let's see what effect that has had on the enemy shall we? Ah look; that seems to have upset the applecart a little. Our friends appear to be having a heated discussion. I wonder if there are any other drones in the sky? I love a bit of shooting practice."

Jonny looked at the screen. Tony and Sully were outside the main gates having a right old argument; shouting at each other with Tony pointing at Sully and then at the gates. The Evoque that came from Bristol with the heavies was close to another camera and had the back door open revealing Will sitting in the back. He was looking pretty sick, with his head resting back against the seat.

Tony stomped over to the vehicle and grabbed Will by the neck of his shirt and deliberately dragged him over to the camera. Clearly this was for those inside the house to see. He then pointed a gun to Will's head and mouthed the word painting. He then let go of Will who slid down onto his hands and knees, retching and trying to hold his jaw in pain. Tony drew back his leg to give Will a kick but was pushed backwards by Sully shoving him in the chest. Sully then turned and then using a stick wrote the word 'painting' in the verge mud beside the vehicle to make sure the message got home. He then helped Will get back into the Evoque.

Lord Henry turned to Jonny saying, "That lad Will is in a poor state isn't he? It looks like you broke his jaw Jonny and it seems Tony Cantana is adding to the injuries. But the message is clear. If we don't give them a painting Tony will execute that young chap. Let's get Sue in here for a chat. Can you go and find her and bring her back to the study?"

Jonny turned and quickly strode up the hall to the Kitchen. He opened the door to a barrage of questions about the explosions. Talking above the din and knowing it wouldn't answer all their questions he shouted, "Nothing to be alarmed about. All sorted. Sue can you pop into the study his Lordship would like a word?"

He noticed that his mum and Devlin were missing. He turned to Sandy and asked, "Where is Mum?"

She replied, "Devlin and your mum have just gone out to check on the horses. She wanted to make sure Wiggy was OK after all the noise."

Jonny nodded and gave a comforting wink to Sandy before following Sue back to the study. Bryn also returned after extinguishing the fire on the E-Type Jaguar.

Henry Looked up from his computer screen and smiled as Sue entered the room. She was followed by Bryn fresh from his fire extinguishing duties. Lord Henry's expression changed from a smile to a worried look and asked, "How bad is it Bryn? Much damage?"

Bryn replied, "Could have been much worse Sir. Most of the upholstery and soft top has gone and it looks like there is damage to the dashboard and instrumentation but the basics appear to be sound."

Lord Henry looked down and said, "Bugger. That was all original. Anyway we can address that later. Let's get back to the here and now."

He then went on to summarise what had been going on and how the gangsters really just want the painting. After a short silence Sue chipped in with a smirk on her face, "Well then, darling; we should give them what they want, shouldn't we. They appear to have no idea about the Gainsborough or the hidden map. The original overlayed canvass is just about totally removed and is still basically intact. All I need to do is stretch that over another worthless painting and put it back in the original frame. With a few touch ups they will hopefully not know the difference. It will be a shame to lose that antique frame but in the worst-case scenario this should give you more time. What do you think?"

Lord Henry gave an admiring smile and said, "That is what I hoped but I needed your confirmation as the expert."

Sue got up saying, "OK; I better get a move on because there is still much to do and it is not a quick task."

As she left Lord Henry moved on to the next task in typical dismissive fashion saying, "Right then Jonny; let's have another chat with Arthur via computer shall we?"

Now seated in front of his computer he put up the video link to Arthur with Bryn and Jonny looking over his left and right shoulders. The screen showed Arthur looking slightly uncomfortable being viewed by several people and he didn't look at them directly.

Jonny tried to put him at ease by gently saying, "It's OK Arty. We just need to know if you have any more intel for us?"

Arthur replied by turning some of his screens towards the computer camera.

"Um; iit's pprobably better iif I sshow yyou."

One showed a couple of the hoods walking around the perimeter of Mayhew. They had taken their jackets off and looked very hot and bothered. Lord Henry looked closely and said, "Mmmm; it looks like we still have a bit of company. What about the Cantana brothers and Will? Do you know where they are now?"

"Umm it llooks like they aare nnow ddriving bback towards umm BBristol. Bby the wway; umm ggood sshot ggeting that ddroneddown Sir."

Lord Henry smiled as he said, "Thank you Arthur I like to keep my clay pigeon practice up to scratch."

Arthur chuckled replying, "Umm I will gget yyou on mmy game ggroup Sir."

Lord Henry gave a thumbs up to the screen camera and said, "I look forward to it Arthur. Thank you once again; we will talk later."

Lord Henry turned off his computer. It was now gone 4 pm. Rubbing his chin in a thoughtful but mischievous way he turned to Jonny and Bryn and mused, "Well, it would appear we still have some unwanted guests interested in Mayhew. Now wouldn't it be fun if we made it easy for them to come in and see what we do on a farming estate. I am sure that being city boys they will find it quite interesting don't you think? At a guess they should be at the Home Farm gateway in less than half an hour, but I calculate that we could be there in about ten minutes. Mary and Aled keep a good flock of geese and they also have a lovely dairy herd that produces a good amount of liquid slurry that they use to fertilise their fields."

Bryn started to laugh so hard he had to clutch his sides as he said, "Now that's what I call a plan"

Jonny looked bewildered for a moment before he cottoned on to what Lord Henry had in mind, and then he too started to laugh.

Lord Henry stood up and started to stride out the room expecting the others to follow saying, "Right then; let's not hang about you two or we won't get there in time. I'll make one quick phone call to the Home Farm tenants before we leave."

Grabbing a twelve bore that he kept handy, he phoned his tenants and checked that theirmuck spreader was loaded. He then asked them to partly open the estate gates close to Home Farm; just wide enough for someone to walk through but not wide enough for a car. He also asked them to make their way to Mayhew House just in-case things didn't go to plan. Phone call completed they were soon in the Land Rover bumping across country to Home Farm.

Once inside the estate gates the two hoods would have to go through the actual farmyard before they could find the track to the Mayhew Estate grounds, so after explaining what he wanted them to do Lord Henry asked Jonny and Bryn to hide in a couple of outbuildings. He then climbed into a tractor and hitched it up to a loaded muck spreader before driving it a few hundred yards down the track that led from Home Farm to the Estate. Turning it around he parked it parallel to the track in the adjoining field and hid in the cab.

It was not long before the two hoods were walking down through the farmyard and out onto the Estate track. Just before they got to the tractor, Lord Henry started up the engine with the muck-spreader full of cow slurry and started to drive towards them, covering them from head to foot in the fragrant mixture.

For a moment they just stood there in shock, until they saw Lord Henry turning around for a second go.

At the sight of this they turned around and ran back towards the farmyard. As soon as they were half way across the yard Bryn and Jonny unlatched a pen containing a flock of very territorial geese that, on seeing the unpleasant sight of the hapless duo, started to chase them with their necks extended. Honking and hissing, they nipped at the men's legs and the unfortunate pair were slipping and sliding all over the place. One fell over and was instantly set upon by the geese. His mate tried to help him, but struggling in a mess of slippery slurry and surrounded by some very angry geese he eventually fell on top of him who was now screaming and shouting obscenities.

When they were thoroughly covered in slurry and goose shit Lord Henry climbed down from the tractor and walked towards the men with his twelve-bore pointing at them. As he stared at them with steely eyes he called to Bryn and Jonny to round up the geese and put them back in the pen. Then addressing the two shit covered hoods he slowly said, "Right then; get up! And I suggest you behave yourselves because otherwise, so help me God, I will shoot you and feed you to the pigs.

Then looking at Bryn he said, "Bryn; can you get the hose pipe and give these two a quick wash down? Then I'll have a little chat with them."

Once the two were soaking wet but less smelly, Lord Henry, still with the gun pointing at them, said, "I will be brief and to the point. I want you to give your employers a message. You can tell them that we will give them the painting on the condition that they must then leave us alone.

If they fail to keep to those terms I will unleash forces that will make Armageddon look like a Sunday afternoon tea party at the local vicarage. Anyone who tries to destroy a classic piece of motoring history deserves no mercy. Ask them to call us soon and we will arrange for a pick-up. Now get off my land before I set the geese on you again and do not return."

With that the defeated duo turned and ran back towards the exit gates as if the hounds of hell were at their heels. Lord Henry left it a while. Jonny and Bryn joined him and they drove up to the gates to check that it was locked again. Happy that security was in place again Lord Henry pointed the Land Rover back towards the farmyard and on to the track leading back to Mayhew. On the way he asked Jonny to check with Arthur that the two, by now, very damp, hoods were on their way back to Bristol. Arthur quickly came back confirming they were in the back of an Evoque that appeared to be heading out towards the Avon crossing.

As they approached Mayhew Lord Henry said, "Right Bryn. I think we will need to get everyone at Mayhew together again. There is more explaining to do I think."

"I'll assemble them in the hall sir. Fifteen minutes OK?"

"That'll do nicely Bryn. I have a phone call to make first."

It was now gone 5 pm. Bryn and Jonny assembled everyone in the hall and Lord Henry started to explain the outline details about what had been going on.

"First of all I must apologise for the recent, shall we say, 'unfortunate' goings on at Mayhew; and I feel you are due some form of explanation. There are some bad people out there who believe we have something that they think belongs to them. I won't go into detail but it does not belong to them at all. We have a plan to satisfy their illegal claims and get things back to normal at Mayhew while the correct authorities deal with the criminality. Rest assured the powers that be are aware of the situation but I would ask you not to tell your family, friends or others about this at the moment. You are all welcome to stay at Mayhew as our guests if you like until things settle down. Mary and Aled, you will want to get back to your farm. I have made sure the Estate Gate is closed but keep an eye on it. Now if I know my wife well then I bet she has some drinks available. I definitely need one."

Right on cue Sue opened the doors to the garden where a table laden with bubbly and coffee was waiting.

Chapter 14

Give thanks for unknown blessings already on their way.
(Native American saying)

Thursday 6.30 pm
24 August 2017
Mayhew Estate

It was gone 6.30 pm before most people had left the gathering. Jonny, Sandy, Devlin and Jacob were the stragglers, staying outside in the early evening sunshine enjoying some of the Prosecco that was left. Looking at his watch Devlin got up and said, "Well, I suppose I had better start the dinner Sandy or we won't be eating tonight. See you in about an hour."

Sandy took his lead and said with a cheeky grin, "Right. So I'd better get showered and ready then. I'll be there hun."

They said farewell to Jonny and Jacob as they walked away—Devlin to his flat and Sandy to her room. With hope in his voice Jonny said, "So, are you busy tonight Jacob?"

The answer was not one he wanted to hear.

"Sorry Jonny but I have my brother popping over."

Feeling pretty confused Jonny replied, "Why do I get the feeling that you don't want to be alone with me? I thought we got on well. I fancy you and I know you have feelings for me. What is the problem?"

Jacob turned his head to look over the gardens and muttered, "To be honest I have never had a same-sex relationship and I am scared. I really do fancy you Jonny but I am pretty confused about my feelings. I love being with you. Can you just give me time?"

Jonny reached over and took Jacob's chin and turned his head to face him saying, "Why didn't you tell me?"

Jacob looked at him and said, "You just assumed I was gay Jonny. I wasn't ready to explain my feelings to you until now."

Jonny smiled and took Jacob's hands. Looking steadily into his eyes he said, "I can give you time. You are worth it. My 'gaydar' is usually spot on. If you have any questions just ask me. I have really been out since I was a kid and this is who I am. All I ask is that you don't string me along if you conclude that this is not for you. For fuck's sake let me know."

A relieved Jacob said, "I promise you Jonny. I just need to sort through my emotions first. Do you fancy a walk around the gardens?"

Jonny replied, "I will give it a miss sweetheart. Just being in your company makes me as horny as hell. I have a massive boner right now, so I had better go and exercise my right hand."

Ruefully getting up and rearranging himself he leaned down and gently kissed Jacob on the lips before saying, "You are gay Jacob. I know it and I think you do as well."

He then turned on his heels and walked back towards the house without a backward glance, leaving Jacob as confused as ever.

Back in her room Sandy was getting ready. Although she gave the impression of coolness her body was actually tingling with excitement. Apart from her regular solo sessions, it had been some time since she had a full-on sex session with a man she fancied like hell and who clearly wanted her. The obvious affection and love they felt for each other was there. She wanted to give him everything but had never been with someone so sexually experienced. She knew he could take her to places she had never been to before. So she had to show him that underneath this outward innocence there was a very sexy lady. One who would make this a special occasion for them both.

She showered and freshened up her Brazilian which made her feel oh so good. So as to get used to it she had decided to go hairless down there during her trip to London. She knew something would happen between her and Devlin soon and had time in the Britannia International Hotel to do a proper job before meeting Jonny at the Slap. Now looking in the mirror she moisturised the shaven areas and as she massaged it in her index finger slid between her vaginal lips and hit the spot. She felt the urgency to go further but she pulled up short murmuring, "No. I want to save all of it for Devlin. Tonight is special."

She put on her prettiest underwear; white lace panties laced with red satin ribbon. Not tarty but neither were they staid or boring. She decided not to wear a bra because she wanted Devlin to see her state of nipple arousal and have easy access. Her young breasts were firm but mobile and there could be no mistaking what was going on underneath the buttoned-to-the-waist flimsy filmy-white dress she had chosen. She also loved the feel of her breasts moving across the material when she was aroused.

She decided to leave the top two buttons undone to show a bit of cleavage and looking in the mirror she applied some pale pink lipstick along with a hint of perfume. She thought about heels to show off her legs, but settled on white flip flops.

She smiled in satisfaction at her reflection and left the room. The look she had achieved was innocent but extremely sexy. However, her thoughts were far from innocent. And Devlin was in for a few surprises.

In just a few minutes she was outside the door to his flat. She tapped on the door and was greeted by the wonderful smell of cooking. Walking across the living space to the open plan kitchen she said, "Hiya. That smells yummy hun. I am starving."

Devlin looked up from the tomato sauce he was stirring. Admiring the multitude of movements going on underneath Sandy's dress he said, "Whoa! You look good enough to eat yourself."

With a cheeky smile and a quiet voice she replied, "Oh! You know I might just hold you to that later."

She thought, *That should let him know that her expectations were limitless.*

Changing the subject quickly, she asked, "What are you cooking?"

The reply came as he lifted the saucepan off the hob.

"Homemade meatballs with pasta and a tomato sauce. It's ready now so sit down and I will dish up. There's wine on the table."

As they ate, they chatted like kindred spirits and Sandy updated Devlin about her trip to London and filled in more details about the painting, Aiyana and the bad guys. When they had finished eating, Devlin said, "Bloody hell Sandy. That sounds like one hell of a trip babe. Shall we sit on the sofa?"

Without waiting for an answer, and with another bottle of wine in one hand and two glasses in the other, he walked over to one of the two dark brown leather Chesterfield sofas in the room. As he sat down he said, "Alexa—play Adel"

The room was soon flooded with the smoky sound of Adel's voice. With her hips moving in synch with her breast Sandy purposely and slowly walked over to Devlin and took the glasses and the bottle out of his hands, giving him an eyeful of cleavage as she placed them out of harm's way on a coffee table. She then walked back, kicked off her flipflops and lowered herself onto his lap saying, "I think I've had enough wine for now sweetheart. But I do need some of this."

With that she put her arms around his neck and pulled his lips onto hers. They were soon kissing with some urgency. Their tongues entwined and Sandy felt a hand on her breast, his thumb and finger finding a hard nipple through the flimsy dress material. She wiggled off his lap and snuggled besides him undoing two further buttons on the front of her dress. She then took one of his hands and slid it under her dress and onto her breast, pressing it hard so he would know that she was not a delicate flower but a very sexy lady. Then they were locked in an all-consuming kiss again. Sandy moved her hand up Devlin's thigh until she could feel the bulging outline of his erect cock trying to escape from his jeans. She held it tight and slowly moved her hand up and down its considerable length murmuring, "Mmm. It feels good."

After more intense but loving kissing and caressing Devlin came up for air gasping, "Oh God Sandy; but you are a massive turn-on."

Still with her hand on his cock Sandy said, "Glad you think so. You are not so bad yourself."

She then removed her hand from his groin and undid the remaining buttons on her dress, opening up the front to fully reveal the beauty of her breasts and swollen nipples. Fingering a nipple and looking into his admiring eyes she said, "I think these need some of your special attention now Devlin."

She pulled Devlin's head down on one and she could soon feel his tongue encircling and teasing her nipple until it got even harder and larger. Her own thumb and finger were caressing the other one until Devlin's mouth came across to create more delicious feelings in her body.

She soon felt his hand under her dress, slowly moving up her thighs. She opened her legs slightly when she felt his fingers searching for her hot spot. Although it was what she wanted and was expecting, as he touched her Sandy experienced a feeling like an electric shock had just gone through her body; even though his fingers were just massaging her through her panties. She gasped and automatically pressed her body hard onto his fingers. To show how much she was enjoying the sensation she used her hand to press his working fingers closer to her now highly lubricated vagina. She was ready to cum at that moment but there was more she wanted to do to her lover and more she wanted him to do to her.

She wriggled herself backwards until she was up against the opposite arm of the sofa. Looking at Devlin with her now very sexy and penetrating eyes she slowly pulled her dress up over her head. With her legs resting on the sofa and slightly apart she was just in her panties. Devlin leant forward and gently removed them, mouth open as he viewed a completely shaven Sandy. He dropped her panties on the floor and stood up in front of her. He slowly undressed until he was standing before her completely naked handling his very erect cock. Sandy just lay there with one hand teasing a nipple and the other slowly caressing the shaven side of her vagina's lips. She croaked, "Oh Wow! Now that is a great bod and what a gorgeous cock."

She sat up and reached upward and forward until she had her hands around his very firm and muscular bottom. She pulled him towards her until she could place her lips around his wonderful bobbing erection. She got to work with her tongue, and with one hand holding firmly onto his shaft she slowly moved it up and down, moaning with pleasure along with Devlin who was clearly in his own heaven.

The wetness from her mouth created a sliding action between her hand and Devlin's cock and he felt his balls start to tighten and cried, "Whoa. I think you need to stop a minute Sandy. I am a bit close. I want to cum inside you but not in your mouth. We can save that until another time if you like."

Sandy removed her lips from his cock and gave a naughty smile saying, "Mmm. Now that sounds nice. I'll look forward to it."

She lay back on the sofa again with her fingers either side of her naked vagina and said with a longing smile, "But first I want to know what you think of this. I prepared it as a special treat for this occasion. I will be disappointed if you don't take a closer look. It's my turn now."

Devlin looked down and said, "You are full of surprises. It is beautiful and it certainly deserves closer attention."

He knelt beside the sofa and lifting her knees slightly he parted her legs with his hands. Starting with his lips on her nipples he slowly moved his head down her body, gently kissing her on the way. When he reached her vagina he kissed either side and let his tongue venture towards her clitoris that was now very prominent. He slowly steered his tongue deep between her vaginal lips and felt her press forward and pull his head closer as she gasped in her own world of pleasure. She was moving his head against the thrusts of his tongue and knew that she was ready to cum.

She moved his head away and whimpered, "Oh God. That was fantastic but we must stop now or I'll explode. I now really need your gorgeous cock deep inside me."

Devlin moved to straddle her but she said, "No. Not that way yet."

She stood up and took Devlin's hand, leading him to the end of the sofa where she released his hand and leant forward over the arm rest with her pert little bottom in the air and her legs slightly apart. Turning her head to the side to look at Devlin she murmured, "OK lover. I want you to take me from behind."

Devlin kissed her buttocks and gently presses her excited clitoris. Sandy groaned, "Oh my God. I am so ready for you; I am so worked up so we had better take it slow or I'll cum straight away."

Devlin then put his hand around his enlarged cock and gently guided it inside and held it there, just for a moment, before drawing out with agonising slowness and stopping again. Then without a warning he plunged deep inside her. Sandy squeezed her stomach muscles against it to feel its girth and squealed, "Oh do that again. Pleeease do that again. Ride me like you're riding a horse"

Grabbing hold of her hair and pulling back her head Devlin said, "Anything to oblige my Lady. Is this what you want. God you are sexy."

The reply was, "Oh yes. Oh fuck yes."

He pumped in and out with increasing speed with Sandy synchronising her hips with his thrusts. Feeling the leather of the Chesterfield on her breasts she gripped one of her nipples and groaned, "Oh God; more, more. It's been a long time since oh…"

The tension started to mount in the pit of her stomach until she could wait no longer and cried, "Oh oooh! I am oooh…"

Devlin slammed into her with a groan as they noisily climaxed together.

They stayed collapsed over the sofa arm for a while and Devlin put his arms around her. He eventually whispered, "Oh Sandy that was bloody amazing."

She turned her head and said, "Yes it was wasn't it. Next time I'll do the riding."

He replied with a grin, "That's a date."

He then gently pulled out and handed over the box of tissues from the side of the coffee table. They both collapsed on the sofa in each other's arms giggling and kissing gently. This was going to be a very special relationship.

After a while Sandy said, "Are you ready for more lover? I am."

The reply was quick and enthusiastic, "Oh yes—with you riding me?"

Sandy whispered, "No we can save that for another day. Right now I just want some gentle loving with you inside of me. Let's go to your bedroom?"

They walked hand in hand and Sandy lay down on the bed with her knees raised and her legs apart just waiting for Devlin to enter her. As he did she drew his head down to her mouth and they kissed passionately as they began to move together again. This time the urgency was not there but the joint climax was even more wonderful with both of them murmuring through their erotic gasps, "I love you."

It was a while before they got dressed and opened that bottle of wine.

Thursday 24 August 2017 8.30 pm
Mayhew Estate

While Sandy and Devlin were getting to know each other in Devlin's flat, Lord Henry, Barry Christina and Jonny had dinner together and discussed the day's events and future scenarios. They had finished eating and were all sitting in the main sitting room when Jonny's phone started to ring. They weren't expecting a call from the hoods so soon but Jonny took a quick look at his screen and said, "It's them."

He put it on loudspeaker and answered with a curt, "Yes."

He recognised Sully's barking voice saying, "Hope you all got your ears on cos I ain't gonna repeat myself. Jonny? You will deliver the painting to us at 3 pm tomorrow at the Willcome Inn Bristol. No cops or believe me someone will die. Any questions? No! OK! See you tomorrow."

Then they abruptly hung up leaving no time for questions and the four of them looking at each other with open mouths.

After a few seconds Lord Henry said calmly, "Well, that was short and to the point and a bit sooner than I had expected."

Just then Sue walked into the room. Lord Henry greeted her with, "Ah darling; right on cue. How is our fake top masterpiece coming along?"

Sue answered, "I am pretty sure I have finished touching in the parts that were damaged when I removed it from the Gainsborough. I mixed linseed oil with my paint and used a heat gun to speed up the drying process. That will also help recreate the varnish crazing that was evident. I have dulled back the colours on the additional paint used so it matches the original colours that have faded with age. I have glued it to a modern painting done in the style of an old master and mounted it on an aged replica stretch frame. I have some 'before and after' photos on my tablet. See what you think."

She opened up the photos on her tablet so that they could all see—zooming in on the detail. Lord Henry said, "Well; that looks the business to me. Brilliant! Can it be ready for a handover tomorrow afternoon? We have had a call from the enemy."

Sue looked thoughtful and said, "That should be OK as long as I do not hit problems when completing the reframing. I just need to remount the fake painting and replica stretch frame in the main frame exactly as we found it. I've kept all the wedges and other bits and I have detailed photos of the back of the painting before I removed it from the frame. I should be able to replicate it—even down to the dust marks. Hopefully they won't know what they are looking at for the time being anyway. In fact I think it will need an art expert's eye to spot our fraud.

And judging by what Aiyana told us about how they kept it in their vault, the current guardians don't really know much about its significance anyway. Only that it held a secret that might ruin many of their land claims in the Boston area along with their moral and financial reputation so they couldn't sell it or give it an asset value anyway. So I ask myself why did they not destroy it? The documents they had lodged regarding their claims had been accepted as proof of ownership by the authorities for hundreds of years. I have some new information about that significance and I will tell you later. The painting would of course have a value as Gainsborough's fame increased over the years.

My guess is that it must have been stolen from Robert Davies or his heirs and the theft was probably published in the press at the time. I will delve a bit deeper into the archives to see what I can find. Once they had acquired it they might also have discovered the map but were not able to identify the location geographically but hoped to sometime in the future. This could be another reason why they decided to hide the painting rather than destroy it. Although I hate the idea of losing a bit of antique history I think it wise that we place our fake painting and map back in the original frame. I have taken some hi-res photos of the map for our records. This will enable me to use the professional version of Photoshop to identify more details."

Lord Henry and the others listened intensely as Sue explained her latest thoughts. The silence was broken with Lord Henry saying, "You have been busy and what you say does make sense. I think the sooner we can get the fake back in the hood's hands the better. Jonny needs to be ready with the painting by 2 pm tomorrow; earlier if possible so he can visit Arthur. We need to plan the afternoon in detail and cover all eventualities."

Christina had been listening with a worried frown on her face and abruptly said, "After what happened in London there is absolutely no way that Jonny is putting himself in that kind of danger again!"

A frustrated Jonny said, "Mum; I will be fine. I know the Willcome Inn like the back of my hand. Arthur will have me on his surveillance camera and I will be wired up so if there is anything slightly out of order I will get my ass outta there pdq."

Lord Henry was sitting next to Christina and grabbed her hand saying, "Chrissie; I agree it is not ideal for Jonny to put himself in danger. But rest assured I will put some additional measures in place to try and minimise the threat. Let's get this done and then we can ask Aiyana to come back and involve her in the treasure hunt."

Barry replied, "Good idea. And I've been thinking that I need to get back to the University soon to prepare for the new student intake. I know Christina has to finally edit her article on the Bristol Hippodrome. It would be good to get back to something resembling normal life."

Christina nodded and Sue agreed saying, "And it will be great to meet Aiyana at last. Oh, and by the way, I have contacted a friend of mine to come and have a look at the revealed painting. I am ninety-nine per cent sure it is an early Gainsborough but I need another expert to see it to be sure. Would you like to have a look before we retire for the night? As I indicated earlier I have some new information that I know is going to intrigue you. Let's go to the studio."

Of course they were all keen to hear and see the latest news so they got up and followed Sue into her studio holding excited conversations along the way. Once in the studio Sue dimmed the main lights but switched on a soft spotlight over the easel containing the painting. They all gathered around the stand and gasped at the beauty of the painting. It featured two main subjects, both male and wearing white wigs and a full skirted coat over white silk stockings. One of the men was bowing low with a tricorn hat in his hand. The other was seated with a small table beside him. He was holding up a document in one hand and a feather quill in his other hand. The room was quite ornate with scarlet drapes behind the person seated. Sue explained her thoughts with a smile on her face.

"Checking against other available images on line, if I am not mistaken the person seated is King George II. And I assume the person bowing is your ancestor Robert Davies. I'll explain why I think this in a moment. But first of all you will notice there are two further people sitting next to the person bowing, watching what is going on and both in traditional 'Native American' clothes. One is young woman and the other a child of about three years old."

Sue pointed to the couple saying, "These two are very interesting. Checking on the Internet the costume on the woman indicates she is of very high status—probably the daughter of a Tribal Chief. This sort of dress is only worn on ceremonial occasions. So who is she? My guess is that she is the wife of the person I suspect of being Robert Davies and the child is his son or daughter—difficult to tell from the painting. The pattern on the costumes could indicate which tribe she is from but I have not found any information that gives conclusive evidence. But we have a friend who might know don't we?"

In unison they said, "Aiyana."

Sue continued, "Yes. I don't want to send her a photo of the complete painting yet but I have taken a shot of the dress worn by the woman and her child. I think it would be safe to send it to Aiyana for her thoughts."

Jonny said, "E-mail me the jpg and I'll get it across Sue. I need to update her with a few things anyway."

Sue replied, "Thanks Jonny. I'll send it to you later today. But there is something else in the painting that I want to point out—this document being held up. This is why I think that it is Robert Davies who is bowing."

She took a magnifying glass and placed it over the document saying, "It is difficult to be completely sure. There are a few cracks in the paint and varnish, but I can make out parts of it. I can just about see the words 'land' and 'Massach'; probably Massachusetts. Also the name Robert Davies. Additional readable words are 'given by my hand'. At the top—very clearly—is the King George II seal and the words 'by the Grace of God'. His image is on the left.

"Checking examples of historic documents online, I'm going to deduce that the document in the painting is the deeds to land ownership in Massachusetts in the name of Robert Davies. It is likely that in return for his help in keeping the shipping lanes clear for trade while operating under an official 'Letter of Marque, ' your ancestor was rewarded with a parcel of land in Massachusetts by King George II. It is in line with the trail your father was following Jonny, as well as the information from Aiyana's mother. It was also quite common practice during

Great Britain's colonisation of North America. It is not absolute proof of course, but with a bit of additional research we could find the key. Thinking it through, it is likely that at some time in the past someone in that Religious Community must have known about the Gainsborough and its true significance. Robert Davies could have used it in any claim on the land. Hence their desire to keep it locked away."

Jonny said, "Wow! So Robert was a bit of a hero then?"

"I'm not sure about that Jonny. He could have been guarding slave ships. However, it increasingly looks like he did something that pleased the King and was rewarded for it. Robert Davies was probably keen to document his grant of land in Boston at this time and so commissioned Thomas Gainsborough to paint a picture of him receiving it from George II. No digital cameras back then to do the job Jonny. Robert might have met the artist during smuggling visits to the River Orwell in Suffolk because the date on the painting lines up with Gainsborough's activities in that area during that period when smuggling by pirates was rife. The artist was not known in Court at that time so he probably used an image of George II from another court artist for his painting. This was a common practice but it could make the painting the first Gainsborough to feature George II.

But now you will have to excuse me because I need to do some more work on the faked-up painting for the handover tomorrow. I suggest you all adjourn to the lounge and I will see you in the morning—probably very bleary eyed."

She then noticed Barry looking intently at the painting with his eyes screwed up tight. She said, "Do you have a question Barry? You can come up and view the painting closer as long as you don't touch it."

Barry rose from his seat and approached the painting. Pointing to a little mini-scene painted in the background just above the deeds he said, "Look! What have we here?"

The mini-scene showed a rowing boat on a narrow river moored next to a small building. Nearby was a mansion. Barry continued, "I think this might add more substance to our thoughts about the smuggler's hut. And if this is our hut then there appears to be a mansion where Home Farm now stands."

They all take a closer look and Lord Henry spoke first saying, "Well spotted, Barry. Artists used to place mini-scenes in the background. Sometimes at the request of the person commissioning the painting and at other times to give the image a geographical positioning. It could be important when viewed in relationship with other clues to the mystery unfolding."

They all said their goodnights and thanked her for the amazing work and then obediently trooped out of the studio and back to the lounge for coffee. As soon as he had finished his coffee Jonny said he needed an early night and left them talking about the painting and what it could mean. He thought the Land Deed image on the painting was almost too true to believe. But there it was. And what about the two 'Native Americans? More pieces of this jigsaw were coming together and he thought he must update Aiyana about this latest news once Sue had e-mailed the jpg. Returning to his room he showered and was sitting on the edge of his bed in just his white boxers, full of trepidation about what might lie ahead tomorrow. Looking at his phone he wanted to speak to someone. He didn't want to disturb Sandy and Devlin muttering, "At least someone looks like they're getting some sex."

Most of all it was Jacob he needed to talk to but he had promised to give him space to think things through. However his desire to talk to him was such that he dialled the number and the phone was quickly answered, "Hi Jonny! Are you OK?"

Jonny replied rather guiltily, "No. No I'm not really. Sorry to bother you but I have some serious shit to do tomorrow and I just need someone to talk to. No that's not right either; not just someone—I needed to speak to you. If nothing else I want your friendship Jacob."

Jacob gave the reassuring reply, "Of course you have my friendship Jonny. That's a given. I am always here for you and I will help if I can. So go ahead. I am listening. What's up?"

After swearing Jacob to secrecy Jonny explained what he had to do the next day and, despite his bravado during the earlier meeting with the others, he admitted to Jacob that he was feeling pretty concerned as to how it may all end. However, still keeping up the bravado he laughed and said, "I am too beautiful to die just yet and there are so many things I want to do—one of those being you sweetheart. But just knowing you care and that you are there for me is enough for the moment."

Jacob was very worried and replied, "Oh fuck Jonny! This shit is real. Of course I care. But what if something happens and we never…you know?"

Happy that Jacob was thinking this way Jonny chuckled contentedly and said, "What, discover you wanted to have some boy on boy with me? Well, you will have to just let your imagination run wild. I will call you when it is over."

Jacob answered, "I think about it all the time Jonny. Please keep safe and don't be a hero. Speak tomorrow."

They said their goodbyes and Jonny lay down on his bed feeling much happier that they had spoken. He now felt relatively calm, although with stuff buzzing around his head he still doubted that sleep would be forthcoming. He e-mailed Aiyana with the jpg with a brief message without going into detail about the next day's plans. He then sent a text to Arthur who replied with more positive news that he had already spoken to Lord Henry and they were sorting out some extra security for the next day. Now more relaxed, Jonny closed his eyes and fell asleep straight away.

Chapter 15

Man did not weave the web of life. He is merely a strand in it. Whatever he does to the web, he does to himself.
(Chief Seattle Native American saying)

Day 10 Friday Morning
25 August
Mayhew Estate

Jonny was rudely awakened by the harsh repetitive bleep of his alarm clock at 6 o'clock in the morning. It felt like he had only slept for a few minutes but he had in fact slept the whole night through. Thinking about the day ahead he put on some black joggers and a T-shirt and ran down to the gym to freshen up with a workout. Barry was already there giving the punch bag a serious beating. Jonny said, "Morning Baz. Fancy a spot of kick boxing?"

Barry stopped for a minute and looked at Jonny remembering the last spell of kick boxing that got a bit heavy. He replied, "That would be good Jonny. Do some warm-up moves and I will be with you in a mo. As it happens I need to talk to you about something personal that I hope will please you."

Jonny gave him a quizzical look, nodded and sauntered off to do some stretching exercises. After a few minutes Barry put on some boxing mittens and walked over saying, "Let's work on your foot movement first. Then we can look at your hand direction and force."

Jonny replied, "Sounds good. Let's go."

After some minutes improving Jonny's footwork they started to work on his hands and getting more force into his punches. In between punches Jonny said, "What's this personal stuff you want to talk about then?"

After a few seconds Barry said, "Ah yes. As you know, your mum and I have been seeing each other for many years and have a lot of affection for each other...well, love for each other and ...well; how would you feel if I asked her to marry me?"

Jonny stopped mid punch and put his head on one side looking at Barry with a smirk.

"That's wonderful. I would love for you to get legal and make my mum your wife."

He put his arms around Barry slapping him on the back saying, "Bloody fantastic. Have you asked her yet?"

Looking at Jonny with half a smile Barry replied, "Um well, no actually. I plan to ask her as soon as I go upstairs. But I wanted to talk to you first. I am nervous to be honest. What if she says no?"

Jonny responded with, "Easy. You just carry on as before. Brilliant news. Let's box-step dad-to-be Baz. I need to clear my mind for later today and this works for me."

Continuing with the work out Barry gave a rueful reply and a punch catching Jonny off-guard saying, "Just Barry will be fine Jonny."

They both laughed and continued some more general work before a sweating and breathless Jonny said, "OK. That's enough for me now. Catch you later."

He went upstairs to his room for a shower, with a big smile on his face and humming to himself thinking, *Well, if anything happens to me this afternoon, at least I know Mum will be OK; new friends and Baz as a husband. Yeah she will be OK.*

He quickly showered and got dressed; as always in black tee-shirt and black jeans. Then he made his way down to the kitchen for a spot of breakfast.

Sandy was just putting some coffee in the café tier as he walked in and hugged her from behind saying, "Well then, darling, I am all ears. Let's have the details. Did you get laid, sweetheart?"

Sandy turned and smiled bashfully. Then in a quiet but gushing voice said, "Oh boy; am I'm a bit sore? It's been a while but it was a fabulous night. He is an amazing lover and a wonderful man. Ooh Jonny I am so happy. Did you and Jacob make it hun?"

A slightly jealous Jonny replied, "Not yet babe but I am working on it. I am really happy for you though. He is yummy. Have you seen anyone about the house yet?"

Sandy answered, "No; not yet. But I have only just walked in. Do you want some toast?"

The always hungry Jonny said, "Yes please—and peanut butter."

He then remembered that Sandy did not know about the late phone call yesterday and the plans for the day. In a more serious tone he said, "I need to get you up to speed hun. We had a call from Sully last night. Later today I have to deliver their painting to the Willcome Inn—on my own. Sue has been working on it until the early hours of this morning. To be honest I'm a bit fucking apprehensive, but Arthur will make sure I am tooled up with electronic gear. It will have to be more sophisticated than that we used at the Slap because they will be looking out for it."

Sandy immediately rushed over to give him a hug saying, "Oh shit Jonny."

Jonny continued, "His Lordship is going to provide backup. And that brings me to something I have been mulling over for some time. What the fuck is your brother-in-law into? He knows a hell of a lot more than he lets on."

Sandy thought before she spoke.

"Mmm; I'm not sure hun. He certainly has fingers in many pies and discloses very little. If she does know much about it my sister never lets on either. And I think Bryn knows more than you would think."

The toaster popped up the toast just as Barry and Christina walked in hand in hand, followed by Sue and Lord Henry. Barry clapped his hands and said, "Gather around everyone. Chrissie and I have an announcement to make."

When he had their attention he continued, "As you know we have been a couple for many years and all this drama has made us realise just how much we mean to each other. So I have asked Chrissie if she will marry me and she has accepted."

Raising his voice above the cheers and cries of, "About bloody time."

He continued, "Jonny has also given us his permission."

Jonny shouted, "Yeah. Go Baz. Within a few days I have discovered a half-sister I didn't know about and now I'm gaining a step-dad."

This was followed by much laughter and lots of congratulatory hugs.

Lord Henry said, "Looks like it's bubbles for breakfast then Sue. Wonderful news."

After breakfast, Lord Henry took Jonny aside and asked him to accompany him to his study to go over details of the hand-over and to talk to Arthur. Bryn was already in the room as they entered. Lord Henry sat in front of his computer, turned it on and moved the screen around so they could all see and said, "Right then take a seat and we will have a chat with our communications wizard."

He dialled up Arthur who as usual answered straight away—appearing on the screen within seconds. As soon as he appeared Lord Henry said, "Ah Arthur. Good morning. I know you and I have already talked about this but I have Jonny and Bryn with me now and we are discussing our requirements for this afternoon. Can you let us know where the enemy is at the moment?"

Arthur replied, "Um yes. Um they are all at the Willcome Inn—Will, Ssully and Ttony. Um unfortunately they hhave turned off the CCTV so I ccan't see what's ggoing on inside. Bbut I will ssort out Jjonny with a mmini camera. I also have ssupplied Lord Henry wwith a um Mmicro Drone fitted with a camera."

Jonny said, "Thanks buddy. I owe you big time. Is there anything I can pick up for you on my way over?"

Arthur replied with a smile, "Oh yyes. Chocolate aand um Ppepsi Max please."

Jonny gave a thumbs up to the screen camera. Lord Henry explained that Jonny would be with him at about 1.30 pm. Going over the timescale and the minutia of the hand-over plan so they all knew the details he concluded, "We want to keep this pretty simple—in, hand-over and getting out. But in case it should all go awry Bryn and I will be following. Christina and Barry will also be in Bristol checking up on their properties but I do not envisage that they will be involved in the hand-over at all."

As Jonny left the meeting Lord Henry gave him a tank top made from some very tough tight mesh material saying, "For extra safety make sure you wear this underneath your clothes today Jonny; it's puncture proof. Hopefully all will go to plan, but if things do go wrong it could save your life."

Jonny noticed how serious Lord Henry was and thought, *Shit! He looks a bit worried.*

Back in his room, taking off his black T-shirt, he popped the garment on and checked his appearance in the mirror saying quietly to himself, "Yeah it fits OK and is not too uncomfortable. If Lord Henry thinks it is important then so be it. Let's hope I don't have to test just how good it is."

Putting his T-shirt back on over the tank top he checked that the new garment didn't show through. He decided it did, and so before going out into the gardens to say goodbye to Jacob he put on a black button-down shirt that disguised things better. In fact, he remembered that Arthur had requested shirt buttons.

There was a freshness in the air that made him think of Autumn. He wasn't sure where Jacob was, so he took his time and just meandered around taking in the beautiful Italian style gardens until he spied Jacob engrossed in pruning some plants in the orangery. He leaned up against a tree and just enjoyed the sight of Jacob doing a job he loved. Jacob stopped what he was doing and turned around saying, "I could feel you watching me. How are you doing?"

Jonny smiled and answered, "Just enjoying the view. And I wanted to see you before I left for Bristol; you know, just in-case."

Jacob put down his pruning shears, took a deep breath and walked over to Jonny. He took him by the hand and led him inside to a private area in the orangery. Looking him straight in the eyes he cupped his hands around Jonny's face and kissed him on the lips; gently at first but then with more insistence and tongues entwined. Jonny responded and put his arms around Jacob's bum pulling him close. Through his jeans he could feel the growing hardness of Jacob's erection rubbing up against his own so he pulled away and put his hand on Jacob's crutch saying quietly and with a grin on his face, "Well, well. So I deduce from the reaction of your cock that you like me a little. It would be nice if we could have a little play now but it will have to be later. Sadly I need to get going."

Jacob drew him close again and said, "For God's sake Jonny please be careful. And promise to phone me when it's done."

Jonny turned to go but says over his shoulder, "I promise I will call; and you will see me later."

As he strode away, he heard Jacob mutter a line from Dylan Thomas's famous poem:

Do not go gentle into that good night.

Jonny stopped and turned around and completed the line with, "And death shall have no dominium."

Now feeling happy, but still apprehensive, Jonny made his way back to the house, and into his room to pick up his back pack. He checked that he was wearing the wrist band gift from Aiyana. Looking out of the window he said quietly, "Hope you are with me Great Spirit. I might need your protection."

Right on time a warm breeze rustled the leaves on a Japanese maple tree outside where a beautiful Jay was sitting. A strangely comforting feeling enveloped Jonny and he said, "Thank you Great Spirit. I know you are there."

After fully absorbing the moment he went down to the kitchen where they were all to meet and grab a quick bite to eat.

By 12.30 pm they were just about ready to leave. Bryn and Lord Henry were in a black Mercedes Benz C class with darkened windows. Barry and Christina joined them and were to be dropped off at the University where Barry could check his post and pick up his PT Cruiser. They would then drive to Christina's house to check all was well and get some fresh clothes, and then on to Barry's to do likewise. Barry would swap cars there so he could take his '57 Chevrolet back to Mayhew as Lord Henry expressed an interest in looking at it.

Jonny was in his own Mini Cooper with a canvas carrying case containing the painting on the back seat. He had put on the communication device that Arthur had given him for the trip to London and he also gave a set to Henry and Bryn so they could be in contact.

The drive down to Bristol was uneventful and they made good time. Henry and Bryn parked up in the Gallery car park where he had a season ticket. There was a car park in Queen Charlotte Street that was closer to the Willcome Inn but the thinking was that they didn't want to be too close in case they were spotted by Sully and Tony.

They then walked through Castle Park and headed to the river and along Welsh back. They passed the Redcliffe Bascule Bridge and stopped to check out the area—again not getting too close to the Willcome Inn. Lord Henry had arranged for a 'friend' to do any close monitoring and he was already in position and had a hidden communication device that Arthur had remotely tuned to their private channel. Lord Henry checked that he and Bryn could contact him.

"OK Tom."

The thumbs-up signal was given. They then retired to the 'Riverstation' where they could sit outside and be within striking distance of any action when Jonny arrived.

Meanwhile Jonny had stopped off at a shop and picked up the Pepsi and a large bar of Galaxy chocolate for Arthur. He added some jelly babies, crisps and a sandwich for himself, before completing the journey.

As usual Arthur knew he had arrived and was standing at the top of the metal staircase with his cat Icon winding lithely around his legs. As he lowered the metal ladder that enabled access to the attic he called down and asked Jonny to bring the painting up with him—a bit difficult climbing a step ladder. Once Jonny and the painting had made it to the attic balcony, Icon left via a precarious route that only a fit cat could manage. Once down in the garden he looked up giving Jonny and Arthur a malevolent glare. Putting his arm around Arthur's shoulder Jonny greeted him with, "Hi buddy. It's good to see you. I have your supplies. Lord Henry said you have some little gadgets for me."

Arthur replied, "Umm yyes. Umm llet mme show you."

Jonny followed his friend into the attic room and took a seat. Arthur walked over to his desk where he picked up one of several plastic zip lock bags and drew out two round devices that were about the size of a fifty pence piece. He explained to Jonny how to activate and use them. Because the Cantana brothers would be very concerned that Jonny would be wired up Arthur also gave him a tiny combined video camera/microphone unit in the form of a shirt button. This replaced the existing communication system used at the Slap. Choosing a colour to match those on his shirt he took some time to replace one button on his shirt with the camera unit button. Then using tweezers he inserted a micro sound pick-up inside his ear channel so that it was completely invisible to the naked eye. He then he asked to see the painting and took a lot of time examining it closely before giving it back saying, "Ggood job by Ssue."

He then summarised the latest situation.

"Um the um nnasties are um at the Willcome Inn. Will iis with them. Um and of great interest there is a twin-hull Ppower boat at the Wwillcome Inn mooring. It um arrived this morning. They wwent down to mmeet it and were um handed the keys. Llooks like they are pplanning a quick getaway and high tide is around 4 pm. The ttwo members of the um ddelivery team then ddisappeared. At the um moment it iis only ththose um three in the Inn. Unfortunately all CCTV is still tturned off—inside um and outside the ppremises. As you know I have pprovided Lord Henry with that mmicro drone that we can um ffly. It mmight give some inside ccoverage if um needed."

Jonny said, "I don't know how to thank you Arty. For the first time in my life I am actually very scared. But it is good to know that you are here watching and listening. I need to go now buddy. See you on the other side."

As he left with the painting strapped to his back he received a text from Barry. It read, *All OK at my house. On way to Chrissie's place.*

It was around 2 pm when Jonny waved goodbye to Arthur and got in his car. Before driving off he thought that he'd better reply to Barry's text, letting him know that he was going to get something to eat before going to the Willcome Inn. He then drove to the Queen Charlotte Street car park and put the rear seats down flat. He laid the canvass bag containing the painting down on the deck and covered it with a rug to hide it from any prying eyes. It was a short walk to one of the kiosks down on the quay where he bought a bacon and egg bap before sitting on one of the benches overlooking the river. Arthur's voice came in loud and clear.

"I can ssee you from a CCTV ccamera Jonny. I ccan also um ssee the um rriver from your um bbutton ccamera."

Jonny took out his mobile so it didn't look like he was talking to himself and replied, "Good to hear I am not alone buddy."

Lord Henry also answered with, "We can hear you loud and clear. You have about three quarters of an hour before you hand over the painting. We will be fairly close to you so we can get to you quite quickly if necessary."

Jonny responded with, "OK. And at least we know all my techie bits are in working order so that's another worry out of the way; not as though I expected anything else from Arty. I am just having something to eat before going back to my car.

The Willcome has a few customer parking spaces, so I will pop the Mini there; leaving it unlocked in case I need a quick get-away. But just a thought; what do I do if they realise it is not the right painting?"

Lord Henry responded with a chuckle, "I guess you run Jonny. You run like hell."

Taking a bite out of his bap Jonny said, "Wow thanks. That's filled me with a lot of confidence."

Lord Henry came back, "Don't worry. Sue knows her business. I'm confident that part of the plan is secure."

Jonny sat for a few minutes just taking in the view and he smiled to himself. But it was a smile without humour; more of an expression of a helpless acceptance of his current situation. Watching the Bristolians and others wander past on the quay, some tourists, but many going about their normal daily business, he thought to himself, *There is nothing normal about my business today. But hey, Que Sera.*

With that thought in his head and whistling the tune from *Kismet*, he got up from his seat and strolled back to his car and drove slowly to the Willcome Inn.

It was now just coming up to 2.55 pm. He parked beside a red Evoque that must have replaced the one that ended up in the stream while chasing his mum riding Wiggy. The garage couldn't have dried out the original one so quickly. He took a deep breath and said, "Well, here goes nothing chaps. Into the breach and all that bollocks."

Lord Henry gave the encouraging reply, "We've got your back Jonny."

He retrieved the canvas carrying case and painting from the back of the Mini and with some trepidation made his way to the familiar entrance to the Willcome Inn. He tried the door but it was locked. So he pressed the bell and the door was suddenly yanked open. There was Sully with a sinister grin on his face—well, more of a sneer really. Making a gesture for Jonny to enter he drawled, "Ah Jonny; so nice to see you. Do come in."

Holding the painting out in front of him Jonny replied more in hope than anything else, "Nah, I am in a bit of a hurry. Here's the painting."

Sully's arm reached out and grabbed his wrist, pulling him inside and slamming the door closed behind them. His drawl was now a snarl as he said, "I said fucking come in you twat. Now say hello to my slightly psychotic brother Tony. I think you missed each other when you visited The Slap and he is a bit upset about that. He is also on a promise with your friend Sandy, a date he plans to keep soon. I would advise not upsetting him because he does enjoy inflicting pain."

Tony was sprawled on one of the comfy chairs by the bar window. He was fingering the sharp edge of a huge Japanese sword resting casually across his lap as he sneered, "Hey kid. How are you doin'? Why don't you bring the painting over here so's we can have a detailed look-see? Come on pretty boy. Don't be shy."

You could almost smell the evil in his voice.

Jonny got a hefty shove in the back from Sully and decided it would be a good idea not to argue with him, so he walked—or nearly stumbled—over to the window. It was only then that he noticed Will in the opposite chair looking brighter than he did the other day. But his face was still swollen in varying shades of purple and yellow and he was trying hard not to look Jonny in the eye.

Jonny placed the bag on the table and unzipped it all the way around until the painting was revealed.

With a continuing cruel smile Tony said, "Now you little poof; I assume you are wired. So I just want your friends to know that if you are trying to cheat us I will cut your fucking head off so fast that your eyes will be looking up at your ass."

Jonny held his breath while Tony and Sully inspected the painting. He noticed Sully was paying extra attention to the back of the painting under the frame.

After a while Sully looked up, smiled and said, "Well done, Jonny. It appears that it is all in order."

A slightly relieved Jonny thought, *Great work, Sue.*

He said, "Well then, in that case I will be on my way."

He started to head for the door, only for Sully to shout, "Where the fuck do you think you're going. Stop right there. Until we are safely outta here you stay put."

Jonny stopped dead and turned around to face Sully pleading, "Aw come on man. I've done what you've asked. You've got your painting."

Sully snarled back, "So you think that's it then Jonny? You have been an annoying little fucker and caused us a shit load of grief. Now do as you are told because, as Chuck Berry would say, it's time for Jonny to be good."

Sully laughed at what he considered to be a joke. He was the only one laughing though. Even his brother kept quiet.

Jonny wondered if it would be possible to drop the two of them. He hadn't a clue how and thought better of it when Lord Henry spoke in his ear.

"Just do what they say for the moment Jonny. Don't react. Just go along with them."

Tony jumped up saying, "Come and sit with your Nancy boy pal Will. Sully and me have one or two things that we gotta do."

As Jonny walked reluctantly towards Will, Tony grabbed him and very gently puts his sword against Jonny's cheek, slightly drawing it down about two inches. As he did it words drizzled out of Tony's saliva dribbling mouth.

"This blade is my baby. She gives me ecstasy with the lightest touch. Oh man; I am hard just thinking about it."

He shoved Jonny down onto the seat beside Will saying, "Isn't that nice? Two pretty pansies sitting together. No touching though."

Jonny can feel the blood running down his cheek from the sword blade stroke. He turned towards Will who muttered, "Sorry Jonny."

Wiping the blood from his face with the back of his hand Jonny snarled, "Yeah. Whatever Will."

Tony turned back towards the two lads, threatening them both by lifting the sword above his head as he shouted, "Shut the fuck up."

Sully thought it time to chip in before his brother did something stupid and through gritted teeth he said, "Leave them alone Tony; it's not worth the hassle. Help me count the money for the planned exchange at sea."

Tony reluctantly turned back towards Sully, who was putting two briefcases on one of the round tables that were in the bar. He started to remove wads of cash from one of them and Tony did the same with the other, counting the notes and putting a band around them in hundreds before laying the banded money neatly back in the briefcase. It took some time because there was a lot to count.

Jonny thought, *Probably money from drugs and the massage parlours as well as the club and the Willcome Inn. Sully said 'exchange' so maybe picking up a new supply of drugs.*

When it had been sorted and packed, Tony started to stride off in the direction of the gent's loo's saying, "Right then ladies! A quick trip to the boy's room and then we are off."

Turning to Will Jonny muttered from the corner of his mouth, "His blatant unfunny homophobia is starting to piss me off."

Will whispered, "For fuck's sake just leave it Jonny. He means what he says about taking your head off."

Lord Henry's voice also came in his earpiece.

"Just do what they say for the moment Jonny. Don't do anything rash."

When Tony arrived back in the bar, Jonny thought, *I need to do something. That fucker is itching to do some damage with that sword. Maybe if I rush him I can get that sword away from him. But what about his brother?*

His brain was working in overtime when Sully said, "Right, my turn for a piss, Tony. Try and just watch Jonny without hurting anyone, will you."

Tony just sniggered as he watched his brother leave the room and then walked over to Jonny and Will until he was about three feet away. Jonny took a look in the direction that Sully went and thought, *Now.*

He launched himself at Tony with the intention of grabbing the sword. But he underestimated just how fast Tony could move. Uttering a Samurai scream, Tony slashed forward in and arc catching Jonny across his middle. Jonny felt his breath leave his body with the force of the blow and sat down heavily on the floor. Doubled over retching and feeling dizzy, out of the corner of his eye he saw Will jump up shouting, "No."

There was then a loud explosion and as Jonny looked up Tony hit the deck like a stone.

Still on the floor himself Jonny looked down at his stomach. But there was no blood; just a cut shirt exposing the puncture proof material of the tank top given to him by Lord Henry. He could also hear Lord Henry and Arthur shouting, "Jonny are you OK."

Jonny caught his breath and muttered, "I am fine; I think."

He looked up to see Sully, gun in hand, bending over Tony with Will stood next to him. Will stared at the body in shock. In full panic mode he shouted, "Fuck! Fuck! You've killed him. Sully; you've fucking killed him."

He then looked at Jonny and said, "And I saw Tony slice you with that fucking sword. Why are you not in two fucking halves?"

Sully turned around and looked at Jonny as if he had just recalled he was there. Still with the gun in his hand he was very pale. His eyes looked haunted as he took a step towards Jonny who was still on the floor. Grabbing the top of Jonny's arm he pulled him up straight and looked at his abdomen and torn shirt. With a puzzled look he grunted. He then put the barrel of his gun at Jonny's temple and said, "I think that was your ninth life ass-hole. We are leaving and you are going to be our passport. Either that or you are dead."

He turned to a still shocked Will and said, "I was not going to stand by and let my psychopathic brother carve you up. God knows why but I have feelings for you. Grab the money and the painting. We need to leave now."

Tony pressed the gun hard against Jonny's temple and frog-marched him towards the door. Deciding that discretion was the greater part of valour, Jonny did not put up a fight at this point. Sully growled, "Will! Just in case Jonny has some friends or cops outside stay very close to me. Lock the door behind us and let's get to the boat as quickly as possible."

As all three exited the Willcome Inn and started walking towards the quay, Lord Henry's voice came in Jonny's ear.

"Jonny. Don't react, but we are to the left of you. Try and keep as calm as possible. While he has that gun at your head we can't do anything."

The sleek and fast looking twin-hull powerboat was moored at the quay. Will boarded first and put the painting and the brief cases securely underneath the controls at the front of the boat. Jonny was next to board with Sully right behind him, now with the gun pressing between Jonny's shoulder blades. Shoving the gun hard Sully instructed Jonny to sit on one of the bench seats on the inside edge of the boat saying, "Now sit there and don't move while I cast off."

Turning to Will he said, "Right here are the keys. Now start the fucking engines."

Sully casting off gave Jonny a few seconds to put his hands in his pockets pulled out the silver discs that Arthur had given him. He placed them in palm of his hands. The twin engines of the powerboat barked into life, and as they pulled away from the quay, Sully turned back towards Jonny and sat down.

Looking back to the quay, Jonny saw Lord Henry and Bryn running down towards another boat. Sully also saw them and raised his gun in their direction. For a moment his focus was off Jonny who had time to rub the discs in his palms together. He jumped up behind Sully and slammed them on either side of his face before he could shoot. There was a satisfying crack and Sully stiffened before falling forward, dropping the gun overboard and into the River Avon. Jonny saw his chance and dived overboard. Swimming for his life he reached the embankment, to be hauled out by Lord Henry and Bryn. Grimacing as they got him on dry land Lord Henry said, "Thank God you are OK. You had us worried for a bit. Come on let's get you to your mother's apartment and out of those wet clothes."

But Jonny pulled away and heading back towards the Willcome Inn he shouted, "NO! I can't. Tony has been shot. He's lying in the bar and probably dead."

Henry yelled at him saying, "Stop! It is being sorted Jonny. Don't worry about it. Everything is under control. Let's just get away from here; sooner rather than later. There are things we need to put in place because the police will be all over the place shortly."

Jonny stopped and exhaled. He then turned around and looked at Henry and Bryn. With some exasperation in his voice he said, "Just what the fuck is going on? Who are you guys anyway?"

In a calm voice Lord Henry replied, "Jonny, we will talk later. But right now we have to go."

With that he turned away and walked towards Jonny's Mini. Jonny looked at Bryn who beckoned him to follow.

Jonny didn't hesitate any longer and stomped off to his car thinking, *This is bloody bizarre. It's like I am caught up in some crazy spy movie.*

He had left his keys in his Mini in case he needed a quick get-away. He opened the driver's door, but Henry gently moved him away and in his calm but firm voice said, "I will drive. You may be a bit shocked."

Jonny replied, "Yeah, OK. I am a bit shaken up; but I would like some answers."

He started to shake. Partly because he was soaking wet and partly because he started to realised that he had come close to having his life snuffed out. So he meekly walked around to the passenger seat of his car while Lord Henry got into the driver' seat. He noticed a look pass between Lord Henry and Bryn and thought to himself, *There is more to this. I want to know what is going on.*

Bryn told them that he would go and get the Mercedes and meet them at Christina's Clifton apartment.

By the time they were pulling up in front of his mother's Apartment Jonny was feeling a bit calmer and had totally forgotten about the cut on his face. As they got out of the Mini Lord Henry said, "I will come up with you to stop your mother having a fit when she sees you wet and with a knife cut on your face."

Jonny gently touched the side of his face and replied, "Thank you Henry. That means I can jump into the shower immediately without having to ward off a barrage of questions."

Once at the apartment Jonny pressed the button and the door clicked open. Christina and Barry were waiting at the door and were very shocked at the state of Jonny but he didn't stop to explain. He headed straight for the bathroom leaving the explanations to Lord Henry who put his arm around Christina and manoeuvred her in the direction of the sitting room.

The hot shower was just what Jonny needed and he was soon dressed in some fresh clothes from the wardrobe in his old bedroom. The cut wasn't too deep so he applied some Savlon and put a plaster over it. Feeling more himself he sauntered into the living room.

They were all seated drinking coffee. Barry and Christina were sat close together holding hands listening intently to Lord Henry. But the conversation stopped as soon as Jonny entered. Christina jumped up to hug her son saying, "Oh Jonny. Henry has been explaining everything."

Not knowing how much Lord Henry had said Jonny gently patted his mother on the back and said, "I am fine mum; don't panic; all is cool. A coffee would be nice though. Oh and can I have some toast?"

He flopped down on one of the sofas and said, "God I am hungry. So, what's next?"

Barry said, "Your mother and I are going to stay here for a night or two. But Henry would like you to go back with him and we are all meeting up at Mayhew on Sunday."

Jonny came back with, "That's fine with me. I've got a date with a Rose tonight. My phone is ruined though. Evidently it didn't like being fully immersed in river water. Do you have Jacob's number by any chance Henry?"

Henry took his phone out of his pocket and thumbed through his contact list before handing it to Jonny saying, "There you go. It's ringing."

Jonny took the phone just as Jacob answered hello. A hopeful Jonny said, "Hi. I made it out alive. Scarred and wet but still here. My phone is ruined which is why I am using Lord Henry's mobile. Do you still want to see me tonight?"

Jacob eagerly replied, "Yes please. I would like that very much."

A relieved Jonny said

"OK. I will see you later. I'm at mum's place and I have an old phone around here somewhere. I will put my chip in it. Hopefully it will work. I'll give you a bell later."

Jonny then heard the words he had been waiting to hear as Jacob said, "Oh, before you go Jonny. The answer is yes"

Jonny smiled and before handing the phone back to Lord Henry he said, "Thank God."

Christina came back from the kitchen and handed Jonny a plate of toast and coffee which he wolfed down as if he hadn't eaten for a month. Christina put her hands on her hips and said, "I swear my child has worms. He never puts on a pound."

With that she ruffled his hair fondly and said, "I love you my son. But you do like to bump up my anxiety levels."

Once Jonny had finished his toast and coffee he went to find another mobile phone. As soon as he had returned Lord Henry got up and turning to Christina and Barry said, "Right! We had better go now. See you both on Sunday."

With that he quickly chivvied Jonny out of the apartment and down the stairs. Bryn was waiting outside in the Mercedes he had retrieved from the Gallery car park. Lord Henry strode towards it saying, "Leave your car here Jonny. I need to talk to you and the back of the Mercedes is secure."

It sounded more like an instruction so Jonny followed Lord Henry into the back seats. Once sat down he placed his now dry mobile phone chip into one of his spare phones. The swim in the river Avon had ruined his main unit. Once the phone had gone through its start up, he noticed he had a message from Aiyana. It said that she had consulted with one of the Native American historians and it would appear the clothing worn by the Native American in the painting was indeed of her tribe. The message went on to indicate that there is not much written history about the tribe; only oral history and folklore, but there is a story of one of Aiyana's ancestors via her mother's side going to England so those in the painting could be ancestors of Aiyana.

He thought, *Great. Another part of the puzzle is being revealed. I must tell Lord Henry.*

He glanced over to Lord Henry to let him know, but he was busy finishing a text. When complete Lord Henry logged into a laptop that he then gave to Jonny before doing the same with another that he kept himself before saying, "Right then; time to talk to Arthur I think."

Arthur's face soon appeared on the screen and before they could greet them he said, "Um Hi. You need ttossee this. It's hhappening now south of Pportishead; a mmile or so off sshore."

The screen in front of them changed to show a bird's eye view of the twin-hulled power boat used by Sully and Will alongside a huge motor yacht; obviously with a very rich owner and one capable of Transatlantic or Pacific crossings. It even had a helipad, a stern port facility and needed a fairly large crew.

White oblong packages were being transferred from the motor yacht. Will and Sully were busy placing them into the hulls of their powerboat that was in the port area. When this was done, Will handed over what looked like the painting and Sully gave them cases containing the money. With all that done the two boats powered off in different directions—Will and Sully towards Wales while the larger super motor yacht headed out down the Bristol Channel towards the open sea. Arthur said, "It's um unusual for them to be ddoing this in bbroad daylight. They mmust um be in a hurry to land the stuff bbefore it gets too ddark."

Lord Henry watched with deep interest and said, "You could be right. Maybe they need to catch the high tide in the drop off area? I've already requested that the local boys in blue both sides of the Bristol Channel just let things happen until the local handover because I think we've got the UK Cantana hub on this one. Sully will be done for murdering his brother; an act witnessed by Will and Jonny, and you have it all captured from Jonny's camera and mic.

The Bristol Police are mopping up at the Willcome Inn and have already fished Sully's gun out of the Avon so we can match the bullet in Tony Cantana with it.

We also have CCTV footage of the Cantana brothers outside Matthew Lloyd's Gallery at the time of his murder; so a strong case can be built on that one as well. And other UK hubs across the country are being raided as we speak. Maybe those on the motor yacht already know this and want to get the exchange done ASAP so they can get to sea and back to Boston. I know you have everything recorded Arthur and that might be used as evidence. We have information from other sources that makes us fairly sure about where Sully's powerboat may be heading. The tracker on the painting will tell us where the motor yacht ends up. We are in good order."

Arthur's face appeared back on the screen saying, "The um ttracker is wworking fine on the ppainting. But unfortunately I have tto bbring the drone in nnow."

Lord Henry replied, "Understood Arthur. We've got that covered from Wales now. You can locate its signal via the usual digital site. We will catch up later but keep a watch on things. I now need to explain to poor Jonny a bit more about what is going on before his mind explodes."

He switched off his laptop and took back the one Jonny had been viewing and switched that off. Putting his head back on the seat headrest he took a deep breath. As he looked at Jonny he said, "Right then; I know that there are many unanswered questions, but before we talk about that I have to tell you that I am now going to give you information that means that you are bound by the Official Secrets Act. This is the law and at some point soon you will be asked to sign a document. Are you OK with this?"

A puzzled Jonny just muttered, "Yeah, yeah of course."

Lord Henry felt the need to stress the point to make sure Jonny fully understood the implications of what had been said and the information he was about to receive.

"Jonny I cannot emphasise this strongly enough. Are you sure you are OK with it? It means that you are not allowed to tell anyone about this unless they too have signed the Act and are in the agreed cell. That means your mum, Barry, Sandy, Jacob and Sue. The legal penalty for breaking this law is very serious."

Jonny turned to Lord Henry and after a short silence he very clearly said, "Yes Henry. I understand and I am truly OK with it."

Satisfied that the message had been rammed home Lord Henry continued, "Bryn; you are our witness. We'll do the paperwork later. Right. Now Jonny, you may already know some of this, but hopefully I can now fill in some gaps in your knowledge and clear up a few areas of confusion. First of all Bryn and I work with MI5 and MI6—but not for them. You've probably gathered that Arthur is also part of our cell. To be more specific, sometimes there are tasks to be done from which the main Government agencies like to distance themselves. So in practice you could say that we do work for the Government—but indirectly. And we do liaise with other agencies on a global scale; but again indirectly.

The Religious Community Accountants in Boston are a cover for a major global criminal syndicate with links to gangs all over the world. They have been on the FBI's hit list for years, but although several of their country syndicates have been found guilty of dealing with drugs and people smuggling, resulting in the courts closing them down, with long local jail terms for those involved, there has never been enough evidence to link them to the Boston hub. We have been part of the team investigating the UK syndicate headed by the Cantana Brothers based in Bristol.

Any link to your father was not something on the radar until his body was found in Massachusetts Bay. It took some time, but eventually someone identified him from a mug shot as a person who once worked at a hotel in Boston and they knew about his friendship with Aiyana's mother. But the FBI did not think he was British. His career was then traced to the Religious Community so Aiyana and her mother became people of interest and were on a watch list. There were no clues to any links to you Jonny.

But a year after Aiyana's mother died we got reports that she was researching a relative in the UK; something to do with a painting. Digital traffic from the Religious Community Accountants also showed that they too were interested in this. But we didn't know why, or that the painting had not been originally owned by the Religious Community Accountants because no theft was ever reported. When it was clear that she was planning a trip to the UK with the painting we thought she might help us link the Boston hub with their UK syndicate, the Cantana Brothers. So we took more interest and followed the trail she left this side of the Atlantic.

Arthur wasn't involved at this point although he knew about the Religious Community of course. However once you had asked for his help he thought he had better report it to me. That was just before Matthew Lloyd's murder was reported. After that things started to move very quickly.

Upon hearing about the murder you came to see Sue and it was only then that I became fully aware of your friendship with Sandy. Sue had known of course but I suppose it just didn't come up in conversation. That's why I asked you all to stay at Mayhew because I knew there could be danger. That decision was strengthened once we became more aware of Sue and Sandy's links with Matthew Lloyd. The reference to drugs in the initial Cardiff Police Report about the incidence interested us because the Cantana Brothers also had an Agent in South Wales and we thought that there might be a link.

Arthur went a little off-piste when he was involved in your London escapade and that annoyed me immensely. However, fortunately it ended OK. I think that's enough for now. We are pretty sure that Sully and Will's power boat is heading for the coast near Cardiff where the drugs will be handed over to the Cantana Brothers' South Wales distributer. I have arranged for the officers who handled Matthew Lloyd's murder case to organise the welcome party but I think we may need to apprehend them at sea because they might be planning to hold back the off-load until it is dark.

That will be at about 8 pm tonight. I'm sure it will be the biggest hoist the officers have been involved in and another step up in someone's career, and they must have been pretty peeved when I closed down their involvement in the Matthew Lloyd murder case a few days ago. I think we can safely return to Mayhew and leave things in their hands. I can answer any questions on the way. Bryn I think we should return to Mayhew now."

The car moved off. Turning back to Jonny Lord Henry said, "Perhaps we can continue with that treasure hunt now?"

This reminded Jonny about Aiyana's text message and he relayed it to Lord Henry who said, "Well, I never. This gets more interesting every day. I think as soon as Sully and Will are arrested and locked up we can ask Aiyana back to join us in the treasure hunt. She can stay with us at Mayhew, but don't contact her until we are sure she will be safe."

The Mercedes was now heading along Portway and Jonny thought, *Bloody hell! Official Secrets Act! Does this make me a spook?*

He then remembered that he hadn't had a snort for a whole day. Maybe the adrenalin had been enough. And in truth, he didn't feel like one now.

Chapter 16

I have seen that in any great undertaking, it is not enough for a man to depend simply upon himself.

(Sioux Native American saying)

Cardiff Police Station
Friday 25 August 4.30 pm

Back at Cardiff Police Station DCI David Thomas was sat at his desk. With a bored expression on his face he was scrolling through case notes of various crimes that had been committed around the city, wondering which one to take forward. Pleasurable thoughts of the night before with Ruth kept entering his head. Suddenly the Superintendent burst through his door saying, "DI Chambers is on her way. I have some news for you both."

Just then Ruth hurried in; smiling more than usual David thought. The Superintendent said, "Sit down Ruth. I have just had a call from the top brass and guess what? That case you were pulled off yesterday is on again. They have requested that you two continue on the case and make any arrests. It appears there is a boat expected to land somewhere around Swanbridge Bay late this afternoon.

We have been told that there is a huge drugs haul on board and a crook you identified as being one of the killers of Matthew Lloyd is on board. The name is Sully Cantana. The Serious Organised Crime Agency is involved in a support role as part of a national drugs bust. You will need to be quick and by the time you have finished all the paperwork tonight I'm afraid it's going to be very late. There is a police launch waiting for you down at the docks with armed response. This is your chance. Now go, go, go."

David and Ruth didn't hang about and were out of the room almost before the Superintendent had finished talking. They ran down to pick up some body armour from the stores and then out into the yard. In just eight minutes they were pulling out of the station. With blues and twos flashing and wailing, there was no conversation apart from occasional expletives aimed at a few road users not getting out of their way quickly enough. Within minutes they were screeching to a halt at the dockside. They grabbed their body armour and were soon running down the steps to one of the two unmarked police launches with their engines idling.

They put on the life jackets that were held out to them. After official introductions to the crew David turned to Ruth and said quietly, "Bloody hell Ruth. It looks like we may get our high-profile collar after all."

Ruth gave his arm a friendly squeeze and smiled replying with a wink, "Certainly looks that way Sir. Looks like we are on a roll so to speak."

David picked up on the need to keep to their official titles and said, "Can you get some more information about this case from the Super Ma'am; how many are on that boat and where the drugs transfer is taking place."

Turning his attention to the six armed officers on board he said, "Right then everyone. I am not sure what you have been told, but this is a huge drugs haul; part of a multi-force operation. The people involved are considered armed and dangerous, with one suspected murderer amongst them in the name of Sully Cantana. The boat they are on is a very powerful twin-hulled powerboat—much faster than our police launches so we need to get this right first time. The drugs transfer is said to be taking place somewhere in Swanbridge Bay. We have a police helicopter available to us. We also have a drone in the area. DI Chambers is trying to get additional information so we need to hold fire until we know more. We don't want to frighten them off."

Turning to the boat's helmsman he said, "Keep it slow and can you make sure the other launch follows our lead?"

The helmsman got on the radio and the launches slowly made their way out of the harbour and headed West towards Swanbridge Bay while Ruth waited for more information from the station. It wasn't long before it came through. She said, "OK. I have been informed that a twin-hulled powerboat has stopped just off the windward side of Sully Island—probably so they can't be seen so easily from the mainland so it could be where the transfer is taking place. There are two people on board. There is a small cabin boat heading towards it carrying a further two people. The Serious Organised Crime Agency has been watching a caravan on a small caravan park for a few days. It is just opposite the island. These men are known local drugs dealers and have been staying there with a boat moored nearby. The police helicopter is already in the air simulating a training exercise with the Barry Island lifeboat so as not to arouse suspicion. The drone is also flying nearby on standby."

David mused to himself, *Sully Island eh? What a strange coincidence. It was known as a smugglers' haunt a couple of centuries ago and Sully Cantana is on the powerboat. Maybe it's a good omen.*

David said, "Sully Island has a causeway but it is now close to high tide so it should be completely cut off at the moment. I think we need to catch them passing over the drugs from boat-to-boat otherwise we risk losing those in the powerboat. Those on shore will be small fry and it sounds as if the SOCA boys have them covered anyway. We can interview them later. So can someone message our other boat and ask them to go wide out to sea and come upon them from the West. No lights or sirens. When they are West of the island they should stay as close to the mainland shore as possible to give us the element of surprise. It's a bit shallow even at high tide so be careful.

Wait until I give the shout to intercept over the radio. I want those on board the target boats to be busy transferring the drugs when we hit. As you know we have a drone up there already and the operator will tell us when to go, and at that time he will withdraw the drone to a safe distance. We will get to the powerboat from this side but we need to stay slightly offshore until we pass the caravan park. We don't want those on shore to see us or those in the boats to get curious. Sully Island is very small so we should reach them while the attention of those carrying out the transfer is elsewhere. Once I give the order to intercept I have arranged for the helicopter to be with us within less than a minute."

David then made his way to the bow to let the helmsman know what was going on. They cruised to a safe distance and waited to hear that the second Police launch was in position just West of the island. This didn't take long so both launches waited to hear that the drugs transfer was taking place. It was vital to remain silent because sound can easily travel over the open sea. Just the waves against the side of the launch could be heard along with the slow tick-over of the engine. After what seemed an age the drone operator came through with, "Handover taking place. I am withdrawing the drone."

David shouted, "Go, go, go!"

The Police launch engine roared into life and the bow of the boat lifted angrily. They were quickly around the Eastern side of the island. The other launch could be seen heading from the West pushing white water from its bow, and from the sea the helicopter was also converging on them at speed; almost at wave height. The target boats were tied together bow and stern to enable the drugs transfer and it took some time before those on board realised what was happening.

When they did realise Sully Cantana rushed to the controls of the powerboat to try and make an escape but it was too late. They were just not fast enough because within seconds the two police launches—now with lights and sirens—were quickly on top of both target boats with assault weapons trained on them as they came along side. The helicopter was now hovering above with more weapons pointing down at them.

The speaker on the helicopter bellowed, "We are armed police. Stand still and put your hands on your heads."

When these instructions were obeyed the helicopter pulled back to a support role and the noise level became more suitable for conversation. The launch sirens were also switched off and the drone came in closer again to digitally record everything. David leaned over the side of the police launch and with a big smile said, "Well, good afternoon gentlemen. I am Detective Chief Inspector Thomas. What a lovely afternoon for a boat trip. Now if you don't mind I am going to come aboard with a couple of these nice armed policemen and my colleague Detective Inspector Chambers. We are extremely interested in what you have been doing."

There was absolutely nothing Sully, Will and the two men on the other boat could do. They were caught red handed with the drugs in their possession and after officially being charged with drugs offences they were quickly cuffed and transferred to one of the Police launches which then headed back to Cardiff. David and Ruth plus the officers on their launch secured the drugs and both target boats as crime scenes. Then in a slow convoy, the Police launch and the boats with the drugs on board, also proceeded back to Cardiff just as the sun went down. Those on shore had seen the action and were trying to escape but the SOCA team had them covered. The net had captured them all. Quite a collar.

Friday 25 August 6pm
The Mayhew Estate

It was 6 pm when the Mercedes pulled up in front of the steps at Mayhew. On the way from Bristol, Lord Henry had checked that the Cardiff end of the operation was up and running and all was well. Johnny got out of the car and stretched looking up at the wonderful old building. The front door was open and

Henry's two dogs come bounding down the steps to say a brief waggy 'hello' to Jonny before literally throwing themselves joyfully at Lord Henry. Sue walked down the steps elegantly; as always. She greeted them all, telling Jonny that dinner would on the back terrace at 7 pm. Then, turning to kiss Henry on the cheek she told him that Anthony Brown would be joining them for dinner and he had just entered the main gates.

Jonny didn't have time to ask who Anthony Brown was thinking about his date with Jacob. He thanked Sue and ran up the steps to get a quick wash. Turning to face the drive before he went inside he saw a metallic blue Audi R8 noisily make its way to the front of the house.

Before greeting the driver Lord Henry turned to Jonny and said, "Oh Jonny? Don't make any plans for tonight. We have work to do."

Jonny opened his mouth to protest, but then thought better of it and stomped into the house. When he got to his room he took his phone out of his pocket and called Jacob who answered almost immediately with, "Hi Jonny. I was waiting for your call. When are you coming over? I will cook."

Jonny already felt guilty and replied with sadness in his voice, "Sorry Jacob. I'm really pissed off but I have to stay here tonight for a meeting with Lord Henry. We have some stuff to get sorted after today's activities. Are you free in the morning? I really want to see you. I am wound up like a coiled spring and need some chill-out time with you."

Somewhat put out, Jacob replied, "Yeah; morning is fine. I'll put the food in the fridge. See you at ten."

Jonny's phone then went dead. Jacob had cut him off before he could say anything else. After Jacob's promise of a gay virgin night of passion Jonny guessed his ego was badly bruised by the fact that he had been stood up.

His stomach turned at the thought of upsetting Jacob, but his actions were now limited by others. He sent a text saying, *Really sorry, Jacob. I'll explain more when I see you. I can't wait for ten o'clock tomorrow to come round.*

Feeling helpless, he sent another text, *Missing you already.*

He just hoped Jacob would understand. There was nothing else he could do at that moment because Lord Henry had given his orders. Moments in time can change everything and he just prayed that his relationship with Jacob had not been ruined before it had really started. A quick wash had not improved his mood as he went downstairs and out onto the terrace.

Lord Henry was talking to a tall man with thick grey hair. He had his back to Jonny and was dressed in a navy polo shirt with beautifully cut stone-coloured trousers.

Greeting Jonny, Lord Henry boomed, "Ah Jonny! I would like you to meet Anthony Brown. He will want to talk to you later with regards to what has happened this last week or so. I'll explain why later."

Anthony turned around and looked at Jonny with a piercing blue-eyed appraisal. Jonny noted his neatly trimmed beard thinking that he looked to be about fifty-five. Flashing a big smile that transformed his stony features in a second, he held out his hand saying, "I'm pleased to meet you Jonny. I have heard much about you and your recent adventures. You're a very brave young man by all accounts."

Jonny thought, *Shit, this is one intimidating dude. What a firm handshake.*

Then he nodded before saying with a wry smile, "Thank you. It certainly had its moments."

At that moment Sue and Sandy brought out some antipasti with some rolls of olive bread and lots of side dishes that were filled with tasty looking dips. There were cold meats, olives, and seared artichokes; all looking absolutely delicious.

Jonny decided that he was starving and as soon as Sue told them to help themselves, he did just that. Taking his quickly filled plate he looked around and headed for a spare space next to Sandy where they could have a private conversation. She asked how it all went during the day. Jonny replied, "Yeah, it ended well; sort of. The painting was handed over and the police should be making some arrests about now regarding drug trafficking and stuff."

Sandy looked annoyed and said incredulously, "Oh come on! I want the whole cake hun. You can't just leave me the crumbs. We went through this together remember."

Jonny responded with a sympathetic look. He wasn't sure how much he could tell her anyway and said, "I need to go over things in my head a bit first Sandy. Just give me time, OK?"

Quickly changing the subject he said with a dirty laugh, "Anyway; how is devastating Devlin? Is he as good as he looks or is it padding?"

A frustrated Sandy replied with a grin, "Jonny! I can assure you that it's definitely not padding."

The pre-dinner chit chat continued, awkwardly avoiding the topic of the day's happenings in detail. With Christina and Barry still in Bristol, Sandy, Sue, Lord Henry, Anthony Brown and Jonny were the only diners. After they had eaten dinner and had a coffee, Lord Henry got up and asked Jonny and Anthony to accompany him to his office. They thanked Sue for dinner and casually walked away leaving Sue and Sandy on their own. Sandy gave Sue a puzzled look, but Sue just shook her head and mouthed 'no', putting her finger to her lips as a warning not to say anything. This she did, but inside she was fuming. Jonny looked around to face Sandy and just shrugged his shoulders.

As they entered the study Bryn was already there. Anthony said, "Good to see you again Bryn."

Bryn replied, "And you too Sir."

They all sat down and Lord Henry said, "Right then Jonny; you must be wondering what this is all about. First of all Anthony is here to de-brief us. He is the Commander-in-Chief of FIST which stands for Foreign Intelligence Support Team. This is the agency we work for. Your story will be the most comprehensive Jonny so please start the ball rolling by going back to when and where this all began, starting with the painting at the gallery.

Anthony will probably ask questions along the way. You already know that Arthur is on the team so include your relationship with him. All conversations will be recorded."

Jonny drew a deep breath and started to relay everything that happened to him from the very first day he came across the painting. He answered questions that were put to him truthfully, even acknowledging his liking for cocaine and about his afternoon at the Willcome Inn with his lover Will; plus what had taken place there today. He covered the meeting at Gordano Services with Aiyana and his trip to Soho. He then remembered that his mother was the first contact with Aiyana; also his mother's dangerous involvement with the Cantana Brothers while out riding and so relayed those details. He went on to explain how his friendship with Arthur had helped him with security and his interview with the Police at Mayhew. Finally he recalled the possibility of the painting being a Gainsborough and the hidden treasure.

The monologue with questions took all of forty-five minutes. When he had finished Anthony Brown said, "Thank you Jonny. I would like to meet Aiyana when she returns. Her information on the Religious Community could be very useful. You have an excellent memory for detail, a trait we value highly within

FIST. You are clearly capable of taking control of a situation, thinking on the spot and leading others. You think things through and plan ahead. Your bravery is certainly not in doubt. I would like to congratulate you regarding how you handled some difficult situations. You should be proud of yourself."

A slightly embarrassed Jonny replied, "Thank you. I'm glad you approve."

Anthony Brown continued, "I certainly do approve, Jonny. So much so that when you finish your degree, Lord Henry and I would like you to consider a position within FIST. You would still pursue a career of your choosing, but would always be on standby for the agency. If you decide to go down this route you would need some extensive training with us covering physical aspects, communication techniques, political scenarios and structures, and learn about the responsibilities of being part of a team. That would take place at Lord Henry's Scottish estate. We don't usually make overtures to prospective FIST members so early in a relationship but we are in an unusual situation. Almost by default we have worked together and it went well. But like I said, you must finish your degree first. Those in the world of art tend to have important contacts and having the right contacts is very useful in our line of work."

Jonny was stunned. He didn't know how to react so he started to laugh, as was his usual way of dealing with situations he wasn't quite sure about. But then he stopped himself so his stifled laugh became more of a gasp.

His mind raced as he thought, *God; what a weird week it has been. Starting with a painting and a murder, I then quickly discover my father who I thought was dead had another life in the United States and that I have a half-sister I had no idea existed. After threats to my mother, a kidnap rescue and a chase through Soho, I've ended the week with two paintings—one plain and on its way to Boston and the other likely to be extremely valuable; plus there has been another murder and a treasure map. Now, someone is offering me a job as a secret squirrel. How crazy is that. This Anthony Brown chap even looks a bit like Sean Connery.*

He thought about it looking at Anthony Brown, Lord Henry and Bryn who all had their eyes fixed on him. After a silence, he answered with a broad smile, "Yeah, you know what? I would like to be doing something that makes a difference. So my answer is yes. I think I would like to join the team. In truth I feel part of it anyway."

Anthony Brown replied slowly and with a straight face, "I am pleased you said that Jonny. If you had said no, we would have had to kill you."

The room went silent for a moment as they looked at Jonny's shocked face. The silence didn't last long before Lord Henry, Bryn and Anthony Brown collapsed with laughter. When Jonny had regained some composure and the laughter had died down, Anthony Brown brought out a copy of the Official Secrets Act saying, "I think we had better now get your agreement to the terms of the Official Secrets Act in writing now Jonny. "

Jonny dutifully signed and Lord Henry and Bryn witnessed. They then all shook hands with Jonny and welcomed him as a prospective member of FIST.

Although it wasn't as if it was the official signing up of Jonny into FIST, Lord Henry decided it would be a good idea to open a bottle of Bollinger champagne to toast a successful mission. This was on top of the wine they had at dinner that was followed by a bottle of his excellent single malt whisky. The talk was mostly about Henry, Bryn and Anthony's army days and Jonny found it difficult to join in, so although he commented when asked about something, he mainly just sat back and observed them—thinking about what his future would hold as part of this unique and well-connected team. Eventually, the alcohol and the fatigue took its toll and he fell asleep.

The next thing he was aware of was being helped up the stairs by the three older men who were trying to be quiet. They failed miserably, stumbling and laughing as they unceremoniously opened the door to Jonny's room and shoved him on the bed bidding him goodnight—although by then it was well into the early hours of the next morning although that didn't register with any of them. They saw it all as a sort of unofficial apprenticeship initiation ceremony.

Not realising the time, in his semi-conscious state Jonny groped around to locate his mobile phone and amazingly managed to speed dial Jacob's number. It rang for a while until a sleepy sounding Jacob answered with, "What the...? It's you, Jonny. Is all OK? I was asleep."

A slurred voice on the other end of the phone mumbled, "I jus' wan'a tell you that I fuckin' love you."

After a short silence, a somewhat annoyed Jacob said, "That's very nice to hear, Jonny, but you are clearly very drunk. I will see you hopefully in the morning. Goodnight."

Jonny didn't hear the reply because he had had already drifted back into an alcohol-fuelled but disturbed sleep. Sandy was woken up by Jonny's noisy sleep and the sound created as he fell out of bed. He didn't hear her come in and remove his shoes before pulling the covers over him. She also took his phone and put it on his bedside table before turning out the room light.

Day11 Saturday 26 August 9.30 am
The Mayhew Estate

It was about 9.30 am when Jonny opened his bleary eyes and looked at the clock. After taking a few minutes to work out where he was he remembered that he was due to meet Jacob at ten. He also noticed that he was still dressed. The events of yesterday slowly came back to him but seemed like they had happened to someone else. He tried to shake himself into the land of the living muttering, "Shit! I'm a fuckin' spy—well nearly."

With that he threw off his clothes and slowly ventured into the shower.

Within fifteen minutes he was dressed and running down the stairs—a 'new day and excited' Jonny. Skidding into the kitchen he nearly crashed into Lord Henry and Anthony Brown; each with a glass of Alka Seltzer in hand and looking pretty red eyed. Anthony was certainly looking a bit green around his untrimmed gills.

Now full of the expectations of meeting up with Jacob, Jonny was feeling quite the reverse. The power of youth in recovery is amazing as he started to assemble a cheese sandwich. He laughed as he said, "Hi guys, you look rough."

They look up and gently shook their heads as Jonny completed his sandwich and eagerly started to mop up the alcohol in his body with it—and a bottle of water. With his mouth full he said, "Well. See you later. I'm out on a date."

Lord Henry delayed his departure with a hand on the shoulder saying, "Hang on minute Jonny! Although my head is still a bit fuzzy, there are things you need to know and rules about what you can say now. I have heard from the boys in blue in Cardiff this morning and they are charging Sully with first degree murder. He will remain under lock and key. But both he and Will are up for drug smuggling. I am sure they will find other offences once they start digging but I think Will stands a chance of getting bail.

It means that if you are asked about this case you must only comment on what is public knowledge. You must not say anything about what happened in detail in case it is used in evidence in court. You will probably be a main witness. But that will depend upon what position the other witness to the shooting decides to take—I'm talking about Will of course. You will receive more guidance on this when the time comes. But as I mentioned yesterday, I'm afraid that ban on revealing info applies to Barry, your Mum, Sandy, Sue, Jacob, et al. I will inform all of them about the situation to take some of the pressure off you.

By the way; now things are safer I have sent a text to Aiyana to invite her for the treasure hunt. She said she can't wait and will let you know her flight details soon. She also sent greetings from her tribe. I think I can arrange a flight for her."

Just then Jonny's mobile pinged. He looked at it and smiled before then moving his gaze to Lord Henry saying, "That's great news about Aiyana. I have been wearing those tribal beads all the time and it may seem a bit daft but I'm sure the tribe's Great Spirit was protecting me."

His attention was then grabbed by seeing Jacob at the back door with two crash helmets so with a parting few words and a beaming grin he said, "Anyway; gotta go. I will see you a bit later."

They watch him run out to meet Jacob; wondering how he could be that fresh after all that alcohol. No words were spoken between Jonny and Jacob as they walked towards the bike. They just looked at each other and smiled. After they had put on their helmets they mounted the powerful machine and noisily rode away.

Jacob and Jonny rode to a small wooden one-story house that wasn't far from the Mayhew Estate. It was absolutely beautiful; surrounded by roses of every type and colour. Once off the bike Jonny took a moment to take in the scene and the rich perfume from the roses before turning to Jacob with a lump in his throat saying, "It's gorgeous and very you."

Jacob could see Jonny's feelings for the house were in line with his own and he felt warmed by the kindred spirit. He looked into Jonny's eyes and said, "I'm pleased you like it Jonny. This is my piece of heaven. I can lose myself here. Shall we go in?"

He unlocked the door and purposely took Jonny by the hand, leading him into the little house. The front door opened straight into the sitting room. This was bright and airy and was decorated in pale blues and cream. It had large French doors that opened onto a decking area adorned with multiple pots of more roses. In some ways it was similar to his mother's flat in Bristol without the view of the river.

After he had taken off his motorcycle jacket Jacob turned to face Jonny and said quietly and with some trepidation, "Jonny, I know why we are here and I want it badly. But I am still really nervous."

Recognising the need to demonstrate love and reassurance Jonny moved close to him, and while gently holding Jacob's head he started to kiss him around his brow and cheeks before placing his mouth tenderly on his lips. He said, "We are here because we fancy each other and we want to be with each other. It's as simple as that. Don't be nervous lover and don't make things more complicated than they really are. Just relax and enjoy the moment."

Jacob responded, hesitating at first and then with passion as they entwined tongues with their lips sealing their deep feelings for each other. Jacob felt Jonny's erection. It was hard with Jonny deliberately rubbing it up against his own hardness. He felt Jonny's hand move to his own erection as he said, "Well, now Jacob. It feels like you are ready for it sweetheart."

With that he gently kissed him on the lips again before saying, "Let's enjoy our bodies first Jacob. Where is the bedroom?"

Jacob took him by the hand and led him into a room with large windows that also faced the beautiful rose garden. Standing by the bed that was in the middle of the room Jonny slowly removed Jacob's tee-shirt to reveal a beautiful toned and muscular torso. Running his fingers down both sides of the amazing six-pack he murmured approvingly, "Oh my God Jacob! You are gorgeous. Gardening clearly keeps you very fit."

Jacob smiled but was clearly still nervous and didn't seem to know what to do next. So Jonny continued to take the lead by slowly sliding down Jacob's jeans and boxer shorts, maintaining eye contact with Jacob all the time.

When he had his partner completely naked, Jonny stood back to admire the view. After a while he said, "Wow; come on babe don't be shy. Undress me."

Jacob stepped forward and removes Jonny's clothes, gently touching him with feather light brushes of his fingertips—almost intimidated by Jonny's huge erection.

When they were both completely undressed Jonny smiled and said, "OK. Let's get on the bed. I won't do anything you are not happy about."

He reached down to his mobile and selected a few songs from You Tube. And as the heady blues sound of KALEO singing 'Way Down', flooded the room, he sat on the bed turning to face Jacob as he said, "Here we go. Be prepared to enter Gay Heaven."

He gently pushed him backwards and put his hand around Jacob's penis. And without taking his eyes of Jacob's face he bent over and took Jacob's cock in his mouth.

Jacob took a sharp intake of breath and pushed his pelvis upwards as Jonny got to work with his tongue and his fingers softly stroking the inside of Jacob's thighs. After a while he came up for air and leaned down to take a tube of lube from his jeans pocket, the contents of which he liberally smothered over Jacob's throbbing erection.

Jonny was so ready for Jacob to make love to him. He looked into his eyes and whispered, "God. I would like you to enter me Jacob. Are you OK with that?"

Jacob too was now more than ready and as he watched Jonny lie down he replied, "I am so OK with this now Jonny."

When Jonny was in position on his back with his hips supported by a pillow, Jacob gently guided himself inside. He had imagined this moment many times but the feeling when it happened was all encompassing. At first he started to move very slowly so that he didn't climax too soon. As he moved he was watching Jonny's beautiful face look lovingly into his eyes and feeling his erection against his stomach. Automatically he gradually increased the tempo until he couldn't hold on any longer and climaxed in a mind-blowing orgasm that made him gasp with pleasure. Jonny's orgasm exploded at the same time.

After reaching for some tissues and tidying up they remained in each other's arms for some time, exploring each other's bodies as true lovers do.

They marvelled at the intense feelings they now felt for each other. Jonny said, "I have never felt like this before. As well as an all-consuming lust that I have, you make me feel wanted and loved. I feel like crying and laughing at the same time. What have you done to me?"

Jacob laughed and just kissed him on the tip of his nose. Jonny was about to turn and return the kiss when he is interrupted by his phone ringing. He thought about ignoring it but figured it might be urgent. He didn't recognise the number but answered it anyway. The voice on the other end was very stressed and in a pleading tone said, "Hello, Jonny. It's me Will. I have been arrested with Sully by Cardiff Police. I need to get out of here. Can you help me?"

Jonny was amazed at Will's cheek and replied angrily, "I don't know what the fuck you expect me to do Will. You got yourself into this."

Will continued, "You mean everything to me; you know I was being forced to do what they said. Please tell them Jonny."

Remembering what Lord Henry had said about not discussing the events with anyone Jonny thought before he replied.

"Everyone has his place Will. And you are now in yours. Enjoy the showers mate. I hear it is a free-for-all in those places. Now fuck off."

These were probably not the words Lord Henry would have used himself in such circumstances, but with that a pleased Jonny put down the phone and turned his attention back to Jacob. An old life ended and a new one had begun.

Chapter 17

Healing doesn't mean the damage never existed.
It means the damage no longer controls our lives.
(Native American saying)

Cardiff Police Station
Saturday 26 August

Back at Cardiff Police Station David and Ruth left their respective offices to meet up for a quick chat about the case because they had been summoned to an early and unusual meeting with the Superintendent and other high-ranking Police Officials; not what their weary minds wanted. The arrest and charging process the previous evening had gone well with Sully and Will being held in cells overnight.

It was the early hours of the morning before they completed the paperwork and got to bed. The press had got hold of the story so David had prepared a short statement. But he knew that more would be required during the coming days. As they readied themselves for the meeting Ruth wondered why things were so urgent that a special high-level meeting had been called and said with a sad expectancy in her voice, "Aw David; you don't think they are going to take the case away from us at this stage do you? I feel we are really doing something important."

She was feeling slightly sick at the thought of having to hand it over to others again because it was a big case and she was very proud of what they had achieved so far—especially with her and David in a new relationship. It would feel good to get some success together. David answered in a not too convincing voice, "No, they will just want us to keep them informed as it has clearly been a multi-agency operation. At least I bloody hope so."

They walked into the conference room and were confronted by people they had never met before—apart from the Superintendent of course. However, they were immediately startled as they recognise none other than the Home Secretary sitting at the head of the long table. She looked up from her laptop, smiled, and welcomed them to the room with, "Good morning. Sit down. I bet you are both wondering what on earth is going on? I must congratulate you on the successful arrests you made yesterday, however I am sure you realise this case is so very much bigger than the people you brought in last night; hence the involvement of the Home Office."

Trying to hold back his anger at expecting to be withdrawn from the case again David turned a bright shade of scarlet as he thought, *Here we bloody go, we do the hard graft and someone else takes the credit.*

But then there was a big surprise as the Home Secretary said, "I can see that you are expecting the worst so here is the good news. We want you to continue with your interviews, but before you take any direct action I want you to report your findings direct to the Home Office. Your Superintendent will give you the contact procedures later today."

Through their surprise David and Ruth mumbled their assent and looked to the Superintendent for his OK which came in the form of a nod. In truth they were both feeling a bit overwhelmed with the proceedings.

The Home Secretary looked across the table towards David and Ruth and asked, "I have read your excellent reports from last night. Do you have any additional information for us from your preliminary findings?"

David replied, "Well, yes Ma'am. I have just heard that William Hurst has asked to turn Queen's Evidence. I think the shooting of Tony Cantana by his brother has spooked him. We will be talking to him directly after this meeting."

The Superintendent interjected; looking at the Home Secretary for a conformation nod but addressing David and Ruth. He said, "Ahem, Jonny Edwards name will probably be mentioned. Don't bother bringing him in. I believe he has already been interviewed by others. I think that will be all for now. You'd better see why our William Hurst has had a change of mind. I will see you again at around 1.00 pm."

Ruth and David left the room but it was several minutes before they could say anything. Ruth was the first to speak, "David... that was the bloody Home Secretary...Wow! And we are still on the case. I thought we would be pulled off for certain."

A happy and relieved David put his hand on Ruth's waist and said, "Come on my lovely. Let's go down and have a chat with young William. He seems to have spent the night in deep thought. Either that or his Solicitor has given him some sound advice. If we are lucky we might finish early and go back to yours for some afternoon delight. What do you say?"

Ruth smiled and looked into David's eyes saying, "Oh yes. I think that sounds like a very enjoyable option."

Saturday 26 August
The Mayhew Estate

Back at Mayhew, it was a lovely day—one in which to be really lazy. Jonny was still out with Jacob. Lord Henry was keeping up with the news from Cardiff and making arrangements for Aiyana's transport from Boston. Sue had a visitor who brought good news about the painting, but both Sue and Lord Henry found time to take advantage of the early afternoon sun.

It was early evening when an incredibly happy Jonny got back to Mayhew. Margie and Sue had prepared a venison stew with fresh bread and the amazing smell drifted through the house. As Jonny followed the smell of food down the hall he spied Sandy coming out of the front living room. In his new found love-inebriated state he rushed forward, picked her up and spun her around singing, "I'm in love; I'm in love."

Sandy was laughing and cried, "Put me down you muppet. So I guess you and Jacob got it together at last then hun."

Jonny eventually let her get her feet back on the ground and said, "Oh my God Sandy! I'm definitely in love…Me the commitaphobe. He is gorgeous in every way."

Sandy smiled and gave him a hug saying, "I am so happy for you sweetie. Sounds like the real thing. But let's go and have dinner. That smell promises much. And I understand that Sue has some news about the painting."

They entered the dining room where Sue had put the pot of stew and fresh baked bread on the table. When everyone was there she told them to help themselves. How Jonny managed to wait for that invite to eat was beyond Sandy's imagination. He usually just helped himself uninvited.

After they all had a bowl of steaming hot stew in front of them Sue said, "Some of you might know that I have had a visitor today. He is a partner in a London firm specialising in the authentication of artwork and his special expertise is the work of Gainsborough. One of the most respected in his field, he spent some hours with the painting, and his opinion is that it is a genuine Gainsborough. I was pretty sure, but I just wanted a second opinion at this stage.

I am sure you realise Jonny, that it confirms the painting as being very valuable indeed.

But there are several hoops to jump through before that value can be realised. The next stage is to get a Certificate of Authentication and assign the work an Identification Number. This will not be easy because as far as we are aware the painting has never been shown in a gallery so its history is hidden and very suspect. We will need to prove provenance before we go to that next stage."

Looking to Henry for confirmation she continued, "I think Aiyana is coming back tomorrow with the information we need. Is that right Henry?"

Lord Henry looked up from his bowl of stew and replied, "Ah yes. I have arranged for Aiyana to come back on a private flight from Boston Logan Airport. It is a Business Flight hub. She will already be on her way there. We will pick her up from Bristol Airport with the helicopter and fly her down to Mayhew. So, we should see her about 1 pm tomorrow. She tells me she has that proof and the photo copies she gave to Jonny before she left Gloucester Airport for Madrid a few days ago would indicate that. So we will just have to wait and see."

Jonny chipped in, "It will be nice tie up all the loose ends. And I am looking forward to getting to know my half-sister without the stress of the bloody Cantana Brothers looming over us."

Looking in the general direction of Sue as he ladled some more food onto his plate he said, "Loving the stew Sue. Hope you don't mind me having another go."

They all chuckled. This was his third go and Sandy smiled to herself as she saw that her friend was now clearly back on form.

As they couldn't discuss the criminal case the dinner conversation was again light and easy They talked about the painting of course but then it was more about getting things back to normal after the recent adventures with the Cantana Brothers. Lord Henry was looking forward to the jump season now that the flat season was winding down. He had several horses in training. He also wondered how the preparations were going for their traditional end of season 'Ball' and asked Sue for an update. Sue answered, "All is coming along beautifully. I will get the invites sent out next week for the twelfth of November. I have decided it would be nice to make it a masked ball this year, with a Magnum of Bolly for the best one."

Lord Henry joked, "As long as it is not a 'Gangsters and Molls' theme. I've had my bloody share of those for a while."

Jonny just sat and smiled to himself as, spread out in front of him, he saw the multifaceted lives of these people he now called friends. Until a few weeks ago he was just on the fringe of it with an occasional contact with Sue about art and his friendship with Sandy. Now it was if he was part of the family and more.

When everyone had finished, Jonny and Sandy cleared the dishes away and started making some coffee. Putting her hand up to gently touch Jonny's face Sandy said, "Jonny; you look quite different. Happy, but somehow softer. I can't quite explain it hun but you are different."

Jonny replied with a grin that stretched from ear to ear, "Sweetheart, I can't tell you just how happy I am. My only concern is holding on to it. Hey we can now double date, how cool is that?"

They carried the coffee into the sitting room where they sat and chatted for a while before Jonny said his 'goodnights' and returned to his room.

He took out his phone and texted Jacob, *Goodnight and sweet dreams of me xx*

He waited until he received a text back:

Sleep well. Thank you for finding me and helping me to find myself. See you tomorrow xx.

Feeling very content, Jonny climbed into bed looking forward to seeing Jacob and meeting up with Aiyana again, plus whatever else tomorrow would bring. In the back of his mind he was sure that there were more surprises to come.

Day 12 Mayhew Estate
Sunday morning, 27 August

After a good and restful sleep Jonny woke up on Sunday morning at about 7 am. The first thing he did was to check his phone and he smiled when he noticed Jacob had sent him a good morning text. He returned it with a heart and a smiley face. He thought, *How soppy am I getting.*

After a shower, he dressed, but instead of his customary black tee-shirt, he put on a white one. It was the only one he owned that was not black but he fancied that change was in the air so why not. Mind you, if the treasure hunt was on it wouldn't stay white for long. While he was combing his hair he spied Jacob out of his window. He was wheeling a barrow up one of the paths and his broad shoulders and well-muscled arms were straining against the load. Jonny groaned and rubbed his hand against his already hard penis. He couldn't stop himself.

He muttered, "Calm down fella. Behave. Your turn will come again soon."

Tearing his eyes away from the view his thoughts turned towards his other great love—food. This time it was breakfast and with one last look in the mirror he was out of the door and heading for the kitchen where he put some bread in the toaster and plugged the kettle in to boil for tea. Margie popped her head around the door from the prep-room and wished him 'good morning' before going back to what she was doing. As the toaster popped up the bread Sandy walked in from the hall in her riding clothes. Cheerful as ever she greeted Jonny with, "Hi hun; fancy going riding?"

Jonny looked up and smiled as he buttered a slice of toast. Riding was not his favourite past time. Horses were so big and needed a lot of attention before and after a ride. Anyway, he preferred to spend more time with Jacob. He said, "Yep, but not on a bloody horse. I'll leave that to you and mum. Do you want some tea and toast sweetheart?"

Knowing that Jonny would not really be interested in a ride out, Sandy grabbed the toast and said with a quizzical expression on her face, "Thank you lover boy. I hope you're not going to become a lovelorn bore."

She then pecked him on the cheek and dashed out of the door before he could say anything. But her words made Jonny think. He loved Jacob, but it was important not to exclude other friends from his life or to exclude himself from their lives. An important lesson to learn he thought.

He sat down at the breakfast bar to eat his breakfast, his thoughts turning to going back to Uni. Since he discovered that he had a half-sister who was Native American his interest in their culture had grown. It was not a topic he had aired with anyone else yet but he wondered if there was a chance of getting a grant to study Native American Art combined with frontier Art/Artists. Of course he would need to be in the United States to do it and there would be a lot of travel involved. As Barry was head of the History Faculty atBristolhe might be able to help. His mind continued to wander, *I wonder if Jacob would like to come with me. Ah but I am getting ahead of myself.*

His thoughts were disturbed by Sue entering through the back door with a basket full of fresh herbs and veg from the kitchen garden. She said, "Morning Jonny. How are you today?"

Jonny replied in his typical laddish style, "I am good. You are looking gorgeous as ever."

Sue knew it was just Jonny-talk and changed the subject, "Flatterer. I look a mess and you know it. Anyway I have just spoken to your mum. They will be here at about mid-day."

Standing up and clearing his breakfast plates he replied, "That's great. We can all go treasure hunting in the afternoon."

Sue laughed at his enthusiasm and said, "Jonny don't get your hopes up. There is probably nothing there. But it will be fun and a bit exciting looking; that is true."

Jonny spent the morning wandering around the garden helping Jacob and enjoying the easy way they connected and chatted. It was not long before he heard Barry's big American V8 grunting its way up the long drive. Giving Jacob a quick hug and kiss Jonny said, "I had better go and see Mum and Barry. Catch you later."

He then jogged down the path to the front of the house yelling, "Hi folks. It looks like a good day for a spot of treasure hunting."

Sue and Lord Henry were already outside. Barry was out of his car and with the bonnet up (hood up to American car enthusiasts) was proudly showing off his concourse condition '57 Chevy engine. In truth it had been gently hot-rodded; larger pistons, performance heads, bigger carbs and fuel pump and performance timing. There was also a lot more chrome than you would find on a '57 Chevy purchased new back in the 1950s. A purist would spot all this. But it really was a looker—show and go.

Jonny hugged his mum and moved over to the driver's side—left hand of course. After fist punching Barry and looking at the inside of the car he said, "Nice to see you have brought the Chevy out for a run. Hmm, bench seats, can I borrow it?"

With a look of distain Barry retorted, "Not bloody likely. Not even your mum, who I trust completely, gets to drive her."

In truth he felt rather guilty considering the fun he and Christina had on those bench seats.

Jonny pleaded, "Aw Baz. That's not at all fair!"

Christina laughed. "What do you mean I can't drive it! This is news to me."

Putting his hands on the roof Barry cried with a smile, "Oh, no, no. Is nothing sacred?"

252

Putting his hand on Barry's shoulder Lord Henry said in a solemn voice, "Sorry my friend; but when it comes to women, they will get what they want in the end. Let's unload your luggage and go in for a drink. I want to take a good look over the Chevrolet later. It's a beauty."

The luggage was collected and with Lord Henry in the lead they went straight to the kitchen. Heading straight for the fridge Lord Henry said, "It's not noon yet but I guess not too early for some bubbles is it?"

They were well into their third bottle on an empty stomach, when they heard the thump, thump of the helicopter coming into land on the front lawn.

A slightly dizzy headed Jonny jumped off his stool shouting, "Yay my gorgeous little sis is here."

He had decided that half-sister was not the way he now felt about Aiyana. He had a sister and that was that. But in his excitement he knocked a pile of Sue's recipe books on the floor. Picking them up quickly and trying to regain some composure he said apologetically, "Oh my God. Head rush. Sorry Sue."

Sue just brushed it off as being no problem and they all went outside to greet Aiyana as the beautiful exotic girl was already out of the helicopter and walking across the lawn smiling; her hips and long straight black hair swinging as she walked. Jonny was the first to step forward, and kissing her on both cheeks he said, "Hello darling sis. Welcome to Mayhew. It's so great to have you back in England again. Come and meet the troops. Some of them you already know."

Walking into the house, Christina was struck by the similarities between her son Jonny and Aiyana. She hadn't noticed it when they met at Days Inn. And it was not just physical either. She noticed that people seemed to be drawn to them. Jonny was a few inches taller but in profile they were so alike. Aiyana had typically Native-American beautiful high cheekbones, but the eyes… dear God they have the same eyes; and the wide ever ready to smile mouth. They were their father's children without a doubt. It brought a lump to her throat.

After a quick catch up over another glass of bubbles, Lord Henry covered the recent adventures with the Cantana Brothers and the limitations of what could be discussed because of a pending court case. Sue also updated Aiyana on the painting and suggested they take her to view the Gainsborough before going out to look for the treasure.

Sue led them straight down to the studio where the painting was still in its place of honour on an easel in the middle of the well-lit room. Sue waited for everyone to gather around before whipping off the protective cover with a flourish.

Aiyana gasped and almost in tears she said, "Oh my God. It is absolutely beautiful! These people are my family; and your family too Jonny. I have a formal dress just like that. The bead pattern is the same. Previous generations of tribe elders tell about a girl going to England with a pirate who became a successful and honoured privateer. It is not clear whether she returned, but it is said that one of her children did. Nothing is written down of course but the story could be in some of our old art work.

According to our traditions, hereditary rights, including inheritance and any privileges, are passed on via the mother, not the father as is the norm in the UK. So accordingly, under our culture you are not a direct descendent of those in the painting as such. But as my half-brother you are part of the tribal family and will be considered a co-heir unless any tribe members object. National or International Legislation can of course sometimes conflict with our cultural practices, although in most States in USA, Native Americans are generally left to follow their traditions. But changing the subject, finding that map tucked away in the frame! You are so clever Sue."

They stood around chatting for a while considering the implications and the need for provenance. As time was slipping by, and before Aiyana showed her provenance, Lord Henry asked her if she would like to go over the to the treasure site indicated on the map. The weather was good so getting started seemed a good idea.

An excited Aiyana replied.

"Oh yes please. Can I get changed first though? I will be very quick."

Sandy said, "Come on then. I will show you to your room."

Sandy took her up to a beautiful room decorated in the French renaissance style. Someone had already brought up her bags. She looked about her with wide eyes. Twirling around to look at Sandy she said, "I can't believe I am here; actually in an English country house."

Sandy chuckled and said, "Actually, it's Welsh; but close enough."

Aiyana laughed with her and said, "Clearly I have much to learn Sandy."

Sandy thought, *I like her. I think we will be friends.*

Sandy said, "I will leave you to get sorted out. The bathroom is through that door, I will see you downstairs when you are ready. But be quick because as you will find out, once Lord Henry is on a mission, everything happens at the speed of light."

Chapter 18

Listen to the voice of nature for it holds treasures for you.
(Native American Huron proverb)

Mayhew Estate
Sunday Afternoon
27 August

As promised, Aiyana was quick and it wasn't long before they were finally all in the Land Rover bumping across country to the treasure site. Lord Henry had already organised some tools and the Land Rover had a trailer that was stashed with everything he thought they might need. On the way he explained to Aiyana how they identified the fact that site shown on the map was actually within Mayhew grounds, and the known links of a building, now a ruin, with smugglers and pirates. But further investigation was required to confirm that this was indeed the site on the map.

Once they arrived at the site Lord Henry got them organised with tools to continue the clearance of the area started a few days earlier. At least they wouldn't have to be worried about interference from the Cantana Brothers this time. It was about two hours later when Barry called out that he had found something. He had uncovered a large flat rock embedded in the stone floor inside the ruins. It had heavy duty rusted metal rings on either side.

They all had a go at trying to pull it up, but it was obvious it wasn't going to budge without lifting gear.

Barry said, "I think we need something more substantial. We could fix up a tripod and use the Land Rover to winch it up. Do you have any scaffold polls and a block and tackle back at the house Lord Henry?"

Lord Henry replied as he took out his mobile, "I am sure we do. I will call Bryn and get him to bring it over."

After making contact with Bryn, he returned to the task in hand and grabbed a spike from the tool selection saying, "Once Bryn arrives we can get to work on the slab again but we can get the Land Rover in position now. And to make it easier to get a purchase on the slab, I think we should try and get as much debris cleared away from around it as possible. You can use a spike around the edges like this. There are more in the tool box. After a dose of WD 40, a hand file followed by rough emery paper might clean those rusted rings a bit as well. A grinder might be too heavy handed."

Barry and Jonny soon had the edges of the slab more exposed, and as soon as Bryn arrived with the gear Barry started to set up a tripod while Bryn continued work on the metal rings. Once the tripod was secure, they attached chains to the now cleaner rings on the slab. Finally they attached the Land Rover winch to the block and tackle that had been secured to the tripod.

An impressed Lord Henry said with a smile, "I thought your speciality was History; not Engineering Barry."

Barry laughed.

"A basic tripod and winch have been used for thousands of years. We learned to make one when I was at school. It's still used a lot, particularly when uncovering history at sites. But safety first at all times is the golden rule. Can you start the winch on slow? And I would get back everyone; in-case the winch line or rusted rings break or the tripod collapses. I'm not expecting it too; but just in case."

They all stood back and watched as the winch slowly took the strain. There was a satisfying grinding sound as the slab began to lift, but after an initial pull to break the seal the slab came up at an angle. So Barry gently eased the block and tackle line in that direction by hand. As it opened further, you could see that there was a metal bar frame attached underneath. The frame's fixings lined up with the rings but it too was very rusty. Hinges were attached to one side of the frame but these were just about seized up by rust. But applying some WD 40 during the lift eased them a little although the metal-to-metal grinding noise was more of a screech.

It took some time but once fully open it became clear that the complete slab/metal frame assembly acted like a lid that could be secured from the inside—similar to that on a submarine turret. Security from the outside must have been by a dead lock that had rusted long ago. Barry inspected the mechanism and his eyes were drawn to a breakage in one of the struts. Pointing it out he surmised, "This must have broken during a lockdown process. It's a sheer fracture that would have happened many years ago as the fracture itself has rusted over. It could mean that unless there is another access, whoever was in there would not be able to get out."

Lord Henry commented, "Whoever was responsible for this place certainly rigged up a sophisticated security system didn't they? This must have been an important store of some kind or another."

They were left with a dark hole in the floor. An unpleasant, musty stale air smell drifted out of it. Barry got Jonny to help him secure the slab in the fully open position flat on the floor before Lord Henry slowly released the tension on the winch line. Once the block and tackle line was clear of the hole Jonny switched his phone torch on and shone the beam down the gloomy darkness. It illuminated a flight of stone steps linked to the side opposite the lake.

Lord Henry said, "I have some more powerful torches in the Land Rover. Shall we take a proper look?"

Bryn had to get back to Mayhew but the others were all keen to progress things so Lord Henry handed out the torches to the now very excited band of treasure hunters. He started the descent as the lead out man saying, "Be careful these steps are shallow and it's very narrow."

The steps appeared to be cut out of the granite rock that is so common in this part of South Wales along with coal and limestone. They went down about ten feet until they found themselves in a small room with a rough-hewn floor. Standing at the foot of the steps and facing the lake there appeared to be a rock tunnel leading from the left. It was about three feet wide and after a few yards it curved further to the left. It would be a tight fit to walk through and it seemed to be cut through a coal seam.

Lord Henry said, "I hope nobody is wearing any expensive clothes. Rubbing against the walls of the tunnel could be messy. And be aware of large stones underfoot."

Christina was the first to express concern saying, "I am not sure I like this. Just think of all those tons of rock above us."

Barry was behind her and said in a soothing voice as possible, "Don't worry love. It's been here for a long time and looks pretty solid to me."

Jonny tried to make light of his mum's concern and said, "Yeah mum. But don't make any high-pitched screams or it will all come down…or am I thinking about an avalanche?"

As Jonny laughed a rather stressed Christina replied, "Ha, ha! That's enough my boy. You are not too old for a clip around the ear."

She thought that might lighten the atmosphere a little. But it seemed she was the only one with concerns; still feeling claustrophobic in the narrow walkway. All the others were just excited and Aiyana's inbred curiosity had kicked in as she looked closely at the sides of the tunnel and the marks made by the tunnel makers' tools. They walked for about five minutes. Then the tunnel started to noticeably go uphill. Lord Henry wished he had brought his compass because by now he had lost his land bearings. He was still pondering whether there could be another route to the surface somewhere.

Turning another corner the passage widened and the tunnel walls had been lined with bricks. This larger limestone chamber led to a heavy metal studded oak door with metal bands and metal strap hinges. On the right-hand side were two large gothic style door handles, one either side of the door, with a keyhole below it.

Lord Henry looked around and noticed places for lamps on the walls. Pointing them out he said, "Well, what do you know? This was clearly an important storage facility for something. There is provision for lighting. But any lighting—probably candles or oil depending on how old this facility is—would burn oxygen. So working in this cavernous room would be time-limited, particularly if there were several people down here. My guess is that at one time there was a second access or at least additional ventilation to the surface. In old mines they used to burn fires at the bottom of updraft tunnels to keep the air moving.

"And have you noticed that it is not damp? There are no stalagmites or stalactites formed on the limestone that is still exposed. There is no sign of a steam driven water pump that would have been available as far back as the 1700s. And the air is quite breathable at the moment. If the slab door is the only access it is providing a very efficient ventilation system while it is open and it traps the air while locked down. But why would you want to leave that slab door open once you have stored valuable cargo or your worldly goods away?"

Returning his attention to the oak door, Lord Henry pushed down on the handle but it wouldn't budge. He said, "Can someone pass me the WD 40 spray? And while this release fluid is doing its job, one of you go back to the surface and get me the wheel brace from under the Land Rover passenger seat or one of the tools we used to free up the outside door."

Barry passed the WD 40 spray to Lord Henry and said, "I'm on it."

He turned and quickly made his way back down the tunnel and out to the vehicle. While Barry was gone, they inspected their surroundings further. The brickwork extended about six feet into the tunnel and worked up into an arch surrounding the door.

Lord Henry said, "If those bricks were brought in by the tunnel it would have taken some time to get to this stage. Maybe it was an on-going project for one man that has still not been completed. It's all very curious and there are many un-answered questions."

Barry arrived back after about fifteen minutes and they got working on the door. The wheel brace had a screwdriver end and Barry picked away at the corroded handle while Lord Henry liberally sprayed the simply hung hinges and the door handle mechanism with the WD 40 until they were able to work it loose. Barry pushed down on the handle and miraculously it moved.

Lord Henry said, "OK. Come on everyone push the door."

Jonny, Barry and Henry put their shoulders to the door until it slowly started to creak open. They pushed it ajar about six inches before Lord Henry shone his torch through the gap.

He said, "Ahh. There is another large room the other side! Keep pushing."

They pushed with renewed intensity. When the door was at about eighteen inches, he called a halt saying, "We should be able to squeeze through that I think."

Lord Henry continued to lead, followed by Jonny, Aiyana, Sandy, Sue, Barry, and Christina. Their torches lit the area well enough to see that they had entered a large domed room that was lined with bricks and some brick pillars. The effect was rather like a church crypt and it was if they had entered the wine cellars of a very large building. There were some gasps and exclamations from the assembled company.

Lord Henry said, "Right then let's split up and take a look around. If you find anything don't touch it until me or Barry have seen it."

The room had alcoves set into the walls. They contained different pieces of furniture. Jonny and Sandy wandered around inspecting them, pointing their torches in each alcove. What they saw in one of them made Jonny jump back in alarm and Sandy grabbed hold of his arm and gasped.

Jonny cried out, "SHIT! I think we might have found Captain Davies."

There in the beam of his torch were human remains laying it the foetal position on a wooden bed. The others rushed over to look, except Christine who said she would take their word for it. There was silence as they gathered around the body, almost as a mark of respect. Aiyana made some signs over the body, which was not complete and had obviously been there for some time. It had some clothing material still attached and evidence of leather shoes.

With his history expert hat firmly in place as he gazed at the unfortunate skeleton Barry said, "Wow! Now this is interesting. We will be able to get DNA and should be able to date some of the material. But obviously this needs to be reported to the relevant authorities."

Aiyana mused, "I wonder how he died? There appears to be no signs of foul play."

Barry answered, "There are still many unanswered questions about all of this. Not wishing to sound too callous but this is a historian dream; a body with supporting material to age it and a story to help us understand the possibilities. From what we have at the moment I have a feeling that when the mechanism broke on the exit to the tunnel it locked the poor chap down here. So he probably died of starvation or hypoxemia; that is a lack of oxygen. But I feel the story still has some missing elements and it will take time to get the results back of some tests."

He continued, "This room looks like it could be one in which he kept his own stash of contraband. And if I am not mistaken those are brandy barrels over there in that alcove; another possible method of dating. And that table over there appears to have written material spread on it; hopefully with more clues. I'll have a look."

He rushed off to check it out.

An excited Jonny replied; almost in a bored or matter of fact tone, "Yeah; awesome Baz. I'm completely blown away."

He pointed his torch into another alcove and cried, "Hey, hey, hey, this looks like a sea chest."

He shone his torch at the chest and quickly made his way over to inspect a large domed box with iron bands and three impressive integral locks. He pushed the lid, but it was obviously locked. After a while the others had gathered around him again and rather stating the obvious he said, "I think we need some keys."

An excited Barry had joined them saying, "There seems to be a journal of some sort on the table. It's a bit faded in parts but readable. I need to go over it in more detail so I'll leave it until later. I've taken some photos for records purposes."

After intently peering at the locks he said, "But look at this beauty. What have we here? I've seen chests like this before. If I am not very much mistaken we will need three different keys used in a certain sequence in order to open it. Let's see if we can find those keys?"

Lord Henry interjected, "I think it would be a good idea for me to go back to Mayhew and get some work-lights and a generator with plenty of power extension leads. I don't think it would be healthy to have a petrol engine running in here. It will need to be outside. With all of us breathing it in, the quality of the air in here is already getting a bit questionable. So when I return I will bring an air-quality monitoring gauge and some face masks with oxygen packs.

But right now, I don't know about you folks, but my stomach is saying that some food and drink would go down well. Does anyone want to come back with me? Or if you like, we could all go back to the house and return at daybreak. You probably haven't noticed the time going by but it is now about 8 pm?"

Christina was keen to join him and said, "I would like to have a break and a wash. I think I will come back with you. What about you Barry?"

Barry thought for a moment and then looked at the others before saying, "Mmm. I think Lord Henry is right. It is so easy to lose track of time. We should all go back and see if we can get a few hours of sleep and start again at first light."

They all agreed they were pretty tired, especially Aiyana who had not had any sleep at all because of the different time zones.

Lord Henry said, "OK! We will need to secure the site as best we can. We'll pull this door too and relocate the slab at the entrance. I'm not keen to leave the site unguarded but as long as we are back at daybreak we should be OK. I might ask Bryn to keep an eye on things during the night and I'll warn Aled up at Home Farm that he might see some strange activity down by the lake."

The tired group of people made their weary way back through the tunnel and up the steps where the freshness of the air hit them like a hot shower. Using the block and tackle they lowered the slab back in place before pushing some earth around the edges to reseal it. Finally some loose earth was spread across the floor to disguise any evidence of excavation activity. The block and tackle was dismantled and loaded onto the Land Rover trailer, but they decided to leave the scaffolding poles hidden in some nearby bushes as they would need it the next day. Then it was all back in the Land Rover.

But this time Lord Henry decided it was best to go via the road, accessing it via the nearby Home Farm entrance. As he drove up the short run to Home Farm he suddenly stopped the Land Rover and looked back towards the ruin they had been investigating. He realised that the tunnel they had been investigating could well have led to the Home Farm property. Rather than considering the tunnel as giving access from the ruins to the bricked-out rooms they had discovered; maybe they should consider it the other way round; as also providing access from the rooms down to the hut—now a ruin. This hut would have been on the quayside many years ago. And evidently, before Lord Henry purchased Mayhew and long before Home Farm was built, there was a Manor House there that was destroyed in a fire.

Barry looked at Lord Henry and said, "You seem to be deep in thought Henry. Are you going to tell us about it?"

Lord Henry said slowly, "No. Not yet. I will need to do a little research tonight. But I might have hit on something that could help us answer a few outstanding questions."

He then drove on. The sun had set and the sky was giving the treasure hunters a magnificent vista of vibrant red, orange and magenta. It was a fitting end to a beautiful and happy day. Jonny took a photo and sent it to Jacob with the words, *How beautiful is this, I wish we were seeing it together. xxx.*

He got a text back, *We are looking at the same sky and thinking of each other.xxx.*

Arriving at Mayhew, they went directly to the kitchen where Margie had left some home-made vegetable soup gently simmering on the range. She had also left some home-made bread and butter for dunking purposes. They helped themselves and sat down at the kitchen table talking about the afternoon's discoveries.

Aiyana said, "This soup is pure heaven. Would you mind if I send a selfie of us all to my tribal Family back home?"

They all got themselves at one end of the table with Aiyana in the middle. She placed her phone camera on an extension stick and pointed it at them saying, "Everyone say treasure!"

The result was a happy photo of them all huddled close together and laughing.

She said, "I'll send it over to Boston later when I have time to write a few words to go with it."

Lord Henry rose from the table saying, "Right then. It's now 9.30 pm. Bryn will keep an eye on our site and I have warned Aled up at Home Farm. After we've done the dishes I'm going to carry out a little research. Then I am going to try and get a few hours of sleep. Shall we meet down here at about 5 am?"

They all agreed and slowly made their way to their respective rooms. It had been a long and fruitful day but there were still some mysteries to solve.

Day13 Monday 28 August
The Mayhew Estate

Jonny's alarm went off at about 4.30 am and he was washed, dressed and downstairs at 5 am. Sue and Christina were already up and preparing some breakfast along with some food and coffee to take with them. They were joined by Lord Henry, Barry, Sandy and Aiyana within a few minutes of each other. Sandy and Jonny teamed up to get everyone some breakfast with Aiyana helping to lay the kitchen table. Sue and Christina concentrated on preparing the food for the day. The conversation revolved around the keys to the chest, because they did not want to break the locks unless absolutely necessary. Barry had spent some time thinking about this and said, "We need to check the space around the chest and the body. Sometimes things of value were placed behind some bricks. I didn't see any keys around the body, but I may have missed something. So, I guess our first job will be to check for loose bricks."

Lord Henry said, "OK then; If someone can give me a hand with one of our generators, some work lights and plenty of extension leads, we can load up the trailer and get going. I will meet you all by the front steps in about twenty minutes."

Jonny volunteered to give a hand and he and Lord Henry left by the kitchen door. The pale light of the early morning promised another perfect day. As Jonny and Lord Henry walked by the stables they could hear one of the horses impatiently kicking a stable door with a front hoof as Devlin went from stable to stable giving the horses their morning feed. Walking towards the equipment store Jonny felt content with the direction in which his life was now unfolding.

And it was at that very moment that it hit him. He could not remember when he last had a snort of cocaine. He smiled to himself and with a feeling of self-satisfaction he realised happiness was not achieved by artificial means. It was achieved by the people you love being around you. It would be one of the most important realisations of his life.

They soon had the trailer loaded and hitched up to the Land Rover and drove around to the front of the house where the others were waiting. With the loaded trailer in tow Lord Henry thought it best to take the tarmac road to the main entrance and on to the road leading past Home Farm. And he wanted to point something out to the treasure hunting team. Something he had been researching during the previous evening. Although still early, the day had already begun to feel quite warm when he turned the Land Rover off the road at the Home Farm entrance and suddenly put his foot on the brakes. It caused the passengers to shoot forward resulting and there were a few expletives from the still sleepy crew.

Taking no notice of the complaints Lord Henry climbed out of the Land Rover. Unable to contain his excitement he said, "I did a bit of research last night and I think I know where that underground room is! I want you to take a look at where Home Farm stands in relation to the old ruins we are investigating."

He started to point out the key land marks as Barry stumbled out of the Land Rover. Barry stood by Lord Henry studying the geography that was being pointed out. After a while there was a realisation and Barry said, "I see what you mean Henry. I have some geophysical equipment at the University that we use on approved archaeological digs, I think this constitutes an area of significant historical importance; don't you Henry? I'm sure they would release it to me for this project."

Lord Henry put his hand on Barry's shoulder and laughed when he said, "Oh, indubitably my learned friend. Bring that out to the site as soon as you can. But we don't have to wait because I have brought along a few toys of my own. And I have some more information about Home Farm and a building that preceded it on this site. But I'll go over that later.

I have sorted out a special modular pack to use today because GPS is not reliable in deep tunnels. The pack includes a compass—gyroscope digital mapper. In some ways it's a crossbreed of old school and modern technology with many applications and tricks in its program. I know the accurate map reference for Mayhew and have logged that in as an Ordinance Survey base line. It will tie the digital mapper to that reference and automatically plot the correct references of the tunnel and cavern we are working in, measured by gyroscopic movement and compass fixes. I have also brought some light weight geo physical equipment in case we need it."

They wandered around the area for a while, Lord Henry explaining his thoughts about the tunnel to the others and pointing out some relevant key physical ground features. Aiyana joined the conversation, "This fits in with thoughts I have regarding the marks made by those digging the tunnel. The pick marks indicate that the direction of travel was from the main cavern out towards the ruins by the lake; not the other way round."

Lord Henry said, "Good point Aiyana. I wondered why you were looking so deeply at the tunnel walls yesterday."

Just then Aled drove by on his tractor and greeted Lord Henry who briefly told him about the work going on at the site. After waving him goodbye Lord Henry said, "OK. Time for work I think. Let's get down to the site and unload the trailer."

They got busy setting up the tripod and block and tackle to open up the slab stone door. After checking the generator petrol tank was full, they started it up and plugged in one of the extension leads. Before accessing the tunnel Lord Henry said, "Let me go first because I want to plot the tunnel's track on my digital mapper."

He activated the start mode which gave him an accurate Ordinance Survey starting point map reference. Then, looking at a screen he walked the tunnel as the mapper plotted a track over a digitised Ordinance Survey map. The tunnel's track was illustrated as a red line on the map.

The rest of the team all had something to carry as they made their way down the steps. The additional extension leads were very heavy and having their arms full made it considerably more difficult to navigate the narrow tunnel. Lord Henry had thoughtfully provided them with some head torches that helped, but they had to keep stopping to attach additional extension leads. At least it meant their burdens lightened as they navigated the tunnel.

Finally the band of treasure hunters was in the room at the end of the tunnel—or was it the beginning of the tunnel as Lord Henry's theory and Aiyana's thoughts suggested. Lord Henry logged in the finish point on his mapper and smiled as he saw the screen display. He would need to check it by surface walking the tunnel's mapped route as shown on the screen but it looked like his theory was right.

They plugged in some work lights and switched them on. These made an incredible difference. The inside detail was much clearer and over on one side they could now see what looked like a collapsed tunnel or stairway; more supporting evidence for Lord Henry's theory. And it looked like Captain Davies—if indeed that is who it was—had been trying to remove some of the rubble. However there were some very large and heavy stones and what looked like fire blackened timbers that would be impossible to shift by hand.

Jonny said, "Poor fellow. But at least he had some alcohol to drink."

He pointed in the direction of the brandy in one of the alcoves.

Lord Henry chuckled but brought some order to the proceedings by saying, "Right then! Let's get organised. I suggest we all look for those keys. Jonny, Sandy, Aiyana, and Christina, check out the walls for loose bricks. Barry; I know you are itching to look at the written material on the table. Sue can you check out the floor? I am going to go back up to the surface. There are some phone calls I need to make. And I want to retrace the tunnel route logged on my mapper by walking it at surface level, using the digitally plotted route taken in the tunnel as the base line. I'll place some markers in the ground as I go."

Once he was on the surface he checked that the generator was working OK and topped up the fuel tank. He then followed the route of the tunnel as indicated by the red line on his mapper screen, hammering in the yellow markers as he walked across the fields. He had to retain his positional curser in line with the red line as he walked. As he had expected, it led to Home Farm—to be precise, inside Home Farm barn. This was probably part of the original Manor House before a fire destroyed the complete building—in the 1700s according to unsubstantiated rumours.

He was trying to confirm who lived there at that time and fix the date of the fire. Church records and published news were reliable sources and one of the phone calls he wanted to make was with someone who was checking this out.

Back in the tunnel, the treasure hunters had all set to work looking for the keys, except for Barry who, after putting on some white cotton gloves, sat down at the table and carefully opened the beautiful, embossed leather cover of the book before him. Slowly opening the cover he found that the pages inside were of velum; and to his absolute joy, as he had thought the day before it appeared to be a journal, with each page dated.

On the first page was an intricate drawing of a ship, captioned *My mistress, The Red Charm.* Turning the pages, he unravelled a fascinating account of the life of a pirate and privateer in the 1700s.

He became lost in the words of the captain. He read how he had travelled to the New World collecting goods to trade; sometimes by taking them from another ship—often Spanish or Portuguese Galleons with gold and emeralds from South America. French ships were also targeted.

It was a subject he graphically described in the journal, logging the captured ship's name, her nationality, the captain's name and the bounty taken. Often the ship would give up its bounty with very little fight and they were free to go on their way—particularly after he had been awarded a Letter of Marque by King George II. But sometimes they would have to fight for it. Captain Davies showed little mercy and gave no quarter to the hapless sailors on the wrong side. The Letter of Marque meant that bounty taken belonged to the King, but there was a marginal 'commission' taken. Sometimes he attacked slavers and sold the captured slaves to planters in the Caribbean. In today's world, he would not have been considered a person of high moral stature.

Barry was so engrossed in the Captain's Journal he felt he could almost smell the gunpowder and hear the shouting and clashing of steel. He read about how the captain had traded with early European settlers, and how he met and admired the Native Americans living on the East Coast of North America, trading with them for animal pelts. He visited several harbours around Boston where he met and fell in love with Sokannon, a young girl of a local tribe who would later become his wife and live in England for a while where she bore him a son.

Back at the treasure hunt and right on cue it was another member of a native American tribe that jolted Barry out of his journey into the 18th century and back into the 20th Century. It was Aiyanna shouting, "I have them! They were hidden behind this brick, just as Barry suggested."

With the keys in hand she immediately headed for the sea chest along with the others and was about to try a key when she heard Barry cry, "Stop! Not yet Aiyanna."

He got up from his chair and joined them at the sea chest explaining why.

"If you use the wrong unlocking sequence it could lock the chest in a different way. Then we would have a Devil of a problem opening it without destroying the locks themselves. If you hang on a moment, I will see if the captain says anything about it in his Journal. If he has then it would be near the back I should think."

Barry carefully turned to the back of the Journal. He couldn't find a direct reference to the sequence of unlocking the chest as part of the book. But what he did find was a sad account of the captain's last days, as if in a letter to his son Bleddyn. It was tucked in the back of the Journal and it contained a reference to the lock sequence.

Barry thought for a moment before saying, "I have found this letter. I think I should read it aloud to you all."

They gathered around and when they were all quiet he read these words.

4 June 1765

To my dearest wife Sokannon and my beloved son Bleddyn.

If you are reading this then I fear I have perished. As I am sure you will have discovered by now our beautiful home has been set to fire by those that would do us ill. I found sanctuary down here, in the cellar, but as you may have also discovered the entrance from the house collapsed and proved impossible to remove, Added to this the entrance from the boat house is damaged, sealing me to my fate.

I believe the painting by Thomas Gainsborough has been stolen from the house by people who would not want its existence to be public knowledge because it is part of my claim on land in Massachusetts. It shows our gracious King George handing me the deeds to the land given to me for my services to his Majesty. The painting needs to be recovered because I bequeath this land to the good people of Sokannon's tribe and it might be needed to substantiate the legality of ownership of the land.

The contents of my sea chest will be shared equally between my descendants and the tribe of my wife. I also have my interests in the Red Charm Ship Company that will come to my son Bleddyn on his 18th birthday. This will be managed by my business associate Samuel Courtney until that time. The unlocking sequence to my chest is in two places. The first place is in my head. But I have also written it on a map that I placed for safekeeping within the frame of the painting. I did not visualise the painting being stolen and the map falling into the wrong hands. The map shows where this sanctuary and the chest lie. If you are reading this then thankfully you must have that map. The unlocking sequence is on the map, left, middle and right indicating the position of the locks on the chest.

My dearest Sokannon, I am so tired. I do not know if it be night or day. I fear my time to meet our Lord is nearly upon me. I will lie awhile and write some more on my awakening.

Your ever loving husband.
Captain Robert Davies.

They all stood around in silence on hearing the sad last words of Captain Davies. In truth it was some time before anyone did or said anything. Then Jonny caught sight of Sue taking her phone out of her pocket. As she did so she he noted a sense of triumph in her voice as she scrolled through her photos.

"Yes! I think I've solved the locking sequence riddle. I took a photo of the map before we placed it back in the painting frame. Ah here we are."

She walked over to the chest and knelt down. They all gathered around so they could see her phone screen. She pointed to the photo saying, "Look! There are some numbers in the left corner, in the middle and in the right corner of the map. I noticed these before but didn't know what they meant. I think these numbers and position on the map could well be the code referred to in this letter. Shall we try?"

Barry questioned whether they should wait for Lord Henry to return, but everyone was keen to progress things, including Barry in the end. So Sue said, "OK! Let's do this!"

After liberally spraying some WD40 into the integral locks, she inserted a key into each of the three keyholes. Sandy read out the numbers in the order shown on the map—i.e. left lock. middle lock and right lock. The middle one had the numeral one so she turned that one first. It wasn't easy, but by wriggling it about the key eventually turned. As soon as she had used the last key there was an audible click.

She stopped and looked up at the treasure hunters before thoughtfully saying, "Aiyana and Jonny, I think you should open it as you are kin."

With that she stood up and stepped away so they could get to the chest.

Aiyana and Jonny each took hold of a corner of the lid and slowly lifted it upwards. When it was fully open Aiyana put her hands to her face and croaked, "Oh my God!"

In unison they all gasped as the contents of the chest were revealed. They hadn't really known what to expect, but what was now on display before them set a new top-level marker for the description 'gob smacking.' It was like a scene out of a movie rather than something in the real world. It was nearly filled to the brim with valuables.

After the initial shock had passed Jonny slowly put his hand in the chest and allowed some gold and silver coins to dribble through his fingers. As they listened to the chinking sound of the coins falling back into the chest, with a quiet voice that was trembling he said, "Bloody Hell! This must be worth thousands."

Barry took out what looked like a huge emerald from the chest exclaiming, "You are wrong my friend. A bit more than that Jonny. More like millions."

A more detailed look confirmed that the chest was about three quarters full of what you could describe as proper pirate treasure. There were gold and silver coins from South America of all shapes and sizes; Escudos, doubloons, etc; there were gold bars, Inca gold cups, Columbian emeralds, rubies, diamonds and pearls. As they were rummaging through the haul Barry noticed something else. It was a leather satchel tucked inside the lid of the chest. As he gently removed it he thoughtfully said, "Mmm! What's in this I wonder?"

He carefully opened the flap of the satchel and took a peek inside. Upon noting that it contained several documents, he walked to the table and put his hands back into the white cotton gloves used earlier and slowly drew out the contents. A quick glance over them confirmed their importance. Looking up from the table he said, "Well, this is rather good. These papers appear to be the Official Deeds to the land in America from George II, with an additional clause stating that if in the future any direct descendants cannot be found, then the land should be returned to the local tribes. There is also the official Letter of Marque from George II and a copy of a London News Sheet announcing George II awarding land to Robert Davies. Other documents are included and these require further investigation. And there is even a Native American 'keep you safe' wrist band; the same as that given out by Aiyana during the 'Days Inn' meeting."

Just then Lord Henry arrived back from making phone calls and surface mapping the track of the tunnel. Somewhat disappointed that they opened the chest without him he said, "So it looks like you have opened the chest without me! Anything interesting?"

Sue walked over to him. Grabbing his hand she dragged him over to have a look and with some pride she said, "Ha-ha, you could say that. Guided by a letter found at the back of the journal and the map we found tucked away in the painting frame, I solved the lock puzzle and asked Jonny and Aiyana to lift the lid as they are kin of Captain Davies. And wallah!"

An open-mouthed Lord Henry exclaimed, "Bloody hell! I wasn't expecting that."

Dipping his hand in and pulling out what looked like uncut diamonds, in a more serious tone than normal he continued, "This one must be about five carats. It's worth a fortune. Barry what is the process Jonny and Aiyana now need to go through? I assume all this needs to be catalogued and proof of ownership verified; not to mention the tax man will be interested. I have also notified the police because of the body. Later today they will be sending a team over which will include a forensic archaeologist to make sure the captain is looked after."

Barry thought about it and replied, "What we need to do now is prove Jonny and Aiyana are the direct descendants. I don't think that will be difficult because as well as the documents we have found down here, Aiyana has brought over paperwork signed by her father before his death. We then need to notify the coroner. This needs to be done within 14 days. Contacting the local Findings Liaison Officer is useful. There will be a Coroner's Inquest where all interested parties will be invited including the land owner and museums. A Valuation Committee of experts will put a value on the findings. The valuation can be released in monetary terms by one of the interested parties making an offer or at auction. All this can take up to 12 months I'm afraid."

Lord Henry continued the thread, "I have also checked whether those renting Home Farm would have any claim as it looks like the chest is just below their barn. As expected the rental agreement gives them no rights regarding additional ownership claims. Because the find is on Mayhew land Sue and I will have the primary claim. I have also now found out that the Manor House that predated the Home Farm buildings was owned by a Captain Robert Davies and that there was a fire in 1765. This date lines up with that on the letter found at the back of the Journal. At the time it was assumed that he perished in the fire. This information can be found in news sheets that are held in the local museum. A body was never found. The ownership and his death in a fire is also confirmed by Church records. Pieces of the jigsaw appear to be coming together."

Henry laughed and with a wink and a smile he looked at the treasure he said, "We know and agree that all findings belong to Aiyana, Jonny and the tribe— including proceeds from selling the Gainsborough painting. We just have to go through the correct procedures to release it to them in the most cost-effective way. Mind you I wouldn't mind a little keepsake. But I think I now need to go topside and wait for the relevant authorities to arrive. I suggest you take photos but don't lock the chest again yet. Jonny can stay here and I will ensure we have Bryn acting as security before you leave and the police make the site secure. The rest of us can meet up again at the Land Rover."

"But there is one more job to do regarding confirming the second entrance to the tunnel. We need to know how bad that fire damage tunnel collapse is."

He positioned a small transmitter next to the rubble in the cavern before making his way back through the tunnel followed by Barry. He continued the conversation, "I think the authorities would prefer access via that point rather than the narrow tunnel so we will need an accurate assessment of the work required to open it up again. I will arrange a meeting with Aled and Mary and assure them that I will cover all costs. I will also arrange security guards and fencing around the site. To be honest I will be happier when we can move the chest and other valuables to a safer place."

They walked to the barn and using the light weight geo-phys equipment they immediately got a strong response from a receiver-transmitter placed next to the fire damage rubble so there was an accurate positioning of the collapse point within the barn. Fortunately it was under a part of the barn used for parking mechanical equipment so there would not be too much trouble in clearing the area required to open up the access. It was also in the centre of the barn and fortunately not close to an existing wall so the risk of major collateral damage was much reduced. It was probably a staircase from the kitchen in the original Manor House.

Once they had marked out the collapse point on the barn floor Barry and Lord Henry went over the full story with Aled and Mary. They were quite excited about it all and were keen to help. It didn't take long to clear the barn area and using the geo-phys kit Barry was able to get a more detailed profile of the collapsed tunnel. It didn't look too bad but Lord Henry felt it best to get experts in the field rather than attack the work themselves. Barry said he had a contact that specialised in archaeological work such as this. It was a company used by the University. It was agreed that he should contact them and get time and financial estimates of the work required.

Chapter 19

Looking behind I am filled with gratitude.
Looking forward I am filled with vision.
Looking upwards I am filled with strength.
Looking within I discover peace.
(Native American proverb)

Mayhew Estate
28 August

Back in the cavern area it soon started to get a little crowded as the various experts arrived. The first team to arrive was from the Coroner's Office along with the Police Forensic Team and the remains of the body presumed to be that of Captain Davies was soon taken away. After making sure Bryn was in place Jonny was the last of the treasure hunters to leave and it felt good to be above ground.

He was about to ring Jacob and tell him all that had happened when he noticed the two Cardiff police officers that had interviewed him the other day walking in his direction. They had been among those organising the body dispatch but he had not had time to make contact with them underground. Jonny opened up with a smile and said, "Before you say anything, I am not going to talk about what happened in Bristol or Cardiff. I have already been interviewed Chief Inspector."

David responded with his own smile, "Yes we know that. We just wanted to congratulate you on your find. We have had a quick look in the chest. It is a remarkable find and it looks like you are going to be a very wealthy young man."

Looking straight into Jonny's eyes he continued.

"Yet it is strange, but I get the feeling that it is somehow connected with all that went down some days ago back in Cardiff. However, you seem to have some very important friends."

Jonny returned the look and with a cheeky grin replied, "Ah Inspector, I was simply in the right place at the wrong time; or the wrong place at the right time—

I am not sure which. But whatever, it certainly has been a fast and very eventful ride."

Jonny looked over to his left and saw the one person he needed. It was Jacob, so he excused himself from the two detectives and walked over to Jacob who was standing on the edge of the crowd smiling gently in Jonny's direction. As Jonny reached him, he just put his hand tenderly on Jacob's arm, mindful of the fact that Jacob was not out yet.

Jacob said quietly, "I have missed you Jonny."

All he really wanted to do was hold Jacob to him as he felt an overwhelming rush of emotion, but Jonny's simple reply with a twinkling eye was, "Ditto"

Just then the treasure chest was just being brought up through the opening of the tunnel, with Bryn still guarding it while the contracted Security Guard took care of the tunnel entrance. Jonny said to Jacob, "Would you like to see Captain Davies's hoard before they take it away. The chest is locked but Bryn will have the keys and I'm sure he would open it for us. I know the sequence code if he doesn't."

Bryn and Security cleared it and Jonny used the keys to open it once it had been placed on the ground. Bryn and the Security Guard stopped anyone getting too close. And luckily, Mayhew was able to keep out the various news crews because of its high security walls and cameras, however they were gathering outside the main gate and it did not stop a helicopter buzzing around taking pictures. When Jacob viewed the contents he gasped as he gazed at the incredible find and said, "Wow Jonny; it's like something from a novel."

Jonny noticed Aiyana and waved her over and introduced her to Jacob as his sister by another mother. They had gazed at the beautiful items displayed in the chest for a short time before Jonny closed and locked it, and watched as Bryn and the Security Guards placed it in the back of a high security van.

Glancing around, he sort of felt bizarrely detached from everything going on around him. Henry and Barry were deep in conversation about what needed to be done next; his mum and Sue were sitting on a bank drinking coffee from a flask and laughing in a relaxed manner; Sandy was chatting to the two Cardiff detectives who turned towards Jonny and laughed; Jacob and Aiyana were now talking quietly and also turned towards Jonny smiling. He thought, *Maybe this is what fame feels like. I'm the centre of attention but alone.*

Due to Lord Henry's contacts, he was confident that he would be able to get the various agencies together at Mayhew in a very short time frame and there was no doubt in his mind that everything would be wrapped up speedily rather than in the 'up to twelve months' forecast by Barry. Tomorrow it will have been fourteen days since Aiyana first contacted Christina. Fourteen days that will have changed the lives of these people forever.

Looking up from his conversation with Barry and smiling wryly to himself, he watched Jonny walk towards Jacob and Aiyana who were laughing and talking together like they had known each other for ages. He thought, *What will the future hold for them all now, I wonder?*

Aiyana and Jacob turned towards Jonny as he approached them and Aiyana linked arms with both of them winking as she said, "Hey Jonny! I like your man. Can I keep him?"

Jonny poked his tongue out at her and said, "Nope. He is mine and I am not into sharing."

Jacob laughed at them and said, "Hey, don't I get a say in this?"

Aiyana turned to Jacob and said with a screwed-up nose expression on her face, "I don't think so Jacob. I have a feeling my brother has staked his claim where you are concerned."

Back came the response from Jonny, "Oh yeah. I have certainly staked my claim."

Jacob blushed and Aiyana hooted with laughter saying, "Jonny! Just too much information."

Even though the treasure chest and the body had been taken away, because of the other objects underground security at the site was immediately strengthened with fences patrolled by security guards on duty night and day.

That same evening when everyone had left and the area tidied up and secured, the treasure hunters gathered around the kitchen table eating cold meats and salad and getting a bit merry on Henry and Sue's excellent Bollinger. Christina let Barry know that Isabella had sent a text to say she had just been to pick up her Landy from the apartment. It was needed for a conference she was attending in Bristol so it was convenient to pick it up. Christina had arranged for the keys and Isabella's mobile to be left in a secret place.

Barry nodded and then stood up. Clearing his throat he proposed a toast to Lord and Lady Mayhew, thanking them for their hospitality and help. Lord Henry smiled, inclined his head and winked. Raising his glass he said, "We haven't finished yet Barry. For example we still have to verify that the bones do indeed belong to Captain Davies. There is more work to do on verifying the

Gainsborough paintings authenticity. We will need to get a report from the structural engineer you recommended to see if the cavern and the barn above it are safe. If it is, or any work required is straight forward, I would like to look at the possibility of using the grounds for education and discovery with regards to the history of pirates and smuggling in this area. Maybe we can open the original steps down from Home Farm, providing Aled and Mary agree. They might want to be involved. Anyway, this has all been going around in my head. Would you be interested in helping me with my new project Barry? Maybe the University History Faculty would like to be involved."

Barry replied, "What an excellent idea, I would be honoured to help in any way I can."

The table was buzzing with conversation and it was only Sandy who noticed Jonny get up and walk out to the back of the stables where Jacob waited on his Motorbike. The engine was idling as he held out a helmet. Jonny took it and they both rode out into the night.

It was about an hour later that a fairly tipsy Aiyana noticed he was missing saying, "Hey! Anyone seen my brother Jonny?"

Sandy turned and said,

"I think he has gone to see Jacob."

Aiyana looked around and said, "Jeez; Jacob is so damn hot isn't he? And he's off limits…What a waste; my brother has taste."

They all giggled and she said, "Oh dear; I made a rhyme. I think I had better now go to bed while I can still walk. Goodnight guys. Thank you all so much. I love you all."

The party broke up soon after, with everyone extremely happy. Barry and Christina linked arms and giggling like a couple of children walked up the stairs and entered their bedroom.

Christina started to remove her clothes immediately the door closed; Barry made a grab for her but wagging a finger at him she laughingly said, "Uh uuh not yet lover boy."

She then turned and walked into the shower, giving her bottom a cheeky tap before shutting the door.

Being husband and wife was going to be quite different to the parallel lives they had been living and she felt very secure and at peace with herself. She was enjoying the water slowly running down her body and was engrossed in erotic thoughts as she caressed her body; seeking out the most arousing spots and dwelling there in pleasure. You could say she was feeling quite 'fruity' and naughty.

So she didn't move away as Barry entered the shower and moved his body up close behind her. In fact she pushed her bum out to meet him. He put his arms around her soapy body and placed one hand over a boob and the other down below to find the button of desire. His cock however was pressed hard against her back.

She giggled, "Hello darling; you seem pleased to see me."

He murmured in her ear, "Mmmm, by the condition of this nipple so do you. Have you started without me."

The coquettish reply was, "Might have."

Turning her around to face him, he gently kissed the tip of her nose before placing his lips on hers. After a while, knowing she loved to involve roll play when having sex he said in his most devilish tone, "Shall we play then?"

She looked at him with a raised eyebrow. A cheeky grin appeared and in a bossy voice she said, "Ooh yes. But only if you do as I tell you or you will get punished. And you must call me Miss Christina."

He thought, *This sounds an interesting new game. Let's play.*

Standing smartly to attention with his cock bouncing up and down, he played his role, replying, "Yes of course, Miss Christina. Whatever you say, Miss Christina."

"First I want you to wash me; starting at my feet. So get down on your knees NOW!"

Barry did as he was told and gently washed her feet and ankles, moving slowly up her leg until he reached the top of her legs. He tentatively placed a finger in between but she slapped his hand away.

"Just wash me, I said."

He continued his ascent up her body washing her carefully but lingering over her breasts as he saw the pleasure in her eyes. She then turned around for him to wash her back. He soaped her bottom using his hands in a massaging motion before moving up to finish the wash. Christina then issued another order.

"Now take the shower head and rinse me."

He was now so turned on his cock was aching for attention. He took the shower head and rinsed the soap off her, again lingering at the spots that turned her on.

The stern but lust-ridden Christina looked him in the eyes, slowly ran a finger down his cheek and then stepped out of the shower saying very slowly, "Now you can dry me."

Barry obeyed and still dripping wet, he took a fluffy towel and dried her carefully all over.

Christina then walked naked through the bathroom door into the bedroom.

"OK; you can dry yourself and but don't come into the bedroom until I say so. If you are a good boy, you might get lucky."

Barry quickly dried himself but it seemed ages before he heard Christina call, "You may enter now."

He entered the bedroom to see Christina swinging his and her dressing-gown belts in her hand. She had also put aside a couple of his leather belts and was wearing some black hi-heel patent leather shoes that made her taller and showed off her beautiful long and shapely legs. She wore a matching black patent leather bomber jacket, left open to show a wide matching patent leather belt with a large front metal buckle.

Around her neck she had a choker style string of expensive pearls with drop pearl earrings that swayed as she moved her head. Her bracelet was wide and made from thick white gold links and she had applied some deep crimson lipstick. To parts of her body she had also rubbed in some baby oil so her skin glistened. In a very seductive voice, she said, "I bet you are pleased that I packed plenty of clothes now. Be a good boy and lie down on the bed."

Mouth open at the sight of a Christina he had rarely seen, Barry did as he was told while this newfound vision of beauty and sexual power tied his hands together. She then did the same to his feet. Using the belts, she tied his hands to the headboard and his feet to the base. When she had finished, she stood back to admire her work and his very hard and throbbing cock. Bending over the bed, she poked out her wriggling tongue and murmured, "Mmm; now what are we going to do with this naughty thing?"

As she spoke, she gently tickled the end with her long red manicured nails. Barry groaned and pulled against his restraints but Christina smacked his thigh hard saying, "NO! Don't move."

She then grabbed his erection in her hand and lowered her head and licked it—from his scrotum to the tip—gently nibbling around the rim.

Barry groaned in pleasure saying, "Please Miss Christina; please I need you to sit on it."

He got another slap for his audacity. And this one hurt.

"How dare you tell me what you need. This is about what I want."

She moved up close facing him, fondling her breasts before cupping one upwards so she could lick her hard nipple. With the other hand, she reached deep inside her now very wet thighs, resting on the hot spot and writhing in real pleasure. She was surprising herself at just how much she was enjoying this level of control by displaying herself this way to her man. But she wanted more before climaxing.

She then straddled Barry's legs and folded from her waist. Facing Barry's feet, her open thighs were just a few inches away from his face. She cupped his cock between her boobs, holding them tightly together and slowly moved up and down its length feeling it slide on the baby oiled skin. Barry groaned but couldn't reach Christina with his tongue because of the restraints, just as Christina had planned, although she would have loved to feel it there. He put his head back and cried, "Dear God, Miss Christina; if you don't stop that, I am going to cum."

Chrissie lifted up, turned around and slowly placed herself over his hot and ready erection, taking all of him inside. It only took a few movements before she felt her muscles tighten inside before releasing in a rush of sensation as Barry exploded inside her.

After a short while, Barry said with a grin, "Well, I wasn't expecting that, Miss Bossy Boots."

Christina just giggled and grabbed some tissues before easing herself off his now wilting member.

"It was fun though, wasn't it? I must bring in my riding boots and crop next time."

She started to make her way back to the bathroom while Barry asked politely, "Ummm, Chrissie. Er sorry to mention it but do you think you could untie me now?"

Christina turned at the bathroom door, looked at his helpless state and grinned as Barry cried, "CHRISSIE! Not funny."

Still in the zone, she shut the door, leaving Barry to grunt and struggle with the belts before he managed to escape. He needed to pay for that sort of pleasure.

Day 14 Mayhew Estate

28 August

The next morning saw the younger members of the team do what new young people do when their insecurity and urgency to explore and satisfy each other takes over. Sandy and Devlin had been up and about since 6 am sorting out the stables. They had turned out the horses and were just returning the feed buckets to the feed room when Devlin smiled wickedly as he shut and locked the feed room door behind them saying, "I must have you, Sandy."

Sandy replied with a wink, "I'm sooo ready, hun. Go for it."

Devlin pushed her up against the wall and they melted into a glorious lustful embrace. It didn't take long before they were both naked below the waist and interlocked in full noisy sexual pleasure with Sandy's legs up around his waist as they pumped in unison against the wall. Even though the feed room door had been locked there was still the danger of being discovered but the horses wouldn't tell tales. However, before they could climax, they heard someone whistling loudly outside as if to draw attention.

So they quickly withdrew, got dressed and exited the feed room chatting about horses as calm as you like. They looked around but there was no sign of the spoilsport phantom whistler.

Jonny and Jacob woke up in Jacob's cottage bedroom. It was 7 am and Jonny turned to see a grinning Jacob propped up resting on his elbow and looking down to where Jonny was making a tent of the bedclothes. As he looked, he said, "Good morning, I see you are a morning person. You must have had a good dream."

Jonny looked at Jacob and smiled saying, "Yeah! It's ready when you are."

With that Jacob disappeared under the covers making Jonny gasp as he felt Jacob's lips and tongue make contact with the tent pole.

Christina and Barry's relationship was more secure and they had been awake for a while, lying in bed laughing about their fun and games the night before. They also discussed their wedding and decided it would be nice to have it in the Spring. Barry kissed her forehead, and they cuddle each other, secure in the knowledge of each other's love.

Henry and Sue were drinking coffee on the terrace, enjoying the peace of the morning, and quietly discussing everything that had occurred. They also discussed Barry and Christina's wedding, both thinking that it would be nice to ask them if they would like to have it at Mayhew.

They stop talking when Henry's mobile buzzed. He answered with, "Good morning, Arthur…OK; yes that's all good. I will let the right people know. Keep an eye on it. And thank you for letting me know. We will talk later."

He turned to Sue and said, "Your fake painting is about to arrive in Boston, darling. Evidently, they transferred it to a private plane in Southern Ireland. I now need to get into the study and sort out the next move."

Sue nodded and turned her face up for Henry to kiss her as she said, "OK. I will see you later."

As he got up and walked into the house, he passed Aiyana walking out with a cup of coffee to join Sue. He said, "Good morning Aiyana. It's another beautiful day. We have someone popping in later that would just like to have a chat with you with regards to the painting and the involvement of your parents with the Religious Community Accountants. His name is Antony Brown. I hope that will be OK. He works for our government."

Aiyana replied, "Yeah sure. Of course I am happy to do that."

Epilogue

Endings and New Beginnings

It was now December and very cold. The year had been one of danger, mystery, unbelievable wealth and high passion. Thanks to the high-level contacts of Lord Henry the formal processes of identification and ownership had been speeded up considerably.

Jonny and Aiyana had become rather wealthy young people. Using DNA profiling, it had been proven that Aiyana was a direct relation to the male body in the cavern and dating the remains confirmed other written evidence about the time and manner of his death. The remains were in fact of Captain Davies, so according to his written wishes the contents of the chest did belong to his heirs— Aiyana and Jonny.

Lord Henry used his financial experience and contacts to advise them on the best way to invest their newfound wealth. With his help and the massive funds now available from the sale of the treasure chest and its contents, they decided between them to start a trust to fund a grant for North American Tribal Written and Illustrated Arts; the fund being made available specifically to Native Americans of all tribes. The aim was to delve deeper into the history of Native American culture through its arts, much of it to be discovered in cave drawings and some in illustrations and text prepared by white colonialists. They also planned to document and fact-check the stories held in the minds of the tribal elders.

Jonny, Aiyana and the current Chief of her Tribe asked Lord Henry to Chair the Trustees and continue to advise them. He agreed. Other Trustees were Jonny, Aiyana, Barry and the Tribe Elder responsible for historic and cultural matters. Because their research might throw up info about how the Mafia gained control of the Religious Community finances via the Holding Company Accountants they knew that both the FBI and the Mafia would be taking an interest. They believed that land ownership was the initial attraction, but although current legislation in USA prevented any changes to the initial claims on the land, the accountants did not welcome any deeper investigation in case it influenced other areas of their lucrative business based there.

However, Aiyana had received news about some influential religious leaders of the community wishing to make some payments to the Tribe and find a way of ridding themselves of the Mafia involvement in their finances via the Holding Company Accountants.

Jonny's relationship with Jacob continued, but they would be apart for a while because Jonny had managed to get a special dispensation from his university to study Frontier and Native American Art for six months in America as part of his degree, and also to oversee the trust fund start-up.

Barry's history faculty at Bristol was also interested in supporting the project—highlighting the links between Native American tribes on the East Coast of USA and the West Coast of England and Wales. Jonny's logged criminal history with drugs might prevent him gaining the necessary entrance visa but Lord Henry's contacts were on the case.

Work had begun on the educational buildings at Home Farm and the old entrance to the cavern opened up. All this replaced the original Home Farm barn that was demolished. Lord Henry had built a smart new barn with hard core access on the other side of Home Farm for his tenants Aled and Mary who were now completely involved in the Cavern project. They would become Official Guardians of the new development, maintaining the building and its contents.

Barry was enjoying researching the history surrounding Mayhew and its past roll in piracy and smuggling. He was also taking an in depth look at Captain Davies and was researching his links to the crown along with his involvement with the native American tribe and his marriage to a tribe member.

It was hoped that Jonny's six-month project in USA would enable him to expand their knowledge in this area and find out how and why the initial friendly relationship between various religious communities and the local tribe changed dramatically over the years.

In line with this, Christina decided she would write a book using Barry's notes and the information from Jonny. It would be fiction based on fact.

After much investigation by a panel of art experts organised by the Royal Academy, Sue had received a Certificate of Authentication for the Gainsborough and it had been assigned an Identification Number. It was now officially recognised as being a painting by Gainsborough. There being no other claims, documents provided by Aiyana were taken as proof of shared ownership of the painting between her, Jonny and the tribe. It meant that provided all parties were in agreement, it could be sold and funds released for projects.

However, rather than put it up for auction, Lord and Lady Mayhew decided that they would like to purchase it for their own art collection. It is not an everyday occurrence that works of art of such rarity become available and its links to the estate and the treasure cavern made it an attractive and logical addition. Jonny, Aiyana and the Tribe Elders were in agreement. Lord Henry also knew it would be a good financial investment and they were waiting for an official independent valuation. Its importance to the artistic community meant that they would loan it out to art galleries from time to time.

Lord Henry had been liaising with the FBI with regards to the corrupt firm of accountants based in Boston, with direct links to the Religious Community and the Mafia. The fake painting prepared by Sue was back in their vaults and the transmitter prepared by Arthur was signalling its whereabouts. Clearly Sue's subterfuge was working well.

Devlin continued to work for Lord Henry. Sandy went back to University in Cardiff to finish her degree before taking over the art shop in Bristol purchased with the proceeds of Jonny's newfound wealth. Her relationship with Devlin was still going strong.

The Funeral of Captain Robert Davies

Although there were several different religions alive and well in Wales during the 1700s, after checking the Church records, it appeared that Captain Davies was a Methodist; so when it came time to bury his remains—although the service was simple and multi-denominational—a Methodist Minister was contacted to carry out the service in the Mayhew Chapel in December.

There was a small congregation sitting in the pews behind a small wicker coffin that had been placed on a table in front of the Altar. The gathering consisted of Lord Henry and Sue, Sandy and Devlin, Jonny and Jacob, Christina, and Barry, Aled and Mary, Bryn and Margie; also Aiyana was there of course, with a representative from The Tribe Elders Council called Martin Massasoit. He was the tribe's history specialist and was named after a famous Tribal Chief. He would help Jonny during his six-month project in USA.

The Minister had just led the congregation in the Lord's Prayer. He then turned to Jonny, who stood up and walked to the lectern. Jonny unfolded a piece of paper and said, "I want to read you a poem or song that I think Captain Davies would appreciate. Some of you will know recognise the words. It is called *Sea Fever* and it was composed by John Masefield and published in 1902."

Using his notes only as a reference when necessary, he continued:

I must go down to the sea again, to the lonely sea and sky,
And all I ask is a tall ship and a star to steer her by;
And the wheel's kick and the winds song and the white sail's shaking,
And a grey mist on the sea's face, and a grey dawn breaking.
I must go down to the seas again, for the call of the running tide
Is a wild call and a clear call that may not be denied;
And all I ask is a windy day with the white clouds flying;
And the flung spray and the blown spume, and the sea-gulls crying.
I must go down to the seas again, to the vagrant gypsy life,
To the gulls way and the whales way where the winds like a whetted knife;
And all I ask is a merry yarn from a fellow-rover,
And quiet sleep and a sweet dream when the long tricks over.

He stood for a moment as if in silent prayer. Turning to the coffin, he said, "Sail on, Captain."

He stepped away, saying, "As Captain Davies was married to a member of theAiyana's tribe, she wants to say a few words. Some of you will know that her tribal name is Eternal Blossom."

Aiyana stepped forward. She wore her formal tribal dress, similar to those in the Gainsborough painting.

"Thank you, my brother. This is quite a modern Native American blessing. Similar verse has been handed down by the Tribal Elders through the generations and similar verse was probably used at burial ceremonies when Captain Davies was alive."

She cleared her throat before continuing in a clear voice:

I give you this one thought to keep.
I am with you still, I do not sleep
I am the thousand winds that blow,
I am the diamond glints on snow,
I am the sunlight on ripened grain

I am the gentle autumn rain.

When you awaken in the morning hush,
I am the swift uplifting rush
Of quiet birds in circled flight
I am the soft stars that shine at night
Do not think of me as gone
I am with you still—in each new Dawn.

Aiyana then walked over to the coffin and placed a ring of feathers where Captain Davies's head would be. When she returned to her pew, the organ started to play the opening bars of the sailors' hymn, *Eternal Father*. Although the congregation was small, they raised the roof singing this hymn.

At the end of the service, they all left with the sounds of Elgar's *Nimrod* being played on the organ. Jonny and Aiyana carried the coffin to the newly dug grave in the Mayhew Chapel small graveyard, and watched as it was lowered down while the Minister read the commendation.

Once Jonny and Aiyana had thrown some soil on the coffin, those assembled were happy that at last the captain had been laid to rest. His grave was amongst those of Lord Mayhew's relatives and some Mayhew Estate staff members. Lord Mayhew was having a suitable headstone prepared but the script had not yet been decided upon.

They took the short walk back to Mayhew where Margie had prepared a small but beautifully prepared buffet in the main reception room. There was a much-welcomed roaring fire glowing in the grate. Lord Henry asked everyone to take a glass of champagne from the table. When he saw they all had a full glass in their hands, he asked them to move to where the Gainsborough was hanging. Looking at the painting, he asked everyone to raise their glasses and simply said, "To Captain Davies. We never met; but you have changed our lives forever. Rest in Peace."